ARROW'S FALL

ARROW'S FALL

Joel Scott

Published by ECW Press
665 Gerrard Street East
Toronto, Ontario, Canada M4M 1Y2
416-694-3348 / info@ecwpress.com

Cover design: Michel Vrana
Author photo: © Hilary Scott

This is a work of fiction. Names, characters,
places, and incidents either are the product of
the author's imagination or are used fictitiously,
and any resemblance to actual persons, living or
dead, business establishments, events, or locales is
entirely coincidental.

LIBRARY AND ARCHIVES CANADA
CATALOGUING IN PUBLICATION

Scott, Joel, 1939–, author
    Arrow's fall / Joel Scott.

Issued in print and electronic formats.
ISBN 978-1-77041-427-3 (softcover)
ISBN 978-1-77305-300-4 (PDF)
ISBN 978-1-77305-299-1 (EPUB)

    I. Title.

PS8637.C68617A75 2019   C813'.6
C2018-905345-3   C2018-905346-1

The publication of *Arrow's Fall* has been generously supported by the Canada Council for the Arts
which last year invested $153 million to bring the arts to Canadians throughout the country and
is funded in part by the Government of Canada. *Nous remercions le Conseil des arts du Canada de
son soutien. L'an dernier, le Conseil a investi 153 millions de dollars pour mettre de l'art dans la vie des
Canadiennes et des Canadiens de tout le pays. Ce livre est financé en partie par le gouvernement du Canada.*
We acknowledge the support of the Ontario Arts Council (OAC), an agency of the Government of
Ontario, which last year funded 1,737 individual artists and 1,095 organizations in 223 communities
across Ontario for a total of $52.1 million. We also acknowledge the contribution of the Government
of Ontario through the Ontario Book Publishing Tax Credit, and through Ontario Creates for the
marketing of this book.

PRINTED AND BOUND IN CANADA   PRINTING: FRIESENS   5 4 3 2 1

MIX
Paper from
responsible sources
FSC® C016245

CHAPTER 1

The water had that stark clarity found only in those rare places a thousand miles from the possibility of man; a clear shining medium that brought the ten-fathom bottom so sharply into focus it seemed I could reach down and touch it. I had seen the fish twice now, a leopard grouper in the five-pound range gliding among the coral canyons like a green spotted ghost, its head swivelling lazily as it checked for dangers, its overhung jaw slightly open as it hunted.

I took a deep breath and planed down behind him, my spear gun extended in front of me, the mask tightening on my face as I descended with long scissor strokes of my flippers. The grouper sensed something in the final second and spurted out of sight around the corner of a sheer cliff so sewn with anemones and starfish that it seemed to undulate as I passed.

I turned in his wake and came out on a large plateau that extended beyond my range of vision, and there, just at the edge, a quick movement. I moved out and saw another quick motion, and then another and now the spotted back of the grouper had changed to stripes, and there were giants in the water, and I choked down the scream that rose up in the back of my throat.

The tigers were loose!

I turned and raced back for the cliff, but I was far too slow, and they curled lazily around in front of me, all the time in the world, the circle tightening, and I spun to face them with my spear but there were too many. As I wheeled, one of them grazed me and I spat out the mouthpiece and screamed and turned, but it was the bloodied mask of Jack Delaney that bumped me, his face rough and sandpapered like that of a shark. The skeletal teeth grabbed my arm and shook me like a dog with a bone and I closed my eyes and screamed in shock and horror.

"Wake up, Jared, you're dreaming again."

My eyes flew open and the threshing of the shark changed into my friend Danny shaking me.

"Jesus Christ," I muttered. Sweat poured from my body and the twisted sheet was damp and clinging.

"What was it, the tiger sharks?"

"Yeah."

"I think you should start drinking again. This unnatural sobriety is affecting you."

Danny handed me a cup of coffee and I took a grateful sip. He was serious, a man who had never experienced a hangover or blackout in his life. He refused to understand that it wasn't the same for everyone. I began drinking too much after Jane left and had cut back in the last month.

"You're probably right. What number on the job list are we up to today?"

"Thirty-two. The head hoses."

"Shit."

"Exactly."

For the past three and a half months we had been tied up in New Zealand for the South Pacific hurricane season. It was five months of boat preparation and overhaul for the next cruising season, combined with a few tours by car and the occasional coastal junket on *Arrow*.

Danny MacLean is my travelling partner, fellow Canadian, and closest friend. Half First Nation and half Scots by birth and all Indigenous by choice, he's a big brown good-looking man who is as strong as an ox and the perennial party animal. He considers it his mission in life to rescue me from introspection and ensure I have a good time, the definition of which usually involves alcohol and, sometimes, women. Two years earlier we had salvaged a large amount of illicit cash from the safe of a sunken drug boat that had been pursuing us. It should have been enough for five good years of cruising, but Danny went through money like the proverbial drunken sailor. I tired of being the whiner who moaned about money and joined in. Now there was barely enough cash for another season in the tropics. We'd have to go home and earn some more. It was a prospect neither of us looked forward to.

"We'd better have a good breakfast; we won't feel like eating once we're into the job."

Danny picked up the cast iron griddle and set it on top of the propane burners we hung on the big Dickinson stove when we set out for the tropics. I topped up my coffee and went out on deck to check the weather.

We were ten miles upriver in New Zealand's North Island, moored fore and aft on pilings in Whangarei town basin with a couple of hundred other yachts, many of them offshore cruisers. Most of us had followed the same tracks through Tonga and Fiji and had a nodding acquaintance. Tied up next to us on the port side was a forty-foot American registered Valiant, and Rachel and I exchanged friendly good mornings from our respective cockpits. She was minding the boat while her boyfriend was back in Silicon Valley topping up the cruising kitty. We'd become friendly with her, Danny more so than me; our hulls were barely five feet apart, and I had felt the sway of *Arrow* many a late night and early morning as Danny swung across and back. Women responded to Danny like iron filings to a magnet, and he was never one for resisting the natural laws.

It was a fine morning, cool and overcast with just enough breeze to crank over the wind generator hanging on the mizzenmast and give us enough amps to run the electrics and fridge without having to start the engine. We had done a costly refit in Tahiti two years back after we lost our rig when we were driven over the reef in the Tuamotus, but we hadn't touched the diesel, an old Perkins 4-108 with the Lucas electrics, ill-tempered and flighty, but never quite reaching the point where it had to be replaced. We had a perverse fondness for it, apart from the serious money it would take to replace it with a new one. We tried to use it as little as possible, and then only when it would have been dangerous not to.

"Here, eat up."

From the galley, Danny passed up a plate of bacon and eggs and came up on deck to join me. He gave a reserved greeting to Rachel and she responded equally sedately. The rascals.

"Seen Sinbad this morning?"

"No, but I felt a slight list around five o'clock this morning," I said. "It must have been him."

Danny chose to ignore it. "Is it a mafia day today?"

"Yes. Likely see Basil in another hour or so."

The New Zealand Ministry of Agriculture and Forestry was responsible for defending the shores of their country from the depredations of foreign pets. You were not allowed to land an animal on shore until it had been in quarantine for six months under pain of death for the beast and the loss of a large bond by its owner. In addition, there was a biweekly inspection of all boats with pets confined on board. The inspector rowed among the moored fleet, and the owners would bring their pets on deck for his contemplation, the process often accompanied by acrimony on both sides.

Since it was their country, they got to make the rules, and they widely publicized their aversion to foreign pets: *if you don't like it, don't land here*. Danny and I had no problems with any of this. Unfortunately, Sinbad did.

Sinbad was our ship's dog, a hundred and sixty-five pounds of ugly and muscle. He was devoted to Danny and barely tolerated me, although he did save my life once. We picked him up in the port of Santa Barbara on our maiden passage down the west coast, and he remained with us ever since.

Sinbad grew up on an atoll in the Tuamotus, a free-running village dog belonging to no one, and fed himself for the most part by catching fish. The cruisers loved to watch him working the shallow edge of a lagoon, springing through the water in high stiff-legged leaps with his head on a swivel, then suddenly pouncing to emerge with a fish captured in his jaws. They were less thrilled when he devoured one of the seabirds he varied his diet with.

Sinbad was befriended by an American single-hander who stopped off at the remote island of Ahe in the Tuamotus, and when the cruiser departed he took the dog with him. When the sailor's voyage ended in Santa Barbara two years later, he deposited Sinbad with the local SPCA, and that is where Danny's grandfather Joseph had found him and brought him aboard two years previously.

He was unquestionably the ugliest dog I have ever seen: outsized head, with yellow staring eyes above a flat brutal face with something of the wolf in it. His neck was massive, the skin loose and rumpled above powerful shoulders that ran down to a narrow, skinny rump and short muscular hind legs with broad thickly furred feet that propelled him through the water at surprising speed. His tail was thin, mangy, and rat-like and had been docked by the teeth of a shark. Another attack left a thick network of scars beginning under his chin and running back through his neck and chest like twisted silver ropes. It also took half his left ear, and the remaining flap was serrated in little steps.

When Sinbad looked at you with those hellish amber eyes and uttered his low, eager growl, it was sufficient to turn any man's bowels to water. He still scared me, and I had known him since Joseph first brought him on board *Arrow*.

We couldn't declare Sinbad when we reached New Zealand. It would have been his death sentence. No force on earth could have kept him on board for six months and so, a mile from the customs dock on our way up the Hātea River, Danny dropped Sinbad over the side. He followed us along the shore until we berthed in the basin and then disappeared. It was another week before we saw him again.

I finished my breakfast and went into the galley to clean up. While I worked I tried to think of a valid reason to postpone the head job, but nothing came to mind, and soon we were immersed in it, pumping bleach through the lines to kill the odour and cursing the frozen fittings. We could have beaten the hoses against the side of the boat to get out the calcium buildup, but it was easier to just replace them all. We had calculated three hours to do the job and the immutable law of boats came into play and doubled the time; it was four o'clock before we finished up, dirty, sweaty, and evil tempered.

We took the inflatable and rowed ashore to the marina office with the showers installed alongside, and less than an hour later were sitting in the Balmain, one of the tougher bars in Whangarei. A lot of Māori did their drinking there. Danny was something of a fixture most evenings, and with his First Nations North Pacific heritage, regarded as a distant relative of sorts. It wasn't even an hour before Danny was charming and chatting a pair of adventurous young schoolteachers who had stopped in for a drink on the way home. They sat close on either side of him, fascinated with Danny and his embellished stories about the cruising life. It was clear that a competition was taking place between the ladies, and the loser would get me. I was contemplating an excuse for leaving when a different woman approached the table.

"Excuse me. Are you the captain of *Arrow*?"

She stood before me clutching the briefcase to her chest as if it might afford some protection against the rough trade that surrounded her. She looked out of place and ill at ease in her severe tailored suit.

She was in her mid-twenties and coming in here might have been the raciest thing she'd ever done. She didn't wait for my reply.

"I'm interested in chartering a boat for a couple of weeks to do some research in the Bay of Islands. Sort of a working holiday. May I sit down?" An English accent mixed with something else. Irish?

"Why not," I said.

Danny glanced up, raised his eyebrows at me, and resumed his conversation with the ladies. The three of them were talking in low voices and doing a lot of giggling.

"Would you like a drink?" I asked.

"No thank you."

"My name is Jared Kane." I offered her my hand. She looked at it but made no move towards it.

"Yes, I am aware of that. They told me when I asked about your boat. My name is Laura Kennedy."

I finished my drink and ordered another. She sat on the edge of her seat ramrod stiff and waited impatiently for me to finish with the cocktail waitress. Laura wore no makeup, and her hair was swept back from her forehead and gathered so severely into a bun at the back it was a wonder her eyes weren't slanted. She looked about five feet two and her shape could have been anything under that suit. She might even have been attractive if she'd taken the broomstick out of her bum.

"I'm studying marine biology and I'm doing my thesis on phytoplankton. I need to do some research on the coccolithophores, a branch of diatoms that are only found in warmer waters." She paused to take a breath.

"Sounds absolutely fascinating," I said.

She frowned. Her bun moved up an inch.

"I have relatives in New Zealand, and the Bay of Islands is warm enough for my purposes, so I thought I would come here for a visit and do some research as well. I noticed your boat tied up in the basin and wondered if you would be interested in chartering it out."

I regarded her skeptically. Danny and I had never talked seriously about chartering *Arrow* to anyone. It was just another hare-brained idea we might have kicked around late some evening when we were in drink and calculating the state of our finances.

"Where did you hear that we were considering chartering?"

She gave a small superior smile. "It was just a guess. I know that a lot of cruisers do a little on the side to supplement their travel funds. I'd pay the going rate."

I wondered for a moment if she could be connected to our past troubles with Jack Delaney and his hired killers, and then dismissed the idea as paranoid. It had been two years, and the accent was all wrong. We hadn't tried to hide, and we would have been found by now if anyone had been serious about looking.

"Why do you want *Arrow*? There are lots of regular charter boats for rent here."

We had neither a licence nor a good layout for chartering. *Arrow*, like so many large wooden yachts of her era, had been built for a couple to cruise in comfort and style, with the other accommodations all a bit cramped. Chartering her out was one of those ideas that seemed brilliant late at night after a few drinks, then shrivelled and died in the sober light of day.

"I like wooden boats. They have so much warmth and character."

She said this with an uneasy smile, like an actress who didn't quite believe her lines. *She* could have used some warmth and character though, that was damn certain.

"No kidding. *Arrow* isn't set up for chartering, you know. She's not really all that big or comfortable."

Arrow is an old wooden ketch, British built from a Laurent Giles design in 1965. She's just shy of forty-seven feet on deck with a thirty-five-foot waterline and an eleven-foot beam. She draws six feet with external lead ballast and a cutaway keel and is heavy by modern-day standards but has a tall set of Sitka spruce spars in her and carries a thousand feet of sail. When she is on a good point of sail, she is as fast as most boats and prettier than all of them.

Laura sat there watching me with an anxious look on her face.

"I'm sure she would be just fine. Would you please consider it?"

There was an intensity about her request that was out of proportion, her face flushed, and her hands tightly clenched as if my response were a matter of life and death to her.

"I'd have to talk it over with my partner. I doubt it though; we still have some work to do on the boat before she's ready for the cruising season. I'm sure there are other people who would be glad to take you out. There are lots of cruisers up in the Bay of Islands right now. It would make more sense to charter someone who is up there already. Thanks for the offer."

She sat there biting her lip and staring at me for a few moments, and I thought she was going to say something else, but then she stood up without a word and marched stiffly away and out the door.

"You're welcome," I muttered.

A full drink sat waiting in front of me and I threw it back and started talking to the little brunette school teacher who suddenly found me fascinating.

The drinks warmed and enlivened me, the women were charming and the music loud, and it all swept up and over me and I let myself go and didn't give another thought to Miss Prim and her odd request to charter *Arrow*.

CHAPTER 2

I woke sweating and disoriented and lay in my bunk trying to reconstruct the evening. I could remember nearly all of it. Towelling off the stale alcohol sweat, I slipped on a sweatshirt and shorts and went ashore for a run. Before I had gone a hundred yards, Sinbad drifted alongside. It was one of the few times he kept me company. Jane and I had run together most days, and he'd always accompanied us, gazing up at her with a look of panting adoration on his ugly face as he trotted at her side. Maybe he still thought she was coming back.

We moved along the road in unison, neither of us looking at the other, Sinbad's shoulder level with me as we went along the river road past the chandleries and swung around the loop over the bridge past the stadium. I picked up the pace, extending my legs and concentrating on my breathing, and the two of us moved out in concert, Sinbad's head nodding in counterpoint to his choppy stride.

We ran for an hour, up and down, sometimes sprinting for a hundred yards then dropping back to an easy jog until my breath settled, and then running hard once more until the burn in my legs and lungs was too great, and I had to slow again, Sinbad never more than a foot away the whole time, breathing easily, his tongue lolling occasionally in the sprints, never looking up but conscious of my every change of pace and stride.

A few cars passed us on the way back, but the road was wide and the traffic infrequent. Once in a while a head turned as a driver checked out Sinbad, but nobody paid much attention until the brown sedan went by on the final stretch back to the marina.

The uniformed driver slowed to a crawl and studied us through the rolled down window, his head profiled above the logo on the door. After a minute Basil accelerated and pulled away.

We finished our run and Sinbad peeled off in the last hundred yards, trotting towards the park without a backwards look. I grabbed a shower at the marina, checked for mail, and rowed back out to *Arrow*. Danny was slumped in the cockpit reading a book with the stereo cranked and the big bulkhead speakers pulsing to the rhythms of Cocaine. People were swaying four boats down.

"Out doing your penance, huh?"

He went below and came back with a couple of cold beers. New Zealand brew tastes a lot like big brewery Canadian beer. It's an imperfect world.

"I did number thirty-three already," he said, firmly establishing his moral superiority. "We can take the rest of the day off."

We used to do the jobs on the list at random but found that being of poor character we invariably did all the easy ones first and left the swines until the end. Now we did them in strict numerical order, but you still rushed at some more quickly than others. I looked at thirty-three, a slow drip under the port sheet winch. A half-hour removal and caulking job at most, and thirty-four was a tricky bitch: replacing the leaking lazarette locker hatch seal and clearing the awkward dog leg at the bottom where it drained into the bilge. The sneaky bastard had snookered me.

"I thought you were gone for the day," Danny managed with a straight face.

"Yeah, well, I needed to go for a run. It's been a while. I feel kind of out of shape."

"I know what you mean," Danny said.

The hell he does. He is one of those chosen few who never have to work or exercise to stay in shape. His weight never varies more than a pound or two, and he is the strongest man I know. His sleek tan body looks almost flaccid at rest, but then he lifts something or moves a certain way and you realize that what you mistook for fat is smooth and layered muscle. I had seen the bulked-up men watching him in the prison gym as he worked the weights and pulleys. I can lose him on those rare occasions he accompanies me on long runs, but he blows me away in the sprints. He is amazingly quick for a big man.

I finished my beer and decided to tackle the lazarette and regain some moral imperative. I emptied out the locker and was crouched back against the pushpit peering down inside the black hole with a flashlight when a loud blast sounded a second before a rusty pole jammed between my legs, lifted my ass, and pitchforked me into the void. I hung there inverted, cursing wildly as I attempted to struggle backwards and out, cracking my head smartly against the bulkhead in the process. Suspended in pain and rage, I heard the sound of rushing feet and then Danny grasped my legs and hauled me out.

The first thing that met my dazed eyes was a rust-streaked bowsprit thrusting five feet inboard over our stern. It had gone between the cross braces of the Aries wind vane to assault me. I flung myself down beside Danny, heaving on the bowsprit and pushing out against the obscenity. Ever so slowly it fell back, leaving a heavy brown stain as it withdrew. It was only then that I noticed the placid figure standing on the intruder's bow.

"Thankee, partners. I guess I came in too slow, misjudged the currents a tad. I'll back up, take another run at it."

The accent was North American, east coast maybe, the woman somewhere in her forties with a friendly smile, chunky body, and frizzled hair that stood six inches out from her head in an electric orange halo the exact same colour as the rust that engulfed her boat. She was dressed in cut-offs and a straining halter that contained perhaps a third of her breasts.

She plodded back behind the dog house and there was a loud *ka-thunk* and the boat reversed back out into the channel. She made a complete circle, lined up again, and brought her in at full throttle, the air filled with blue smoke, the transmission screaming in protest as she manoeuvered past the first of the four pilings that were to contain her, caromed off it amidships, and rebounded across to its mate. She had a loop ready and threw it over the piling; the line tightened and stretched, the piling creaked and bent, and for long seconds it seemed it would rip out and she would lunge forward and impale the immaculate Beneteau just forward whose owners crouched white eyed in the cockpit.

Another *ka-thunk* as she took the boat out of gear and then the piling straightened and the behemoth slingshotted back towards *Arrow*. Coughing and half blinded by smoke, we threw bumpers and fought her off again. The woman cast another loop over the second piling, and the beast was contained. She switched off the engine and peace returned to the boat basin.

"That was exciting," Danny said. "You've cut your forehead, Jared."

Her voice drowned out my blasphemous reply.

"Thankee, neighbours. The name is Molly. Have a drink. I see we're countrymen. Actually, I'm a countrywoman." She threw us a roguish wink and chuckled and I saw the Canadian flag on her stern. I'd been hoping she was American. She tossed over a couple of beers, which Danny plucked out of the air.

"Why don't you come over and join us," he said. She was across the lifelines almost before he had finished speaking.

Molly was five years out of Newfoundland on an open-ended circumnavigation. She had started out with a boyfriend, but he had disappeared somewhere along the way, where or why wasn't clear. A common theme among cruisers, but usually it was the woman who bailed. For the last three years, she had been travelling on her own, "although I'm always looking for a good man." She'd spent most of her time in American Samoa, staying in Pago Pago for the hurricane seasons and picking up some casual work in the hospital cafeteria there. Judging from the state of her boat, it couldn't have paid all that well.

Tramp, for that was her name, was the scruffiest, most ill-conceived vessel we'd encountered so far from her home port, resembling at first glance one of that tribe of abandoned derelicts that anchor out in every large harbour the world over, tied to the bottom by a rusty length of chain, their sole remaining act of grace a final disappearance beneath the waves.

Her appearance was a doomed union of poor design and flawed workmanship. There was not a natural curve to be seen anywhere and the badly executed right angle reigned supreme. The dog house that dominated her aspect above the water was in the nature of a rectangle, quadrilateral by accident rather than design, one felt. The windows were square and consisted of rough-sawn chunks of Plexiglas bolted over the cut-outs beneath, with caulking worming out everywhere.

Tramp's hull was hard chine, fabricated from overlapping steel plates of every shape and size, welded up in a rough bead and presenting the scaly appearance of a rusty robotic fish. She had a wide-angled bow and her stern was uncompromisingly square, the mast a steel pipe welded to the forward end of the house and the boom a good ten feet above the water. She looked as if she would sail to weather about as well as a nineteenth century square rigger. The windows were so glazed, it was impossible to see inside the cabin.

"Who was the designer?" Danny asked in an awed voice.

"My ex," she said. "He was a prairie boy, built it in Saskatchewan and trucked her back east on a flat deck."

Now that I thought about it, the house did kind of remind me of the wheat granaries of my youth.

"Pretty little boat you've got here," Molly said magnanimously. "Bit on the frail side maybe." We nodded. *Arrow* weighs over twenty tons.

"Who's the skipper?"

"He is," Danny said.

She shifted her hams slightly on the seat, subtly turning away from him towards her social equal. I inched away. "That so. Where's the little woman?"

"Back home visiting," I quickly lied. "She should be back soon."

She nodded in understanding. "Don't tell me," she said. "Another one of those cruising women who come and go. Mostly go. Am I right?"

This time Danny beat me to it.

"How did you know?" he said.

Molly stayed for another couple of hours and drank several more beers before she left. She had some home brewed Newfie screech aboard and was all for bringing a jug across and having a party, but I managed to dissuade her. Danny was no help at all, saying how great it was to have a fellow Canadian skipper alongside and how he tried to give me companionship, but it was difficult for him, being just a lowly deckhand.

For the next few days, Danny and I worked on *Arrow*, picking off a dozen jobs in rapid succession. Most evenings I went for long runs with Sinbad. He never seemed to be waiting for me or showed any signs of pleasure at my arrival. He simply materialized when I passed by the park and ran alongside without acknowledgement of my presence. We travelled out of the city up into the ridges and along the switchbacks, stopping occasionally to drink from one of the little streams or explore one of the ancient Aboriginal middens. We never saw the inspector again.

At night I read from *Arrow*'s journals, sitting in the saloon under the brass trawler lamp sipping a nightcap as I slowly worked my way through the tiny illustrations and fine copperplate script. *Arrow*'s original owners, Bill and Meg Calder, had spent six years in the South Pacific and three in Fiji where Danny and I planned to spend the upcoming cruising season. Their journals were filled with detailed descriptions of isolated anchorages and villages up in the north end and contained soundings for some of the uncharted lagoons. Bill had been an engineer before he and Meg retired to go cruising, and the journals contained the complete record of *Arrow* and her travels, beginning with Bill's first brief sketches when she was just a dream, right through to their final anchorage on Vancouver Island. Just before Bill died, he and Meg decided that I should have the gift of *Arrow*. They didn't want to see her sold off to an indifferent owner and knew that in spite of my shortcomings I would always take good care of her.

Friday morning I rose early and sat in the cockpit drinking coffee as the sky gradually brightened and the outlines of the boats around us emerged from the darkness and took on shape and substance. I made toast as the light strengthened and fed the leftovers to the fleet of begging ducks that patrolled the waters of the basin. They gathered alongside *Arrow*'s hull, paddling slowly against the current, their necks stretched up in anticipation. I was grateful that Sinbad had so far spared them his attention.

From where I sat I could see him sleeping on the foredeck, his hump profiled against the light. He sometimes came aboard at night, disappearing again in early morning before the marina came to life. It was as if he knew he was not welcome here, but perhaps it was merely his antisocial nature that resented the noise and bustle of the clustered yachts. As the sun's rays touched him, he woke, stretched, slipped over the side, and vanished among the moored boats.

The marina gradually came to life, cruisers appearing on deck with their coffees, the sound of radios tuned to the early morning marine nets, the first flushes of the day from the incontinent who couldn't wait to use the shoreside facilities. I finished my coffee and was climbing up the ratlines with the Fluke tester and wire strippers to fix the steaming light when I heard a knock on the side of the hull. It was the MAF inspector in his little skiff.

"Good morning. Permission to come aboard?"

Without waiting for an answer, he seized the shrouds and swung himself over the lifelines. Basil was a short man, overweight and red-faced with choler and exertion.

"What can I do for you, Inspector?" I asked.

"It's about that dog I saw you running with the other day."

I frowned for a moment, puzzled. "Oh. You must mean that big ugly bugger."

"Yes. That one. What do you know about it?"

"Nothing really. He just tagged along when I went jogging. That can happen with dogs sometimes. He doesn't even like me, nearly took my hand off when I tried to pet him. What is he, a stray?"

He stared at me. "He showed up a few weeks ago, right about the time the cruisers all came in for the hurricane season. Coincidence no doubt. We've had reports about some animal in the park bothering the wildfowl, someone even said they saw it take one of the eels out of the lake."

"Caught an eel?" I laughed in disbelief. "How in the hell could a dog even do that?"

I'd read an article in the local paper about the freshwater eels in the park lake and how they were becoming a problem, occasionally biting off the legs of the waterfowl that paddled above them. Sounded like Sinbad might be redressing the balance of nature. There was nothing he liked better than fishing.

"I don't know. But I'm going to catch him, and if it turns out he belongs to a cruiser, there'll be hell to pay. He's been seen in the marina swimming out among the boats a few times."

He gave me a hard stare, turned and swung back down into his skiff, and rowed away towards a fifty-foot British Moody sailboat five berths down, where a man was holding a yowling cat up by the scruff of its neck while his wife looked anxiously on.

"What was that all about?" Molly asked, blinking sleepily on *Tramp*'s afterdeck, the sun blinding on her hair, the front of her nightgown bulging as she stretched.

"He's looking for some dog, saw me running with one a couple of days ago, figured it might be the one. Asked me a few questions about it."

"Would that be the one that sleeps on your decks most nights?" she asked. "Don't worry, I won't say anything. Now, how about that drink tonight, the one you've been too busy for the last few days?" She smiled sweetly, but it didn't really sound like a request.

In the next eight hours, I crossed four jobs off the list. Danny was impressed by my zeal and agreed to accompany me over to *Tramp* that evening after I volunteered to paint the bottom when we hauled out and gave him his pick of the remaining jobs.

We went over at six and passed a pleasant evening trading stories and drinking the wine and beer we had brought. Later on we sampled the screech Molly brewed up in the still she kept hidden in the engine room. It wasn't terrible mixed with orange juice; potent as hell, I was sure.

Molly insisted we stay for a late supper and served up an east coast boiled beef dinner with all the trimmings, with a dessert of apple crumble and New Zealand cheddar. It was excellent, and she flushed with pleasure when we complimented her.

She was a sweet woman when you got to know her, a genuine character, big-hearted and generous, and I was embarrassed and a little ashamed of my earlier presumption. Danny and I left *Tramp* at midnight, both of us in high spirits from the drink. When I turned in, he was sitting in the cockpit with a glass of brandy trying to decide if he should go visiting ashore.

I awoke to the sound of pounding on the hull. A similar pounding resonated in my skull and the galley clock informed me I had slept in. I pulled on a pair of shorts and stuck my head out the companionway. It was the inspector again. This was becoming persecution.

"What do you want?" I growled.

"It's about that dog," Basil answered. He didn't even pretend to ask permission to come aboard this time, just swung up and over the lifelines.

"Goddammit, I've told you everything I know already. There's nothing else to say." The fascist bastard was getting on my nerves.

"And you're absolutely sure he's not your dog? You have nothing to do with him?"

"That's right. Why don't you go and hassle some of the other boats? Maybe they've got some foreign cockroaches on board you can impound." I really did have a headache now.

"Then perhaps you can tell me what that is on your foredeck?"

He pointed forward.

Sure enough the stupid bugger was laying there on his back, legs splayed out, snoring softly, his morning erection swaying in the breeze. I remembered that he had shown up late at Molly's and gotten into the screech with Danny.

"Well, I'll be damned," I said. "How the hell did that son of a bitch get up there without us seeing him?"

Basil gave me a look of patent disbelief. "Oh. So he's not your dog then?"

"Christ no! Look at the size of that son of a bitch. We're cruisers, how the hell would something like that live on a boat at sea? Can you even imagine trying to feed him?" I laughed in disbelief. "He just ran with me a few times, doesn't even like me."

We walked forward as we spoke, and Sinbad awoke at the sound of our steps, rolled over onto his belly, and watched with narrowed eyes as we approached. He uttered a low growl, and the inspector halted suddenly.

"See what I mean?" I extended my hand towards Sinbad and he growled more loudly, switching his tail back and forth like a disturbed lion.

"The bugger hates me. I can't imagine what he's doing here, how the hell he even managed to get on board. I'll fetch you a piece of line, you can take him with you right now."

The inspector's look of sarcastic disbelief turned to one of concern as I returned with the line. Sinbad was motionless, his baleful yellow eyes fixed on the inspector.

"There you go. He's all yours, Officer. I certainly do admire you. I wouldn't touch that fucker with a ten-foot pole, but I'm sure you handle a lot of dangerous animals in your line of work. Nothing at all for a man of your experience."

The inspector took a small hesitant step forward and Sinbad rose to his feet and thrust his head towards him, his growl rising a notch and the hairs on the top of his hump standing suddenly out on end.

"I'll just leave you to it, Inspector."

I turned and quickly ascended the ratlines to the spreaders. Basil glared up at me and then took a quick step backwards as Sinbad snaked his neck towards him. Sinbad stretched to his utmost and then took a step forward as the official retreated. The two of them moved down the boat in halting choreography, every precise backwards step of the inspector matched by Sinbad's careful stalking. At the end, Basil broke and turned and ran the last three steps with Sinbad on his heels. He jumped the lifelines and landed awkwardly in the skiff, seizing the oars and rowing frantically for long moments before he realized he was still tethered by the painter. There was no question of untying it now, as Sinbad had a bight in his mouth and was straining backwards to haul him in again. The inspector pulled out a pocket knife and cut the line and the dinghy shot away. He turned his head and looked up at me, his face red with anger and shouting, but I couldn't make out the words.

"I guess we had better step up our departure plans then," Danny said when I told him. "What say we check out of the marina, tell the manager we're heading north, and go into the yard for a quick haul out? With any luck the inspector won't even know we're there until we're gone. We should be fine."

Two hours later we were on the hard, blocked up, pressure washed, and carrying out an inspection of *Arrow*'s hull. Her bottom paint was still in decent condition, a light sanding and one coat over would do us for the next twelve months. There was a nasty ding in the lead ballast at the forward end of the keel where I had misjudged a coral head going through a pass in the Mamanucas, but it was mostly cosmetic. A few blows with a hammer to reshape the lead plus some fairing with thickened epoxy and it would be good as new.

It took two days of steady work to get everything more or less shipshape. I sorted out the dent in the lead while Danny pulled out and repacked the stern gland stuffing. The drip was running a little fast, and we were near the end of the adjustment. The cutlass bearing was worn, but it would last until the next haul out given the limited amount of time we spent motoring. We pulled the through hulls and changed two of them, replaced both zincs, and greased the Max prop, slapped on the bottom paint and were done.

Danny doesn't need much of an excuse to celebrate, and we called up Molly and the three of us went out for a final dinner and night on the town before heading north to Opua.

When we returned to the yard at midnight, we found that somebody had broken into *Arrow* and ripped her insides apart.

CHAPTER 3

Danny was headed up the ladder and into the cockpit with me following close behind when he suddenly halted and uttered a curse. He picked the shattered companionway board with the padlock off the deck and stared down into the interior. I moved in beside him and saw outlined in the harsh yellow light from the yard arc lamps a scene of wild confusion. It looked like every drawer, cupboard, and shelf on the boat had been emptied and their contents thrown into a pile on the cabin sole. The shelves that attached to the forward bulkheads had been ripped off their mounts, and books, charts, and manuals were mixed with clothes, food, and supplies in an unholy mess.

We stood there for a long minute and then went inside and lit the oil lamp. A half-filled bottle of Scotch lay on its side amidst a tangled pile of clothes and Danny poured out a couple of drinks. We sat and stared at the mess.

"Shit! The money."

We cleared a space by piling everything in one end of the cabin and lifted the bilge covers. I thrust my hand down and up behind the steel floors and felt the duct taped package that held our remaining funds.

"Still there." The money was tainted; we had obtained it by suspect means and never declared it, and it would have been begging for trouble to deposit it in a bank. Somebody would have wanted to know where we had got all those crisp new thousand-dollar bills.

"What did they take?" Danny said. "Looks like the electronics are all here."

They're usually the first thing stolen. It only takes a minute to remove the GPS, radios, or even the radar monitor, and they're all expensive, portable, and readily disposed of in any port.

"The Steiners are still here too."

Danny pulled the expensive binoculars out of the mess, blew the flour off them, and checked to see that they weren't broken. I sat there sifting aimlessly through the debris, my mind whirling. Every time we thought something was missing, we found it somewhere else and threw it into the pile. The search had been quick and brutal, done by someone who didn't give a good goddam for pretty old wooden boats.

"So what the hell were they after?" Danny said. "Nobody has reason to think we carry any amount of cash on board, and there are a lot of more expensive boats around to hit. If it was kids, they would have taken the liquor. I haven't heard of anybody else being ripped off."

"No. These guys were looking for something all right. But what?"

They hadn't broken into the outside lockers, or opened the bilges or engine compartment, or any of the other obscure hiding places found aboard any large boat. So they expected to find whatever it was inside the living space. From the looks of the saloon, they had flown into a rage when they hadn't. There were signs of frustration everywhere, marks on the bulkheads where things had been thrown, a bottle of ketchup exploded against the heater, the wine glass rack hurled fully loaded into the forward cabin. Or maybe they were just destructive.

I reached down and picked up the little Purdey over-and-under we hide in a map cylinder, with old charts cut up and plugging the ends. Usually, we declare it but hadn't bothered in New Zealand. The intruders hadn't discovered the other weapons hidden in the false post by the chart table and under the panel at the foot of Danny's bunk. We had used them in a war against people who were trying to kill us a while back and hadn't got around to getting rid of them yet. Maybe we'd hold off on that for a bit.

"I suppose there's no question of reporting the bastards to the police," Danny said.

"I don't think so. We don't stand up all that well to close scrutiny and there's not much that they could do anyway. Especially if nothing is missing. We'll ask around in the morning, see if anybody noticed anything. Too bad Sinbad wasn't in the neighbourhood; we might have had a corpse to identify. You seen him lately?"

"Not since we moved into the yard. He'll show up once we're back in the water. I think he can pick up the vibrations of *Arrow*'s engine from five miles away."

Danny picked up the bottle and refilled our glasses. We sat there amidst the wreckage and I felt a slow wrath building. We didn't need any more trouble on this trip. We'd already had enough to last us a lifetime.

"I can't face this mess tonight; let's tackle it in the morning."

"Yeah."

We scrounged around in the mess for clean sheets and turned in. It occurred to me that what they were looking for must have been fairly large as they hadn't opened any of the smaller food containers, only the big ones. So, larger than a quart? That was a big fucking help. Although, it probably meant it wasn't money. I didn't know if that was good news or bad news. I lay there listening to Danny's gentle snores trying to think what they could have been after. It wasn't random violence or petty thievery, I knew it instinctively, deep in my bones, as certain as the knowledge that whatever this was about, it was only the beginning. When I finally slept, my dreams were dark and confused.

We'd planned to leave the following morning, but it was another two days before we had everything cleaned up and ready to go. In spite of all the mess, there was little serious damage, and no visible signs of our visitors remained other than some new varnish and a few hairline cracks. When we'd restored everything to its proper place, we found nothing missing, and in some ways that was more disturbing than an actual theft; it suggested that we were specifically targeted.

Danny went around the yard a final time to see if anybody remembered anything from the night of our break-in while I went to the marina office to check for mail. The manager handed me a fax from Bob Sproule, the Canadian lawyer who had married Bill Calder's widow and was now retired and living in England. We'd become good friends since that day we'd first met with our backs up when he told me I'd inherited *Arrow* from the Calders in spite of all his advice to the contrary.

Jared,

All is well with both of us and Meg sends you her love. We are still hoping to get out and meet you for that cruise this summer. A strange thing has happened. Our house was broken into last week while we were in Spain on a brief holiday. While it appeared at first that nothing was missing, we discovered yesterday that the thieves had taken the first three volumes of *Arrow*'s journals that Meg had copied when she left the boat. I thought I should let you know, though I have no idea why they were taken. There were some quite valuable first editions right alongside them that were ignored.

I can't think of anything that would prompt the theft. The only thing that Meg has done lately that relates in any way was to present a slide show at the yacht club last month about *Arrow*'s voyages, which included a display of some of the souvenirs she and Bill had collected over the years.

All the best. Looking forward to seeing you and Danny in the near future.

Regards,
Bob

The journals! That must have been what they were after. They occupied so little space I hadn't even thought about them. I jogged back down to the boat to check. They were gone. All *Arrow*'s history, the descriptions of hundreds of anchorages, the wonderful sketches of people met and places visited, all lost. Meg would be devastated.

Danny came up the ladder and saw from my expression that something had happened.

"What?"

"The journals," I said. "They're missing."

"Oh shit. I forgot all about them. Sorry about that Jared. I'll go get them right now."

"What do you mean you'll go and get them, you idiot? I just told you they've been stolen."

"No, I lent them to Rachel. I'd mentioned the journals to her and she asked me if she could borrow them for a few days. I didn't think you'd mind, and you weren't around at the time to ask. I was supposed to pick them up before we left the marina. What with the break-in and all, I forgot all about them."

I whooped and clapped him on the back. "Marvellous! That's what they were after, Danny. The journals. We lucked out, old buddy. Here, read this."

I handed him the fax.

"They stole Meg's copies of the first three books and what they wanted wasn't there and they came for the rest."

I waited while he read the fax. He looked up at me, his face thoughtful.

"Interesting. What could be in those journals that's so important?"

"I have no idea. I'm going to phone Bob, though, and see if I can't find out. Hold on. That woman. The prissy one who wanted to charter *Arrow*. Remember her? What was her name? Laura something?"

"What woman?"

I hadn't told Danny about the strange offer to charter *Arrow*, it hadn't seemed important. "Laura Kennedy," I said. "The woman in the business suit who came up to me in the bar the night you met Dianne. Asked me if we wanted to charter out *Arrow*. Said money wouldn't be a problem for her and she thought we might be interested as a lot of cruisers do some chartering on the side to earn a little extra cash. Seemed odd at the time. I told her I'd talk to you about it. I forgot."

"Did she say why she wanted to charter *Arrow* in particular?"

"Said she liked old wooden boats, but that was a crock. She wasn't a very good liar. It must have been the journals she was after, figured she would get on board and read them."

"Well, maybe. That was a vicious search though; she didn't look the sort to rip things apart like that from what I remember of her."

"Yeah, well you didn't talk to her. One cold fish, that lady. I'm going to phone Bob, see if he has any thoughts about all of this."

"I'll collect the journals from Rachel. Maybe I should make copies for Bob and Meg."

"Good idea. We'll stow the originals somewhere safe."

We walked downtown, and I wasted a few coins checking the hotels for a Laura Kennedy before I gave up on it and dialled through to England. Meg answered.

"Jared. How nice to hear from you. Everything is fine with you and Danny, I hope?"

"Couldn't be better. I just called to see how you were. I got the fax, thought maybe you'd like me to send you a full set of copies."

"I'd like that. Strange isn't it? We're quite sure there is nothing else missing. I had foolishly left a gold necklace in my dressing table drawer; they never even bothered with that. We probably wouldn't have known for ages except the books were out of order. Bob spotted it immediately."

"Out of order?"

"Yes." I could hear the smile in her voice. "I think maybe time is sitting a little heavy on Bob's hands since he retired. He's always looking for projects. He has all the books in his study organized by author and subject and they were out of order. He saw it as soon as we got back, and he went to put away the ones we'd taken on the trip. When we called in the police, they found where the lock had been forced on the patio doors."

"Well, I'm glad it turned out all right."

We talked for a while about our plans for the cruise in August. She asked about Danny and I told her that he was fine. I'd phone again when we arrived in Fiji, and I'd be sure and tell her if there was anything she could bring out for the boat.

"Just hang on; I'll switch you through to the study."

A brief pause and then Bob picked up the phone.

"Hey Bob. What are you up to, colour-coding the magazines?"

"Laugh, you disorganized clot. You received the fax then?"

"Yes. It came just after someone ripped *Arrow* apart looking for something. Nothing was taken, but the journals weren't on board at the time. We'd lent them out to a friend."

"Really. That was fortunate."

You could almost hear the agile brain ticking over in the next few seconds of silence. "It must have something to do with Meg's talk at the club. She took her copies of the journals with her and read some passages from them."

"Yes. You mentioned she also took a box of souvenirs to the club. Was anything missing from that?"

"It was still in the trunk of the car. We hadn't gotten around to unpacking it yet, so it stayed at the airport the week we were away when the break-in occurred. I hadn't even thought to look in there. It could have been something in there couldn't it, and maybe the journals to tell where it was found? What about them? Will they be safe with you?"

"Danny is making copies as we speak. I'll forward a set and maybe you and Meg can make some kind of connection out of all of this. We'll stow the originals on board where nobody will find them."

Wrapped in cloth and shoved up beside the barrel of the Ithaca shotgun in the false post, they would be safe short of the wholesale demolition of *Arrow*.

"Did you tell Meg about your visitors?"

"No. I figured that was your call, didn't want her to worry."

"Yes. I suppose I'll tell her. She's got a lot of confidence in you and Danny. Is there anything else?"

"A woman last week who wanted to charter *Arrow* for some research on her thesis on diatoms or some such. She wasn't very convincing and didn't have a good reason for wanting *Arrow* in particular. We've never advertised her as a charter vessel. She said her name was Laura Kennedy. Probably phony, but I thought there might be some connection with the yacht club. English, mid-twenties, very prim, no makeup, black hair pulled back in a bun. Good looking perhaps, if you favour the repressed schoolmarm type."

"I don't really know anybody at the yacht club, that's Meg's turf. I'll ask her about it. Not very likely, but it's a place to start."

"I don't have anything else. We're going to start drifting north tomorrow, should be in Opua in a couple of weeks. They have a post office there if anything comes up and you want to get in touch. I'll give you a call when we arrive."

"Okay, Jared. Take care. Talk to you soon."

I replaced the receiver and walked down to the print shop where Danny was finishing up. We had them wrap up the copies and air mail the package to Bob. Afterwards we walked down to one of the little cafes for lunch. I couldn't wait to get back to the spicy foods of Fiji; in parts of New Zealand, they consider black pepper an exotic spice. We had a couple of pies and then went over to a bar where we started shooting pool and drinking beer.

The locals checked our strokes for a while and then offered to play doubles for drinks. We spent a pleasant afternoon, mostly at their expense, Danny keeping the game close and losing occasionally so they didn't get discouraged and me plugging along. Afterwards we picked up some ribs for the barbecue and went back down to *Arrow* to ready her for departure on the morning tide.

When we were finished Danny rowed ashore to say goodbye to Dianne while I paid a final visit to the little martial arts club and worked on the mats and heavy bag practising my katas. I concentrated on speed and height, letting the anger seep out and disseminate with every jarring impact; *mae geri, mawashi geri, yoko geri*, all the kicks in quick sequence and then into the punches and reverse punches, faster and faster until I was lathered in sweat and my breath was rasping and uneven and my mind a blank and empty slate.

One of the instructors came in later on, and we worked on sparring and free sparring, alternating roles as attacker and defender in rhythmic flowing sequence. He was a big self-exiled Englishman, better than me but not by much, and we had been doing this for months and knew each other's moves so well we fought almost even. I started to tire, and I gambled and feinted for his head then tried a low sweep. He was waiting and caught my leg and threw me and it was over. We made our bows and I showered and changed and went back to *Arrow*. I took a glass and a bottle of Scotch and went out into the cockpit and sat under the stars reading the journals and searching for answers.

I found none.

CHAPTER 4

We were back in the water early the following morning to catch the first of the ebb. A few minutes after the old Perkins growled reluctantly into life, Sinbad materialized from the mangroves along the river and swam out to our towed dinghy and sprang aboard. He came and stood close by me and stared up as he shook himself off. He looked ravaged, with fresh scars on his muzzle. I ignored him, and he stalked up to the bow, flopped down, and was asleep before we were a mile down the channel.

The wind was light, on the beam for the most part, and with the big genoa up we were just able to maintain steerage and make three knots with the help of the current. We weren't in a hurry anyway. We still had a month to kill before it was prudent to leave New Zealand and head north to the warm water. It felt good to be on the move again, even if it was just idling down the muddy Hātea River. An ex-girlfriend told me once that the desire to be constantly moving and changing venues was childish and immature, and demonstrated a clear inability to form permanent relationships.

Hard to disagree.

We moved slowly past the warehouses and docks that fringed the upper reach of the river, some of them with the big offshore tuna boats tied alongside for their annual refits, their bows towering forty feet above *Arrow*'s decks.

Danny proclaimed the sun over the yardarm and pulled a couple of cold ones from the fridge. I accepted mine gratefully and sat there steering with my foot on the tiller, leaning back against the cushions and letting the peace and tranquility enfold me. There is something so fundamentally right about moving silently through the water with the aid of cloth and tall sticks, something so innately satisfying and appropriate to the inner man that I can no longer conceive of an existence without sailing. There must be some hidden instinct, some racial memory implanted in the genes and handed down unbroken since the first man on a log put up the first scrap of hide to trap the wind; a secret, unrecognized yearning, lying dormant sometimes for generations and then connecting immediately to the first raising of a sail.

There are birds who fashion their complex nests from strange esoteric materials and whose offspring have been taken away in their eggs, and their offspring's eggs for generations hatched and raised confined in cages. Once released to the wild, the freed birds fashion their nests again in the strictest compliance to the patterns of their forebears. Not taught, not learned, but an essential part of their being lying in wait for an opportunity.

We moved past the last of the warehouses and out into the floodlands where the river wandered and tracked through acres of mangroves. The channel was marked, but the mud drifted and changed the course with the tides, and a boat with *Arrow*'s draught was only certain of water a scant boat's length from the guideposts. It was on the slow, lazy curves where the danger lay. We had to continually check to make sure we weren't drifting inside the invisible line that connected the markers; there is little the locals appreciate more than the sight of a grounded yacht with a foreign flag slowly heeling and settling embarrassed into the mud on a falling tide.

We came out of the swamps and into the first of the bays on the way to the sea, the water more salt than fresh now, the land smell changing into something more saline and bracing. A small chop sprang up as the wind veered forward and worked against the tide's last ebb. We hardened up the genoa, *Arrow* took on some heel and her speed increased, and for the first time in months we heard the hiss of water split by her hull, and the creaking of planks and rigging as she worked and flexed after her long rest.

We slanted past the refinery docks and their attendant tankers; Calliope Bay opened to port, and we moved around the shallow bank and into the anchorage. Danny dropped the headsail and kicked the Danforth over on the last of our surge and *Arrow* ran on a hundred feet into the bight of Home Point and snubbed up hard before I turned her bow into the wind and dropped the main.

It was a lovely spot, well sheltered by the undulating green slopes of the sheep-dotted hills that surrounded it. We were the only boat in the anchorage apart from a skiff moored out in front of the farm at the head of the bay. Behind us a trawler steamed up the channel, its decks awash with shining fish, the seagulls screaming in its wake as the crew dressed the catch and threw the offal overboard.

"I wouldn't mind some fresh fish myself," Danny said.

He went forward and untied the little wooden skiff and lowered it into the water on the spinnaker halyard. Sinbad opened a lazy eye at the activity around him and then settled again.

I went below and took down the old Peetz trolling reels on their stubby rods and picked up the tackle box and a cooler of beer. When I returned Danny had the sail rigged and we headed off towards the little spit that jutted off our bow a hundred yards distant. I put on one of the silver spoons and rigged a white feather and for the next hour we drank beer and tacked up and down without even a nibble for our efforts. Finally we gave up and anchored over a deep edge and jigged up a dozen cod-like little fish in minutes.

"That'll do," Danny said. "There's bacon and a bag of green mussels left. I'll cook up chowder with them and some of the fish. Sinbad can have the rest."

We went back to *Arrow* and ate a leisurely supper at the little cockpit table. Afterwards we played cribbage until the light faded and then went inside and cleaned up.

I was about to turn in when I heard a boat edging cautiously into the anchorage and went up on deck to have a look. They were playing a spotlight ahead of them as they felt their way in and it caught and held *Arrow* in its loom for long seconds before they moved slowly past. A big power boat, but I couldn't make out the name. They anchored well inside, right in the bight of the spit. When we got up in the morning, they had already left. It was silly to worry about every boat that shared our anchorage.

For the next ten days, we worked our slow way north, resting in a secure anchorage each night, and sleeping in each morning. The wind held from the southeast and it was day sailing of the finest kind, the breeze always aft of the starboard beam between ten and fifteen knots, a light swell, and *Arrow* relaxed and going nicely under the working jib and main. Apart from the occasional fishing boat, there was little traffic that tight into the coast. In the distance, a steady stream of container ships, tankers, and the occasional freighter loaded with Japanese cars on its way to Auckland.

The only sailboats we saw were two big black maxis beating down the coast in contest the third night out, something to do with the America's Cup and New Zealand's ongoing campaign. They are hands down the finest sailors in the world, and like most amateurs, I relished their David-like victories against the moneyed Goliaths from the United States and Europe.

Each night we stopped at a different spot, sometimes sailing for only an hour before heading back into the coast again to thread our way up a tiny river, or work our way through the rock piles that cluttered the bays. We passed Pataua, Whakareora, Tutukaka, Rangitapu, Mimiwhangata, Whangaruru Harbour, and then Whangamumu

Harbour — the names as vibrant as the Māori culture that birthed them — and finally cut inside Tiheru Island on a surfing beam reach, the aptly named Dog formation as clear and unmistakable as a commissioned sculpture, before we turned the corner into the Bay of Islands.

Three times on the run up, a power boat came in after us and anchored after dark, and each time it left before daylight. They didn't put out an anchor light and kept the shades drawn over the windows. It wasn't carrying commercial fishing gear, but apart from that, it was impossible to pick out any details. Sport fishermen most likely, early to bed and up before dawn to catch the morning bite. Their twin engines had the deep-throated rumble of Jimmys.

I spent my time going through the journals, taking note of any mention of objects retrieved or seen as I worked my way through them. It was a daunting task as they were so detailed, so many days and locations, but I found *Arrow*'s history fascinating and the time flew by. It was hard to believe the Calders had overlooked anything of value. They were avid and knowledgeable collectors, and Meg had become something of an expert on marine history and archaeology; like many cruisers, the Calders had researched and dived on many of the famous old wrecks in the South Pacific, and spent weeks searching out the rumours of others as yet undiscovered.

We were still well ahead of the earliest hurricane-safe departure date for Fiji and decided to spend a few days hanging out in Te Puna Inlet, up behind the Hen and Chicken Islands. It was shallow in there, but we had excellent charts and a local had told us where we could pick up shellfish. A light swell was pushing up through the exposed entrance and we went in tight against the south side in late afternoon, running down the fifteen-foot edge until it shoaled up, and then laying in against the islands. We found good holding in mud and sand and backed down hard to set the anchor.

The wind died with the daylight and it became eerily still, the only sounds the soft break of waves on the beach and a breaching school of small fish beside the boat. As the sky darkened, the earth turned another degree and the full moon rose from the waters behind us and captured *Arrow* in liquid silver light. It seemed we were caught out of time as we slowly revolved through the eternal wheel of the universe, the constellations sailing across the sky and us huddled below on our tiny craft suspended on a thin skin of water, humbled and insignificant. It was midnight when we went below, and still not a breath of wind, only the echoes of a far distant engine moving past the inlet entrance.

It was flat calm the next morning and a four-mile run to the shellfish beach, so we took the British Antichrist off its bracket on the pushpit and fastened it to the stern of the inflatable. The little Seagull outboard would push us through the water at three knots if it chose to run. Danny had just overhauled it but that never made any significant difference to its performance; it was governed by more complex and eclectic criteria, the fundamental tenet being that it operated in an inverse ratio to the need of its services. As the weather was settled, the waters smooth, and we could manage nicely without it, I had little doubt the motor would run superbly.

Danny wound the cord and pulled, it fired immediately and we headed up the inlet. Sinbad had left earlier, swimming ashore and working the beach in high stiff-legged jumps, his head jerking around as he searched for the telltale flashes that would indicate breakfast. I watched him for a while, but he didn't catch anything and soon disappeared around the corner. The chart showed a little reef extending out behind that looked like it might have some good tide pools as well as the long-legged cranes that sometimes fished them.

We spent the day at the head of the inlet, gathering a bag of clams and mussels and going for a hike. We followed an old trail that ran up the big hill that faced the inlet, winding across it in long parallels before it finally emerged at the top. In the distance, we could see a half dozen boats spread out in the scattered coves and bays, and beyond them Opua opening out with a hundred more. The tips of *Arrow*'s masts were just visible, and a white power boat was slowly cruising up the channel towards it, a red inflatable towing behind. It made a long lazy turn and disappeared behind the island.

We sat in the shade of the big pines, drinking beer and eating the sandwiches we had packed. By the time we finished, clouds had arrived from nowhere and the temperature had dropped ten degrees. We jogged down to the beach and headed back to *Arrow* in a light drizzle, the wind rising and the dinghy slapping and uncomfortable in the short chop. When we were a mile from *Arrow*, the Seagull choked and died and we paddled back to *Arrow* with the long wooden oars we'd customized, cursing British technology.

Danny tied off the dinghy and I vaulted over the lifelines and slipped in a wet red pool on the cockpit seat. Blood, a lot of it, and Sinbad's tracks right through the centre, leading up to the rail and disappearing. The stains along the rail were thin and watery with the rain, but under the dodger the blood was thick and viscous. It was smudged in spots, and a shallow arc was traced in one corner, half repeated near the seat.

Danny swung down beside me and gently touched the blood with the tip of his finger.

"How long you figure?" I asked.

"Hard to say. Not more than a couple of hours I'd guess." He stood up and scanned the shore. "I'd better go and look for him. He must have cut his foot on a shell, or maybe a piece of broken glass on the beach. I wonder why he didn't stay on board?"

I went below but he hadn't been down there. No tracks, everything intact. We hadn't locked up. With Sinbad around we didn't think it was necessary. Boats were dead easy to break into anyway, we'd already proved that.

When I went back on deck with the binoculars, Danny was in the dinghy untying the painter, his head cocked and listening.

"What?"

"Just a distant boat engine. Thought I heard Sinbad for a second." He untied the line and sat down at the oars.

I took a quick sweep with the Steiners and then swung back again.

"Hold it, Danny. I think I've got him."

I took a cloth and wiped the rain off the binoculars and then looked again. It was Sinbad all right, swimming around the corner of the island with something shiny and black clamped in his jaws.

"He must have got hungry, went back ashore, he's been hunting again. Looks like he's moving pretty well, can't be hurt too bad."

It wasn't until he was alongside that we realized that what he had in his jaws was half of a diving flipper. He held it in his mouth the whole time Danny ran his hands over him checking for damage, and then Sinbad went up to the bow and ripped it up into small chunks and began eating it, growling softly. I fetched his stainless bowl and poured a beer in it for him to wash it down with and set it by his side.

"Good dog, Sinbad." He raised his head and stared at me, then snaked it slowly towards me, the lips drawn back over his teeth to the gums, eyes glowing. He didn't look like he was waiting to be petted. I returned to the cockpit.

"The guy must have come aboard just before Sinbad got back," Danny suggested. "Or else he didn't see him on the bow and Sinbad jumped him. He would have taken his flippers off before he went below."

"Yes," I said. "There's no moisture below, nothing out of place. Maybe the power boat towing the inflatable we saw."

"Could be," Danny said. "We should head into Opua, there could be some news from Bob and Meg. Might even get a lead on somebody who injured himself and had to get stitched up."

He stood up and stretched, a hard smile on his face. "Maybe they'll decide to come and visit us again when we're at home and can entertain them properly."

"It's only three hours away. Be dark by then, but we can find our way into the anchorage easily enough with the range lights and radar. Pretty crowded anchorage I'm told. We'll tie up alongside somewhere tonight and get anchored out in daylight."

Before I'd finished speaking, Danny was at the bow cranking up the anchor. Ten minutes later we were beating up the inlet and then we made the headland and the long swing to starboard with the wind on the beam. In another half hour we turned again, and it was a sleigh ride down the middle of the channel, the small spinnaker up and straining, keeping the range lights in the white aspect, making the occasional radar check for traffic. A cruise boat passed us, loaded down with noise and lights, and we tucked in behind and followed it into the inner harbour.

We tied up on the outside of a big steel schooner flying the Swedish flag with a farewell party in full swing on board. The skipper said it was fine to spend the night as long as we were clear by ten o'clock the following morning when he planned to leave.

Danny and I went ashore and did a quick tour of the docks. There were no white powerboats with red dinghies tied up visible, and we couldn't begin to check the hundred odd boats hidden in darkness out in the anchorage. When we did, it was a fair bet there would be a half dozen that fit the general description and no way to tell which, if any, was the one. We gave it up for the night and went back to *Arrow*. As we crossed the schooner's decks on our return, we were ambushed by the Swedes and spent the rest of the evening drinking aquavit, eating a smorgasbord, and trading opinions about the best places to spend the upcoming cruising season.

I left at midnight, only the skipper and Danny remaining now, the two of them sitting in front of a table holding an ice bucket with two half-empty bottles of aquavit buried in the cubes and a couple of hundred dollars in U.S. bills alongside. They were smiling fixedly at one another, each pouring from his own bottle, drink for drink, and two more bottles lying in wait. I shuddered and went down to my bunk.

I awoke at first light, picked up the binoculars, and climbed up the ratlines. After ten minutes I had six possibilities: four New Zealand boats, an Aussie, and one fouled flag I couldn't make out. A mild breeze dimpled the waters in the harbour, and I rigged the skiff out with the little main and jib and walked up to the bow.

"Morning, Sinbad. How you doing?"

He opened one eye and regarded me.

"You want to go in the skiff, Sinbad?"

His ear twitched.

I knew he recognized the word skiff. He liked to clamp onto the rudder with his teeth and tow along behind when we sailed it.

"Skiff, boy, skiff."

He started a growl deep in his throat and held it, his eyes watching me, his tail slowly sweeping back and forth. I could see a piece of the flipper underneath his forepaws.

"Here, Sinbad." I rolled a piece of the hamburger I'd brought with me into a ball and threw it to him. He caught and swallowed it in a single motion.

"Good boy. More?" He watched me intently. I rolled another ball and held it up then threw it. He dispatched it as effortlessly as the first, the hungry yellow eyes never leaving me.

"Good boy, Sinbad. More?"

I took the last ball of meat and threw it off to the side. He moved across and snagged it and in that second I reached down and grabbed the last small piece of the flipper.

"Good boy, Sinbad. More?" He stared at me and then the flipper. "Yeah, Sinbad. More?" I waved the flipper back and forth and he growled low in his throat and crouched, his eyes no longer on the piece of rubber, but staring into mine.

"More, Sinbad? Skiff, Sinbad, skiff." He took a step towards me, his growl increasing a pitch as I stepped backwards. His chin was almost on the deck now, his whole body vibrating with purpose.

"Skiff, Sinbad, skiff," I shrilled.

"What the fuck are you doing, Jared?"

Danny, smiling and clear-eyed, emerged on deck with no trace of the night's debauch.

"I thought I'd take Sinbad and check out some of the powerboats," I said.

"Good idea," Danny said. "Sinbad, get in the skiff." Sinbad rose from his crouch, trotted past me, and sprang lightly into the skiff.

"Assholes," I muttered as I climbed down and elbowed Sinbad off my seat.

We checked the four nearest boats with red inflatables, sailing within a few feet of each without any interest at all from Sinbad. When we went by the fifth, he raised his head from off the transom and stared at it briefly, then looked away again.

"One more," Danny said. It was the one farthest from the docks, tucked into the little bay that ran off the southeast corner of the anchorage. As we approached, the stern flag billowed out and I saw it was New Zealand's, with a small red ensign flying off the masthead on the upper deck above it indicating English crew aboard.

Danny swung the tiller and we tacked across its bow without any sign from Sinbad. He looked like he was going back to sleep.

"Maybe downwind," Danny said. He jibed and ran within ten feet of the stern. As we passed, Sinbad raised his head and growled.

"Inconclusive," Danny said. He ran a hundred yards downwind and then beat back up to the boat. Sinbad sat up and growled again.

"Maybe," Danny said.

The boat was the *Kiwi Maiden*, registered in Auckland with all the charter gear installed, half a dozen rod holders and some expensive looking tackle padlocked in, two radars, two fighting seats, and enough antennas to furnish six sailboats.

"What do you think?" I said.

"Looks to me like this is a fine spot to anchor, lots of swinging room, out of most of the wind, interesting neighbours. Let's move over here, see what happens. I'll buy you breakfast first. I made a couple of bucks last night."

Halfway back to the docks Sinbad slipped over the side and swam off towards the shore. He emerged onto the beach, shook himself off, and loped away with a purposeful stride.

When we'd finished breakfast and walked back to the boat, the

Swede Danny had traded shots with came out onto the deck of the schooner, pale and trembling, and said we were welcome to stay another day as he had decided he wasn't ready to leave just yet. I thanked him but said we were going to anchor out while there were still some good spots available. Danny invited the captain over for drinks later on, but he blanched and refused.

We untied *Arrow* and ran across the channel towards *Kiwi Maiden*. No one was visible on deck and Danny took *Arrow* close past her at full revs and then swung around into the wind a hundred yards off her beam. I kicked over the anchor and laid out a five-to-one scope. Danny backed down hard, the Perkins smoking a bit as he gave it full power, and then he cut the engine as we grabbed and held against full reverse. We watched until *Arrow* found her spot with the wind and tide. We were well clear, even when the tide changed there would be a couple of lengths' swinging room. I went below and brought up coffee.

"Somebody is watching us," Danny said. He stood up and waved and the big man on the power boat waved back and went below. He must have weighed two hundred and fifty pounds. A short while later another giant came out on deck, stretched, and casually turned towards us. Danny gave him a big wave as well. While he was doing this another man came out and looked over at us. Oversize.

"Who the hell are these guys? All Blacks rugby players on a fishing charter? There must be eight hundred pounds of beef there," I said. And then another man came out on deck with his coffee. He was tall, slim, and elegant in white slacks and a navy turtleneck. One sleeve was rolled up and there was a bandage wrapped around his arm from wrist to elbow.

"Well, well," Danny said. "Now there's a bit of a coincidence, don't you think?"

Danny stood up and waved enthusiastically, the big shit-eating grin firmly in place. The man stared back across the water, his face impassive.

"Maybe this isn't such a great idea," I said. "No sense asking for trouble."

The man turned and went below.

Danny regarded me in surprise. "Who's looking for trouble? We're just anchored here, that's all. No law against that is there?"

He turned away and gazed towards the powerboat again. He made no effort to hide his interest, just stood there sipping his coffee and staring. The men had all gone back inside now.

Half an hour later it began to rain, one of those sky darkening, pounding New Zealand thunderstorms, and we went below and did some work on the VHF radio. It was picking up static and it was likely the antenna connection stuffed in tight behind it. It required disassembling half the nav station to get at it, and it was late afternoon by the time we finished. We were just cleaning up when we heard their outboard start. Danny stuck his head out the companionway.

"One, two, three, four. All the little piggies going to market. How nice. I think we should go over and check out their boat. Turnabout is fair play."

"I don't know, there could be someone left on board. And they might come back."

"Trust me, Jared."

He gave me what he thought was a reassuring smile. He looked crazed. I tried to think of something to stop him, and in that hesitation, he took my silence for approval.

"Okay then. It will be dark in a while. We'll have a little drink while we wait."

He got out the Scotch and half filled two tumblers and we sat there while the light faded, and I tried not to think about the size of those guys. But we'd keep a sharp lookout, and we'd be careful, and they'd never know we'd been there.

We took the Avon inflatable, its shabby grey Hypalon near invisible in the dark, and paddled across. We bumped alongside, and Danny knocked sharply against the hull. We waited, but there was no response. We swung aboard, keeping our profiles low. I tried the cabin door and found it locked. I'd expected this and worked on it for several minutes with the stiff wire and vice grips I'd brought along.

"Let me have a go," Danny said. "You're not going about it the right way."

He took the vice grips and rapped them smartly against the glass pane in the upper half of the door. The glass shattered, and he reached inside and turned the knob and opened the door.

"Nothing to it when you know how," he said.

So much for the invisible in and out. I followed him through the door and looked around. It was a standard powerboat layout, galley to starboard as you came down the steps, saloon just forward and two small cabins up in the bow with the master cabin aft alongside the engine room on the port side. The skipper's bunk was in the wheelhouse on the upper deck with the chart table directly across. Danny searched the cabins while I checked out the chart table. It was covered with the usual assortment of clutter, parallel rules, dividers, tide tables, an assortment of pencils and half a dozen charts of the North Island. At the top was NZ 521 covering the run from Whangarei up to Cape Brett. A track was pencilled in with several of the anchorages we had used marked off, but that was to be expected. They were the best ones and would be used by most boats. No dates. I rummaged through the shelves under the chart table looking for the log book. Most skippers kept them and the boat was reasonably shipshape and tidy, it had to be somewhere. I located it tucked up behind the radar, pulled it out, and flicked through the entries. Very brief, just a couple of lines for each day, a lot of gaps. But then I saw the one I was looking for.

Ship's log
Saturday March 20th
Ran 3 hours 315 at 8 knots. *Arrow* layed in for land 1700 hours.
Followed in after dark.

I replaced the logbook and called Danny.

"It's them all right. They mentioned following us in the log. Nothing else though. You find anything?"

"Just the one passport in the master cabin. Englishman. Lord Barclay Summers. Landed in Auckland March first. I took down all the details. He's the one with the bandage. The others are likely all Kiwis. No passports lying around anyway."

"Right. Let's get the hell out of here then, before they come back."

"Not to worry. All of them going ashore this time of night, they're most likely staying for dinner and a few drinks. Not a bad idea, I was thinking we might join them. It's a small town, they'll be easy to find."

He gave me the sweet and charming smile he used on women.

"Never mind trying your big shit-eating grin on me Daniel MacLean," I said as we went out the cabin and closed the door behind us. "We're not messing with those oversized motherfuckers. My momma didn't raise no fools."

An hour and two drinks later we were cleaned and shaven, wearing tidy loose-fitting gear with runners on our feet, not sandals, and on our way into town.

Now that we knew for certain it was them, I was almost looking forward to it.

CHAPTER 5

We tied the skiff alongside the red Zodiac with the twenty-five horse Yamaha and the name *Kiwi Maiden* stencilled on the transom. Danny stepped down inside and bent over the motor while I kept a nervous watch. He stood up, pocketed his jackknife, and we headed up the hill towards the bar and restaurant.

"I shut off the vent in the fuel tank, slit the feed line. That will stop them for a while."

If they were chasing us, we'd need all the help we could get. We managed three knots in flat water with the Seagull. We trudged along. Danny finally broke the silence.

"Okay then. If we get into it, and I'm not saying that we will, but if we do, let me start and I'll take out two of them. You handle the wimpy Lord Summers and one of the others. Agreed?"

"Agreed."

It didn't really sound all that bad. Danny would have surprise on his side, and I'd seen his work before. He'd take the first man out before they even realized, and I couldn't imagine anyone going one on one with him for very long. The Pom would be easy and then it'd just be the other big lout. I had no intention of fighting clean when outweighed by eighty pounds. Nothing above the waist for the first ten seconds.

"Tell me again Danny. Why are we doing this anyway?"

He glared at me. "C'mon, Jared, you fucking well know why. We have to teach them a lesson, get them off our backs. They'll know we're on to them anyway when they get back to their boat and see the cabin door. Now is our best chance. If we're smart we might learn what they're after."

There was a flaw in all of this of course, if he hadn't busted the glass and advertised our visit, etcetera, but what the hell. He was right. The bastards had ripped *Arrow* apart, they deserved some trouble. I rationalized, as I had in the past, the violence that was to come. I breathed deeply in and out as we ascended the steep hill, letting myself get loose and focusing on the faces of the four. They were all fixed firmly in my mind, the supercilious Englishman uppermost. He would be the one in charge. I felt a cold chill of anticipation.

We walked through the door into the first tavern and there they were right in front of us, all four of them, seated around a table covered with pies and chips and pots of beer. The Englishman was sitting back a little from the other three, what looked like a pink gin suspended elegantly in his hand. He was taller than I'd thought, and not really slender either. Actually, he looked damned fit. At close hand, his face was older and harder beneath the fashionably long blond hair. He looked up and saw us and a thin smile appeared on his face.

"Well, well, our colonial Canadian neighbours on the old wooden sailboat. Won't you gentlemen join us for a drink? I'm sure we can find something in common to talk about."

The voice was rich and plummy, the smile languid, but I saw nothing easy about his eyes. They were bright and hard and watching. He seemed half-drunk and reckless already. His forearm was wrapped in a light gauze.

Danny was smiling and seating himself when I reached across the table and gripped the bandage hard. The Englishman's face suddenly went pale.

"I hope you had a rabies shot for this," I said. "Dog bites can be dangerous."

The man beside him pushed back his chair and started to his feet. Without releasing my grip, I elbow-smashed him and he flew sideways and down. Summers pulled back and away from me and I was just taking the first step towards him when he floated up in the air and drop kicked me in the chest and I hurtled back across the table and down among the pies and glasses.

The Englishman didn't bother coming after me, just waited for me to get up, facing side on, taking little dancing hops on the balls of his feet, an assured half-smile on his face. Out of the corner of my eye, I saw Danny backed up against the wall. One of the men came at him and Danny hit him with a chair. The man never even slowed down. I struggled to my feet and the Kiwi I'd hit was waiting and kicked at me and I partially dodged but his boot caught me a glancing blow and I was down in the broken glass again. Something burned across my ass and I felt a sudden dampness. I hoped it was hot pie and catsup.

This wasn't going well.

"No," the Englishman said sharply. "Kane's mine. The other one."

So they knew our names.

The man threw me a glance of pure hatred from a face that was already puffed and bleeding then lumbered off towards Danny. I was glad this affair hadn't been my idea. I turned back and moved in on Summers. He had his injured arm pulled back and I kick feinted for his thigh and then went for it. He took a quick sidestep and kicked me in the chest again then spun and took me under the arm with the pointed toe of his shoe as I was falling.

I lay there trying to clear my head, wishing I hadn't had those last two drinks. The bastard's hair wasn't even mussed. He kept taking weird little sideways two-legged hops, faster and faster now. Any hope I had of somebody stopping the massacre vanished when I saw the bartender pulling the tables away from the combat zone, and the customers all leaning back against the bar with interested faces, as if this were a scheduled entertainment enacted solely for their enjoyment.

"Come on, laddie. Let's finish it."

He smiled at me and stepped over to one of the ladies at the bar and casually took a drink from her glass. She smiled coquettishly at him. Maybe the son of a bitch was overconfident. He should have been, from all I'd done so far. I chanced a quick glance over at Danny. One of the men was down and looked out, one was weaving around holding his head, and the other was lying on top of Danny, pounding. A sudden heave and he rolled off.

I turned back and Summers was coming for me with those little mincing hops again. Thai style maybe. All I knew was I didn't know a fucking thing about it, and this was a hard way to learn.

I crouched a bit and staggered, and when he went up again with that easy toying smile I spun under the scything foot and clenched one hand on his groin and the other on his arm and swung with his momentum and pitchforked him head first into the bar. I was after him immediately and when he started to get up I spun and kicked him in the back of the neck as if I was punting for the winning fifty yarder in the last seconds of the Super Bowl. He flew back into the bar and stayed there, lying at the feet of the customers. They glared at me in disapproval. I went across the floor in time to side kick the man who had been holding his head just as he jumped onto Danny's back. He fell off to the side and I chopped him twice on the way down and this time he wouldn't get up again.

Danny's face was cut and bleeding, and his nose looked out of true. He and the last man were squared off toe to toe pounding each other, great sighing breaths issuing from their chests as they fought. The other man was heavier than Danny and I watched Danny hit him again, burying his fist right in the gut, and the man groaned softly and dropped to the floor.

"Behind you," Danny mumbled, bent over against the wall and sucking air in long gasping breaths. I turned too late and the Englishman was there again, and I felt the burn across my arm as I moved. No smile now, just an ice-cold rage in those staring blue eyes and a broken bottle in his hand. I retreated in small backwards steps as he stalked me. Danny picked up a chair and moved alongside.

"No. Stay out of it."

Watching Summers now I could see the whole room delineated in my mind, every inch of the floor space around me and all the glass and bottles behind me. My arm burned and then chilled and I heard the separate drops of blood as they fell and knew the pattern they made on the faded linoleum. I circled backwards and past the wreckage with never a thought of a wrong foot and he was in slow motion now, caught and broken already.

I felt the frozen smile starting deep inside and coming slowly out, and the calming cold the rictus brought, and I knew before he did when he would take the sudden sidestep feint and move across, and I was already there and waiting. I took the offered arm and broke it cleanly, the snap overloud in the silenced bar, and as he stood there in shocked disbelief I smashed the arrogant face and then again, until it was a bloody mask and still I wouldn't let him fall and hit him again and then he slowly crumpled and went down.

I stood there panting and timeless in the centre of the hushed room and something touched me and I spun away and wheeled and it was Danny.

"Time to go, Jared," he said. I watched him, puzzled for a moment, and then he took my arm and we left for *Arrow* together, the room still and quiet behind us.

"Goddammit, I told you to let me start it, Jared. Why the fuck didn't you wait?"

Danny was having a difficult time talking, leaned back in the chair with cotton batting stuffed up his nose while I sewed up the long gash above his eyebrow where he'd been head-butted. I'd already put six stitches in his lip, and between that and the nose, he was just barely intelligible.

"Keep quiet. You'll have your chance when I'm finished. My ass needs at least a dozen stitches."

A wide strip of adhesive tape was holding the edges together at the moment; we'd decided that Danny's cuts, being more visible, should be attended first. I'd sprayed them with a local anesthetic and he was taking long careful swallows of Scotch at frequent intervals. I had sewn the cut in my arm up myself. I prided myself on my tidy needlework and hoped he'd take the same professional attitude when his turn came.

"The asshole wasn't going to tell us anything anyway. You could see that."

"Okay, probably not, but I could've taken one guy out straight away, made it more even," he said.

"How was I supposed to know the Englishman was Bruce fucking Lee come back from the grave? You're the one who called him a little wimp. Now be quiet or you won't be pretty anymore. I don't think your nose is broken though. It looks pretty good. The guy must have punched it straight again."

I tied the last stitch off, took a drink of Scotch, and stifled a snicker.

"Fuck you," Danny mumbled, but his shoulders heaved and then we were both laughing. We kept it up until the first stitch went into my rump and then it was only Danny who was laughing.

We finished the bottle and opened another when Sinbad came back aboard and we knew that we wouldn't have to stand watch. Not that we were worried anyway. The other side had to be in even worse shape. By the time we went to bed, neither of us was feeling any pain. When we rose up in the morning and made our slow and careful way out on deck *Kiwi Maiden* was gone, and a Tayana 52 from California had anchored in her place.

"I'll flip you for the mail run," Danny mumbled. With his swollen lips and two black eyes, he was unrecognizable as well as unintelligible.

"Forget it, I'll go. You look like something out of a horror movie."

The low had passed through, and now at slack tide the water was near flat. I climbed carefully over the side and into the skiff. Crouching slightly and facing forward, I propelled myself slowly but steadily towards the dock with even backhanded strokes of the oars. There was a delicate moment when I climbed out of the skiff onto the dock, but I managed with some discomfort and no untoward sounds of ripping.

A fax from Bob Sproule was waiting at the post office.

Hi Jared,

Stranger and stranger. Meg has been trying to remember what was in the box of assorted items she took to the yacht club to illustrate her talk. She is almost certain there is a silver plate missing. It must have been taken when Meg was showing the slides. She thinks nothing else was taken although she can't be sure. But we did find something else missing from the house — some old coins that were on the mantle in the study. An assorted lot, nothing of any value, most of them covered in coral or eroded by sea and sand. Certainly taken in the break-in. As for the mystery woman, surprise! A Laura Kennedy signed in at the yacht club guest register on the night of Meg's presentation, but no one remembers her or knows who she was. Meg is still making enquiries, and perhaps we'll get lucky. Odd that the woman wouldn't have used a different name when she tried to charter *Arrow*.

I hope things have settled down for you and you haven't had any more unwelcome guests. The journal copies arrived this morning. We are looking forward to reading them together and perhaps helping unravel some of the puzzle. There have to be some answers in there somewhere; perhaps they can tell us where Meg and Bill came across the missing silver plate and coins. Meg sends her love.

Best wishes,

Bob

It didn't make any sense. Why would Laura Kennedy steal the silver plate? All she was doing was drawing attention to herself and whatever it was she was looking for. Using the same name at the club and in her dealings with me was stupid and amateurish, and Lord Barclay Summers didn't strike me as either a careless or a stupid man. Laura Kennedy seemed an unlikely tool for him to use, but they had to be connected in some way. There were too many coincidences. I stood there pondering for a while and then thought to hell with it all.

It was time to get out of New Zealand. A few weeks early perhaps, but it would be very bad luck if we were hit by any major weather on the way to South Minerva Reef. We could spend a safe month there well south of Fiji and Tonga, and by then the dangerous hurricane zone to the north would be clear of storms and all this aggravation would be long behind us. Nobody would find us in South Minerva.

I went to the corner phone and called the customs number in Whangarei. They said the next clearing day in Opua was on Friday, three days away, unless of course we wanted to pay the travel time and clear earlier. I said Friday would be fine. When I told the customs officer our boat's name there was a long pause.

"*Arrow*. Yes, I've heard of you. There's a man here who talks about you all the time. He's looking forward to meeting you again."

"Give my regards to Basil too," I said.

I went back down to the dinghy and rowed gingerly back to *Arrow*. Danny read Bob's letter and we kicked it around for a while, but he had no better ideas than I did, and we finally gave it up and spent the next couple of hours working through the duty-free forms for the liquor. The cheapest booze starts at ten New Zealand dollars a litre and rises slowly up from there, with no limits on the amount you can take out of the country. Apparently they send a statement of your excesses to the neighbouring countries, but I'd never heard of anyone having a problem with customs when entering Fiji.

We went absolutely berserk.

We passed the next two days finishing up the last few little jobs that remained on the list and stowing everything away for the passage to South Minerva. After four months of being tied to the pilings with only the one sheltered run up the coast, nearly everything on the boat was sitting loose. When we hit the offshore swells and the boat started to roller coaster, anything not fastened down would destruct, or disappear over the side. It's scary how things can shift around and take on a separate life of their own at sea. Once, when I was in a spring storm off the Aleutians in a sixty-foot halibut longliner, the boat dropped off a wave so precipitously that a cauldron of soup bungeed tightly on the stove inverted inside its restraints and drained into the flame pot below.

In the evenings we went out for supper and had a few drinks with the locals. We gave the bartender a couple of hundred dollars to cover the fight damages, and by the look of surprise on his face, it seemed likely that the other side had paid him off as well. There had already been another brawl in the tavern between the crews of two draggers who had tangled their gear on the fishing grounds, and we were old news. The *Kiwi Maiden* hadn't been seen since the evening of the fight, and the general consensus was that they had returned to Auckland.

On Friday morning we rowed into the main dock to pick up our supplies and clear for Fiji. It didn't surprise me that Basil was behind the desk with the customs officer. He went on the attack immediately.

"Your dog has been seen up here."

"I keep telling you, he's not my dog. He doesn't like me and the feeling is mutual."

Inasmuch as anyone could be said to own Sinbad he belonged to Joseph, Danny's Grandfather.

"What about your friend then?"

"Why don't you ask him yourself?"

Danny was carefully ticking off the sea stores against our list and when he heard his name he came over and smiled down at Basil. With his battered face and blackened eyes, it was not a reassuring sight. He crossed two beefy arms across his large chest.

"What dog?" he said.

Basil looked at him and turned away. The customs officer filled out and stamped the forms and passports and handed them back to us.

"I'll be coming out this evening to do the final shipboard inspection," Basil said. "You're under suspicion of having an illegal animal aboard. Don't leave before I come out or I'll have the Search and Rescue on you."

We carried the cases down to the dinghy dock and loaded them into the skiff. Danny raised the sail and we edged out across the channel, moving slowly through the anchored boats. Halfway across, Sinbad swam out from the end of the bay to meet us, his glistening hump rising out of the water behind him like some primeval sea monster. He grabbed onto the transom with his teeth and trailed out behind, slowing our progress by half. Over his back I could make out the form of Basil on the docks, binoculars raised to his eyes. He remained there watching until we were back to the boat.

Danny tried to get Sinbad to leave and managed to pry him loose from the transom once, but the beast was having no part of it. He knew from the changes in our routines that we were readying for sea and was taking no chances on being left behind. When we arrived at *Arrow* he stalked up to the bow and threw himself down with an air that said try and move me. I was nowhere near that foolish and went below and began stowing.

It was just getting dark when Basil came out. Danny had been watching for him, and as soon as he spotted the white MAF inflatable leave the dock he went forward and spoke to Sinbad in a low urgent voice then grabbed him by the loose folds of his neck and dropped him over the side. To my amazement, Sinbad paddled away and vanished into the darkness. So far, so good.

Basil bumped alongside, and I took his line and tied him on to a cleat. He sat there smiling up at us, one hand holding the collar of a sleepy-eyed Alsatian and the other clutching a shotgun.

"Who's this?" Danny asked. "One of your hostages?"

"No. She's my own dog. I bring her along with me for company on the drive up from Auckland sometimes." He smiled. "She's in heat at the moment.

"The gun, of course, is for that wild dog. I've noticed he hangs around your boat a lot. My bitch will bring him in. Would you like to see the dangerous animal form giving me permission to destroy him?" He held out a piece of paper.

I could feel Danny tensing up alongside me.

"I'll take your word for it. Come aboard and do your search then."

The idiot didn't realize the danger he was in. Danny was literally swelling up before my eyes. If Basil fired that gun we were all going to be in trouble, but him first. The bitch had raised her muzzle and was sniffing the air with an interested look on her face. Basil patted her on the head and stepped up onto *Arrow*, still holding the shotgun. He did a quick tour of the decks, even checking underneath the hard skiff stowed just forward of the cabin. With a final look around, he disappeared below.

"If he takes a shot at Sinbad I'll kill him myself," Danny hissed through clenched teeth.

"Just hang tight. He'll be gone in a few minutes."

Basil appeared in the companionway, a look of disappointment on his face. You could tell he'd been hoping for an opportunity to blow Sinbad away right in the middle of *Arrow*'s saloon.

"Well, I guess he's not here right now," he said. He climbed back into the inflatable and seated himself and absent-mindedly scratched the bitch's neck. Her gaze was focused somewhere over his shoulder.

"Goodbye then," I said.

"I think I'll just sit here and wait for a while if you don't mind," he answered, polite for the first time.

Danny reached over and cut the painter with his knife.

"I mind," he said.

The boat drifted slowly away. "You could get in trouble for that," Basil hollered.

"Asshole," Danny said.

Basil stood up and began cranking the motor in short vicious pulls. It finally fired once then hesitated and died. Sounded like he'd flooded it. The wind and tide had him now and he was moving rapidly away. He was cursing and pulling the cord and didn't see the dark humped object in the water swimming swiftly towards him. I grabbed the binoculars to watch. The Alsatian was standing now, looking over Basil's shoulder as he crouched over the motor, her tail wagging in steady encouragement. Basil suddenly noticed her actions and stood up and turned in one motion. He uttered a scream and reached for the gun and just as he raised it there was a loud explosion.

"Fuck! He's shot him," Danny screamed. "I'm going to kill that cocksucker."

"No! That was one of the tubes."

I had seen it all, the great jaws rising out of the water and closing on the pontoon, the material exploding around them in quick deflation, and Basil teetering frantically for balance before he went over the side with the gun. His head was just visible as he swam for the docks in the distance.

Behind him his Alsatian bitch stood in the semi-collapsed inflatable, forelegs braced against the remaining sound tube as Sinbad thrust strongly into her from the rear.

"I guess we can haul anchor and leave now," Danny said. "We've had our MAF inspection."

CHAPTER 6

Smooth azure seas, the swell from the southwest in long rolling billows, and quartering them with full sail, *Arrow*, leaving the land under clear skies and a steady glass, the water parting so eagerly before her that there is scarcely a wake. As the land receded, the sea started to change, becoming more heavy and powerful, the waves and swell holding the same aspect and size, but denser and weightier now, pregnant with the pressure of ten thousand open miles in every break and curl. *Arrow* responded with an increased stiffness, the pendulum roll of her passage more measured and constant after the frivolities of the coast and bays; a small gust hit her, she tucked her shoulder, then gathered and moved in nodding concert to that slow rocking cadence as old and comforting as the cradle.

We sensed the land slipping away from us with every seaward mile, our motions and gait more rolling and fluid, our inner clocks beginning to slow and adjust to the new maritime rhythms. We ran the whole of the first day without touching a sail or sheet, sitting quiet in the cockpit as the North Island shrank down and vanished beneath the curve of the earth until there were only the stacked clouds to signify the land beneath. As the day wore the birds gradually left us and returned to their terrestrial roosts, and we were alone in the lonely sea. The last clouds disappeared over the horizon, the last faint smell of shore, more imagined than real, vanished as the wind veered and now the crossing had truly begun. We had a light supper and I took the first watch.

Ship's Log March 6 Day 1   2200 hours
Position 34 58 S 174 30 E. Winds out of southwest at 15 knots. Steering 015. *Arrow* running with winged out jib at 6 knots. Barometer steady at 1016. Some scattered cumulous clouds. Southerly 2 metre swell, very comfortable. We should put up the spinnaker, but it's just too damn nice, we're just too damn lazy, and we're in no rush no how.

The sky is absolutely brilliant this first evening. Strange how it always seems so much brighter when you are at sea. Even in the most lonely and deserted anchorages a hundred miles from the nearest possibility of a loom of lights, the stars have less lustre, as if some aspect of the neighbouring land absorbs and dulls their glow. Perhaps it is because the stars occupy the entire area of your outlook at sea; there is nothing else to draw the eye as they stretch overhead and down into the water from horizon to horizon. They always impinge upon your vision and you are constantly aware of their changings as they tilt and wheel across the sky from one watch to the next.

Transfixed by that cold analytical light, the frail ambiguity of our situation, suspended on a thin film of water rotating in the universe among the dead and distant stars, seems both humbling and presumptuous.

Ship's Log March 8 Day 3   1200 hours

Position 31 26 S 176 40 E. Winds out of southeast at 25 knots. Steering 015. *Arrow* doing 7.5 knots with wind on beam, nicely balanced with reefed main, #2 jib and mizzen. Just enough spray to drive Sinbad off foredeck. Glass dropped 05 millibars on a knock, down to 1004, now rising again after a small front went through. Big oil tanker diagonally crossed our bow a mile off last night, Danny called repeatedly on VHF, no contact made. Caught 30 lb. yellowfin. Sinbad gorged, may sleep for rest of trip.

Constantly surprised by how casual the big ships are about keeping radio watch. Do they just not bother talking to the small boats, or is there really no one there? I have this vision of the crew gathered around the TV set watching *Seinfeld* reruns while the ship ploughs through the night at 16 knots. The bastards wouldn't even feel the bump. Danny suggested we take the Winchester and put a couple of rounds through the wheelhouse windows to catch their attention.

Ship's Log March 9 Day 4   1200 hours

Position 28 42 S 178 15 E. Winds out of southeast at 25 gusting to 30. Steering 015. Put in second reef and dropped mizzen to reduce weather helm. Seas building, 3 metre swell. *Arrow* corkscrewing, motion still reasonably comfortable at 6.5 knots. Glass 1010 on a slow rise. Seems like we've been out here for weeks already.

How quickly the body adapts to the shipboard routines again; watch on watch, 3 hours on 3 hours off, the days and nights blending together so seamlessly that the differences blurred and vanished. Arising from deep sleep at the touch on your shoulder, a quick splash on the face, and then the first hot taste of black coffee, your senses already assessing the sounds of the night wind in the rigging and the heel of the boat, so that when you clip on your safety line and climb up on deck you're already half in tune. Moving from the red glow of the cabin out into the dark, the eyes slowly adjusting, everything faster and sharper out here, the foam curling along the rail, the sheets bar tight and singing softly, the thrum of the mast coming down through the decks and vibrating underfoot, the wind blowing away the last traces of sleep as the small resentment of a summons from a warm bunk fades, and the endlessly fascinating task of driving a 20 ton wooden boat through the universe with wind and cloth and lines consumes you.

Ship's Log March 10 Day 5   0600 hours

Position 26 02 S 179 40 E. Almost back in the western hemisphere. Winds remain southeast at 25 knots. Can't make South Minerva before dark, slowing down to put us 10 miles off at daylight. Steering 015. Glass 1014. Looks like a nice high building.

Standing at the tiller under the stars as the daylight rises up from the sea like a thin grey blanket that gradually covers and dims the lustre overhead. Slowly the sky assumes colour and body before the rising of the sun; grey to white and then the palest blue before the hint of rose on the rim to the east begins to strengthen and incarnadine. *Arrow* moving slowly now under the jib, edging barely east of north as the light increases off our starboard bow and then the quick bright flash of dawn, the sky all sudden blue and there, just before it, a telltale break of white, the rising of the twin lagoons of South Minerva.

Pub. 126 Sailing Directions (enroute) for the Pacific Islands: South Minerva Reef (23 56 S 179 08 W), consisting of two united atolls about 4 3/4 miles long in an ENE and opposite direction, has large detached blocks of coral lying on the W reef which dries 0.9 m (3 ft).

The thin white line of breakers gradually assumed size and strength as we made our slow way towards them. From the spreaders, the atolls appeared surrounded by pearl necklaces in the blue water, the volcano that created them long since sunk beneath the waves. Our British Admiralty hand-drawn chart showed the pass on the north side just beyond the junction of the two atolls and running due east into the farthest lagoon. We waited for the sun to rise higher above the horizon before we made our way in, eyeball navigation now, the chart predating the pinpoint satellite positioning by a century, and as usual on old charts, the latitude very close and the longitude off considerably.

Sinbad lifted his head from the cockpit floor and sniffed the air, then moved to the bow and stood watching as we slowly rounded the west end and began to work eastwards. The swell subsided as we gained the lee and the changed motion brought Danny yawning and stretching onto the deck.

"Morning. This the right place then?"

"Looking good so far. Should be a break in the reef in another couple of miles. Don't see any masts in there, maybe we'll have the whole place to ourselves."

The colour of the water changed as we moved inside Herald Bight, a dozen shades of blue, each indicating a different depth, from the dark azure of the deepest water up through the spectrum to where the pale blues changed to greens and then to yellows and finally brown over the just submerged tips of the bommies, those towering coral pinnacles that rise perpendicular from the bottom.

Danny went up the mast and stood on the spreaders as we worked our way slowly through the pass, the seas breaking on both sides, the water so clear I had to keep checking the depth sounder to assure myself we really were in forty feet, and Danny calling down warnings about little reefs that were three fathoms under the keel but appeared close enough to touch. It might have been the clearest water we'd ever seen.

We exited the pass and I swung *Arrow* forty degrees dead into the wind and dropped the jib. The Perkins groaned reluctantly into life, sounding unnaturally loud in the lagoon as we motored the last three hundred yards and dropped anchor in five fathoms of water over a patch of white sand that looked so near you might step down onto it. Danny let out scope and I reversed hard and the Bruce caught and held. I switched off the engine and as *Arrow* sprang up over the anchor before the wind pushed her back again, you could see the chain all the way down to the stock, the flukes buried, and a school of tiny silver fish swimming through the settling grains of sand just above. Danny tied the half-inch nylon shock lines onto the rode and then back to the big Samson post, suspending a long-looped bight of chain that flashed in the sun like tiny linked mirrors.

The reef enclosing the lagoon was barely two hundred yards wide and a scant five feet above the water, the top near table flat save where the seas breaking on the outside edges had carved canyons, gullies, and tide pools into the coral. Sinbad swam ashore and began to work them, wading into each in turn, only his head visible sweeping from side to side and then the quick lunge and the jaws thrown back as he swallowed.

Now that *Arrow* had anchored the increase in heat was palpable, and for the first time since we had left New Zealand we took off our sweaters and long pants.

"Now this is nice," Danny said. "I think I might not move any farther than from here to the fridge and back for the rest of the day, get into the lobster tomorrow."

He peeled off the rest of his clothes and stretched out naked on the cockpit seats, his big body an even, deep shade of brown save for where the old knife scar ran its crimson pattern across his belly and up into the swelling chest above. The son of a bitch could lie out for hours in the hottest tropical sun without a worry, his First Nations ancestry giving him the needed carotenes for protection. My northern European forefathers, on the other hand, had bequeathed me a skin which was always pale white or flushed pink, in spite of careful applications of lotion and measured increments of sun.

I rigged a canopy over a corner of the cockpit and settled in with that sense of accomplishment that always accompanies a successful landfall, no matter how placid or uneventful the journey. It's a complex feeling, comprising equal portions of relief, gratitude, and surprise.

For the next two weeks, we enjoyed South Minerva, our days settling into a lazy pattern of reading, diving, and spearfishing. The lagoon was alive with fish: sweetlips, coral trout, snappers, wrasse, and the ubiquitous parrotfish abounded on the reef edge, while juvenile tuna and schools of mackerel patrolled the placid waters within. A trio of grey reef sharks visited occasionally, scavenging the fish offal and meal leftovers we jettisoned. Although not particularly dangerous, they weren't conducive to casual dips over the side. Sinbad was incensed by their presence and sat with his head over the side of the boat, his eyes never leaving them, growling softly the whole time. He had been savaged by sharks when he was a pup in the Tuamotus and never forgot. Once, when we threw stale bread overboard and the sharks rose to the surface, he launched himself over the side and got his teeth into the tail of one of them and hung on for several feet as it fled for the bottom.

In addition to the usual white tips and reef sharks there were the occasional tigers, larger and less wary, sometimes approaching within twenty feet to watch us with their staring senseless eyes before cruising slowly away. We always left the water when we saw the tigers. We spear fished quickly and carefully, rising immediately to the surface and holding the threshing fish high out of the water on our return to the dinghy and moving to a different location after each kill. Even the merest trace of blood in the water was sufficient to bring the sharks in and start them on their restless circling.

A Fijian fisherman had been killed by a shark in Naviti when we were there. He had tied the speared fish on a line around his waist, and a shark had come in and taken his thigh off. He died from shock and loss of blood in less than fifteen minutes. During our layover in New Zealand, I'd read every book the library had on sharks and their behaviour, and it was clear that nobody had any real absolutes. Don't excite them and don't mess with them were the basic rules, and many people had dived for years among them without ever experiencing aggression. They were never going to convince me.

It took us a week to refine our lobster technique and it was Sinbad who showed us the way. The moon was nearing full, and every day more of the reef was exposed with the lower tides. We'd been hunting the pools and canyons on the windward side, some of them almost ten feet deep, and sometimes a lobster was tucked away out of sight under a rock or in one of the deep crevices. We put on masks and snorkels and Lycra suits and swam carefully around checking out the underwater retreats. When a wave broke over the reef and into the pools, or pressured in through one of the connecting channels, we had to dive to the bottom and hang on to avoid scrapes from the coral. The scratches were more like burns than abrasions, warm to the touch and slow to heal.

We'd been catching two or three a day, enough for a modest feed, when on one of our walks Sinbad started growling and scratching along a honeycomb of reef just exposed by the spring tides along the outside perimeter. He'd found a den of lobster in the coral, small parts of their coloured shells visible through the holes. We lay down on the coral and reached in and pulled them out, returning the gravid females and throwing the males to Sinbad who quickly removed their heads. In short order there were a dozen tails lying in a neat pile in front of him. We took them back to *Arrow* and feasted, and after that we were never short of the shellfish.

At the end of the third week, an English boat with an older couple on board came in and anchored nearby, and we rowed over and gave them a feed of lobster and stayed to drink their homemade beer. After that the boats came in at the rate of one a day, and a cluster of four from Southern California which, judging from their chatter on the VHF, had seldom been out of sight of each other since leaving San Diego two years earlier.

Although we'd picked our spot randomly from a mile of locations with similar bottom and shelter, the herd instinct took over and every boat that came in anchored just out of swinging room of the previous arrival. I'd been guilty of it myself; you assumed that the incumbents, having first choice, had selected the very best spot available, they were obviously happy with it, otherwise they would have moved, and the closer you approached their ideal position, the better off you were.

When there were a half dozen boats next to us we picked up and moved half a mile and were alone for another three days until the morning we woke to a fog horn and a shrill whoop. I looked out the port light and made out a rusty black hull with a buxom carrot-topped figure waving from the bow. Molly had arrived.

"Well, boys, it's almighty good to see you. I wasn't sure if you'd still be here or not. You'd just left when I got into Opua."

She was seated beside me in the cockpit, her flushed face beaming from ear to ear. She had scorned coffee and was already downing her second beer. As it was her landfall beer it would have been impolite not to join her, but I engaged slowly and cautiously. I don't drink well in the mornings.

"How was your trip across?" Danny asked.

"Great. Ten days from Opua. That's a record for me."

I worked it out. Under eighty miles a day and considered a good passage. *Tramp* was not a quick boat.

"How's the lobstering?"

"Good. We've been having them most days. We'll go out this afternoon at low tide, catch a few."

"I haven't had a good feed since I left Newfoundland. My ex ran some traps. Never made much money, but we ate well. I used to go with him, do the hauling while he ran the boat."

She took a long drink of beer, the muscles in her arm flexing as she raised the can. She was one powerful lady, no doubt about that. She was wearing her habitual garb of cut-offs and a halter, bulging somewhat, but all of it looking hard as India rubber, no hanging slack anywhere. Danny eyed her thoughtfully and I suspected what was going through his mind. He was a better man than me.

"You look like you've lost some weight since I saw you last, Jared. Tell you what, we'll have a few more beers, do some lobstering, then I'll cook up a big east coast feed for us all." She threw her arm around me and gave me a motherly squeeze. "How does that sound?"

"Sounds great," Danny said. He went below and pulled another three cold ones from the fridge.

"Parrrrrrrtttttttty tiiiiiiime!" Molly screamed, head thrown back. Danny grinned and raised his can and we all clinked together and saluted.

It was four o'clock by the time we set out on the fishing trip, packing a cooler of beer and a plastic bag for the lobster. None of us was feeling any pain by then. Sinbad trotted along the outside edge, head down as he ran back and forth in his searching pattern. He suddenly stopped and began growling and scratching.

We congratulated him, and in minutes had picked up a dozen lobsters, all of them in the two-pound range. Molly saved a few whole for her broths and Sinbad wolfed the rest down to their tails. We put them in the cooler alongside the remaining beer and paddled back to *Tramp* where Molly insisted we try her latest batch of Newfie screech and served boilermakers all around. I had a small shot and it almost lifted the top of my head off. I tried to stick to beer but by then it was too late, my thirst didn't really want to.

Besides, I hadn't had a decent session in months. I was in the middle of the ocean on a boat with two good friends. How much trouble could

I get into anyway? It wasn't like those times ashore where I woke up the next morning in a strange place with eight hours and sometimes my money missing from my life.

"Just time for one more, luv." Molly gave me a roguish wink as she fetched up the bottle. "Supper will be ready in half an hour."

I held out my glass.

Dinner was superb. Molly served the shellfish dressed with a white wine sauce and shallots. She still had fresh vegetables left and accompanied it with a salad and rice and mushroom casserole. The drinking had given me an enormous appetite and I ate until I could barely move. We had wine with the dinner and then screech served out of shot glasses for liqueurs. It tasted almost smooth now.

The food and drink made me sleepy, and I sat on the edge of the bunk slumped half over the chart table talking with Molly. I think Danny was at the sink doing the dishes. It was all a bit confused, and at one point Molly asked me about Jane, so I guess I must have mentioned her. A feeling of maudlin depression settled over me and I babbled away while Molly sat close, her arm around my shoulders, and then it all got confused and faded away and I think someone said what was needed was a good full-time woman, it might have been Danny joking although I might not have seen him for a while and I said I should be going . . .

I awoke with the sudden heart-pounding awareness of the recently drunk, already sweating in those first few seconds from alcohol and guilt, frantically trying to orient myself. I was lying on my back staring up at a rust-streaked surface, my left shoulder jammed against a scarred piece of Plexiglas. It was just breaking first light. A strange unearthly sound rose beside me in sharp ascending notes, then settled back down the scale into a soft bubbling gasp. I turned my head slowly in the forlorn hope it might be Danny.

There, on the outside of the berth, garbed only in a light shift, flat on her back and snoring loudly was Molly, her giant breasts less than a foot from the ceiling.

Jesus. Oh, Jesus!

I had absolutely no recollections, but that meant nothing. Over the years you learn the real terror of drinking lies not with the hangover, but in the anxious days that follow the event when you nervously wait for friends or strangers to approach and gleefully recount horrendous events surrounding you of which you have no memory. I took deep shaky breaths trying to clear my head. Danny might be asleep. There was still a slim chance I could bluff it out.

My problem was that the berth was less than six feet long, and with Molly stretched out between me and freedom, there wasn't the space to flank her.

I would have to go over the top.

I slowly turned my head and studied her. She was snoring loudly, her knees drawn up so that they almost touched the cabin roof above the berth. The air in the confined space smelled of pure alcohol and I still felt half drunk. There was some swell in the lagoon, and *Tramp* was rolling.

I turned carefully over onto my stomach and raised myself on my arms until my head touched the ceiling. Ever so slowly I drew up my left leg and stretched it across her body. There were only a few inches of berth between Molly and the outside edge and my foot crept down and planted itself and then my hand up over her full belly and down. Slowly with infinite caution I transferred my weight until my feet and arms carried it all. Back and ass glued to the ceiling, suspended on my shaky quadruped I worked my way up and started to move across. I had just sufficient clearance above her chest and I was staring into Molly's face beneath me and just going to make it past when that under-ballasted top-heavy pig of a son of a bitching mother fucking boat took a quick roll and my foot slipped and I crashed down. Molly's eyes flew open in surprise and then a sly smile spread over her face.

"You little rascal," she said. "Didn't get enough last night, eh?"

The powerful arms wrapped me and crushed me into her. I broke loose and ran up the stairs, Molly's roaring laughter following me every step of the way.

"Just kidding, Jared," she yelled.

The dinghy was gone, and I dove over the side and raced back to *Arrow*. The thought of sharks never even crossed my mind until I was back on board. By the time Danny came out on deck I had the anchor aboard and stowed and was heading out the pass under full sail.

CHAPTER 7

Ship's Log April 11 Day 2   1800 hours
Position 21 10 S 179 30 E. Wind east by south at 30 knots.
Steering 335. 175 miles last 24 hours. *Arrow* making 7.5 knots
under reefed main and working jib. Conditions rolly, some water in
cockpit, put in second reef at change of watch. Glass still dropping.
Talked to big charter boat, says 40 knots and gusting forecast this
evening. A nervous time for the boats in Minerva.

A wild night. *Arrow* going like a train under cloudy skies with only the
occasional glimpse of moon, the wind aft off the starboard quarter and
every once in a while a sharp bang as a sea breaks on the stern and the
spray reaches up and catches us under the dodger. Wind vane handling
it nicely. We've got the number two jib and three reefs in the main,
nothing to do but hang on and enjoy it. Holding thirty-five knots most

of the time, saw one gust up to forty-five but that was the peak. Not building though, hopefully just a shallow trough going through.

Kandavu Island came up on the radar an hour before sunrise and we had to decide whether to continue on for Suva or shelter in its lee. Foreign boats are required to clear customs before dropping anchor in territorial waters, but most countries will allow for prudent seamanship in the unlikely event we were seen and reported. In any case the wind dropped off by the time we reached Kandavu and we had only the occasional gust in the high twenties and decided to push on. The sky had cleared with little cumulus clouds scattered above us, but over Suva they were banked high, with the darker sheets of stratus below.

It was the Great Sea Reefs on the leeward side of the main islands which sustained Fiji's reputation as one of the finest cruising grounds in the world. Stretching from Navula Point on the west side over two hundred miles northeast to Cape Undu was an inland sea averaging fifty miles across filled with islands, reefs, and anchorages and contained on its seaward side by a long arc of reefs which gave shelter to the whole. Much of the area was uncharted, and the existing charts were dated and carried warnings of inaccuracy. Once we entered the area we could wander for weeks without seeing another boat, eyeball navigating through the reefs and anchoring in a different spot every night. Nobody was going to find us in there.

"Looks like it's raining in Suva," Danny said. "Why am I not surprised."

We'd spent a fortnight in Suva the previous season and it had rained most days. The high windward side of Viti Levu receives several times the rainfall of the arid western regions. It is covered with rainforest vegetation from the coast inwards past the first low range of mountains at which point the landscape changes, flattens, and hosts the sprawling sugar cane fields which form the main support of Fiji's economy.

"Remember *Cantata*? The Crealock 37 from California? They waited in Suva for two weeks for a good day to leave before somebody finally told them the weather ten miles out had been fine the whole time." Danny grinned. "I love that kind of shit. And they only wanted to go to Kandavu anyway."

We cleared the northern end of Great Astrolabe Reef and jibed onto our new track. Danny went below and plotted our position with the GPS and laid the course for the leading beacons that would line us up for the approach through the fringing reef that guards Suva Harbour and gives protection from swell to everything but a pure southerly.

"Thirty miles to go. Let's throw up some more sail and make sure we get in early enough to clear. I want to hit the bright lights tonight. Besides, there's a charter Beneteau coming out of Kerry Pass on Astrolabe."

With those words Danny moved onto the foredeck and dropped the little number three jib we had changed down to during the night. He pulled out the heavy medium-sized genoa and hanked it on and hauled it up. *Arrow* shivered for a moment as the sail filled, and then it ballooned out with a crack and *Arrow* began to pick up speed. We waited for a couple of minutes as she worked her way along and then I went aft and raised the mizzen. It put some weather helm into the tiller, but *Arrow* gained a half knot in speed on the beam reach.

The Beneteau was half a mile away on a converging course, idling along under main and working jib with sunbathers sprawled all over the decks. If it was who I suspected it was, they obviously hadn't seen us yet. We were slowly overhauling her when a girl in a bikini came up out of the companionway and pointed at us, sparking a sudden flurry of activity. A couple of hands ran up onto the foredeck and in another minute a red spinnaker appeared on the deck and then blossomed out in front of her and her bow lifted, and she began to run. The wind was just aft of the beam and the big sail fluttered as they struggled to keep it filled when she rounded up coming off the swells.

"What do you think? Should we go with the spinnaker as well?" Danny eyed the Beneteau, trying to determine if she was gaining on us.

"Let's make the bet first."

We knew her now, the *Enterprise*, one of Kirk Mellor's charter boats that operated out of Suva and Lautoka on the west coast, and the man himself was at the wheel looking back over his shoulder. We'd shared a few beers with Captain Kirk the previous year at the Royal Suva Yacht Club. A Brit, smooth as silk with all the charming patter you'd expect from someone who made his living selling. He and Danny had hung out together for a month before we returned to New Zealand for the hurricane season. Kirk was a keen and competitive sailor and would hate nothing more than being bested by an old wooden boat. I went down and switched the vhf onto low power.

"*Enterprise*, this is *Arrow*. Drinks at the club tonight for first in?"

"Jared, you crafty bugger. Trying to sneak past me, eh? I thought for sure the old girl would founder on one of the New Zealand legs. I'm absolutely amazed to see you back again. What's my handicap?"

Danny grabbed the mike. "You're homely and you like plastic boats. Isn't that sufficient?"

"Danny." Kirk's delighted laugh boomed over the radiophone. "Glad to hear you're still aboard. There's a lady here you'll want to meet. Christy. She's standing beside me right now." One of the bikinis turned and waved. "How about the loser pays for dinner and drinks at the club tonight? I can round up a date for Jared too."

"Sounds good to me, but I can't speak for Jared," Danny said. "He's involved in a pretty heavy relationship at the moment. You see, he met this Canadian yachtswoman . . ."

I snatched the mike away. "You're on, starboard beacon at the end of Levu Passage," I said and slammed it back into the bracket. "Now, let's catch that son of a bitch."

The Beneteau had gained another hundred yards and was a good ten boat lengths in front of us and three hundred yards upwind. Definitely in the controlling position. She was shorter than us at forty-one feet, but had a longer waterline and would be faster downwind in light airs. With the wind anywhere near the beam, *Arrow* could hold her own.

Once she heeled beyond fifteen degrees, the overhangs extended her waterline and she increased her speed accordingly. The wind was down to a steady fifteen knots now, settled fine aft on the starboard beam. It was *Arrow*'s best point of sail, and we were in with a chance.

"We'll set the big light air genoa and the mizzen staysail," I said. "On this course we should do as well as with the spinnaker and might be able to hold it longer on the way in."

It was a bit heavy for the genoa, the sail maker had said a maximum of twelve knots but what the hell, it was a race. With the wind aft, the mizzen staysail would do some of the work and the apparent wind on the sails would be less. There were too many things to go wrong with a spinnaker in a jibing race when there were only the two of us. Danny was bull strong and cat quick, but even so. There was still a decent easterly swell and the *Enterprise* suddenly broached slightly and spilled the air out of her sail. It filled again with a loud crack. Everyone on board was staring up at the big sail, and Kirk's crew were playing the sheets constantly.

Danny hung the block on the end of the winged out mizzen and ran the sheets while I pulled out the mule and fastened the tack and clipped on the halyard. I hauled it up and it bloomed in shocking bands of purple and white and we felt the difference immediately in the sound of the wind in the rigging and the increased heel of the deck. The notes were higher now, more pitched and keening. Danny went forward and pulled down the foresail and stuffed it below then clipped on the big genoa and I ran it up and sheeted in, and the bow lifted slightly as it filled, and *Arrow* settled back and over, and the spray arced past her bow in a misted rainbow and fell into her wake. I looked up towards *Enterprise* and took her bearing.

"Even most of the time, but we're gaining a bit when she spills air," Danny said after a while.

"What, about fifteen miles to go?"

"Something like that. Well under two hours at this clip. Looks like the wind will hold."

We were hovering around seven and a half knots, with occasional surfs when we caught a wave.

"I'll switch on the radar. It will show us if we're gaining."

For the next hour we ran almost even, but then the wind went forward ten degrees and Kirk had to drop the spinnaker and we slowly began to reel him in. He ran her right ahead of us and covered religiously as we closed to within a hundred yards. He had all his crew sitting on the rail and the frequent looks back over his shoulder showed how seriously he was taking the match. Five miles out from the pass I tried to roll him over, but he luffed us up then broke away again. Twice more we tried going under and each time he held us off, the two of us edging farther to starboard with each attempt. The niceties of yacht racing such as not sailing below your course to the mark had no place in this contest.

The reef was clearly visible on each side and directly ahead, the breakers defining the perimeters, a mile on the port hand and half that to starboard, the passage narrowing quickly now, funnelling in until the last hundred yards between the beacons and then hauling sharply to starboard and into the harbour.

"All he has to do is hold this course, keep covering us and then make the quick tacks through the pass," Danny said.

"Yes, if we tack with him. If we get right up on his stern and hold our course a couple of lengths past his tack we might be able to get in front of him."

"He won't tack until there's no room left for us. He'll wait for us to go first."

"Then we won't. There's room, and then there's room. He's got clients on board. He might not want to scare them too badly. The tide's up now, I figure we can go in to within a boat length of the breakers, the chart shows eight feet of water at low tide. The little coastal freighters all hug the line there, cheating on the swing up to Suva Point. We'll crowd him, see if he'll break first."

"Sort of like white line chicken, only with boats instead of cars," Danny said.

I stood braced with the tiller between my legs, concentrating on the boat ahead. We were gaining ever so slowly, the mizzen staysail sheeted in hard and shivering as the wind edged slowly forward another couple of degrees. It was doing very little now, but maybe we could use it to dummy *Enterprise*.

Kirk's head swivelled around and I waved to him. We were less than fifty feet apart now. I saw the look of thoughtful calculation on his face, and I hoped he was remembering that *Arrow* outweighed him by ten tons. Our bow was just threatening to overlap his stern. Pretty soon we'd find out just how badly he wanted to win this race.

"Mind, no going over the reef this time," Danny said.

"No. The stakes aren't high enough."

We were only playing for drinks and glory now, back then it had been for our lives. I wished Joseph were present. He would have loved this. Danny's grandfather was a very old man, but his appetite for life was fierce and you underestimated him at your peril. He'd saved *Arrow* and all our lives two years past.

We were just three hundred yards from the channel now, the breakers booming in our ears and the rollers building as the water shoaled and lifted us towards the reef on their surge. It would be a bad time to miss a tack.

"I'll slip the sheets, fall back just behind and then scream for a tack, swing the bow while you drop the mizzen staysail and we'll see if he goes for it. Another hundred feet."

It was a decent plan in theory. But looking ahead at the reef, I wasn't so sure. The water was turbulent under the swell and it was hard to pick up the edge. I wondered how much water the Beneteau drew. Certainly not less than *Arrow*, and Kirk would be keyed up, ready to go at the first sign. Slowly I eased the mainsheet and took some way off her, until our bow was just clear on *Enterprise's* stern.

"Tack!" I screamed and shoved the tiller across and the bow started to swing. Danny slipped the mizzen halyard and gathered the sail into his arms and threw it on the cockpit floor.

"She's gone," he yelled and *Enterprise* swung onto the other tack and I hardened up and drove *Arrow* towards the reef for an endless thirty seconds and then we tacked hard and quick onto starboard, *Arrow's* momentum carrying her across without a pause and we were beating back hard to the *Enterprise* with right of way, everything sheeted tight in and the rail down in the water and the spray coming onto the decks in driving, sluicing sheets.

Danny threw back his head and howled like a wolf and Sinbad rose from the deck and caught it up and then the three of us were baying as we thundered down on the *Enterprise*, nothing in it for speed now, both boats going the same and I could see Kirk calculating our course and thinking he might just make it clear, but it wasn't quite there and he wouldn't bluff us off, but just in case, Danny brought out the rum and we tilted the bottle back and drank it down in turn and howled once more and let the madness show.

In another minute he tacked away, and we went across the channel with him and covered, and then twice more he went again while we waited seconds to be sure before we followed, and then we were through the pass and by the beacon a full two lengths in front. We'd won.

We turned the corner and dropped the sails and ran up the yellow quarantine flag as the harbourmaster directed us over to King's Wharf. At the first sound of the diesel, Sinbad slipped over the rail and headed towards the mangrove swamp that bordered the port side markers. He emerged on the beach, shook himself, and disappeared into the bushes.

The best thing about Suva Harbour was the yacht club that nestled in the northeast corner. The harbour itself was dirty, of indifferent holding, usually overcrowded, and subject to swell during the southernmost swings of the trades, but the Royal Suva Yacht Club made up for all of this. Housed in an old wood-framed building of considerable charm, the interior walls were covered with pictures from its early days when it played a prominent role in the social structure of the British colony. It had a good restaurant and an excellent bar which served as fine a gin and tonic as could be found in the southern hemisphere.

Flushed with victory and feeling morally obligated to drink and dine as heavily as possible at Kirk's expense, we treated ourselves and tied up at one of the club's berths for the night. The price was reasonable and it would spare us the hazardous dinghy ride back to *Arrow* at evening's end. We signed in and had a quick drink with Roland, the grizzled Fijian bartender, before luxuriating in the club's showers. When the last lingering memory of salt was flushed away, we went back aboard *Arrow* and changed into clean whites for the evening.

"I couldn't believe you buggers would go in that close," Kirk said. "I thought for sure you were tacking away when you faked."

He raised an arm and ordered another round of drinks, his handsome face flushed with wind and drink, his other arm around the stunning creature he'd introduced as his lead hand. Kirk's crews were usually female and always attractive. He selected them from the passage crews who left the cruisers in Fiji each season and wanted to extend their sailing holiday with a chance to earn some money. It was an agreeable arrangement for everybody. Kirk was always fully booked and had told us earlier he had just bought a fifth Beneteau to add to his little fleet.

"That was nothing," Danny said. "Sometimes we don't even bother to tack, just go straight on over the reef."

He winked at me and turned back to Christy, the statuesque blonde who hadn't taken her eyes off him since they were introduced and now had her arm proprietarily linked through his. She laughed in delight at his sparkling wit.

My date was a stolid German girl, earnest and sincere, the daughter of one of Kirk's regular clients, and, I suspected, his subtle revenge upon me for winning the race. Her father owned a BMW car dealership in Suva, and you didn't have to be a genius to figure out that most of his customers were found among the wealthy Indians who controlled the majority of business and trade in Fiji. She'd been lecturing me about the unfairness of the legislation that had prevented them from owning property or forming the government since we'd first met two hours earlier. She was sincere, and her arguments had merit, but I was beginning to wish we'd tacked sooner. I was trying to keep the glaze out of my eyes when I overheard Kirk talking about one of his charters.

"— so that takes care of three of them, and the new one looks like it might be chartered to an Irish professor for a good part of the season. I'm not real crazy about it though, his daughter wants some conversions to the stock layout, which I'd have to change back after they're done. I could probably get it eighty percent chartered anyway, without the hassle. Besides, his daughter is a royal pain in the ass."

"Would the professor's daughter happen to be Laura Kennedy by any chance?" I asked.

"You know her?"

"We met briefly in New Zealand. She was interested in chartering *Arrow*. I would love to see her again."

"They're staying in town somewhere. I'm not sure which hotel, but she runs past the club every morning, seven thirty, regular as clockwork. I've seen her a few times when I went in early."

Kirk's office was a small room in the back of the yacht club about the size of a large closet. He paid a modest rent and they picked up his messages and did his secretarial work when he wasn't there.

The evening wasn't a total loss after all. The food came, and the lamb curry was rich and spicy hot and the Fiji Bitters flowed in an unending stream. I finally got Marlene off local politics and she told me of her other passion, the collection and identification of marine specimens from the inland sea. She was studying marine biology in Dresden and was home for six weeks between terms. The evening passed quickly enough, and when the other couples left to sample the Suva night life, I stayed and had liqueurs and coffee with Marlene and then walked her slowly home in the scented dark and wished her a formal good night at her door.

Chapter 8

When the alarm went off at six thirty, I'd already been awake for an hour. I was alone on the boat, which didn't surprise me. Kirk had a bachelor pad in one of the new high-rises and Danny had stayed there on occasion the previous season. As for Sinbad, we might not see him the whole time we were here. It was annoying that he abandoned his guard duties in port, but there was little we could do about it. He always seemed to be within earshot, though, and the first sound of the Perkins grinding over would be sufficient to fetch him loping towards us. For all I knew, he could be watching now.

I drank two cups of strong black coffee and had a cold shower to banish the last cobwebs from my brain. I walked out behind the club-house and did some slow stretches on grass still damp from evening rain. Behind the club the morning traffic flowed into the city for the day's work, a steady stream of buses, taxis, and cars moving past me and the prison just ahead.

A mixed group of guards and prisoners walked past the club, the only difference between them the uniforms, no sign of weapons and all of them smiling and chatting indiscriminately. Fijians must be the most mellow and likeable people on God's earth.

A group of runners moved quickly past, men in their twenties wearing club sweatshirts and led at a fierce pace by a close-cropped warrior with tattooed legs. Three hundred yards back in black lycra, was a woman running. I couldn't make out her face, but the ramrod posture was unmistakable — Laura Kennedy. As she came closer I saw that she was wearing that same look of serious determination as the first time we'd met. She was breathing hard and her strides were short and choppy as she moved past. She didn't look as if she were enjoying herself but rather as if this was just something else to be endured before the next task appeared. I wondered if she ever smiled, or, God forbid, laughed. I gave her a hundred-yard lead and then moved out behind her, heading away from town towards the cemetery in the distance.

It was a fine balmy morning, the air still fresh and cool and the scent of wet grass and frangipane carrying on the land breeze that washed over me and out to sea. As the sun climbed, the wind would falter and swing before steadying in the forenoon and blowing back in over the land. I kept my distance, letting the muscles stretch and warm, breathing in deeply until I settled and the old unconscious rhythms of blood and pace began to move within me.

Laura Kennedy was proceeding steadily on, lacking the grace and stride of the natural runner, eating up the distance with a square choppy step that never eased or varied. I wouldn't have believed that anyone could run with so little upper body movement. Her shoulders were shiny with sweat, her long black hair done up in a ponytail and hanging down her back.

I extended my stride and began to move up behind her. When I was twenty feet back and knew she was aware of me, I slowed down and held the distance there.

She didn't turn, but her gait became stiffer and she picked up the pace for a hundred yards and I stayed with her and then she slowed right down and I stuck there twenty feet back. I could tell she was furious, and finally she stopped altogether and spun around with hands on hips and her face all flushed and angry.

"Morning, ma'am," I said and moved past her.

Her mouth opened to speak and then a faint look of puzzlement appeared, and I was by and speeding up before she could utter a word. I stretched out and sprinted away and there might have been a vague call behind me but I ignored it and held on for another quarter of a mile until the sweat was rich and flowing and then I dropped down a couple of gears and kept at it; up and down and up again until the furthest thing from my mind was Laura Kennedy and the only reality the burning acid in my thighs and the bursting need for air.

Three miles out, a road appeared to my right and I swung off along it and turned again and worked my way back to the yacht club, going slowly now, jogging past the bungalows and tenements, and sometimes little kids coming out and running with me for a few yards, their faces lit with laughter.

After showering I checked for messages at the club. There was one from Danny saying he wouldn't be back tonight. Kirk was throwing a party and I was invited. Drinks and a swim at the complex pool beforehand, and a barbecue on the terrace afterwards. Call and leave a message if I wanted a date with Christy's friend. I thanked the girl behind the desk and went back aboard *Arrow* to wait.

I had the jib out on the dock hosing the slides off with fresh water when Laura showed up. She'd taken some pains with her appearance, her hair was combed out along her shoulders, she was wearing a bright silk blouse and tie skirt, and there might even have been a pale trace of lipstick. She came up and stood behind me as I continued with my work.

"Good morning," she said at last.

I turned around. She had a strained smile on her face.

"Hello," I said.

"I'm Laura Kennedy. Do you remember me?"

I gave her a long assessing look. "No," I said.

She flushed but the smile remained.

"It was in New Zealand, Whangarei. I wanted to charter your boat."

"It must have been someone else. We don't do charters."

Her lips thinned, and a gleam of anger appeared in her eyes.

"I wanted to charter this particular boat. *Arrow*."

She enunciated the words carefully, as if speaking to an idiot.

I shrugged. "If you say so, lady." I shut off the hose and began folding the sail.

"I recognized you when you were out running and went by."

"What were you doing out there?" I asked.

She frowned and started to respond and then thought better of it.

"Never mind," she said, the words clipped out like little stones. "The point is, I would still like to charter your boat. We'll pay good money."

"Who's we? You and the little hubby I guess, huh. What are you, newlyweds?" I winked. "Want a little romance, eh? Deserted lagoons, soft nights, the warm waters lapping on your naked bodies? I guess I can understand that all right."

I leered.

She stood up ramrod straight, all hints of softness gone. "It's for my father and me," she grated. "He's a professor of marine archaeology and I'm helping him with some scientific research."

"Scientific research, eh? I don't know as *Arrow's* very scientific. She's only an old wooden boat, you know."

"I am aware of that," she said wearily.

"I'll have to ask my partner of course. He's away for a while. Look, I've got an idea, why don't you come out for a sail with me and have a look around *Arrow*? I'm taking her out to check a jib we had recut. Only be gone for an hour or so at most."

"Well, I don't know," she said doubtfully.

"I understand. She's probably not right for you anyhow. See you around."

I went aboard and turned the key and pressed the starter button.

The Perkins whined for a few revolutions and then coughed into life. I stepped back onto the dock and began casting off lines.

"All right, I'll come with you," she said.

She went forward and untied the bow line and coiled it in her hand before putting it inboard.

"Let's go then."

I waited until the bow swung with the wind then gave a quick burst of throttle and *Arrow* pivoted out and away from the dock and we headed out into the bay. There was a splash off the point ahead of us and Sinbad came into view, swimming towards us. I shifted into neutral and *Arrow* glided towards him as I tied a line on the skiff and lowered it over the side and into the water.

"Tie it off the stern," I said to Laura.

She walked the dinghy back along the rails and fastened the painter onto the pushpit just as Sinbad arrived. I heard her gasp of surprise as he swung himself into the skiff and then sprang under the lifelines and past her. He came into the cockpit and glared at me, uttering a low throaty growl. He shook himself over me and stalked off to the bow.

"What was that?" Laura whispered.

"Our guard dog. Sinbad. He ripped up a guy who came on board uninvited in Opua."

I watched her, but her expression didn't change.

"No shit," she said.

I threaded my way through the anchored boats and then put *Arrow* onto the course for the pass. The wind was light, and just forward of the beam.

"Can you steer?"

"I've done some dinghy sailing."

"Principle is the same."

I gave her the tiller and ran up the mainsheet and jib and set them, then reached across and switched off the engine and we were doing a lazy three knots across the harbour.

"This is nice," Laura said.

She had a genuine smile on her face.

"Yeah. You want a beer?"

She glanced pointedly at her watch. "No, thank you. It's a bit early for me."

I went below and brought up two. "I'll just have one for you then," I said. I opened the first and drank it down and threw the empty back down the companionway. It clattered at the bottom and Laura started nervously.

Good.

"Just head on out the pass. There'll be a little more wind out there and I can see how the jib sets."

I smiled at her and raised the second can in salute then popped the tab and drank. She gave me a worried glance but didn't speak. We were going through the pass now. The tide was slack and the wind down and it was near flat.

It wasn't until we were through that the wind picked up around the point and laid us over ten degrees and the trades swell started to build. It was beautiful sailing but it wasn't flat anymore, and as the wind came forward I hardened up the sheets and the heel increased and all of a sudden it was all very different.

"Shouldn't we turn around soon?" Laura asked after a long silence.

An occasional bit of spray was coming aboard now, and her blouse was damp in spots.

"In a bit. Let's talk about the charter first. Sure you're not ready for a beer now?"

"I'm sure."

"How about a journal then?" I said.

She turned towards me, mouth agape. "What did you say?"

I went below and grabbed a journal. I threw it towards her and she flinched away and it struck her and fell to the deck.

"There. That's what you wanted, isn't it?"

She stood up suddenly and *Arrow* luffed up into the wind as she released the tiller. I took a drink of beer and we sat there for a while,

Arrow rocking gently and the sound of the flapping sheets and sails loud in the silence.

"I don't know what you're talking about," she said finally.

"Meg and Bill Calder's journals. The ones you heard about at the yacht club in England the night Meg gave the talk. You know, when you stole the silver plate. Before you stole the journals from Meg's house."

Her face turned white and she sat down. I sipped my beer and watched her.

"I didn't steal any journals," she mumbled. "I want to go back now."

"Tell me about it first."

She looked away. "There was no harm done," she said. "Please take me back now." She was trembling.

I felt a little sorry for her, and then I thought of the ruthless search of *Arrow*; the ripped books and smashed pictures and broken shelves.

I grabbed her arm. "Tell me," I said.

She raised her chin and looked me full in the eye. "No," she said. "I want to go back now."

I shrugged. "Okay, then."

Before she knew what was happening, I had picked her up and dropped her over the side. By the time she came sputtering to the surface, *Arrow* was twenty feet distant. She started swimming towards the boat and I hardened up the sheets and moved slowly away. She followed for a bit and then turned without a word and headed back towards the pass. She had a good workmanlike stroke and looked comfortable in the water — even in her clothes and shoes. The pass wouldn't always be visible though, down there in the trough of the swell. I settled back into the cockpit where I could keep an eye on her. It wouldn't do to drown her.

After twenty minutes she began to labour. What little form she'd had was gone and her head was rolling with every stroke. I jibed and cruised down past her a boat length off.

"Any time you're ready to tell me," I yelled.

Her head swung across and she looked at me for a beat. Her face was pinched and white. She turned back and started swimming away again, but in the wrong direction. She had heart though; you had to give her that. I kept on past her for a bit, then tacked and worked back up and across again.

Sinbad had been watching her from the bow and as we went alongside he jumped into the water and swam towards her. She saw him at the last second and gave a choked scream and splashed hysterically away. Sinbad followed her with a puzzled look on his face. He often came swimming with Danny and me.

Laura was trying to tread water and wave at me and yell at the same time and a wave caught her with her mouth open and she went under. Sinbad went down with her and when she surfaced again his grinning face was before her. Even better than swimming he liked to free dive with us when we spear fished. He could get down to twenty feet and we had talked about getting a little harness with weights for him so he could get down the additional thirty feet that Danny and I sometimes achieved.

Laura didn't know any of this, of course, and wouldn't have been interested at the moment anyway. Her eyes were closed now, and she was choking and then she went under again just as *Arrow* and I got there. I jumped down into the skiff as we drifted past and grabbed her under the arms and lifted her into it. She lay gasping on the floorboards then opened her eyes just as Sinbad threw his paws over the transom and hauled himself aboard. His weight tipped the little boat and as she jerked up she lost her balance and fell across him. She screamed and fainted dead away as Sinbad struggled frantically to get out from under her. It was another five minutes before I managed to get her up into the cockpit.

Laura's face was chalk white, her breathing shallow as she shivered unconscious on the cockpit seats. I put on a kettle of water then stripped off her sodden blouse and skirt and rubbed her down with a heavy towel. Lying there pale and helpless she looked like a teenager. I wrapped her in one of the Mexican blankets just as her eyes fluttered open. She stared wildly around until her glance fell upon Sinbad eying her quizzically from the opposite seat.

"Please, don't set the dog after me again. I'll tell you everything."

"Deal. Here, drink this."

I handed her the hot rum I had mixed up. She took a drink, coughed and choked, then drank again.

"Lips that have touched liquor never shall touch mine," I said.

"What?"

She looked at me, then down at the blanket and blushed furiously.

"I had my head averted the whole time. Your secrets are still safe from the eyes of man."

She glared at me then took another defiant drink and shivered some more as she pulled back as far away as she could from Sinbad who was stretching his neck tentatively towards her. She looked pathetic and I felt a sudden shame about the whole sordid business.

"Look, I'll let you in on a secret. The dog likes you. He wants to make friends."

"Really?"

"Really. It's me he doesn't care for."

I held out my hand towards Sinbad and he growled deep in his throat and drew his lips back from his teeth then turned towards Laura again. She put her hand out slowly and he butted his head against it then rolled over onto his back, his pathetic stub of a tail beating on the seat.

"That's funny," Laura said. She smiled and scratched his belly.

"Hilarious," I said. "Take the tiller."

I went below and pulled out a clean pair of jeans and a T-shirt from my locker and threw them on the seat beside her.

"Get dressed, we're going in."

I raised the jib and let out the main and we slanted back through the pass towards the clubhouse. Laura went below and came back out a few minutes later wearing her wet clothes.

"Suit yourself," I said. "Sure you don't have a couple of journals hidden under there?"

She glared at me but didn't answer, just stood as far away as she could get from me, looking ahead to the docks. We didn't speak again the whole way in. As I brought *Arrow* alongside she stood up to leave. I grabbed her by the shoulder and pushed her down onto the seat.

"We're not done yet," I said. "Wait there for a minute."

The dog growled softly.

"Fuck you, too, Sinbad," I said.

I jumped onto the dock and tied *Arrow* up then came back aboard. Laura was curled up in the corner of the cockpit staring out to sea while she absentmindedly stroked Sinbad's head. I stood waiting until she looked up.

"I want you to listen to me very carefully," I said.

She turned her head away and I took her chin and faced her back towards me. She paled and a tear trembled in the corner of her eye. I didn't let it bother me.

"It ends right now," I said. "It's finished. You call your bully boys and tell them it's over. I don't know what you're after but we don't have it and my friends don't have it. If I hear that Meg and Bob have any more trouble from anybody I'll come after you no matter where you are and you will pay for it. Believe me. Tell that fucking ponce Barclay if I ever see him around *Arrow* again I'll kill him. Do you understand me?"

"Barclay? What Barclay are you talking about?" She looked at me in amazement.

"Lord Barclay fucking Summers. The bastard who did this."

I rolled up my sleeve and showed her the faded scar that ran from shoulder to elbow. I could have pulled down my shorts and showed her the one on my ass as well, but I refrained.

Her hands went up and cradled her face and then she closed her eyes. "Barclay," she whispered. "Oh, Jesus. What a fucking mess."

She rocked slowly back and forth, and then the tears started to come and suddenly she was sobbing like a child, looking straight at me and the tears pouring down her face and onto the wet blouse. She started to shake and the crying never slowed, those big hazel eyes just filling and refilling and her hands clamped to her temples as if to contain the pain within. Finally she stopped and lay back exhausted.

I mixed her another hot rum and handed her a towel and waited while she slowly pulled herself together, the long shuddering breaths gradually easing.

"I'll tell you," she whispered at last.

CHAPTER 9

Doctor Padraic Kennedy had been a professor in the department of Marine Archaeology at the University of London. His work was researching shipwrecks in the South Pacific during the eighteenth century, and his overwhelming passion the unsolved disappearance of Jean-François Galaup, comte de Lapérouse, the celebrated French navigator and explorer.

The comte had sailed from Botany Bay in Australia on February 7, 1788, captaining the vessel *Boussole* and accompanied by *Astrolabe*, the other ship under his command. He wasn't heard of again until nearly forty years later when British naval captain Peter Dillon heard rumours of an old shipwreck in Vanikoro Island in the Santa Cruz group. Dillon sailed to the island, located the wreckage, and obtained sufficient proof to determine that it was indeed the remains of *Astrolabe* and *Boussole*.

Subsequently he ascertained that Lapérouse and several of his crew survived the shipwreck and built a small sloop from the remains of the two vessels. A year after the disaster they set sail from Vanikoros Island in their little craft and disappeared without a trace.

The mystery of Lapérouse had always fascinated Kennedy, and

gradually it formed into an obsession. After the death of his wife, he took early retirement on a small pension from the university and spent his days trying to discover the secret of Lapérouse's final resting place. He'd done his research with the original logs, diaries, and journals from the Maritime Museum in Greenwich and the Musée National de la Marine in Paris, and supplemented this with the records of the East India Trading Companies, sea captains' logs, and various accounts of early French merchant traders and explorers who had covered the area in the late 1700s.

He concluded from all of this that Lapérouse had not sailed directly towards New Caledonia as was previously assumed but had instead been island hopping down the New Hebrides when a series of cyclones issuing from the monsoonal trough over Papua New Guinea had struck and carried him and his crew south and east to shipwreck and destruction.

Kennedy bolstered his theory with a projection of the extraordinary series of cyclones that had ravaged the South Pacific in 1787, as well as drift pattern sequences based on those storms a colleague at the university had programmed on a computer for him. He became convinced that Lapérouse's second and fatal shipwreck was somewhere on the Great Sea Reef of northwest Fiji. It was an eccentric theory at best, and one unsupported by his colleagues.

Doctor Kennedy had spent the last four years travelling around the north coast of Fiji interviewing the chiefs and headmen of the isolated villages and searching their histories and local legends for some reference to the wreck that he was convinced had occurred there. Laura occasionally accompanied him on his journeys.

The previous year, Kennedy had become certain he was getting close when one of the old villagers told him about the legend of a ship that had appeared far out beyond the reef on a stormy night with all lights blazing and disappeared in a ball of fire. The chief had showed him an old silver plate dating from the eighteenth century, severely eroded by weather and time, but upon which the words "in gratitude

1775–82" could still be seen engraved on the rim. The good doctor was convinced.

He knew that Lapérouse had received a silver service from a grateful American government for his distinguished service in the war of American independence, and it would undoubtedly have graced his wardroom when he was at sea. It was as near conclusive proof of his theory as he could hope for without the actual discovery of the wreck.

Unfortunately, the plate had been recovered decades earlier, handed down through maternal grandmothers, and no one knew from which village it had originally come.

It could have been any one of many along the northern coast, and every one of them with dozens of miles of surrounding reefs. Laura had seen Meg's silver plate at the yacht club and realized immediately that it was similar to the one in her father's possession.

"So you just decided to steal it," I said.

"No. I borrowed it to see if it was a match. I was going to try and bring up the engraving with some acid and then I was going to send it back. You don't understand. My father has ruined himself with this obsession. He's lost his position, his reputation, and his money. His pension is a joke. He has nothing left. This was a chance to vindicate him, to give him back some pride. I would have done more than borrow a silver plate for a couple of weeks to accomplish that."

"Well you did do more, didn't you? You stole the journals from Meg as well, although I guess maybe you were just borrowing them too," I said.

"No. I don't know anything about that. That must have been my ex-boyfriend. Barclay Summers."

She had a sad, ashamed look on her face, as if just tasting the full fruits of her betrayal. "And I thought he liked me for me, the condescending asshole," she spat out.

"I can't say I really cared much for him either," I said. She didn't reply, just stared off into space, her fingers absently tracing the scars that ran along Sinbad's head and back.

"I met him last summer, through my father," she said finally. "He skippers the *Golden Dragon*, the famous sailboat. You've probably heard of it."

What sailor hadn't? Over two hundred million dollars' worth of the latest technology wrapped up in two hundred forty feet of grace and beauty, she was one of the most celebrated sailboats ever built. Her picture had appeared on the cover of every major yachting magazine in the world.

Built of steel and aluminum, the *Golden Dragon* had been launched three years past to intense interest and acclaim. Although she carried a permanent crew of seven she was so automated it was said that one man alone could sail her well. Everything was powered, from the in-mast sails and hydraulic winches that responded to the touch of a button to the computer centre that controlled her navigation and steering systems. Even her trim was calculated and balanced automatically by pumps that pushed the water and fuel from her tanks fore and aft, or port and starboard as the computer decreed. Everything about her was an expression of the modern quest to reduce sailing from an art to a science.

The purists had decried her, but it was difficult not to admire her grace and beauty, for this fantastic science fiction machine was encased in a clean sleek hull that was as fast as any monohull in the world other than the flat out racing maxis.

Her owner, Robin Waverly, was every bit as famous and charismatic as his boat. Rising from humble beginnings in the East End of London, he had made his fortune in real estate and parlayed that into a media empire and then a shipping line that carried his name. Waverly was the darling of the press, one of those modern-day financial buccaneers who are so celebrated and admired. He was frequently surrounded by hints of scandal and rumours of imminent financial collapse that never came to pass.

In his mid-fifties, he looked younger and, in the grand tradition of freebooters, had become something of an adventurer and philanthropist. The *Golden Dragon* was the ultimate expression of that new stage, and the world press carried reports of his voyage to southern Antarctica and his race eastwards around the world in a near record circumnavigation with all the breathless titivation they accorded the latest rock star's love affairs. The last I'd heard he was carrying a boatload of British scientists along the west coast of Africa to plot the maritime effects of the escalating erosion of the Sahara.

"The *Golden Dragon* was cruising in Fiji last season," Laura said. "Robin Waverly had heard about my father's theories and research, and he invited us aboard for drinks one evening. Of course my father was flattered. Here finally was somebody important who took him seriously, someone who was a celebrated explorer in his own right. I hadn't seen him so happy and outgoing for years. We spent the night as guests aboard the *Dragon* and in the morning Robin offered to take us around for six weeks and do some diving on some of the spots where Daddy thought the wreck might be. It was a great opportunity for us and we took him up on it. That was when I first met Barclay."

"Did you find anything?"

"No. But we covered only a small fraction of the possibilities. That's why when I returned to England and happened to hear Meg's talk and saw the plate, I was so excited. I don't really know why I took it. One minute I was in the corner going over the souvenirs on the table and the next minute the plate was in my purse."

"You could have just asked. She would have lent it to you and told you where they picked it up if she knew."

"I didn't want anyone else to get the credit for my father's discovery, and I didn't know if I could trust her. In retrospect, I should have told her."

"When did Barclay find out about the plate?"

"It was a coincidence. He'd phoned me up earlier, said he had some information for me about Lapérouse. We had already arranged to meet, even though we'd broken up by then. He'd been so interested and helpful on the yacht, diving every day with me and some of the crew, organizing the search patterns. I felt I owed it to him. He said he really wanted to see the plate. He came back to my flat." Her voice faltered for a moment.

"We had a disagreement. He left with the plate. But I never knew anything about a break-in at your friends' house. Or at your boat either. I really did want to charter *Arrow*, get to know you and maybe tell you about everything. Or maybe just read the journals on a pretext if that seemed a better idea." She shrugged. "That's all there is."

"Not quite. What makes this find so important that Summers would fly all the way out to New Zealand and risk a prison sentence just to get a look at the journals? The silver service wouldn't be worth all that much. It must be something else."

She shook her head. "I can't think of anything specific. Of course there were always rumours about Lapérouse's last voyage."

"Rumours?"

"You know. The usual fancies. That he was carrying a vast sum of money on board from King Louis to bribe and overthrow one of the British colonies, that he was carrying some Russian treasure from his earlier visit there, a gift from the czar. Take your pick."

"What does your father think of all this?"

"He's not interested in any of that. He just wants to locate the site and recover the artifacts."

"Assuming that there is just the silver service, maybe a few other bits and pieces, what might it all be worth, best case?" I asked.

"Say twenty, thirty thousand pounds tops. And then with the Fijian salvage laws and maybe some French rights and you'd be lucky to end up with a quarter of that."

"Summers probably wasn't worried about splitting it up, but even so, it seems hardly worth the trouble he's gone to. There has to be something else."

Assuming that Barclay was working on his own of course, and not representing his boss. Was Waverly's ego so great that he needed to receive full credit for the discovery? The location of Lapérouse's final resting place would be a major historical find and media event. The person credited with that would be celebrated, even famous. And Waverly certainly didn't shun the limelight.

But I caught the whiff of something else in all of this: the unmistakable siren scent of money — undeclared, tax-free, untraceable wealth and the power and greed it could unleash. I'd cast that trail before and there was no mistaking the stench. I'd stake my life on it. Maybe I already had. I could still see the look on Summers's face when I'd left him broken on the bar room floor.

Laura and I sat back in the cockpit letting the sun wash down over us, suspended in one of those brilliant Suva spaces where the sky was perfectly clear, and you could imagine you would never see a cloud again. In ten minutes it might be raining.

"Tell me about Summers."

She stirred from some distant reverie and frowned.

"Barclay is from a well-known family, has two older brothers, so not much chance of him inheriting the family estate. Rumour has it there was a huge row in the family a while back and they haven't spoken to Barclay in years. He receives an annual allowance of fifty thousand pounds, but that's chicken feed in the circles he moves in. He wants and expects the best of everything. When the *Golden Dragon* was being built, he ran into Robin and they became friends and Robin offered him the job of captain. Barclay was a keen sailor. He'd done some offshore racing and the position was perfect for him." She paused for a moment, and I wondered what she was thinking, but then she charged on. "Robin admires him for his toughness; they're more friends than boss and employee. Barclay left university and joined the Special Air Service as soon as he was of age. He was there for fifteen years and made the rank of major, but something happened in Northern Ireland and he was forced to resign his commission. He's bitter about that, told me once when he was drunk that the service was his real family and they'd turned their backs on him when all he'd done was protect his men. It was one of the few times I've seen him completely serious about anything. Usually he has this easy-going, cynical, half-smiling, half-mocking attitude."

I nodded, remembering him in the pub.

"I guess I was pretty easy for him, not much experience with men, naive."

She paused and glanced at me. I bit down on my lip and stared out to sea.

"He was attractive, charming, even my father liked him, although he thought he was too old for me. Barclay was fun to be with. Everything came easily to him. He knew everybody and had lots of clever stories about the jet set. You could see how they all respected him. One day towards the end of our trip on the *Golden Dragon*, they were bringing the motor launch on board and one of the crew slipped the line on the drumhead and the boat smashed down into the deck. Barclay went ballistic. He screamed at the man, slapped him until finally the guy went after him and then Barclay just cut him up with his hands and feet. It was horrible. The deck hand was just a kid. Nobody interfered. I just stood there in shock and then it was over, and Barclay was acting as if nothing had happened."

"Was Waverly there?"

"Yes. He seemed upset at first, but then he said you had to make some special allowances for Barclay because of his past. It was almost as if he was proud of him. Called him a hard man. After that I stayed away from Barclay, that side of him scared me. Then he phoned me in London a couple of months later and apologized. Said how sorry he was about us and he had some information about Lapérouse and could he buy me lunch to make it up."

"What was his news?"

"Nothing really. Some French artifacts they'd retrieved on a dive after we'd left. Or so he said. They were clearly too recent, though, obviously turn of the century."

"So you told him about Meg and the journals and *Arrow*."

"Oh yes. Everything. I was even stupid enough to bring him back to the flat to show him the plate." She paused and a bitter smile twisted her face. "He took it. Afterwards I realized I couldn't very well go up to Meg and confess I'd taken the plate, but I didn't have it anymore. That's when I decided to fly out to New Zealand and try to charter *Arrow*. Meg had mentioned you and Danny were in Whangarei in her talk at the yacht club, and it sounded as if you could use the money. You weren't very hard to find."

I thought she was telling the truth now. So far as she knew it anyway. She looked exhausted, and I felt a twinge of guilt. So what to do?

"I think we should talk things over with your father. Compare notes. Maybe over lunch."

"You just tried to drown me and now you want to have lunch together?"

"I figured you for a swimmer. Don't forget I still have the journals. If you don't play nice you won't get them. And then your father will never find Lapérouse's wreck."

She studied me.

"You can relax, you're not my type," I said.

"I had you figured more for the blonde bimbo model. Feel threatened around any woman who has a brain in her head."

"Don't underestimate yourself." I winked and she flushed red from the neck right up to the roots of her hair.

"You son of a bitch," she stammered. "A gentleman wouldn't bring that up."

"Who said I was a gentleman? So, are we doing lunch or not? You must be starved after all that exercise. Running, swimming, no wonder you're in such good shape."

There was a long pause. "I'll have to shower and change first," she said at last through gritted teeth. She really wanted to see those journals.

"Fine. Say an hour then, Laura. I can call you Laura, can't I? And you may call me Jared. After all, since we're going to be partners, we don't want all this formality."

"Partners?" She regarded me with horror.

"The notion will grow on you. You'll see."

"Over my cold, dead body," she said.

I picked up the journal and flipped through the pages. "Just think. The answer could even lie in this very one. Right here at our fingertips just waiting to be discovered. I can imagine how excited your father will be. By the way, did you tell him about the stolen plate?"

She looked at me as if I had crawled out from under a rock.

"No, I didn't think so. Well, we had better get our stories straight hadn't we? Don't want Daddy to think his little princess is less than perfect."

She spun away and marched up the dock, the broomstick firmly in place.

"One o'clock then, partner," I called after her. "Don't be late now. We don't want to start our new relationship off on the wrong foot. Your father can chaperone."

She never replied or gave any indication that she heard me, just kept walking away in that rigid square shouldered stride and disappeared without a backwards glance.

CHAPTER 10

I walked up to the club and spent half an hour talking with Roland the bartender about the big win by the Fijian rugby team over the New Zealand All Blacks in the World Cup quarter finals. I'd given up on Laura and was about to order lunch when she walked through the door in company with a tall gangling man in his late fifties or early sixties with a shock of iron-grey hair showing out from under his baseball cap. Laura was dressed in a severe close-necked blouse and three-quarter length tailored skirt. She strode across the room and took my hand and shook it firmly.

"Jared. Thanks for waiting. Sorry we're late. This is my father."

"That's okay. Pleased to meet you, sir." I extended my hand and we shook politely. He had a sharp, unseamed face under the grey hair, surprisingly young looking.

"Let's sit down and order first," Laura said. "Waiter!"

She raised her hand and two of them converged on her with menus.

"I think the special, please. Same for you two? Yes? Three, please. And another beer for Mr. Kane and one for my father. Perrier for me. Thank you."

She turned back to us and smiled. I could see she'd done the power lunch thing before.

"I've told Daddy how I heard about you at the yacht club in Cowes at Meg's lecture. How I thought I recognized the silver plate and she gave me your address and you agreed to meet me in Fiji. When you phoned and said you were here this morning, I could hardly believe it. I didn't want to tell him earlier and raise false hopes."

"That was sensible," I said.

"I couldn't believe it when Laura told me." Kennedy smiled and shook his head. "To think after all this time and there's no evidence, and then suddenly two plates turn up from totally different sources. It's just amazing."

"I can scarcely believe it myself," I said.

"I can't wait to get a look at the journals. Laura said someone attempted to steal them from *Arrow* after they took some copies from your friends' house."

"Yes, that's right." No wonder Laura was late. She'd done a lot of creative explaining.

"And you think it was Barclay Summers." The shrewd brown eyes were watching me closely.

"There's no proof of that, but yes, I believe it was him."

"Hmm."

He drank down his beer and held up the empty bottle to summon another. Laura watched him nervously. "So the question is, was Robin Waverly aware of this or was Barclay acting on his own?"

"Yes," I said. "That's the question."

"Hmm."

He turned away again lost in thought. He suddenly swung back towards me. "I think it's safe to assume Waverly is involved. I doubt Summers would jeopardize his position with him on some freelance venture. So, you want to be partners with us then. Why?"

"We have the boat, some dive gear. We're at loose ends, we'd as soon dive in one place as another. We'll give you the journals anyway, maybe they'll lead us to it. If not, what do you have to lose?"

"You haven't answered my question. Why?"

The waiter appeared with our lunches and we ate in silence for a few minutes. The prawn curry was searing, and we ordered more Fiji Bitters to wash it down. The professor was sweating heavily and quaffing steadily along with me, but the Ice Maiden just spooned it serenely in as if it was sherbet.

"Okay," I said. "Let me lay it out for you. I think something more is going on here than you're aware of, and you're in over your heads." Laura shook her head and glared at me and angrily began to speak. The professor raised his hand and motioned her to silence.

"Hear him out, love," he said.

"They went to considerable trouble and expense to find us in Whangarei, break into *Arrow*, and then track her all the way up the coast to Opua for a second attempt. It might just be Waverly's ego involved in finding a historic wreck site, but I doubt it. He must have known he could have acquired the journals openly, through Meg. She would never have refused a legitimate request from someone of his stature. He could have had other authorities support his quest, maybe even invited Meg and Bob to join him for that matter. He chose not to, and it was only by a fluke that we found out what they were really after. Summers and Waverly didn't want anyone knowing what they were about. The only thing that warrants that kind of secrecy is money or treasure. Illegal, readily disposable, tax-free riches."

Laura was shaking her head impatiently as I spoke, and now she exploded into the pause. "That's bloody ridiculous. You don't know that. You're just making wild guesses based on some ludicrous macho thing between you and Summers."

I waited for her father to speak.

"I am inclined to agree with you, Mr. Kane," he said. "Please continue."

Laura glared at him.

"What I propose is that we share equally in any recoveries we make. We supply the boat and the diving gear, the provisions, everything. We have enough money for three months, we were going cruising anyway, and it won't be much more expensive to feed four than two. If the journals help find anything and there's some money due, we'll recompense Meg out of our share. If there are just the usual ship items on board, including the silver service, nothing out of the ordinary, then we just take the expenses for the trip out of it, you keep the rest."

Laura stared at me, eyes narrowed.

"How do we know we can trust you?"

"You don't. But we could go out and look without you, and besides, what have you got to lose? You need to hire somebody to take you around in any case. I think these are very dangerous people, and you may not be capable of dealing with them."

"And you are, of course," she sneered.

"Well, you haven't met my partner, Danny, yet. He's quite capable. You've met Sinbad, of course."

"Who's Sinbad?" her father inquired.

"The ship's dog," Laura said. "Meanest looking fucker you ever laid eyes on. Sorry, Daddy," she added quickly as he looked over with eyebrows raised.

"My daughter and I will have to talk about this, Mr. Kane. I must say, it appears a very generous offer."

"Good then. I'll have to discuss it with Danny as well, but I'm sure he'll agree. The truth is we have only enough money for a few more months of cruising, and any chance of avoiding going back home to work is worth taking, however slim."

"What is it you do?" Laura asked sweetly. "Some kind of menial work, I'll bet?"

"We're commercial fishermen."

She gave a small superior smile.

"A fine honest job," the professor said approvingly. "I always wanted to go to sea myself."

He ordered another round of beer and we drank them under Laura's disapproving stare. She sipped her Perrier with a sanctimonious air that I found intensely annoying.

"I have a great idea," I said. "Why don't you two come with me to a little informal gathering tonight and meet Danny? It will give us all a chance to get to know one another and see if this venture has any chance of working out. After all, four of us on a relatively small boat, we'll be in pretty close quarters." I winked at Laura.

She smiled glacially. "That's very kind of you, but I'm sure Daddy has a lot of work to do and I . . ."

"Nonsense, my dear. We'd be delighted, Mr. Kane."

"Please call me Jared, sir."

"I'd be honoured, and you must call me Padraic. Let's drink to that." He raised his bottle to me and took a long pull.

"The tropical heat requires a steady consumption of fluids, you know," he said.

"Yes, I've noticed that Padraic. *Slainte.*"

It was three o'clock by the time Laura finally got the professor away from the club. She threw a vicious look over her shoulder at me as she ushered him out the door to the waiting taxi. We'd agreed that I would drop by their cottage and pick them up around nine. I phoned Kirk's apartment and left a message on the machine that there would be another three people to barbecue for. He had a freezer full of cheap beef fillet that he smuggled in from Vanuatu at ridiculously low prices, and I'd bring a couple of bottles of the duty-free whisky from New Zealand to trade off.

I stretched out on the cockpit seat and thought about what Padraic had told me about the rumours of treasure that circulated around

Lapérouse. Something was nagging at the corner of my mind, something I'd read or heard recently, and I felt I was getting close to it when the beer caught up to me and I drifted off to sleep.

The sun was down when I woke to the sound of early evening mosquitoes buzzing in my ear. I had just time enough for a quick shower and change and then it was off to pick up the Kennedys. They were staying at one of the cheaper resort complexes north of town set back a few blocks from the water. Laura answered the door looking fresh and cool in a white cotton dress. Padraic was dressed casually in khaki shorts and a Chicago Bears T-shirt that matched the cap perched on his mop of hair.

"You look lovely, Laura," I said.

"Thank you, Jared," she replied.

"I hope I'm not overdressed," Padraic said. He winked at me over Laura's shoulder.

"These little get togethers are usually pretty casual."

The last one I attended ended up with half a dozen people in the pool playing water polo with somebody's set of falsies in the early hours of the morning. I couldn't envision Laura in that scenario. Padraic, maybe.

We drove across town and pulled up in front of Kirk's building. You could hear the music pulsing from the street. Laura got out and looked around, a frown on her face.

"Isn't Kirk Mellor's apartment here?"

"That's right. It's his party. I didn't realize you'd been here," I said.

"I had lunch with him here when we were discussing his charter," she snapped.

"Of course, you did. Let's go up."

I tucked my hand under her elbow and she pulled away and marched up the stairs.

"You sure you just met her today?" Padraic whispered. "It usually takes a bit longer for her to dislike a man so much."

"I'm a fast worker," I said.

Laura opened the door and the wall of noise hit us like a sledge-hammer. There must have been thirty gyrating bodies jammed into the living room, many of them dressed only in bathing suits. Danny was in the middle of the pack, swinging Christy around his shoulders in an intricate series of movements that culminated with her spinning up to the loft style roof screaming in fear and delight. He saw us and dropped her back down to the floor and came over. He was dressed only in cut-offs and sweating freely, the rivulets coursing down the twisted scars that covered his stomach.

"Jared," he roared. He grabbed me by the waist and threw me towards the roof then waltzed me around the floor.

"Put me down, you stupid son of a bitch," I snarled. "I want you to meet someone."

"What? A date, Jared? I would never have believed it. A looker too. I'm impressed, old buddy. The name is Danny, ma'am. Daniel MacLean at your service."

"Laura Kennedy. And I'm not his date."

"Marvellous. Let's dance then."

He picked her up and whirled her out onto the floor, her protests fading into the general cacophony. I watched them go as Padraic appeared at my side carrying a couple of beers. He passed me one and we clinked them together and drank.

"That's your partner, I take it."

"Yes. He's a little high-spirited at the moment."

"I noticed."

We watched as Laura's body rose four feet above the dancers before she dropped and disappeared again. I couldn't see her face. Probably just as well.

"Those are nasty knife scars on Danny," Padraic said.

I looked at him in surprise. Most people bought the fishing acci-dent story. He smiled at me.

"Ireland has a bloody history, my boy. I left there when I was eighteen and went off to University in London, but I'd seen enough by then."

115

"Yes. We had some trouble a couple of years back. Some people after us and trying to kill us. Not our doing, just in the wrong place at the wrong time. They cut up Danny, but we got away and he should have died but he didn't." I paused and then thought what the hell. You either trust him or you don't. "And then they came after us and we ended up killing them. In the same circumstances we'd do it again."

He nodded. "I saw Barclay Summers a few weeks ago, you know. I was giving a talk on British naval exploration in the seventeenth and eighteenth centuries." He shrugged. "It's mostly how I pay my way nowadays. He was there and came up to say hello afterwards, asked how things were going. He had his arm in a cast."

"There was a fight up in Opua after they tried to board *Arrow* the second time. His side lost."

"Barclay Summers is a dangerous man. He was in Ireland for a while, extremely ruthless, much hated by the locals. There was some talk about a British murder squad although nothing was ever proved. It was rumoured that Summers was the leader. He resigned from the service. It was that or be cashiered, the stories said."

"Not the ideal son-in-law then," I said.

"It was never anywhere near that," Padraic replied. "He was smooth, experienced, just swept her off her feet, and she didn't realize what he was like. We didn't know much about him then. She's still angry about it. She's not very experienced you know."

"No kidding? And here I thought she was a real swinger."

I took the bottle of Glenfiddich and poured us a large drink.

"She's had a sheltered life. Her mother died when she was young and I've had the raising of her. I was away a lot, there were different women, you know," he gestured vaguely with the glass. "She's very determined, quite successful in her own right. She was taking fine arts courses at Dublin University when I left my job and the money dried up. She went out and landed a position at Sotheby's as a trainee appraiser; within three years she was one of their best people in her specialty, antique glass and silver. She opened her own shop in Chelsea a year later. It's what we live on mostly now. She has a partner who runs it while she's out here with me."

I watched Laura while he spoke. She was talking to Danny, the two of them laughing. She lifted her head and saw me looking and her face sobered. I could read the appraisal in the level hazel eyes. Base metal. I smiled at the thought and she tossed her head and turned away.

"Laura is opposed to us joining forces," Padraic said.

"Well, maybe Danny will change her mind," I said. I took the bottle and poured myself another glass. The liquor hit the pit of my stomach and burned and I closed my eyes and basked in the glow. Someone had turned on the gas barbecue and the sizzle of burning meat filled the air. It smelled rank and nauseous to me and I took the bottle and moved away. The professor followed.

"You drink like an Irishman," he said.

No, the Irish drink to enjoy themselves, I thought.

I looked out at all the bright smiling people on the floor, and the couples standing close and talking in the corners and I knew I would never be one of those and the blackness rose dark and inarticulate and I took a long drink straight from the bottle now and it burned and cut its way through to the bottom. For a moment something was very clear to me but then it faded.

"My turn," a voice said and a big brown hand took the bottle. Danny raised it to his lips then passed it across to the professor.

"Danny, meet Professor Padraic Kennedy. Laura's father."

They shook hands. The bottle was back with Danny now.

"I've got your steak on, Jared. It'll be ready in a minute. Come on, Professor, there's one for you as well."

"I'm not hungry," I said.

They each grasped an elbow and moved me to the buffet table.

"All right goddammit, I'm coming. See, I'm eating."

I picked up a roll and took a bite. Danny stayed beside me while Padraic got the steaks and returned with our plates.

"I guess you really are Laura's father after all," I snarled at Kennedy. He smiled and started to eat.

"What do you mean he's my father after all?" Laura, appearing out of nowhere, a bright facetious smile on her face.

"I mean, he's a tight ass as well," I said, but in a low voice that Padraic drowned out with some ridiculous Irish bullshit about her eyes. She gave me a skeptical look and began eating her salad in dainty little bites.

"So I understand we're going to be partners then," Danny said. I looked up in surprise. "Laura told me all about it, sounds good to me. Better than cruising aimlessly around snorkelling and spearfishing all year. Maybe a little action, a little money."

Laura watched me closely, a mocking little smile on her face.

"Actually, I'm not so sure that some spearfishing and snorkelling and lazing around wouldn't suit me just fine," I said. "This could be dangerous, you know. For all of us."

"Well, yeah," Danny said. "So?"

"So they should understand that. This isn't a game. Somebody could get hurt, maybe even killed," I said. "Once we start this there is no telling where it might end up. They should know that going in." I turned to Laura. "I told you once you were out of your league. I still believe that."

"You're scared," Laura said. Her father watched me silently.

I felt the frozen smile coming to my face. "You don't know the first fucking thing about me, lady," I said softly, moving up close to her. "You should keep that in mind."

Her face paled and she drew back. I turned and walked out the door.

A taxi was parked at the curb, but I strode past and after a few yards started to jog and then broke out into a hard run. It had rained again, and the air smelled sweet and fresh. The sound of my sandals slapping the pavement and the sighing of my breath were the only sounds in the night. Racing alone in the darkness, moving in and out of scattered pools of light, the tenseness gradually spilled out of me and I extended my stride and ran faster still, half-drunk and high on whisky and fresh air, my heart pounding like a drum. As I turned onto the coast road, a shadow came out of the brush and ran alongside and I bent down and gave the great head a cuff. Sinbad growled and drew back his lips and I laughed and cuffed him again and he snapped at my hand but missed and never changed his stride or moved away.

"You ugly old bastard," I said. "You're just a goddammed fake, aren't you?"

He turned his head and stared at me, the yellow eyes glowing wetly in the reflected light, the ears cocked and listening as we ran, and I cursed him steadily and he growled in reciprocation, and maybe the closest thing to love I would ever feel was for the misshapen creature that ran so close beside me in the night.

CHAPTER 11

I awoke to the sound of wind soughing in the palms, the morning dark and rain-filled, the low moving cloud so dense the clubhouse a hundred yards distant was scarcely visible through the port light. My head ached with a low throbbing pain, my spirits as black and depressed as the weather. *Arrow* surged against the floats, rolling along the oversize fenders strung down from her lifelines, her motion quick and loose. I went on deck to tighten the spring lines and was soaked through in seconds, the water moving in driving horizontal sheets that swirled and pulsed at the caprice of the wind. I stripped off my sodden garments and turned into it, letting the stale sweat of whisky-soaked dreams wash away under the lukewarm drumming beat. After long minutes I went below and towelled dry. I was on my second cup of coffee when I heard a knock on the side of the boat. I dropped the top companionway board and there was Laura, dressed in running gear, her body slicked with rain and sweat. Little tendrils of steam rose from her bare shoulders and she had a bright smile on her face.

"Good morning. Want to join me for a run?"

"No."

"Come on, don't be a grump. It'll be great."

"Go away."

My legs were sore from the night before, and besides, running was supposed to be enjoyable. This woman didn't know the meaning of pleasure. What the hell was she doing here anyway? I went back inside. She knocked on the hull again.

"How about a cup of coffee then?"

I stuck my head back out the companionway.

"Look, Laura. We don't like each other. That's okay, I've never believed that everyone has to be bosom buddies. I'm Canadian, not Californian."

"I want to apologize for last night."

"Forget it. Give my regards to your father. In fact you can take him the journals. Wait there, I'll get them."

I went back inside and took the copies out and was putting them in a waterproof bag when she came down the companionway stairs.

"Does this mean we're partners then?" she asked.

"No. This means you and your father can use these however you please. If they're useful, then you can decide if you owe something to Meg. We're out."

I passed the bag to her and she set it down on the table in front of her and poured herself a cup of coffee.

"Why don't you have a cup of coffee, seeing as you're on board anyway?" I said.

"Thanks, I will. Do you have any milk?"

"No."

"Black is fine then."

She took a tea towel and spread it on the lounge cushions before seating herself. She didn't look like she was planning on leaving anytime soon. I went to the fridge and took out the milk.

"Thank you, Jared."

"You're welcome."

We sat and sipped our coffee in silence.

"Nice boat."

"Yes."

"I spent a lot of time with Danny last night."

"That's nice. Wasn't it a little crowded with Christy?"

She took another sip of coffee and now there were spots of colour just above her cheekbones and the determined smile slipped a fraction.

"I mean talking to Danny. At the party after you left. He was furious. Told me I should have my ass paddled."

"That's just part of the quaint Haida courting traditions."

"Goddammit, shut up, Jared. This is hard enough for me. Daddy was right there and he never said a word. Danny told us about what happened with the jewel robbery. How you got him off, the Lebel brothers, everything, right up to the end in the Tuamotus. He said he owes you his life."

It wasn't really that simple. If not for Danny and his family taking me in when I came out of prison all those years ago, I would likely be dead now, or lying sodden and hopeless in an east end gutter. Theirs was not a quick reckless act like helping Danny, but an unflinching love and acceptance that never questioned or faltered. They were my family now, the only one I would ever have. I would lay down my life for any one of them.

"We look out for each other. Like I said, forget it. Take these to your father, see if there's anything in there to help him."

She picked up the bag and stood to go. "All right then, Jared. But promise me you'll talk to Danny about coming in with us."

"I'll talk to him."

She stared at me as if wanting to say something more, and then she turned and left. I watched her go up the dock in the driving rain, looking small and fragile in the running outfit. She disappeared, and I went below and listened to the rain drumming on the deck. Her words had brought it all flooding back; the brothers, Delaney, Chuck and Eddie, the mad flight and the circling tigers and the final deaths. Ghosts filled the cabin.

I stripped down and practised my katas in the gloom of the saloon, wheeling and striking in the narrow corridor, my eyes closed, shadow dancing just short of the whipped mast support, taking my invisible opponents in turn with feints and shadow kicks, and then gradually extending. I was stiff and awkward at first but then the rhythms began to establish, and the movements became less practised and more natural and I let my feet and hands extend as the oiled sweat encased my body and the column shook beneath my blows. Never looking, I let my mind expand and delineate the narrow space, spinning and whirling and striking, searching for the faces that revolved just beyond the edge of my inner vision, faster and faster now, the sweat rolling over my closed eyes, my body running with moisture, the edges of my hands and feet focusing and narrowing into knife edges of dimly felt pain as they pounded the column.

I worked until the breath ran ragged in my lungs and my hands and feet were blocks of wood, separate and detached, functioning with a life and purpose of their own, and there was nothing in the universe but the ghosts, the column, and the pain. They moved and danced forever beyond my reach, that wrecking crew all dead now, their bodies ripped and blown, rent by the savage teeth of sharks, and only the gaping grins of skeleton jaws remaining, mocking and untouchable. And there, drifting off to the side, Jennie and her father rocking in slow embrace, their bleached bones entwined and drifting three thousand fathoms below the light forever. And all of it or none of it my fault.

I slowed at last and shuddered to a halt. I opened my eyes and the haunts withdrew and I was left only with the pain rising up from my hands and feet and the cord-whipped column oiled with sweat and faint pink streaks. I cleaned everything and fell down exhausted into my bunk.

"Wake up, Jared. You going to crash all day? It's happy hour." I rose out of deep dreamless sleep to the sight of Danny's hand wrapped around a glass six inches in front of my face. Over his shoulder I saw legs in the cockpit.

"We've got company. Padraic's here with Laura and they've brought snacks and a pitcher of martinis. Have a drink, it will wake you up."

I sat up, took a drink, and choked. It was straight gin with just the faintest hint of vermouth and bitters.

"Jesus. Let me guess. Padraic mixed these, right?"

"No, as a matter of fact, that's my recipe," Laura said from the companionway. "I enjoy a good martini now and then."

She was dressed in a wraparound skirt and white silk blouse that brought out the pale gold colour of her skin. She had her hair tied off her face with a vivid yellow ribbon and the whole effect was striking. If I hadn't known her, she would have been attractive. She took a sip from her glass and smiled at me. Laura having a determined good time.

I went forward to the head and splashed water on my face and put on a clean pair of shorts and a T-shirt. When I went on deck everybody was laughing at a story Padraic was relating. The wind had died out completely, and the late sun was beaming down upon the three of them in the cockpit. Sitting around the table in their whites with the half-filled pitcher of martinis in front of them and the vivid green backdrop of the palms behind, they looked like an advertisement for the cruising life. The air of close complicity among them was tangible. I sensed that issues had been raised and settled in my absence.

"So Connor said to the dean, 'Right then, if Dylan is so damned sure about it where's the bloody empties then?'" Padraic raised his arms in an open-handed gesture and the three of them fell about the cockpit seats in gales of mirth.

"Here, Jared, let me top you up. You've got some catching up to do, we were in the club for a while." Padraic wiped his eyes with a crumpled handkerchief and filled my glass to the brim. I took a polite sip.

"Daddy was just telling the old chestnut about the time Dylan Thomas went to Trinity College for a poetry reading," Laura said.

"Who's he?" I said.

Danny sighed and passed me the sandwich tray. They were cut into perfect little triangles. The sight of one of them in Danny's big hand almost restored my good humour. I took a bite.

"Damn, they're not cucumber," I said.

"Look here, Jared," Laura began, but Padraic smoothly overrode her.

"We were talking with Danny about the trip earlier on, Jared. I'm very excited about it. The more I think about it the more convinced I am that there really is something valuable down there, something I have somehow missed. You hear so many stories about treasure in my business that you become skeptical. But there are still fortunes out there waiting to be found, and people still do come across them occasionally. There's an expedition off southern New Zealand right now zeroing in on a find rumoured to be worth millions of pounds. Why not us?"

His face was flushed with enthusiasm and drink, his hands waving emphatically as he spoke.

"Would it mean that much to you?" I asked.

"The finding of Lapérouse's ship is what I've been dreaming of for the last ten years, just to show the bastards I was right all along. Of course the money would make a big difference as well, never mind rubbing a little extra salt in their wounds. God knows it's been tight this last little while. I could pay back Laura, set her up."

"A dowry," I murmured. "Yes, that could make a difference all right."

Laura's chin rose as she pretended not to hear.

"I have the general vicinity now. I'm certain of that. If I can just get something out of those journals of yours, narrow it down some more, we could have it inside of a couple of months."

I wasn't so sure. Even if you had it limited to a five-mile square area, it could still take a long time and you might never find it. Or, for that matter, you might come across it and not recognize it for what it was. Coral grows an inch a year and it was possible that after two hundred years the outlines of the boat would be so softened and blurred that they might be unrecognizable. Coral only grows to a depth of around one hundred and fifty feet, so there was a possibility the sloop could still be there, deep, hardly changed, looking much the same as when it sank. The Brits had hauled up King Henry VIII's warship a while back and it had been amazingly well preserved.

But if Lapérouse's little ship was down in the dark where the coral couldn't grow for lack of light, the recovery of artifacts and treasure would be infinitely more demanding, if not impossible. At least for us. Diving below a hundred feet would open up a whole range of nasty possibilities: diuresis, inert gas absorption, never mind good old fashioned bends or decompression sickness, which can occur at any depth over thirty feet. The deeper you dive the less time you can stay on the bottom without a decompression stop. At one hundred and fifty feet, your bottom time without ascent stops is five minutes, starting from the time you leave the surface. If you stay at a hundred fifty feet for half an hour, your ascent time is thirty-five minutes with two decompression stops on the way up. For longer stays the ascent time increases exponentially. Deep diving is risky and only a fool would enter into it lightly.

"Do you have a compressor?" Laura inquired.

"No."

We'd never needed one, preferring to free dive for the most part and rely on the occasional tank fill from resorts or other cruising boats that carried compressors and paid some of their expenses by filling tanks. We'd need to buy one if we teamed up with the Kennedys, as well as some extra tanks to hang at the decompression stops. Maybe even a little hookah on a floating platform to work some of the shallower depths. We could run a couple of fifty-foot hoses off it, water visibility was good in the areas we would be searching, that would let us cover anything down to the seventy-five-foot level. I sat there, my eyes half closed, working it all out. I realized that I was resigned to the expedition, maybe even looking forward to it.

"Show me the areas you've worked so far, where you think the wreck might be."

Padraic uncapped the map cylinder he had brought along with him and pulled out a half dozen charts, from the small-scale DMAs to the detailed Australian surveys that covered one mile to the inch. Even the most recent carried warnings of inaccuracies and uncharted reefs, testimony to the complex and fragile nature of the Fijian seascape. The previous year an Aussie boat with GPS, radar, and all the latest charts had tried a shortcut through the reefs and ended up lost in a coral maze, running up blind alleys and unable to find a clear channel before finally going aground on a falling tide after sunset. That had happened in fine weather. When the winds kicked up, it could be a nightmare.

Padraic took the small-scale chart that showed the northwest corner of Vanua Levu and spread it out on the cockpit table. It was shaded in different colours and filled with dates and notations.

"Okay. The broad red line delineates the possible area where Lapérouse might have been shipwrecked."

He picked up the compass dividers and ticked off twenty minutes of latitude on the side scale of the chart, starting at the southernmost end of the red line and walking them up and around the corner counting each step aloud.

"One, two, three, four, five, six."

"Jesus," Danny said. "That's a hundred and twenty miles of coastline."

"Yes. But that's where he might have come aground. The black line is where I think he is most likely to have hit the reefs."

He walked the dividers again. Three steps. Sixty miles.

"Still too much to search," Padraic said. "I found the memorial plate in Laini, and the people there thought it had likely come from one of these four villages."

He circumscribed an area of fifty miles that extended past each of the villages and then went out to enclose the furthest sea reef. The distance between Vanua Levu and the reef varied, but was in the neighbourhood of ten miles, with a series of other reefs in between with occasional gaps. It was likely that Lapérouse had hit the external reef, but he could also have been driven up and over it by the force of the storm, and on to one inside before plunging to the bottom. I knew from personal experience that it was possible to take a wooden boat over a reef without destroying it entirely.

So, an area of approximately five hundred square miles, less the actual land area above the water at low tide. Maybe twenty percent. That left four hundred square miles of ocean bottom that dipped and twisted and doubled back on itself in a thousand canyons, drop-offs, and switchbacks. Padraic pointed to the grids that marked the areas the *Golden Dragon* had searched the previous year. I stared at the chart and tried not to show my dismay. They had covered perhaps the fiftieth part of it, and I knew without being told that they wouldn't be absolutely certain they hadn't gone right past the wreck without recognizing it.

It was easy to see how people spent their entire lives and all of their fortunes searching the rumours of treasure. The thought of heading out into that vast wilderness and going over the side to look for a boat that wouldn't be much over thirty feet long filled me with a sense of futility. I could see by the expression on Laura's face she felt the same way.

"What we need is some kind of a fix from the journals. Even if they don't mention the plate, there are records of their trips in Fiji, all the places the Calders visited. We'll cross reference them. With luck there won't be all that many inside this area." I gestured to the circle Padraic had drawn.

"How about the Calders' charts?" Laura said. "Do you still have the originals from their trips? Most people mark them up. It might show us what areas they visited."

"Good idea," I said. "Bill never bought new ones, just updated his old ones from the notices to mariners. I've never looked at his large-scale charts for that area. I'll dig them out and you can take them back with you. Danny and I will work on the boat, get the supplies in, and see about extra tanks and a compressor."

"So it's partners then," Padraic said with a smile.

I looked across at Danny and he winked. "Let's go for it, Jared. I feel lucky and we just might be able to keep this idle worthless lifestyle going for a few more years. The thought of that alone will get me going every day. Jesus. Just imagine if we do find something. It will be incredible."

He raised his glass. "Partners."

We touched our glasses and drank to the venture, Padraic beaming at the three of us like a proud father. Laura was smiling, and she had a look in her eyes that I hadn't seen there before. It might have been happiness or maybe just relief. I thought that for perhaps the first time she had someone to share the responsibility for her father with, someone who began to understand the pressure she'd been under. I touched her on the shoulder.

"Don't worry, Laura. If the boat is there, we'll damn well find it for you both."

She frowned and moved away from me.

"About the expenses," she said. "Dad and I have discussed it and we will split them down the middle from the beginning."

A faint look of surprise appeared on Padraic's face. I suspected this was news to him.

"Great. Does that include the booze? Danny and I drink a hell of a lot of booze."

"Everything," she replied stiffly.

"Down the middle," I said.

"Yes."

"Great. Remind me to throw that cheap New Zealand Black Heart rum out tomorrow, Danny. We can afford the good stuff now."

Danny nodded. Laura continued unabated in that same prissy accountant's voice.

"About the compressor, tanks, any extra equipment we'll need, just save the bills. We can sell them when the partnership breaks up and split any loss."

"Down the middle."

"Yes."

"Great. What about when we have friends aboard. Women, you know?" I winked. "Should we just keep track of what we use and replace it, or would you rather have an itemized list that you can deduct from our share?"

Padraic jumped smoothly in. "I'm sure we can work out all the little details as we go along, Jared. That's not important just now. Let's have another drink to celebrate this momentous agreement. To Lapérouse!"

We drank to the comte.

"Do you think we should draw up a written agreement of partnership?" Laura inquired the second she lowered her glass. "You know, to prevent any misunderstandings later on."

Danny's arm was outstretched on the coamings behind me, and before I could respond his hand was on the back of my neck and squeezing.

"I really don't think that will be necessary, Laura," Padraic said. "Why don't you just mix us up another jug of those wonderful martinis, darling?"

"That would be lovely, darling," I echoed.

She snatched the jug up and marched below. The sound of slamming locker doors rose up moments later.

"How long before you're ready then, lads?" Like many Irishmen, Padraic's accent seemed to increase with every drink.

"A week at the most. There's not much to be done on *Arrow*; we had an easy passage from New Zealand. We'll look around for a used compressor and extra tanks first thing. Kirk might know of something, maybe even sell us one of his from the charters."

Kirk liked to replace the toys every couple of years. The charter business was one of glitz and image, and he was one of the best at it. We'd bought a headsail for *Arrow* from him the previous year at less than half the original cost, just because it was looking a trace shabby. In fact it was fine, and we both knew it, but he depreciated his gear shamelessly, and his little fleet was always immaculate among the competition. He told me he was selling the sail for the same reason he would never employ me, even had I been the best skipper in the whole of the South Pacific.

"You just don't fit the image, Jared," he'd said with mock sadness, looking down upon me from six feet two inches of sailing chic. "I might be able to do something with Danny though."

I smiled at the memory. Kirk had a sense of his own absurdity that never deserted him, even when he was at his most pompous.

"What's so funny?" Laura asked. Speaking of pomposity. She'd brought the jug back and refilled all the glasses, under tight rein again. The gin didn't seem to be bothering her at all, she'd been matching us drink for drink. Padraic and Danny were bent over the charts, heads together, tracing the grid lines along the outer reefs, Padraic talking rapidly and Danny nodding occasionally in agreement.

"Nothing. How much diving have you done?"

"Not much. Barclay gave me a few lessons on board *Golden Dragon* last year; he has his Divemaster certificate and is a qualified instructor. There's a complete dive shop on the boat. Waverly keeps everything aboard for his guests, and Barclay would take them out and instruct them if they were novices. Robin boasted that he could fit out anyone from what was on board. He even had suits and masks in children's sizes."

"Sounds like quite an operation."

"It is. He entertains a lot, and some of it is for business. He says he's retired, but he still makes deals all the time. Many of his guests are older, nose to the grindstone types who have worked hard all their lives and it's quite something for them to suddenly be on board a world famous superyacht. They're treated like royalty, the diving, jet skis, gourmet cooking. A lot of them were like little kids who had never played before."

Like you, Laura, I thought. *You would have been so very, very easy for a man like Barclay.*

"Of course it was all good for business too. Robin was frank about that. It's difficult to be quite so hardnosed in your dealings when you're enjoying yourself on your host's yacht, having the time of your life at his expense. And there were the women too."

"Women?"

"Yes." She frowned, lips between her teeth. "Robin always had different girlfriends. You read about them all the time, but there were always extra women aboard as well, beautiful, immaculately groomed, cultured, but not attached to anybody. And then a different group of people would come out but the women would still be there. Or maybe one or two new ones."

"Maybe he was just running a high-priced exclusive whorehouse," I said.

"Jared!" She giggled. "No, it wasn't that. I think they were there as part of the whole image. It was strange. We'd all sit around this huge teak dining table, it must have seated forty people, with Robin at the head. He'd steer the conversation, set a topic and everybody would discuss it, including the women who were invariably smart. And beautiful," she added wistfully.

"Maybe your father can give us some insight," I said.

"They were hired help," Padraic said. "Robin paid them to be there as hostesses but they weren't under any obligation. If they liked someone, that was different, but it was up to them."

"Probably a tax-deductible business expense," Danny said. "Lifestyles of the rich and famous. Anyway. I have to go. I'm meeting Christy for dinner at eight o'clock. Anyone want to join us?"

"Not me," Padraic said. "I'm going to start working on the journals tonight. I've waited long enough. Laura, why don't you and Jared go with them? My treat."

He fumbled for his wallet. I waited for Laura to shoot the idea down and by the time I realized she was waiting for me to speak, the silence was already too long.

"Sounds fine," I said quickly, "but Dutch treat, Padraic. We're partners remember."

And that way it wasn't a date either.

"Dig out those old charts if you like. There's some leftovers in the fridge; help yourself to anything you want. You know where the liquor is."

We left him rummaging among the chart cylinders, a large Scotch to hand. The three of us walked up to the clubhouse, and a few minutes later Christy arrived in her little Honda. Laura and I squeezed into the back seat and we drove out to a Thai restaurant that Kirk had recommended. By the time we finished, I'd drunk sufficient to find Laura charming. It didn't hurt that she was wearing that outfit. Danny and Christy went on to a nightclub and I walked Laura back to her motel. She shook my hand firmly and told me she'd enjoyed the evening and shut the door in my face. And here I'd been thinking she was a bit of a cold fish.

I arrived back at the yacht club with the wind scudding dark clouds across the moon and the imminent threat of rain. I'd just stepped onto the dock when the squall struck and chased me the last few feet to *Arrow*. To my surprise Padraic was still aboard, slumped over and sleeping on the cockpit table, the charts all stacked beneath him, cap askew, the thatch of hair already damp from the rain.

CHAPTER 12

"Padraic, wake up. It's raining."

I shook him roughly and he moaned and raised his head from the layer of charts spread out on the table. His eyes were red and unfocused, and there was a spill of Scotch on the cushions beside him.

"Jesus." He ran a cautious hand over his head. "I must have passed out."

"Come on, let's get you inside."

I pulled him to his feet and he groaned as he levered himself up and gingerly eased down the companionway stairs. His face was white and greasy.

I poured him a glass of water and handed him a couple of ibuprofen. "These will help."

"Thanks. I feel like shit."

"That's fairly normal after you've been beaten up," I said.

He raised his eyebrows but didn't speak.

"If we're going to be partners, Padraic, I think it is time we all levelled with each other. Laura has this idea of you as the dedicated historian, searching only for recognition of your theories and acceptance among your peers. That may be partially true but there's something more, isn't there? No offence, but you don't strike me as the selfless scholar sacrificing all in pursuit of his lofty ideals. You seem a little too fond of your creature comforts to throw everything away for the sake of having your name appear in a historical society paper and fifteen minutes of fame."

"What makes you think I've been beaten up?"

I reached around and prodded him gently in the kidneys. His face paled and he flinched away.

"The way you're moving. The spilled drink on the cushions but the glass standing on the table. If it fell when you passed out, how did it get up there again? There was somebody else here. Besides, you're not the type that passes out. Trust me, I know my drunks."

"You're quick, aren't you? Laura said as much. Get me a drink. The bastards beat me hollow."

His face was grey and pinched, and for the first time he looked his age. I poured him a glass of Scotch, and he raised it to his lips and drank it down like holy water.

"That's better." Some colour came back into his face. He sat there with his head down, taking in short careful breaths.

"Do you want me to take you to a hospital?"

"No. I've had worse in bar fights. Not for a long time, mind you." He smiled ruefully and helped himself to another drink.

"Who was it?"

"Summers, of course. Who else?"

He said it had all started the previous year in Suva. The Kennedys were looking for a cheap dive boat to take them out to the searching grounds. The established charters had become too expensive for them, and they hoped to find a cruiser who would do it for a cut rate. Waverly had been in the yacht club and heard about the professor and his daughter who were searching for the legendary wreck. He'd invited Padraic and Laura aboard the *Golden Dragon* for drinks and become interested in their project. He said he was spending a month cruising in Fiji with a few guests aboard and told Padraic that he could easily accommodate his search as well; the *Dragon* was completely self-sufficient, and it made little difference to Waverly where they went, the scenery and sea conditions in one area of northwest Fiji being as near ideal as another.

The idea of supporting the professor appealed to Waverly, and it would add some spice to the trip. It was the kind of thing he was interested in, research of a sort, and some publicity if they were successful.

"It sounds like a generous offer."

"Yes, it was. And at first I think that's all it was. But then I made the mistake of getting a little tight one night and telling Waverly about my other theory, the one I don't advertise. About the gold Louis."

He leaned back, organizing his thoughts.

"Peter Dillon, the British navy captain, who found the wrecks of *Astrolabe* and *Broussard* in the Santa Cruz Islands, made an official report to the British government about what he discovered; most of the crew killed, and the building of a small sloop by the survivors. Dillon meticulously searched the island and beaches, even did some shallow diving among the reefs, and made a detailed list of what they found. It was all pretty standard stuff, what you might expect to find from two fully equipped boats that were driven onto the reefs and broken up; cannons, muskets, swords, some cast iron utensils the natives had reclaimed, an anchor, even a gold cross that the chief was wearing. The only thing that was unusual was a small bag of coins, although nobody realized it at the time."

Padraic took another drink and continued.

"All of that is common knowledge. Some of the artifacts recovered by Dillon were returned to the French government in later years and are on display in the Musée National de la Marine in Paris. While I was over there doing my research, I found a curious little sidebar on the recovered gold Louis stating that they were minted in 1787. But Lapérouse left Brest on his final voyage in 1785, so how could they have come aboard? It was just one of those little anomalies that sometimes occur when you're attempting to reconstruct the past. Puzzling, but probably not important. But then later on, I came across an account of Lapérouse's brother who left France in the summer of 1787, one of the many aristocrats who foresaw the bloody revolution impending, gathered up their valuables, and fled the country.

"He left on a small merchant ship with his family for an unknown destination and was never heard from again. It was always assumed the ship had been lost at sea with all hands, but I found the story of a survivor picked up by a British whaler in 1787 buried in the naval intelligence reports of that year. He was half-mad, babbling. He said he was off the *Espérance*, the ship that Lapérouse's brother had chartered. They had met with another vessel off Macao in the fall of 1787 and off-loaded three heavy chests from their hold onto the other boat. The French seaman died before the boat reached England."

"You think the other boat was Lapérouse's."

"It would make sense. He was in Macao at that time. Perhaps it was his share of the family estate."

"Even if you're correct, it was likely lost in the first wreck in Santa Cruz."

"Not necessarily, but yes, probably. Which is why I don't understand Waverly's actions. He must have found out something else."

"It is Waverly as well then, and not just Summers?"

"Yes. Waverly was interested in my talk of the possibility of treasure, but only in a casual way. A man like him, wealthy and with the perfect set-up for treasure hunting hears a lot of stories, receives a lot of propositions. You know what it's like; there are a hundred lost treasure accounts out there. I could see that he didn't put much credence in mine. When we left the *Dragon* I asked him about the possibility of becoming partners and searching together again, but he turned me down. Wished me every success but said he wouldn't have the time this year, he would be in the Caribbean."

"But then he approached you again," I guessed.

"He contacted me a few days ago, just before I met you. Said he had been trying to reach me, his plans had changed, and he was going to be in Fiji for the season. Wanted to discuss a partnership similar to what I'd talked about last year. I was ecstatic, but when I told Laura she just went white. Wouldn't hear of it. I put my foot down finally, said we had to take the offer; it was our one great chance to find the site. Waverly has unlimited resources, his support meant everything. That's when she told me about Summers. He raped her."

I closed my eyes. "When?"

"A few weeks ago, I'm not sure exactly. She had broken off with him on the boat, he phoned her up one day in London, said he had some information that might help in our search. They agreed to meet for lunch. They went back to Laura's flat and he knocked her down and raped her. She finally had to tell me."

"Did she report him?" But I knew she wouldn't.

"No. But she did go to see his boss. Robin Waverly. He just laughed at her, called her a silly cunt who didn't know what she wanted and changed her mind halfway. Why else would she invite him to the flat after he'd been screwing her all last season? But of course it wasn't like that at all. They were just inside the door, she had the plate to show him. There was some kind of argument, he smashed her to the floor and assaulted her. After she told me about it there was never any question of joining forces with Waverly. I told him I wouldn't work with him if the *Dragon* was the last boat on the planet."

I felt an aching sadness for Laura. He couldn't have picked a better way to hurt her. I wondered where Summers was at this moment. Padraic was talking again.

". . . was his way of persuading me I should reconsider my position. Said it was only a warning. Next time he might pay another visit to Laura."

"What do you want to do now?"

"I don't know." There was a sad defeated look on his face. "I wish to God I'd never started on this fool's errand. What can the likes of us do against Waverly and his crew?"

"You might be surprised."

I took a long drink and looked out over the water. Sinbad came jogging down the dock and leaped aboard. He stood a minute in front of Padraic who kept very still, then turned and gave me a low growl before moving up to the bow and flopping down. Padraic's eyes never left him.

"Sinbad," I said.

"I've heard."

"Tell me exactly what happened tonight."

"I was going over the charts, having a drink. It couldn't have been more than an hour after you left. There were two of them, Summers and a crewman from the *Golden Dragon*. He asked permission to come aboard and I told him to fuck off, we had nothing to say to each other. He just laughed and they came into the cockpit. He said that Robin wanted me to reconsider his offer. He would give me a thirty percent finder's fee of the value of anything recovered."

"That's generous of him," I said.

"Waverly would fund everything, we would share the credit for the discovery. Summers said my share could make me a millionaire several times over. I asked him what made Waverly change his mind and he just smiled, told me not to worry about that. My job was to help locate it, and they would do the rest. I said I wasn't interested and that's when he hit me. The other man held me, and Summers worked me over. He said not to worry, there wouldn't be any permanent damage, they'd done this to a lot of Irishmen. They were laughing. That's when I passed out."

I glanced around the cabin. Nothing out of place, no signs of a search, the hollow post that hid the journals undisturbed. Maybe they now thought it was better to let us work out where the gold was and then just take it from us.

"The first thing you have to do is talk to Laura. Tell her what happened tonight. Tell her that you've thought there was gold from the beginning and now it seems certain."

Padraic's face fell.

"Don't worry," I said. "She'll survive the shock of finding out you aren't the Albert Schweitzer of marine archaeology. I'm afraid she's not really Mother Teresa either. When you're finished, ask her to tell you everything. From the beginning. There've been too many secrets for too long."

He looked at me in surprise. "What do you mean?"

"Never mind. Just tell her I said so. Then get a good night's sleep and check out of the motel first thing tomorrow morning. If you decide to have nothing more to do with any of this, get hold of Waverly. Tell him you've given me everything — your notes, all your research, the sites you've searched, everything. That should get the pair of you off the hook."

"And what about you, then?" Padraic asked.

"It's personal now. That bastard has been aboard my boat three times uninvited. Danny will be with me. Whatever we find, you'll have your share. Fifty percent. You have my word on that. We can draw up an agreement if you like."

"Go on."

"If we find anything we'll take our expenses first," *and maybe a tad more*, I thought, "and then we'll turn it over to you and you will be the official finder, notify the government, negotiate your salvage rights, all the bells and whistles. Once it's above board and out in the open there won't be any more trouble with Waverly."

"And what if we don't choose to withdraw?"

"Then you and Laura move onto *Arrow* right after you leave the complex tomorrow morning and do exactly as I tell you. I'm in charge while you are aboard. But either way, you check out tomorrow. Onto a plane and out of the country or onto *Arrow*. We can't protect you sitting over there. And stay together."

"All right."

He rose slowly to his feet, an old man now. I took his arm and walked him down to the parking lot. We woke up one of the drivers asleep in his cab and Padraic climbed in and left. An hour later

Danny came back aboard and we sat talking until the early hours of the morning.

I woke to the first rays of sun coming through the port light and the smell of a freshly brewed cup of coffee under my nose.

"Rise and shine, sport. There's work to be done."

One of the truly annoying things about Danny is that the son of a bitch is always cheerful in the mornings. He was drinking two to my one a few short hours ago and here he was, fresh as a fucking daisy. I shook my head tentatively. Not too bad. Swinging out of my berth I slipped on a pair of shorts and went topsides with my coffee. At this early hour my body could still handle the rays. By nine o'clock I would have to put on a long-sleeved shirt. You don't get many gene gifts from the Scots.

The ship's clock said seven twenty-five. I settled back and watched the traffic flowing into the city carrying all those people with settled lives, important responsibilities, meaningful goals, and worthwhile objectives.

Poor sods.

The early-morning runners were heading the other way, out of town and along the highway that framed the bay, a few masochists taking the road up into the hills. The football team passed by strung out in a long line, the tattooed giant at the head setting a killing pace. A hundred years ago he would have been one of the fierce head-hunters that raided the outlying villages, raging up the coast in the big war canoes of his people.

Behind the group a lone woman runner moved steadily along. I looked at the clock. Exactly seven thirty.

"Son of a bitch!"

"What?"

"Laura is out running by herself. I told Padraic they were to stay together."

I stormed below and grabbed my Nikes and a T-shirt. "I'll kill her myself. She won't have to worry about Summers."

"Well, Padraic doesn't really look like much of a jogger to me," Danny said.

"Laugh, you asshole. We talked about this last night. How can we protect her if she won't listen to us?"

"Aye aye, Captain. Shall I rig the gratings for the flogging?"

I didn't reply. There was no point and I needed to save my breath. Laura was fast disappearing in the distance. I called Sinbad who raised his head, looked at me, and settled back into sleep. He wasn't really a morning person either. I trotted down the docks and headed out onto the highway in pursuit of Laura.

She was five hundred yards ahead, running with an unvarying grimness and determination that about summed her up. There was no sense of the grace or harmony that emanates from many runners, but rather the body language of someone with an unpleasant task to be performed as quickly as possible. I kept her in sight until my legs loosened up and then gradually overhauled her. By the time I reached her, I was almost calm.

"Good morning."

"Good morning."

"How are you this morning?" I asked.

"I'm fine, thank you."

"That's good."

We ran in silence for a while.

"Did you have a chance to talk with your father last night?"

"Yes."

"And what have you decided?"

"About what?"

I ran in silence for another hundred yards. I was not going to lose my temper here.

"About leaving Fiji."

"Oh. We're staying."

"And?"

"And we're moving onto *Arrow* as soon as I get back."

She hadn't looked at me once. Enough is enough. I took her arm and dragged her to a halt.

"Look at me, Laura."

She brought her eyes up. She didn't try and free her arm.

"What did you talk about?"

"Everything."

"He told you about the treasure and the threats and the beating last night by Summers?"

"Yes."

"And you told him about taking the plate and Summers stealing it when he raped you."

She didn't even flinch, just that same dull impassive stare. "Yes."

"So now there are no more secrets. Everybody is in the picture and we're going to go out and find Lapérouse's sloop. And maybe make some serious money."

"Yes. Can we run some more now?"

She sounded like a little girl asking Daddy for an ice cream cone.

"Okay."

We ran steadily on, neither of us speaking. We ran side by side, almost touching, but I doubt she was even aware of me. The last time I glanced across, tears were tracing down her cheeks.

"Tell me what's the matter, Laura."

She just shook her head and we kept on at the same even pace. But of course I knew what the matter was. Summers. And Laura out here running alone to prove to herself that he hadn't damaged her, that she was still in control of her life. Even after what he'd done to her and Padraic. In a way, her father's beating might have been almost as difficult for her as the assault by Summers. A father was a child's natural protector, the barrier between them and the nasty things outside. My parents died when I was nine, and the nasty things had come in with a vengeance, and the worst of them was the grandfather I had gone to live with, but I still knew how it was supposed to work and carried deep inside me the talisman of my father.

"Danny and I can protect you, Laura, but you have to cooperate. For a while at least you have to stay with one of us all the time. You're too vulnerable when you're alone."

She nodded, the tears tracking slowly down her face. "For how long do you think? A month? A year? The rest of my life?" She still spoke in that same lifeless voice.

"I know how you feel, Laura, but none of it is your fault. The wolves are always out. Sometimes it's our bad luck to cross their path. You have to get past that, otherwise they win."

She didn't reply, just kept running at that same steady relentless pace, punishing herself ruthlessly. I knew all about that. Sometimes I was surprised I hadn't been born Catholic, that would have made it perfect. They actually come into the world guilty. I thought about it for a while then took a deep breath and swallowed the gall and spat it out.

"I was raped in prison, Laura. By two brothers when I was eighteen."

Her head didn't turn and she didn't say anything, but I knew she was listening. I told it for the first time.

It had been a case of aggravated assault that put me into prison, but there'd been extenuating circumstances and everyone assumed I would get off with a suspended sentence. I likely would have if my grandfather hadn't stood up in court and told the judge he would no longer have me in his home or be responsible for my actions. It was the first time he had spoken my name since I'd torn the rattan cane he disciplined me with out of his hands and broken it across my knee three years earlier. The judge was of the same generation as my grandfather and went to the same church. He sentenced me to two years. My lawyer was embarrassed and outraged by the sentence and pleaded with me to appeal and guaranteed we would win, but by then I didn't care. I took the time.

I thought I was pretty tough, but of course I wasn't, and the Wakosky brothers caught me on the prison work party out behind the cow barn as easy as a pair of hawks taking a chicken. I fought hard and even broke the older brother's nose but there were two of them and they were big men, and that just finally made it worse for me. They had done and I was laying there stunned and bleeding listening to them talk about how maybe they'd better drown me in the dugout now when the big Haida came around the corner with the axe handle in his hands. They didn't stand a chance against Danny.

"What happened to them?" Laura asked.

"They'd been pretty tough boys. When they finally came out of hospital, they weren't so tough anymore and people were waiting."

I was one of them. I was in the hayloft with Dieter the day he fell through the trapdoor onto one of the stalls below and broke his back. I heard later that somebody pulled his plug in the nursing home. After that they transferred his brother to another prison before somebody killed him too.

"You have to hang in there, things go around. Just keep telling yourself that none of it was your fault."

Sometimes I almost believed that myself. But the truth was that when the wolves took a piece of you, you sometimes never got it back.

"I know all that. But it's not so easy is it, Jared?"

She touched her fingertips lightly to my wrist for a few seconds and then withdrew them. We came to the little bridge and turned and jogged slowly back towards her motel. We didn't speak again. I waited outside while she and Padraic packed and settled their bill, then we climbed into a taxi and went to the yacht club. Padraic paid off the taxi and we carried their luggage aboard *Arrow*.

CHAPTER 13

We spent the rest of the day stowing gear and organizing the Kennedys' cabin. Unused space aboard boats accumulates objects in a marine variation of Parkinson's Law, and there was enough junk lying out in *Arrow*'s spare cabin to require the restowing of every drawer and locker in the entire boat. It was happy hour by the time we finished and Padraic proposed we go up to the clubhouse for drinks. He was showing few ill effects from his encounter with Summers. Now, if only Laura could bounce back. I could see she was making an effort, talking and laughing with Danny who could cheer up the Devil himself.

The club was having their midweek barbecue special, serving up grilled lamb and seafood on their outdoor grills. After a couple of drinks it smelled irresistible and we ordered the yellowfin tuna with sides of lamb chops to share. It was a pleasant evening, we were all a little excited at our prospects and the moon and stars were out with just enough breeze to keep the insects away and blow the smoke from the grills out to sea.

We finished our dinners and Padraic told us about his one and only scuba training session, explaining, "Sometimes, on men of rare intellect, the body's balance in water can be askew, thereby offsetting the natural order of things."

"His feet kept floating up above his head!" Laura giggled. "Everyone was laughing so hard they were choking, even the instructors. They finally had to take him out of the pool."

She broke off suddenly and her face paled. I turned and saw the heavily built man striding towards our table and knew immediately it was Waverly. He had the tailored clothes, immaculate tan, and air of self-satisfaction that wealth and power bring. His blond streaked hair was just beginning to grey at the temples. Cut fashionably long, it combined with a rakish close-trimmed beard to lend him a piratical appearance. His powerful body showed the effects of regular workouts at the gym; the one aboard the *Golden Dragon* would be world class.

Waverly stood well over six feet, with heavy shoulders bulging a beautifully cut navy blue blazer, and large square hands. His faded blue eyes were sun squinted and intelligent, and he looked like what he undoubtedly was: a tough, powerful man at the top who hadn't been particular about how he'd arrived there. There was a smile on his handsome face as he approached with hand outstretched.

"Padraic, Laura. So good to see you again. I'm terribly sorry about the misunderstanding with Summers. Let me say at once that he completely exceeded his authority."

You had to give it to him, the man had balls of brass. To my amazement Padraic stood up and shook hands with him. Laura turned her head away and after a brief pause before her, he swung towards me.

"I don't believe we've met. I'm Robin Waverly."

"Jared Kane."

The eyes flickered in recognition and he extended the big hand. We shook, and he squeezed down hard but I left my hand limp and unresisting and my face blank. He backed off with a faint mocking smile. He turned to Danny.

"Pleased to meet you."

"I'm Daniel MacLean."

Danny rose to his feet and extended his hand with a smile. His body looked smooth and almost flabby against the other man's chiselled bulk. "I've heard a lot about you," he said.

Their hands locked.

"Really?" Waverly returned the smile. "And just what did you hear? Nothing too awful, I hope."

"I heard you were a supreme asshole," Danny said.

The smile was still in place and he was still holding Waverly's hand. He looked completely relaxed, his forearm smooth and brown as a piece of polished mahogany. You had to know him to see the shirt suddenly stretched and too small. The tendons were standing out on Waverly's wrist as he strained, and a sudden sweat appeared on his forehead. His smile was long gone.

"It's been nice talking to you," Danny said, "but I really think it's time for you to leave now, don't you?"

Waverly jerked his head in assent, his face a rigid mask of rage and pain. Danny released him, and he pulled his hand back. It was a blotchy white, with livid red bars spreading across where Danny had gripped it. He spun on his heel and walked away from us, cradling his hand against his body. As he passed the bar he snapped at a pair of burly men in ship's whites who downed their drinks and followed him out the door.

"Good thing I softened him up for you," I said.

"Yeah. Thanks. What was that anyway? The old Gandhi grip?"

"Goddammit, it's not funny. That man is dangerous, and you deliberately antagonize him, and now you're sitting there grinning like a pair of bloody idiots." Laura glared at me.

"What are you looking at me for?" I said. "I didn't do anything. I was about to ask him to sit down and join us for a drink when Danny chased him away."

She dismissed me with a contemptuous glance and turned quickly towards her father who became suddenly fascinated with the bottom of his drink glass.

"And you. You actually shook the son of a bitch's hand. I'm surprised you didn't get up and hug him."

"Well, you see . . ." Padraic began, but Laura slammed down her drink on the table and stormed off.

"I'm going to my cabin." She threw the words over her shoulder as she marched away. The three of us watched her stamp down the ramp onto the dock and vanish aboard *Arrow*.

We sat there for a time and tried to get the fine mood back, but it had sickened with Waverly and died with Laura. I didn't want her on the boat alone and before long we were all back on board.

Three hundred yards off *Arrow*'s stern a magnificent yacht had pulled in and anchored during our absence. The polished masts of *Golden Dragon* were so high she mounted flashing strobes on them as a warning to aircraft, and her broad decks carried both a seaplane and a Bell jet helicopter forward of the main cabin. All her lights were on, and beautiful gowned women and men in formal dress stood around the aft deck with drinks in their hands. Through the large port lights other couples were visible, and white coated waiters moved among them carrying trays. It wouldn't have surprised me to see a grand piano inside there and somebody in a tux playing it. It was a staggering display of beauty and wealth, and the people aboard the *Golden Dragon* were conscious of the admiring eyes upon them and smiled and postured just that little bit extra for their audience.

She was one of the newest of the second-generation yachts from the Italian boatyards to carry the radically altered DynaRig of the original *Maltese Falcon*, the unstayed carbon fibre mainmast rotating a full three hundred and sixty degrees, the boom in this newest version extending forward past it to carry the jib as well as the main. Her mizzenmast was similarly rigged, the jib in this instance acting almost as a mizzen staysail.

The sailboat was highly controversial when she was being built, attracting many comments about the eccentricities of the ultra-rich, but she'd proved herself over three years and sixty thousand miles, winning every leg of the around the world rally. When she went around the Horn the wrong way, in some of the worst weather seen there in years, the critics were silenced, and she was accepted as the wave of the future, and her owner was hailed as the prophet of the new age of sail. It was a role Waverly relished, and he combined the glamour and romance of the sea with his new-found philanthropy and scientific pursuits to silence many of his former enemies.

Even the media backed off from their previous harsh judgments and began to affectionately refer to him as a modern-day buccaneer. It appeared that like so many other merchant princes whose early fortunes had been built by questionable means, Waverly had put his ruthless business ethics behind him and moved on. There was even talk of a knighthood.

Looking at the *Golden Dragon* and seeing what it represented in terms of status and power, it was hard to imagine we could conceive of going up against her, and ridiculous to think we could prevail. One of her carbon fibre masts alone was twenty times the value of *Arrow*. She carried a full crew of professionals aboard with launches, compressors, sea sleds, and a state of the art mobile underwater camera, as well as charting and depth sounders so advanced they could pick out a lobster hiding behind a rock on the bottom. I'd read that the *Dragon* even had a decompression chamber aboard so that after deep dives they wouldn't have to set up air dumps at different levels and wait there for the specified times but could go straight up and decompress on board while the boat moved on to new territory.

"Awesome, isn't she?" Danny passed me a drink.

"Yes."

"First class gear, professional calibre divers, sleds, all the bells and whistles."

"So they say."

"The absolute best equipment and people that money can buy."

"What's your fucking point?" I said.

"I was thinking we need something to give us a bit of an edge."

"The journals might do that."

"Yeah. Those too. Something else as well though. I've got an idea. Let me think about it for a bit."

"I'm just the fucking captain. Why should you tell me anything?"

"Cheer up, Jared. We'll kick their ass, you'll see."

Danny, forever the optimist. This time, though, I felt we'd bitten off more than even he could chew. I stayed on deck for another hour, gazing over at the brilliance that was the *Golden Dragon*. I listened to the music and laughter, watched the beautiful people and tried to convince myself that we were doing the right thing. I wouldn't let myself think about the old man dreaming of fame and fortune down below, and his bitter daughter lying awake in tears and gall.

In the morning Danny and I set about making *Arrow* ready for the trip. We were taking enough stores aboard for two months, so we could conduct our search without having to run in for supplies, and thereby reduce the chances of being spotted by Waverly. Laura took over the provisioning while Danny and I set about converting *Arrow* from a cruiser to a workaday dive boat. The biggest problem was where to house the compressor and the extra bottles of air we would require. It's difficult to make even minor structural changes on a wooden sailboat without compromising her integrity. We finally removed part of the bulkhead between the tiny workshop and the hanging wet locker and made it into one room. It was cramped, but adequate. We considered storing the bottles on deck in containers, but they would have been underfoot in normal conditions and dangerous in a rough sea.

Danny and I completed the alterations and set off on a buying trip. We left Padraic at the chart table with the journals, the little Purdey over-and-under loaded and ready beside him, and Sinbad asleep at his feet. He was in fine spirits and said he would cheerfully shoot dead the first son of a bitch who came aboard uninvited. I thought that we were done with threats and bullies, and if they came aboard again it would be secretly, in the night and in force. The best way to guard against that was to depart Suva for the hunting grounds as quickly as possible.

It took the better part of the day to find everything we needed. Captain Kirk came up with a hookah and half a dozen dive bottles that were still in test but scratched and unsightly. He sold them to us for half their new value and directed us to a French cruising couple who were selling their compressor to secure funds for another season in the tropics. We ended up buying all their dive gear for spares as well. If we were forced to go deep, we would need complete backup systems for the two divers who went down. Once you went below one hundred feet, the dangers and difficulties multiplied, and everything had to be doubled up. None of us had done any serious deep diving, and we would need to be careful. I knew just enough about it to realize I didn't know very much.

We piled everything into the back of the Toyota pickup we had borrowed from Kirk and returned to the club. I helped Danny load it aboard *Arrow* and left him to deal with the stowage while I accompanied Laura to the supermarket. She was brisk and organized and soon had shopping carts piled high with the staples we would require for the trip. There were a few disputes and she won the majority of these. I held fast for the canned corned beef I wouldn't think of eating ashore but loved with a passion at sea and gave way to low fat butter substitutes and something that was labelled as turkey bacon but looked like pink bologna. We finished and went back to the docks and transferred it to *Arrow*. To my amazement there was a formal embossed invitation awaiting us. Drinks and dinner aboard the *Golden Dragon*.

"Delivered an hour ago," Padraic said. "Handed to me by a smartly dressed young man in ship's whites and gloves no less. Apparently he is their entertainment co-coordinator. I'm not kidding."

"Are you sure it wasn't dated before our little encounter with Waverly yesterday?"

"Nope. Sent today. Note from Robin on the back saying he hopes we can all attend. It's addressed to the four of us and says we are welcome to bring along friends if we wish."

"How about Sinbad and a couple of fucking Uzis," I said.

"Oh there's no need for anything like that," Laura said. "I'm quite sure he will be on his best behaviour."

"Well, it's academic, as we're not going," I said.

"Speak for yourself," she snapped back, vicious as a wet cat. "I don't recall anyone appointing you entertainment co-coordinator on this boat."

I gaped at her in amazement. "I'm the captain and I'm responsible for your safety, and I'm telling you, you are not going aboard that bloody boat." I turned towards Danny and Padraic for support. "Just ask them, they will tell you; it's absolutely ridiculous."

I waited for them to speak. Padraic was staring thoughtfully over at the *Dragon*, and Danny was trying not to smirk.

"Say something," I snapped at him.

"Jawohl, mein Fuehrer," he said, his hand rocketing skyward as his heels clicked together.

"Asshole," I muttered.

"Shall we say six thirty then?" Laura asked.

"Summers will be there," I said and immediately regretted it. Padraic glared at me and turned and stalked off below. Laura followed him, her face pale but her head held high.

"I think you handled that really well, Captain," Danny said.

"Fuck you. Pour me another drink."

"Jawohl, mein Kapitan," Danny replied. "By the way, in all the excitement I forgot to mention that I met an old friend of yours. She's coming over for drinks anytime now. We can bring her along."

"Yeah? Who would that be?"

"Molly," Danny said with a wicked grin.

"Oh, Jesus." I buried my head in my hands. "Make that a double will you please?"

❀

Resplendent in a flowered pareu, a spray of frangipane in her flaming red hair, and Tahitian jelly sandals on her feet, Molly blew into the cabin like a scented whirlwind. Hugs and kisses for us both and a saucy slap on the bum for me alone.

"You little rascal," she said, "slipping away like that."

I muttered something about a falling glass and compressing isobars. Out of the corner of my eye, I noticed Laura's raised eyebrows as Danny made the introductions. She had changed into a plain white gown and sling sandals, while Padraic was wearing long slacks and a sport shirt. Resigned to the inevitable I'd shaved and changed as well. What I had wanted to do was retire to my cabin with a bottle of Scotch and get really drunk, but as Danny had pointed out, we couldn't forcibly restrain Laura and Padraic, and we couldn't very well let them go alone. Besides, we might learn something.

Know thy enemy.

"So, tell me all the news," Molly said. "What have you been up to? Danny mentioned something about going on a diving expedition, treasure hunting and such. Sounds terrific. I'm an experienced diver, you know, did it on the east coast for a living one time as a matter of fact. There isn't much I haven't done in my life, you know." She winked broadly at me. I glared at Danny.

"Well, you certainly have the lungs for diving," Padraic said gallantly.

"Why thank you. So, you're a professor are you? Of what, if I may be so bold to ask?"

She went over and seated herself beside Padraic and the two of them began an animated conversation.

"Who the hell is that?" Laura hissed in a low voice.

"An old friend."

"Why does she think she's invited on the trip?"

"Actually," I said, "it might not be such a bad idea. Another boat, an experienced diver, more equipment and storage. We could use it as the diving base, and *Arrow* for the support ship. She could be a big help."

"Look at him," Laura said, scowling at her father next to Molly. "His eyes are practically popping out of his head."

"She's quite a nice person," I said, "once you get to know her."

"Yeah, I'll bet. And just how well do you know her, Jared?"

"We spent some time together at South Minerva Reef," I said. "She sailed her own boat there."

"What's her boat called?"

I looked down at my glass.

"*Tramp*," Danny offered.

"Ha!" Laura said.

I lifted the drink to my lips and drained it.

CHAPTER 14

At 1900 hours precisely *Dragon*'s launch pulled alongside, crewed by a pair of hard-looking men, incongruous in their dress whites. We boarded, rose up in brief acceleration, and a minute later were berthed at the *Dragon*'s gangplank and handed aboard. A steward was waiting at the top of the gangplank and escorted us into a large saloon off the main entertainment area.

In spite of my resolve to remain unimpressed, it was hard not to goggle at the opulence. Everything was in superb taste, from the white leather lounges and gold-plated bar fixtures to the paintings on the walls: Gauguin, Degas, Picasso, a millionaire's ransom in that one small area alone. Waverly was celebrated as one of the world's great collectors. The steward left us and moments later a stunning blonde in a black strapless gown swept into the room.

"Good evening. Thank you so much for coming. I'm Elinor and I'm your hostess for this evening. You are Professor Kennedy of course, and you must be Laura. That is a simply beautiful dress. You must tell me the name of the designer." Her smile was warm and sincere, her accent upper-class British. "And you're Jared Kane and Daniel MacLean. I don't believe I know the lady."

Molly introduced herself and Elinor complimented her on the Fijian pareu she was wearing. It was all very well done.

"And tell me then, just what are the duties of a hostess?" Danny enquired.

"Well, first off to see that you all have drinks," Elinor replied, "and then maybe we can talk about the rest later."

She smiled and pressed a button in the wall and the steward reappeared. He took our orders and left.

"He'll only be a minute," Elinor said. "Would you like a quick tour of the boat while we're waiting? Yes?"

She glided out the door and we trooped off in her wake.

"There are thirteen different hardwoods used in the interiors, and the carpets alone cost over a million dollars. Jean Luc Marais was the interior designer and he insisted that each cabin have different materials and its own ambience, as well as its own art. The paintings alone could stock a small gallery, never mind the statues and other objets d'art."

It was like walking through a small palace, the indulgence and sense of privilege overwhelming. If this woman had been coached to intimidate, she was certainly succeeding in my case.

We passed through a small corridor and came out into a large room filled with fighting masks, spears and shields, and other implements of war. I recognized Fijian axes, Vanuatan throwing spears, some large carvings from the Marquesas with the peculiar diamond chip finish, the three-dimensional see-through carvings of the Solomons, and dozens of other artifacts, all of them catalogued with brief descriptions in a brochure available for guests.

"This is the South Pacific room," she said.

We paused for a moment while she spoke briefly about some of the more important exhibits, and then moved on, down a flight of stairs, and into the lower levels.

I had a brief impression of shining stainless steel and copper, with two men in peaked chefs' caps chopping on hardwood blocks and plunging baskets into vats of bubbling oil. A cloud of steam rose up and was swept away in the exhaust fans and we moved on once more.

The engine room was as clean as the galley, huge twin diesels higher than a man could stand and twelve feet long. The smaller engine twice the size of *Arrow*'s throbbing in the corner must have been the generator. Off again to the crew quarters, lodgings for a dozen men with their own galley, saloon, and entertainment centre. Everything first class, overwhelming, nothing I could imagine improving on.

"I'll leave the wheelhouse for Robin, he loves to show it off to his guests."

Elinor smiled and led us up a different set of stairs and back into the reception area. A silver tray with our drinks was sitting on the coffee table, and she picked it up and passed it around.

"Any questions?"

"How many crew aboard?" Danny asked.

"Usually seven, plus the two chefs and a pair of stewards. Right now there are ten as we've taken on some extra hands for the season."

"What are their qualifications? It would sure be something to crew on a boat like this." Danny was at his most charming.

"Oh, they vary. I think you may see some of them tonight. I understand Robin has scheduled an entertainment in your honour. Maybe I could put in a good word for you, if you're really serious."

"You don't know my qualifications yet," Danny said with a smile.

"Isn't it about time we joined the others?" Laura snapped.

"Of course. Forgive me. Please come along."

Elinor took Danny's arm and the two of them swept out of the room. Padraic bowed to Molly and she took his arm and they marched grandly out behind. Laura snatched my arm and we trudged stolidly after them.

A dozen couples were in the main saloon, standing about talking in small groups or seated in the occasional chairs and love seats scattered around the room. The floor was teak and holly with richly textured oriental carpets spread about beneath the furniture. Waverly was off in a corner in deep conversation with an obese elderly man accompanied by a beautiful young woman. When he saw us, he smiled and raised a hand and came across to meet us. He was dressed in the same whites as the crew, with an officer's epaulettes on the shoulder. It was odd, a rich powerful man who seemingly had everything money could buy but still needed the authority of fake command.

"I'm delighted you could all make it. And who is this beautiful young lady? I don't believe I've had the privilege."

He bowed over Molly's hand with an exaggerated theatrical gesture, much to her delight. He couldn't have been more charming. It was as if the encounter in the club had never happened. He didn't offer to shake hands though.

"And you've all had the mini tour? Excellent. Here, let me freshen your drinks."

He gestured, and a steward brought new drinks for us and took away the old ones.

"Come and meet the rest of the guests."

Waverly led us around the room, standing quietly until he was acknowledged, and then presenting us. A couple of the men's names were vaguely familiar; I recognized none of the women, who were without exception young and beautiful. Waverly didn't seem to be attached to any specific one; they all greeted him politely with chaste affection. Summers was nowhere to be seen. I was grateful, for Laura's sake.

"I think we're ready to dine now," Waverly said when the introductions were over.

He pressed a button in the panelling, and what had seemed a solid wall covered in an intricate reproduction of Gauguin's *Riders on the Beach* collapsed inwards upon itself and revealed a massive dining table with chairs along both sides and waiters standing by in attendance.

"A little trompe-l'œil," Waverly said with a smile, pleased by our reaction. He walked to the head of the table, the guests following, and when he nodded his head the wall unfolded into place once again and we were enclosed in a separate room.

The meal was excellent. Five courses, each accompanied by its own wine, and each one a clever variation of a native Fijian dish blended with the best of European cookery, from the tiny oysters served with fiery peri-peri sauce to the final roast suckling pig glazed with truffles and century-old balsamic vinegar. I never expect to have a better meal.

The conversation was equally rich, smoothly carried by Robin Waverly and the women, and most of it was about the South Pacific. He talked about Cook and Bligh and Bougainville, and the lesser known explorers Kotzebue and Bellingshausen, managing to work in an account of his own voyages in the *Golden Dragon* along the way.

Then he spoke of the art of the South Pacific and illustrated his talk with examples from his own walls, including some that he had unearthed on his travels. He included all the company in his conversation, but it seemed that his attention was focused mainly on our party. He was smiling and urbane and knowledgeable, and you couldn't have asked for a more charming and attentive host, but there was something forced and unnatural about it all, and the whole performance made me uneasy.

Halfway through the dinner, a slender Asian girl appeared and sat at the empty chair alongside Waverly. He acknowledged her presence with a nod and then ignored her. She took no part in the conversation and seemed bored. Her hair was cut short and curved delicately across her cheekbones in little wings, and she was dressed in a simple white cotton kimono. It was impossible to guess her age, and it wasn't clear whether she even understood English.

A plate was in front of her, but she disdained the food as she did the other diners until the beef course, when a serving of blood red steak was put before her. She ate it eagerly, in small quick bites, her teeth ripping the flesh into little chunks, which she swallowed almost without chewing. Waverly regarded her with a faint, almost paternal smile. When she finished she rinsed her hands delicately in the finger bowl and took no further interest in the proceedings.

We had desserts and then brandy, and most of the men and Molly smoked hand-rolled Cuban cigars, which Waverly dispensed. I had eaten and drunk well and was looking forward to getting back to *Arrow* and a good night's sleep. We had a lot of work remaining before we could leave, and in spite of Waverly's apparent friendliness, I wanted to be out of there. I knew in my heart he was our enemy, and I wouldn't relax completely until we were a hundred miles distant from him, lost among the reefs and passes of a remote lagoon.

"Are you ready to go?" I asked Laura.

"Yes, please," she said.

She had lost whatever bravado had impelled her to come in the first place and now was anxious to leave. The same couldn't be said for her father and Danny, the two of them seemed to be having the time of their lives along with the two women who hadn't moved from their sides since the evening began. Danny and Elinor had the conspiratorial look of lovers soon to be, while Padraic and Molly had discovered a joint love and were deep into the *Golden Dragon's* supply of Bushmills whisky. He had been telling her stories during Waverly's monologues, and her raucous laugh had drawn several annoyed glances from him.

Waverly suddenly clapped his hands and the painted wall folded away once again and we were looking back into the main saloon. The furniture and rugs had disappeared, and a thin rolled up tatami mat lay in the centre of the room with a stack of white towels alongside. I felt a sick awareness rising in my stomach.

"I thought after such a splendid meal we should have some entertainment," Waverly said. "I know at least one of our guests has some martial arts experience, and our good captain has arranged a small demonstration on behalf of himself and the crew."

The little Asian girl beside him suddenly sat up and clapped her hands, her teeth gleaming and her eyes alive with interest. Waverly laughed.

"Yes, Phueng. Perhaps later."

She gave him a dazzling smile and returned her attention to the mat. Three men emerged from a door off the saloon and moved to the centre of the room. One of them was Summers. Laura drew in her breath and her hand crept into mine. Summers bowed to the assembly and unrolled the mat. It was about twenty feet square. The contestants stripped off their shirts and went to opposite corners of the mat and stood with their arms crossed, waiting impassively. They wore only short trunks and were barefoot. They were well matched physically, both somewhere in their thirties with lean hard bodies and chiselled faces. One man had a series of scars running from his shoulder to his waist that could only have come from a burst of machine gun fire. His life had been spared by inches.

Summers muttered a low command and the two men met in the centre of the ring in a blurring flash of movement; thrust, kick, and parry following so fast one upon the other that it was hard for the eye to follow. They sprang apart and then came together again and the scarred man was down on his back and then up again in an instant.

Summers held up his hand and they immediately stopped.

"Saunders's fight I think," he said, and the blond man bowed and retired to the side of the ring and another man came out, this one bigger, a giant almost, with a bald head and a scant greying goatee. Fat swung from his belly, and he looked soft, but I knew he wasn't. He had the scarred, misshapen knuckles of a brawler and his nose was flattened against his face.

Summers raised his hand and the first man came in hard, striking the big one in the gut and moving out again and the other just took it and swayed back, his cruel head bobbing and his eyes never leaving the other. Suddenly the large man pounced and there was a sharp crack and the other man's face exploded in blood and he fell back to the cries of some of the women. I glanced at Phueng, and her eyes glowed and grew larger, and she gave a small sigh of pleasure.

Summers held up his hands and the fighters stopped, and the vanquished went and stood beside the first man, no sign of the pain he had to be feeling showing on his battered and bleeding face. Summers handed him a towel and he applied it without a word.

And so it went. The big man, Turk, lasted two more rounds and then he was taken out by a man half his size who was quick as a mongoose. He was using a form of Judo and setting the big man's weight against him, and finally he threw him heavily enough to stun him and it was over.

The fighting was hard and vicious, with no holds barred, but they were hard men and I had seen it all before. Summers was quick to step in and there didn't appear to be any serious damage, or even animosity. It wasn't to my liking, but I could understand it. I would have bet money that there wasn't a single man among them who hadn't fought in some vicious little war in a remote part of the world, and if they weren't brutal and efficient they wouldn't be here now. This was just part of the game, of staying ready for when the next thing came. It was not all that different from the martial arts people paid to watch on television.

The reaction of the guests to the spectacle was varied. The men were all avid observers except for an obese man who I had been told was a French banker. He deliberately turned his back on the fights and talked to his companion throughout. Many of the women gasped at the viciousness of some of the bouts, but none was uninterested, with the exception of Elinor. After a scornful glance at the male posturing, she returned her attention to Danny.

The final winner was a young German with a shaved head. He had drawn the straw for the last bout and his opponent was tired and couldn't compete with the fresh man's quick attack. He staggered the other man with a series of kicks and then finished him with a vicious chop to the back of the neck.

He bowed to the applause and received a handshake and an envelope of prize money from Waverly, then lined up with the other men. There were eight of them now, including Summers, standing in a row by the mat. The sense of controlled discipline about the whole exercise was striking. Three of the men were bleeding, and one of them had clearly broken his collar bone, and yet they remained there, motionless as statues while Waverly inspected them with a proud look in his eye, for all the world a Caesar reviewing his legions.

"That was splendid," he said and led another round of polite applause from the company.

"And now," he said, "something special."

He whispered to Phueng and she gave him a dazzling smile and stood up and stripped off her kimono and danced out onto the mat. She was completely naked, her lithe, androgynous body carrying all the grace of youth, her face as old as sin. She glided over and stood before the men and spun mockingly in front of them, postured and leered and made obscene gestures and they all stared straight ahead, but now the smell of fear was in the air whereas before there had been only adrenaline.

I couldn't take my eyes off the girl and knew that everyone else was the same. Even Elinor had turned and was watching with an expression of fascinated contempt. The girl moved up to one of the men and rubbed lasciviously against his waist and then looked down and laughed, a high pealing laugh that filled me with horror, and then she danced away again and stood in front of the young German champion, as he must have known she would.

He stared straight ahead, and she rubbed him and murmured and the sweat was running down his face. She took his hand and he glanced despairingly at Summers who only smiled, and slowly he let her lead him into the centre of the mat.

She released him and stood back, and I saw him summon his courage, and the resolution form and stiffen as he lunged for her in a lightning-fast movement, but she drifted away light as silk, smiling, and he only looked clumsy. She leaned forward as he passed and touched his face and the blood sprang out and I saw the long-filed nail I hadn't seen before. He blinked and lunged again and she swayed sideways and her head went close to his and when she drew back she left a track where she had licked the blood from his face and she made a sound like a purr and her body arched in pleasure and the room was filled with sex and madness.

I closed my eyes in horror, but I was caught as fast as the others and soon I watched again. She was carving him now, a slight golden matador posturing and cutting, and he was staggering and dazed, his movements slow and confused, and all the time the darting tongue and flashing hands. Summers cast a questioning glance at Waverly, but he was rapt, his eyes riveted upon the scene before him, his breath panting in soft heaves.

I broke loose and took my brandy glass and hurled it at the obscene sight. It struck the woman's back and broke, and she spun and turned those dull and glowing amber eyes upon me and I knew I looked at death. Summers took three quick steps and stood before me, eyes blazing.

"Yes, perhaps that is enough for this evening," Waverly said. "Stand easy, Barclay. Take Gunther to the infirmary, please, gentlemen."

The previous combatants who had remained standing at attention beside the mat throughout the whole performance took the dazed young German, wrapped his face and arms in towels, and led him away. Waverly spoke to the girl and she pouted and put on her kimono, her head twisted back as she left the room, her eyes upon me like a cat's on prey.

Waverly turned towards me with a smile.

"You shouldn't get so excited, Captain. Much of it is theatre, you know. The men take drugs for the pain, and they're well compensated for their trouble."

"You are one sick son of a bitch," I said.

"As you have curtailed our evening's entertainment, perhaps you would care to engage Mr. Summers in a little demonstration for the guests," he went on unfazed. "I am sure he is quite keen. I understand he was at a slight disadvantage last time you met. Something about a dog bite if I remember correctly."

Summers remained in front of me, his face impassive, his eyes burning.

Laura's nails dug into my hand.

"I don't think so," I said.

My head was spinning from the drink and the smoke, and the girl had released demons into the room. I needed clean air, and space to breathe.

Summers's lips drew back in a mocking grin, and he leaned towards me.

"Perhaps we could compete for the tart," he murmured in a voice only the three of us could hear. "I see you're fucking her now. Not that she was all that great, mind you. Except for the last time of course. That was outstanding."

I looked at the sneering face and my world spun, and I was lying by the dugout dazed and bleeding and then the stifling smell of hay in the barn and the oppressive dust-filled heat and the stillness of the other prisoners circled around us as the rage built and consumed me like a prairie fire.

"This time I'll kill you outright, Wakosky," I murmured, and the face in front of me grew puzzled and a hand was pulling at my shoulder and I pushed away and there was a crash and Danny yelled and then I was up and had Summers by the throat and hurled him across the table and he slid across in a crashing of dishes and fell.

He rolled and came up smiling, much quicker than I remembered, and he kicked me twice before I spun and took the leg and jack-knifed him down but he rose again as if on springs, so light for a heavy man, the dust from the hay clouding the air around him, but Wakosky was much thicker, and I pondered this and he hit me again and I fell heavily and he danced away, changing shape. I rose and crouched and caught him in the throat as he came in, and he buckled and fell and I grabbed a fallen knife and leaned down and stared at his face and his eyes changed into the blue of my grandfather's and I screamed in rage and terror and brought the knife towards him but Danny was there holding me now and Summers rolled away.

"The demonstration is over," Danny said.

Waverly looked at us and I saw him calculating, but there were guests, important people, and he was no fool, and he smiled and the tension left his body.

"Perhaps we can do this again another time," he said. "I hate to leave things unfinished and I am sure Captain Summers feels the same."

We turned and walked away, Padraic, Molly, and Laura in a tight group, her father's arm around her, and Danny and I bringing up the rear. We went outside and there were two uniformed men waiting in the launch and they took us back to *Arrow* without a word from anybody. Molly left and the others went down below and then Danny came back out with a bottle and glasses, and we sat in the cockpit drinking in silence.

"Do you want to talk about it?" he asked me once.

"No."

He nodded and poured another drink and we sat there for the longest time.

I put the evening away and pulled the covers over it and buried it back down deep and held it there until the alcohol and the tiredness dulled it down and then I closed my eyes and slept. I woke once, and Danny was still there, talking to someone in a low voice, and it was just breaking dawn. I squinted my eyes and it was Elinor, dripping wet in the cockpit, and this struck me as strange, but I fell asleep again before I could make any sense out of it.

When I woke again I was alone and hoped I had dreamed it all.

CHAPTER 15

"I thought you were going to sleep forever."

I took the cup of coffee and grunted my thanks. I noted a slight bruising on Laura's left cheek. I felt like shit.

"Sorry about last night," I muttered.

"My fault. I should have stayed out of the way. I suppose you were sort of defending my honour."

I fumbled around the cockpit for my sunglasses. The cloud cover was thin, and it was exceedingly bright.

"Or don't you remember?"

"I remember."

"Why do you always drink so much?"

Jesus Christ. "Look, I said I was sorry."

"Do you want some rum in your coffee?"

"No."

"How about a Caesar then?"

"Look, I'm not an alcoholic. I just like to enjoy myself once in a while. Summers last night, that had nothing to do with drink. We don't like each other very much."

"What did you call him?"

"Summers."

"No. Last night. Something else."

"I don't know. Asshole, maybe. What does it matter? He was out of line and I lost my cool. Forget it."

She stared at me, her face thoughtful.

"What time is it?"

"Ten o'clock. Everybody else has been up for ages."

"I think I'll go for a shower."

I stood up and looked out over the harbour. The *Golden Dragon* was gone.

"They left an hour ago. Dropped all their guests ashore before they pulled out," Laura said.

"Good riddance."

I'd drop over to Port Control, see if I could find out where they had cleared out to.

I went down below to grab some clean clothes and a towel and halted in surprise. Danny and Elinor were sitting at the table drinking coffee.

"What's she doing here?"

"She swam over early this morning. You said *Hi* to her."

"I thought I was dreaming. But what's she doing here?"

"Hi again," Elinor said. "I decided I didn't want to stay aboard that boat any longer. I don't know why I didn't leave when my friend Susan did a month ago. I don't particularly like any of them, and Waverly gives me the creeps. And that Thai woman he keeps. Phueng. Ugh." She shivered. "After you all left last night he told his guests there'd been a change of plans, they would have to leave."

"And that included you?"

"No. I was crew. But he was angry with me about last night, as if some of it was my fault because I was with your lot. I don't trust him."

"I'm not sure I trust you," I said.

"C'mon, Jared. Relax. She's all right." Danny glared at me.

"Waverly selected you to be our hostess?"

"Yes."

"Why was that?"

"I don't know. The others were taken, I guess."

"Taken?"

"You know. They were with the other guests."

"And you weren't with anybody."

"That's right. Not right then. But I have been some other times. I don't have to make excuses to anybody," she said, standing up. "I just needed to get away from the *Dragon*, and I didn't have anywhere else to go right away. I'm leaving now."

"No. I apologize. If Danny wants you to stay, you stay. It's his call," I said.

"What would you like to do?" Danny asked her.

"I'd like to stay aboard *Arrow* and help you beat that arrogant, manipulative bastard," she said.

With her makeup washed off and her hair pulled back in a ponytail, she bore little resemblance to the sophisticated woman of the previous night.

"Beat him at what?" Laura asked.

"Recovering the treasure. I heard them talking about it."

"Welcome aboard, Elinor," I said. "Now please tell us everything you know."

She'd been a crew member aboard the *Golden Dragon* for ten months. She'd met Waverly at a ball in London, and he'd invited her aboard for a trip and she'd stayed on. It had been novel and exciting, and although she only earned a couple of thousand dollars a month, there were no expenses. Even her wardrobe was paid for as long as she helped Waverly entertain his guests and obeyed his simple rules. The position also offered an opportunity to meet and mingle with some of the world's richest and most powerful men. Her friend Susan had married one of Waverly's guests two months earlier.

"He told us to think of ourselves like privileged courtesans of a royal court. We were there to amuse and entertain the guests, and anything beyond that was at our discretion. He was very clear about that. He threshed a French diplomat who crossed the line with one of the girls and had him dumped naked on the docks in Papeete. It made the papers, although they said he had been attacked and robbed by locals."

"When did you hear about the treasure?"

"When we were in Tonga, five weeks ago now, I was in among the stacks in the reading room, looking up some books on Fiji, when the two of them came in. Waverly was furious, shouting at Summers, said if he had done his job they would have the site by now, not be sitting around waiting for someone else to lead them to the spot. Summers said it wasn't his fault, just bad luck. He said that at least the coin proved it wasn't a wild goose chase."

"It has to be one of the coins he stole from the Calders," Laura said. "They must have identified it as the same minting as the one Captain Dillon found at the original wreck site on Vanikolos. My God. Lapérouse's treasure actually does exist. I don't think I ever really believed it before."

"It would seem that it does," I said. "The bad news is that they think we know where it is. The sooner we get out of here and disappear, the better. Padraic must have some idea of where to begin looking. Where is he, by the way?"

"He and Molly went to check out *Tramp* a couple of hours ago," Danny said. "They were talking about setting it up for diving, free up some space on *Arrow*."

"Ah."

Laura stared at me, eyes narrowed.

"Good idea," I said. "I should have thought of it myself."

❁

We left at noon, sailing in company out of the harbour under a trade wind sky, *Tramp* doing surprisingly well under a hundred thirty-five genoa and main. Padraic had remained aboard with Molly, the two of them boisterous as kids, and even Laura succumbing to Molly's generous nature and high spirits. We were overnighting up the coast, and when Padraic told Laura he'd decided to move some of his things on board *Tramp* for the journey, she'd remained silent. I thought the move might be more permanent; Padraic had a rich bawdy streak that flourished in Molly's presence, and the two of them were as thick as thieves. Sinbad had taken a liking to *Tramp*, and after spending his time equally between the two boats in harbour, opted for *Tramp* for the run north.

We decided to begin our search at the village where Padraic had found the plate. We drew up a search grid and figured it would take about two weeks' work to check out the area. That was with two teams of divers working six-hour days, which was probably too much, even if most of the diving was in water as shallow as it showed on the charts. There were a couple of deeper spots where we might only get in four hours of searching in a day. But the thing to do was get started and see what developed. It was all a long shot anyway. We would either get lucky or not. What the hell. I decided to try and forget about possible problems until they actually presented themselves and just enjoy the trip.

As *Arrow* moved leisurely along, Danny and Elinor sat on the aft rail, ostensibly handling the fishing lines we trolled for supper but paying more attention to each other than their duties. Elinor was proving a welcome addition with her sunny good humour and infectious laugh. A Sussex girl of good education and family, she had been doing the society scene in London before signing on with Waverly as the result of their chance meeting.

"This is sweet," she said. "The *Golden Dragon* is so damned big and automated, it hardly seems you're sailing. It's more like being a passenger on a cruise ship where everything is done below decks out of sight, and the whole idea is to make you feel as if you're still ashore, only with a seaview. There's scarcely even a list with the water ballast pumped back and forth."

"Tell me about her."

She came and sat beside me on the rail, her chin cupped in her hands, staring aft to where *Tramp* ploughed along in our wake, falling back now in the freshening breeze.

"Waverly insisted the women become familiar with all aspects of the boat so we could instruct the guests and conduct tours. When I first went aboard, I spent a week going around to each area of the ship and spending a shift with the crew who worked there: the engine room, the nav station, even the galley. It was like an initiation. Waverly quizzed us on it afterwards, and those girls who hadn't paid attention were let go. I'd done some sailing before I went aboard, club racing, that sort of thing, so I had some idea. He let me take the wheel for the occasional watch and tune the sails. Of course, it was a lot different than I was used to, with the computer graphics in front of you, and the controls for the sails just buttons that managed the sheets and outhauls, and everything specified to the last degree. It was interesting though, and the rig is very efficient. In this kind of a breeze we'd be doing close to twelve knots."

Almost double *Arrow*'s speed. If we got into trouble with the *Golden Dragon* we weren't going to outrun her, that was damn sure.

"Did he ever hook up with any of the girls?"

"No. Not when I was aboard anyway. He always had somebody alongside, usually a celebrity, a model or an actress, but they seemed more like decoration, a testament to who he was. Trophies. The only person he seemed close to was Summers."

Elinor shrugged. "Some of the girls speculated about the two of them, but I think it was just talk. Most of them had made a play for him at one time or another and been brushed off."

"Oh there's something there all right," Danny said. He had abandoned the fishing and sat beside us listening. "I saw a lot of that sort of thing in prison, although I don't speak from personal experience. Mind you, I did kind of fancy Jared, cute little white body and all, and towards the end of my term, I must admit I was tempted once or twice."

He winked at me.

"You were in prison?" Elinor asked.

The tone of her voice suggested this was just another of Danny's many attractions.

"I've led a wicked life, my child," Danny said. "Come below and I'll show you some of what I've learned."

He seized her arm and led her away over her giggling, half-hearted protests. Laura snorted and retreated to her cabin and I went back to studying the charts of Kandala.

We arrived at the village on the second evening and anchored off the beach in five fathoms of water. There were a dozen bures running along the arc of the bay, set in amongst the palm trees and banyans that grew thickly on a small ridge running down to the water's edge. Children playing in the shallows spotted us, and in less than half an hour the headman arrived. He recognized Laura from her previous visit and accepted the gift of tobacco she'd brought with a grave smile.

I made the formal request for hospitality, showed him the stamped permits from the ministry, and gave him a kilo of kava as our greeting present. We accompanied him back to shore for the Sevusevu ceremony and squatted on the mats while they pounded the roots into pulp and mixed them with water in a clean cloth, the whole turning into a muddy broth that was passed around in coconut cups.

It wasn't offensive, just different, and had never done much for me although others swore by its narcotic effects. I'd presented a bottle of Bundaberg to the headman along with the kava root, and we chased the yaquona down with a swallow of rum.

Afterwards we walked around the village and handed out small presents we'd brought for the children and visited with their parents.

The chief insisted on holding a feast in our honour that evening and sent some men out spearfishing while others gathered shellfish. Danny and I joined in the fishing, much to the amusement of the Fijians whose skills in the water were infinitely superior to ours. They seldom missed with their spear guns and were extraordinary free divers, many of them staying under in excess of three minutes, disappearing into the depths below us like sleek coppery fish with quick powerful thrusts of their flippers as Danny and I struggled in their wake.

Padraic had gone off to talk to the chief about our search for the wreck and see if any of the elders had recollected anything new about the silver plate since his last visit.

"Nobody remembers anything about it," he told me later in the evening when we had feasted and were sitting around the fire watching the women dance. "No idea where it came from, although they seem pretty certain that it wasn't from this village. Not much help."

"Never mind. We'll get organized in the morning and start the campaign. In the meantime, let's just enjoy ourselves."

I reached over and poured a tot of the punch we had made into Padraic and Molly's glasses, and she promptly topped them up with some of her homemade screech. She'd wanted to add it directly to the communal bowl, but I had absolutely refused. We needed to maintain the goodwill of the local chiefs if we were to have any chance at success in our search, and inducing alcohol poisoning among their young men would not be helpful.

Some of the men were now dancing with the women, their heel drumming rituals keeping pace with the thrusting hips and driving rhythms of the log drums, the blatantly sexual nature of the dance creating a small tinge of embarrassment between Laura and me. She'd chosen to sit with me at the feast, not I think for the sake of my company, but rather because her father and Molly, and Danny and Elinor were such obvious couples, her presence among them would have been an intrusion.

"They really are quite uninhibited, aren't they?" Laura said finally with a nervous laugh.

"Yes," I said, "especially that couple over there."

She looked to where I pointed and saw her father and Molly pounding their pelvises with enthusiastic abandon just off the edge of the light from the fire.

She frowned and sprang to her feet.

"Hey, take it easy, I was only teasing you. They're just having fun. Sit down."

I pulled her hand and she sank back down on the sand beside me.

"You really can be an asshole," she said.

"Yeah, I know. I'm sorry. You want to dance?"

She looked at me. "Yes, sure, come on." She jumped to her feet, tugging at me.

"I was only joking," I said.

"I know," she said smugly. "You'd rather be dead than get up there and make an exhibition of yourself, wouldn't you?"

"Well, I wouldn't go that far, but yes, it's not really my thing."

"And just what is your thing, Jared Kane? You seem to know a lot about me, but I know practically nothing about you. Except you drink far too much as a rule, and you're not really as tough as you like to pretend."

She sank back down beside me, still holding my hand.

"Well, there's not really that much to tell. Just a simple fisherman who inherited a sailing boat through undeserved good fortune and set off to see the world with his friend."

"Elinor told me something about that. Not quite all that simple was it?"

"No, there were a few problems there at the beginning, all right. But we got by them eventually with a little help from Danny's grandfather. Joseph. I miss him."

"What about your own family?"

"Nobody left. My parents died when I was young, along with my little sister."

My grandfather didn't count. The day in the court room when he disowned me was the day he'd died for me. He might be in his grave now. I couldn't have cared less.

"That must be tough."

"I don't know. Maybe. But Danny's family took me in at a bad time, they're blood to me now. I could do anything, commit any crime, and they would still welcome me with open arms. I suppose that's what family is."

When they took you in you occupied a special place in their hearts, and nothing could alter that. I'd never imagined love and commitment to that degree. It was why the People hadn't crumbled under poverty, hardship, and the persecution of indifference and contempt, but only become stronger.

"Tell me about Joseph."

"It's hard to explain. He's a very old man, but that has nothing to do with who he is. It's simply an incidental fact. He's one of my closest friends. He has gifts, and seems to understand everything without saying much of anything."

I didn't try and tell Laura that Joseph didn't even speak English to me. That would have been really hard to explain.

"Just how old is he?"

"Nobody knows for sure. Maybe close to a hundred years old."

"It's hard to imagine you having much in common. I mean, a centenarian Haida and a young Caucasian." She laughed.

"Yeah." *Drink and women*, I could have said, but didn't.

Laura threw back her head and gazed up at the stars. It was light enough to read by.

"It's different out here isn't it? As if none of the ordinary rules of life apply. Just suppose we do find treasure, I mean loads of it, enough to make us all filthy rich. What would you do with your share?"

"I don't know, I haven't really thought about it. Nothing too different I suppose. Spend a few dollars on *Arrow*, rig her out exactly the way I'd like, maybe a new diesel, set up the family if they'd let me, although they're all doing well enough."

"No trips to Europe, the capitals, the Riviera, see some of the high life?" Laura asked.

"Probably not. I feel most comfortable here, on *Arrow*. She's my world; she can take me anywhere I want to go. So far she's given me all the excitement I can handle."

"Yes, I suppose that's true. And tomorrow we start the search. It's hard to believe in it sometimes. That it's even real. But I have to, for my father's sake. I don't know what he'd do if he didn't have this."

I looked over towards where Padraic and Molly had been, but they'd vanished into the darkness.

"Well, it looks like Molly might be creating some new interests for him," I said.

She punched me on the forearm. "Be nice Jared, you've been doing pretty well up to now. Don't go and spoil it."

"No," I said, "I don't intend to."

Her eyes looked up at me and she smiled tentatively, and I leaned down and kissed her, and her eyes widened for a second, and then she put her arms around me and returned the kiss. We broke it off and she smiled again and said, "Just put your arms around me and hold me Jared," and I did, and we sat there quietly until the end of the dancing when the fire and drums died, and then I walked her back to the dinghy and we rowed back to *Arrow*. There wasn't even an awkward moment as I held her hand and led her down to my cabin, not until the time later when she said, "Please, Jared, I'm sorry. I can't," and began weeping inconsolably.

I tried to comfort her as desire ebbed and was replaced by pity, and I knew for certain then that I would kill Barclay Summers, and the thought consumed me, and long after she had fallen asleep I lay there holding her in the night and pictured his face, and what should have been love faded to despair and a burning desire for vengeance.

CHAPTER 16

By ten o'clock the next morning Danny and I had moved the dive gear aboard *Tramp* and set up a basic schedule with Padraic and Molly. There would be two teams of divers, each partner always in sight of the other, and both teams with an observer above them in a dinghy with a lead line down while they worked. We'd use a system of buoys to mark the areas being searched and move them for each ensuing dive. Daniel and Elinor made up one team and I'd alternate with Molly and Laura on the other, Laura sticking to the relatively shallow areas until she gained more experience, and Molly accompanying me on the deeper dives. Padraic had final responsibility for charting the dives and setting up each day's program.

I was uncertain about Laura's morning after reaction to the evening's events; I'd untangled myself at first light and slipped silently away and left her sleeping. She finally appeared with a wan smile and a tentative glance in my direction, and I walked up and kissed her on the cheek and wished her a good morning. Padraic smiled upon us, so that was all right. Later on, Laura came and sat beside me as we worked out the day's diving details, her hand creeping surreptitiously down and squeezing mine.

"Right, let's get started then."

Danny and Elinor jumped up from the table and went out on deck and began putting on snorkels, masks, and fins. The water was relatively shallow, nothing deeper than fifty feet in the grid, and so clear we could get by with free diving to start with. Later in the day when we became tired, we'd use the hookahs. We'd bought a second one from a Dutch boat that was selling off its gear prior to returning home. Each unit was mounted on a free-floating platform with a pair of fifty-foot air lines attached and would allow us to search the shallower depths without the complications of tanks.

We eliminated any area that was heavily fished by the villagers who were familiar with every rock and reef. There was no chance they would have failed to spot any wreckage. There were other areas less visited, where the fishing was uncertain, and we concentrated our efforts there. Diving this shallow was more fun than work, and that was the way we wanted it for the first while. Let everyone get comfortable in the water and learn their tolerances, building confidence for the deeper, more dangerous dives that would follow later on.

Snorkelling in the sheltered lagoons was a picnic, the water placid, the currents nonexistent, the only sharks the occasional small white tips who moved away at sight of us. When we moved outside the sheltering reefs into the treacherous passes where the erratic tides sucked and whirled, and the predators moved like flashing silver knives through the roiled waters, it would be much different.

The days passed like a vacationer's dream: rising early to a light breakfast and then into the water, the first slight shock of contact quickly disappearing as the water formed an insulating layer between our skin and the neoprene suits we wore for protection from the sun and the coral reefs we swam amongst. Most coral stings, some varieties merely a mild nuisance, others, like fire coral, inducing real pain, and sometimes a violent and dangerous reaction.

The reefs were stunning, huge living forests of every hue and description, rising near to the surface in tangled masses before falling away into long kaleidoscopic canyons and valleys that we swam through like entranced children, caught up in the beauty and majesty, almost expecting any moment to come upon a ruined castle, or an enchanted civilization.

There were corals and sponges of every colour in the rainbow, from the pale delicate white of sea fans swaying to the slightest current, to the dark glossy eruptions of stony brain coral, clinging to the calcified skeletons of their forebears. Table corals, tier upon tier supported by a single delicate stem, hanging on an impossible slope like roped climbers; whip corals surrounded by their tiny proprietary reef fish, so delicate an errant flipper could destroy them in a careless second. Lettuce leaf coral, and fire coral, and staghorn coral, and then the numerous others whose names are known only to the scientists, all of them intertwined and alive, competing for their space on the huge living organism that is the coral reef.

And the countless indescribable fish, always so many more than you first expect. Wrasses and cleaners and parrotfish; butterfly fish, needlefish, angelfish; clowns, surgeonfish, unicornfish and Moorish idols; morays and triggerfish, and squirrelfish and rabbitfish and hawkfish and conefish; and a dozen others too small and quick to identify, had we even known their names. And then the bigger species, jacks and groupers and snappers and a glistening school of barracuda glimpsed so sudden you caught your breath before they wheeled and were gone in unison, all separate parts of a single hunting intelligence.

Swimming with Laura was best of all, she had excellent conditioning and could stay under for a full two minutes, smiling innocently under her mask at me as I struggled to stay with her, and desperately pointed upwards. Her slim body knifed through the water with little resistance, and scorning wearing a diving suit, she grew only more tanned with every passing hour.

"The black Irish," I gasped one day as she laughed at my struggle into the clinging suit, sitting on the edge of the inflatable with only a bikini on, and that no bigger than it ought to be. "When the skin cancer gets you, you won't be laughing, never mind the fire coral or the jellyfish."

"Not a chance, boyo," she said. "My mother was part Spanish, don't you know."

She looked it, sitting there smiling like a Castilian princess, only her hazel eyes, which seemed lighter every day, suggesting the northern part of her heritage. As she grew more open and free in my company, she seemed more vulnerable, her soul shining out of those remarkable eyes, and it became so I couldn't even tease her. It was she who now took the Mickey and me who just smiled and accepted it, knowing how delicately poised it all was and how easily it could come crashing down with a single misplaced phrase.

We quit late each afternoon and congregated in *Arrow's* main cabin, dining on fish and fruit and the vegetables we traded for with the villagers. A few drinks and then we turned in early, Danny and Elinor later than the rest of us. Sometimes they went off to the village to party, but she was seemingly as immune to the effects of debauch as he was, and they were invariably the first up and the brightest.

After that first night I'd been uncertain as to the sleeping arrangements and lingered in the cockpit over a nightcap with Danny, letting Laura make up her mind. She walked boldly up to me, grabbed my hand, and told me it was time to go to bed.

"Okay," I said.

"Night, kids," Danny said. "Sleep tight."

Even he had backed off from his usual ribald self, sensing it was a delicate time.

When we went into the cabin and shut the door, Laura put her arms around me and kissed me and said it would just take some time and would I please be patient with her.

"Okay, but easy on the hugging and kissing, and put on a good Catholic nightgown if we're sleeping together."

"Oh, we're sleeping together all right, Jared Kane. Wasn't there an old American custom called bundling where the couple slept together without actually making love?"

"Yes, but it was in a cold northern climate, and they were wearing several layers of clothing. And the women weren't as beautiful as you."

She smiled demurely and put on a diaphanous gown and lay down in the bed and waited, and when I lay down beside her, she kissed me again and whispered in my ear to be patient, and hugged me and held me then, and finally drifted off to sleep, and it was all very sweet and touching, and I didn't really mind after all.

But in the middle of the night when I awoke to the sound of her sobbing as if her heart would break, great tearing sounds coming out of that slender body, and the thin sheet all wet with tears, I felt a minding so great it consumed me, and I lay there silent and helpless and pretended to sleep and swore black vows of repayment in the consuming darkness.

In the morning, everything was fine again with no remaining trace of the grief that had overpowered her in the night, and she was laughing and light of heart, and you wouldn't have guessed she had a care in the world. We went out and dove together and had a wonderful day, as if the night was only a bad dream, but then the following night it was the same as her defences crumbled and vanished in the lonely morning hours, and I lay beside her silent and powerless, with no solace or comfort to offer her.

It took ten days to complete our search of the area, and then it was time to move on to the next village and begin the process all over again. Taneki lay twenty-two miles west of us, a lovely three hour run on a bracing beam reach, and we were all in high spirits as we raced out through the encircling reefs and hit the open water for the outside run. *Arrow* seemed to relish it as much as the rest of us, putting her shoulder down and bucking along the quartering swells with a quick sidling motion as she rose up and came down off them.

The women were tending the boat, Elinor at the tiller while Laura worked the sheets, both of them quick and competent and a study in contrasts with Elinor's patrician blond beauty set against Laura's dark elfin presence.

"A pair of beauties, to be sure," Danny said.

It seemed like everyone was starting to sound Irish now. He leaned back against the rail beside me and sighed in pure contentment.

"I don't know as if I really care whether we find any treasure or not right now. This life is pretty good already," Danny said. "Finding gold might mean we'd have to start doing some real work."

"True. The money would be nice though. We don't have all that much left, if you recall."

"Not to worry. Elinor says she's quite comfortable, has a nice trust fund annuity from Daddy. Says she can keep us going indefinitely."

"Kept men," I said.

"Yep."

"Dependent upon the capricious whims of a woman, losing all pride and self-respect as we grovel for her money and approval," I said.

"Exactly."

"I could probably handle that."

"I thought you might."

Danny reached into the cooler at his side and brought out two beers and popped the caps.

"How's it going with Laura?"

"Pretty good between us. There's still the Summers thing though. She's not over that, maybe never will be. Cries some nights."

"I've never cared much for rapists," Danny said. "I've always considered it as the most personal and damaging of injuries you could inflict on someone."

Danny could still surprise me. Our eyes met, and I knew we were both thinking of the Wakosky brothers. I suddenly realized it might well have been him who pulled the plug on the one I'd put into the nursing home in Mission. The thought hadn't occurred to me before. Danny was certainly capable of it. I stared at him.

"What?"

"Never mind. It doesn't matter."

We lay back and drank our beers and discussed the new area and how we should approach it. It was deeper, running between fifty and one hundred feet, and we'd have to use the tanks. Some of the spots looked tricky on the charts, deep, narrow gullies big enough to conceal a small boat but tight enough to cause some concerns when we went down. We would be closer to the outside edge, and there would be currents and swell running through at the higher tides.

"If you lose your concentration or you're unlucky, you can easily get swept up against the coral," Danny said.

I agreed. Some of it was razor sharp, and the cuts always became infected. Apart from that, it was never a good idea to put blood in the water. People were killed every year by shark attacks in Fiji, and for some reason the attacks were more prevalent in the northern parts of Vanua Levu. Nobody knew why.

"There's the pass," Elinor yelled.

Danny looked forward, then suddenly straightened and pointed ahead. "Look."

The upper half of a pair of golden masts, towering skywards from inside the lagoon.

"The *Golden Dragon*," Laura whispered, and the carefree spirit that had enveloped *Arrow* vanished like smoke and was replaced by a sense of foreboding.

"They won't have seen us yet. Heave to and we'll wait for *Tramp* and decide what to do."

Danny sprang up and dropped the mainsail while I took down the genoa, the way slowly coming off *Arrow* as Laura brought her into the wind and we sat there bobbing in the swell, nobody speaking and all of us staring at the long-tapered masts as if they held the final secrets of life and death.

"There would be no point in them coming after us right now," Padraic said. "The mere fact we're here will tell them we haven't found anything yet. They'll realize we're still looking and just keep an eye on us while they conduct their own search."

We were gathered around the big table in *Arrow*'s salon, *Tramp* tied alongside with a half dozen fenders to keep her rusty hull off *Arrow*'s topsides.

"I agree," Molly said. "Makes a lot more sense to leave us alone until we find it, and then just take it away from us."

"Which wouldn't be too difficult, considering that they probably have ten crew aboard," I said. "Why don't we just go off somewhere else and look? One place is as good as another at this point. God knows there are enough of them to check out."

"There's only eight crew aboard now," Elinor said. "Waverly let the others go when the guests left."

"Oh well, only six mercenaries plus Summers and Waverly then. Maybe we should just go straight in there and kick their asses right now."

"Now now, Jared, relax. We're just having a discussion here. Nothing has been decided yet." Danny patted my shoulder. "Let's hear what everyone has to say."

"There's a hundred square miles to cover in this grid," Padraic said, "all of it divided up by reefs and islands and bars. Shouldn't be too difficult to keep out of each other's way." He pointed to the chart. "They're anchored here. It's reasonable to assume they started in the northwest corner and are proceeding southeast. We begin at the opposite end, twenty miles distant, and work back towards them. We chart and eliminate all the areas where they're searching. Seeing as they're here, why not take advantage of it? They were bound to run across us sooner or later anyway."

"Sounds good to me," Molly said.

"Why not," Elinor said, and Danny nodded with her. "They'd be fools to bother us now, and Waverly certainly isn't stupid."

"What about you, Laura?" I asked. Her eyes had barely left the *Dragon*'s masts since we'd first seen them.

"Let's go for it," she said at last. I might have been the only one who detected the tremor in her voice.

"Okay then. It's agreed. We'll go through the pass, head up through Landas Channel, and anchor in tight behind Vatele Island in the southeast corner. What have you got for guns aboard *Tramp*?"

"Nothing," Molly said. "I never thought it necessary."

"Well, we can remedy that," Danny said.

He went below and carried up the canvas covered bundle we had bought in Suva and unwrapped it on the cockpit table.

"Jesus," Padraic said. "The last time I saw a load like that, I was a member of the provisional IRA."

"Just in case somebody comes visiting," I said. "They may still think there's information in the journals that they can locate the treasure from, even if we can't. Better safe than sorry."

It wasn't really much of an arsenal, but it was the best we could do under short notice in a strange country. A couple of pump shotguns in waterproof bags, a converted Army Springfield 30-06 with a cross-hair scope, and an old pair of battered .38s.

"The shotguns are for the dinghies when we're diving," I said. "Keep them loaded and handy in the waterproof cases. The Springfield you can stow aboard *Tramp*. It's a decent weapon with good range. The pistols were just thrown in as part of the deal; they might be all right if you can get close enough to hit something with them. They're for you and Molly. With luck you'll never have to use them."

"What about yourselves?" Padraic asked.

"Oh, don't worry about us," Danny said. "We've still got a couple of goodies stashed here and there."

As we emerged from the pass into the inside waters, a busy scene unfolded in front of us. The *Golden Dragon* was anchored a half mile off to starboard, three Avon Ribbies with fifty-horse Yamahas spread out around her, each with a dive flag hoisted at the stern. As we motored by the nearest of them, two men in scuba gear and tanks popped up alongside it and climbed aboard. One of them pulled off his mouthpiece and snorkel and picked up the VHF radio from the console and began talking. A few minutes later, they pulled into *Tramp*'s wake, a quarter mile back.

"Seems like they're going to keep an eye on us," Laura said.

"Looks like."

"Up theirs," she said, and raised a finger and gave them the salute.

We ran along the inside edge of the reef at a steady five knots, Danny standing on the lower set of spreaders keeping an eye out for uncharted bommies. The tide was full, and the fringing reef on the port side was masked by a foaming line of breaking waves that extended ahead as far as the eye could see in a long gentle crescent. To starboard the water was a deep, brilliant blue, fading to green and then brown as it shallowed up, and then it deepened to azure again, all in the space of a hundred yards. A scant few boat lengths farther along and another reef rose up just beneath the surface and the whole pattern repeated again, browns and blues and greens in infinite variety, over and over for miles, all of the coral constantly changing and growing and dying and none of it accurately charted.

"God, it's beautiful," Laura said.

"Yes, it is."

But dangerous too. I could feel the pressure on the tiller from the force of the waves breaking on the reef as the back eddies and currents twisted around *Arrow*'s keel. There were stories of divers working the inside edges getting caught in the undertow of an uncharted hole through the reef and slashed to ribbons in a split second. Unfortunately, the inside edges were the most likely spots to find Lapérouse's boat. If he'd crashed on the reef in a storm, the boat would have likely been swept over and inside. After that it was anybody's guess where it might end up.

If we were wrong, and it was on the outside of the reef, there was no chance of finding it, the boat smashed to splinters centuries past, the gold buried beneath the crumbled reefs, or slid down a hundred fathoms into the eternal deep.

Danny's shrill whistle broke into my thoughts as he pointed a course twenty degrees to starboard around a bommie that rose up to within five feet of the surface and was only a faint shadow from the deck. We swerved to miss it and then another whistle from Danny, this time for a beer. Elinor went up the ratlines and delivered it and stayed up there with him.

"They make a nice couple," Laura said, watching with a trace of wistfulness as they laughed and clowned around on the spreaders, the two of them sure-footed as monkeys. Danny had Elinor under one arm, threatening to drop her over the side if she didn't release the beer she had taken and refused to give back. "It must be nice to have such a happy go lucky disposition."

"Don't be fooled. It's not always fun and games with Danny. He can get pretty serious when it's called for. He's had his bad times too."

I'd been with him once when he'd shut down all systems and drifted fatalistically towards death. Joseph had brought him back at the last possible moment with a combination of massage, shamanism, and bullying. Now there was a man we could have used on this forlorn search. Maybe Joseph could have fashioned some of the wizardry that he seemed capable of dredging up whenever things were blackest. Looking at the thin line of boiling surf on the one side, and the limitless miles of reef broken sea on the other, I realized again what an enormous task we faced.

Danny called down, motioning towards the little island emerging off our bow.

"Vatele Island," Laura said, pointing it out on the chart spread out beside us. "Stay on this course until it comes abeam, and then you should see the channel that takes us around in behind open up; twelve feet of water at the shallowest point and then anchorage in forty feet in sand."

We ran *Arrow* down and found the channel and went through, *Tramp* following close behind, and the dinghy with the two men in it keeping their distance beyond them. When they saw us safely anchored, they cranked up the throttle and disappeared back down the channel in a cloud of spray.

"I guess we should stand watches," Danny said as he watched them disappear around the corner.

"How about we tie the two boats together and let Sinbad take care of both of them? Nice and flat in behind here as long as the wind doesn't shift. If it swings around, we can split up easy enough. I'll see what Molly thinks."

Not that she was risking anything in her steel juggernaut. The worst that could happen to *Tramp* was that her hull would get a little white paint on it from *Arrow*'s topsides.

Molly agreed, and after tying alongside, set off with Padraic in the inflatable to check out the area where we planned to dive the following day. Danny and Elinor went spearfishing while Laura and I rigged up the awnings and lounged and read in their shade. I felt I'd missed something in the journals, some means of correlation between the lists of objects they had recovered and the plate from Lapérouse.

Many of the uninhabited islands and isolated reefs the Calders had visited were unnamed, and it was a tedious process with a chart in one hand and the journal in the other trying to retrace the early voyages of *Arrow*. Sometimes, faced with a lack of identifying names and an imperfect position in those pre-GPS days, Bill had resorted to drawings of the terrain that surrounded him, with their bearings written alongside. Sometimes these had proved useful, but more often they could have been any one of a dozen different spots, as there were so few landmarks that stood out. One palm tree looks much like another, and many of the islands' outlines were beaten down to similar profiles by the prevailing wind and wave action, never mind the hurricanes which had savaged them in the decades since Bill and Meg had been there.

"Listen."

I couldn't hear anything at first, only the distant roar of the surf on the edge of the barrier reef. Then, something else, a faint, low whine that escalated into the snarl of a high revving engine. Laura pointed up and I saw it glinting, coming out of the sun. A seaplane. Laura picked up the binoculars and focused them.

"The *Golden Dragon*," I said, and started below for the rifle.

"No, not them. Their plane is yellow."

This one was pale blue, heading directly towards us fifty feet above the water. At the last possible second it pulled up and screamed over us, missing the mast by only a few feet. I caught a glimpse of a seamed brown face in the passenger seat before the plane turned and landed into the wind and taxied back towards us.

"What now?" I said. "Some old chief whose sacred ground we've violated?"

I stood watching, the shotgun cradled under my arm as the plane came alongside. A dignified figure in brown wool fisherman's pants and a red flannel shirt stepped down onto the pontoons. He took the kit bag passed down to him and nodded gravely in our direction as the seaplane taxied alongside and tied off.

Joseph.

CHAPTER 17

Danny had phoned Joseph from Suva and told him about our expedition, and he'd decided to come out and join us. He had our rough itinerary, and it was a simple enough matter to charter a seaplane when he arrived in Nadi Airport. He'd spent a mere two hours searching and a thousand dollars U.S. to find us. I knew the latter for a certainty, as his first act upon arrival was to hand me the bill for the pilot's account.

He was unchanged from the last time I'd seen him two years earlier, the proud carriage strictly erect, the grave brown eyes showing no sign of the humour that lurked within, the outstretched hand steady as a rock. When we embraced, the faint odour of pipe smoke and cedar that defined him to me.

He made a slow tour around the foredeck then seated himself in the cockpit, Sinbad resting at his feet, and began talking quietly to Danny.

"He's come to help us find the treasure," Danny said. "He's been having strange dreams."

Padraic glanced at Molly with raised eyebrows. When Danny had told them that Joseph was fluent in the English language but chose not to speak it, they'd stared at him as if he'd arrived from another planet. I could see the effort they were making not to smile.

"Dreams about what?" I asked.

"They're confused. A long tailed yellow bird, sharks and snakes. He hasn't figured it all out yet."

"Sharks and snakes," I said. "That figures. Why can't he dream about something cute like dolphins or sea turtles?"

I knew all about Joseph's dreams, and they came true far too often for my liking. The big yellow bird wasn't all that hard to decipher.

Joseph looked at me and murmured something to Danny, who burst out laughing.

"What did he just say?" Laura asked.

"It doesn't translate all that well," Danny replied. "Something about a little white bird who squawks and makes droppings."

Much mirth all around. Joseph leaned over and patted my shoulder, his eyes gleaming.

"Ask him if the yellow bird in his dream might have been a dragon," I said, and the laughter stopped.

Joseph stared thoughtfully at me and puffed on his pipe. He resumed his conversation with Danny, and then the two of them stepped down into *Arrow*'s inflatable, fired up the Honda, and took off in a long arcing plane down the lagoon in the direction from which we'd come.

"He seems pretty sharp for an old man," Padraic said, watching them disappear in the distance.

I nodded in agreement.

"Is he some kind of medicine man, witch doctor, something like that?" Molly asked.

"Something like that."

"How old is he, anyway?"

"Close to a hundred," I said.

"No," Molly said in a shocked voice. "He doesn't look anywhere near that old. Are you sure?"

"Not absolutely, no."

"I thought so. They probably didn't have good records in those days."

"True."

"I mean, a hundred. Jesus, Padraic, that's like thirty years older than you, for Christ's sake," Molly giggled.

"Thirty-four years older than me, actually," Padraic said stiffly.

"No offence, love. You know what I mean. How did he ever manage to get out here on his own anyway?"

"He's pretty competent," I said. "You don't want to judge him by his age."

I knew a few people who had done just that, and some of them were dead now.

They asked a few more questions about Joseph, curious about how an old man could just up and leave his home and fly halfway round the world like that. I explained that in the First Nations culture the elderly aren't relegated back to the status of children with advancing age but are respected and treated according to their individual merits. They didn't really understand. Eventually they tired of the subject, and Padraic brought out the charts, and we began to lay out our dive schedule for the following morning.

Danny and Joseph returned just before dark. They sat down with the charts we had been working with, and Danny spoke while Joseph sat listening, his eyes half closed, his fingers gently tracing the contours of the reefs and lagoons. Once, he stopped and tapped the chart with his finger and asked a question, and Danny answered him, and he paused, considering, and then his fingers began their restless searching again.

"Well, what does he think?" I asked. It was midnight and the others had retired for the night. I stayed below with Laura until she fell asleep and then went up and joined Danny and Joseph in the cockpit.

"He doesn't think it's here," Danny said. "The treasure. Not on the charts we showed him, anyway."

I stared at Joseph. He regarded me calmly and took a small sip from the glass of Laphroaig in his hand.

"Not here," I said.

He nodded.

"Is he sure?"

"Not absolutely," Danny said.

"Not absolutely," I said.

Joseph shrugged his shoulders.

"What the fuck does that mean?"

"Keep your voice down, Jared. You'll wake the others."

"Not absolutely sure," I whispered. "That's a big fucking help, isn't it?"

"He hasn't had enough time; it will take longer before he knows for certain."

"How about if he takes the plate Padraic found. Would that help?"

Joseph shook his head. No.

"Where did you two go today?"

"Down to the other end of the lagoon, round where the *Dragon* is working. Joseph wanted to take a look at the area, see the boat up close as well. He says that's not the place. He knows because of the sharks. There aren't any sharks down there."

"What about this end?" I inquired. Sharks are territorial and will often congregate in just one of two otherwise identical areas for no apparent reason.

"There are a few down here," Danny said.

Joseph shrugged and raised his hands in apology.

"A few?"

"Quite a few. Sharks, that is. Maybe not any snakes though. He's not sure about the snakes yet."

We'd seen a few sea snakes in our travels, swimming along the surface of the water, and once we found one lying dead in the dinghy. They were small and brightly coloured, and their bite was said to be the most poisonous of all the vipers, but as their mouths were tiny, and their teeth were set well back, I'd never considered them much of a threat. If you were foolish enough to force your little finger down their throat, of course, you might get yourself into some bother. I'd never heard of anyone having trouble with sea snakes in Fiji.

"Joseph says we should keep to Padraic's dive schedule for now. He wants to poke around a bit, and then he'll know better what to do."

"He can use the sailing skiff, we'll stick the Seagull on the stern for when the wind dies."

Joseph nodded in agreement and said something to Danny.

"He'll take Sinbad with him," Danny said.

"Good. Let's have another drink then."

We passed around the bottle while Joseph gave us the latest news about the family, Danny translating for me. Annie's latest boyfriend had been a French Canadian who ran a trap line in the interior of British Columbia and actually assumed that she was going to join him in the enterprise. When she stopped laughing, Annie asked him if she should bring along a couple of spare sets of false teeth for chewing on the hides, and then threw him out. We finally turned in at three o'clock in the morning, and it seemed only minutes later that Laura was shaking my shoulder and telling me it was time to rise up.

"We're going to start slowly, work our way down to the deeper spots gradually, nothing over sixty feet today, is that clear?" Padraic inquired.

We nodded in agreement, sitting around the big table with our coffee as Padraic outlined the day's program. Molly was our designated diving expert, and he had run everything by her first.

"The charts don't show anything over seventy feet in this particular area, but they may not be totally accurate. There could be some deeper depressions that have been eroded since they were drawn."

Considering that most of the charts for this area were around fifty years old, and one, a hand-drawn sketch by a lieutenant in the British navy, a hundred and thirty-five years old, it seemed at least possible.

"You've all set your alarms for sixty feet?" Padraic asked.

We all nodded again. It was the third time he'd mentioned it.

"All right then, team, let's go!"

I thought Padraic was getting a little carried away by it all, but he was thorough as well as enthusiastic, and that was all for the good. We crossed over to *Tramp*, loaded the inflatable with the dive gear, and set off, Molly and I in one boat with Laura as our monitor, Danny and Elinor in the other, overseen by Padraic.

Thirty minutes later, we arrived at the southeast corner, set our first buoy, and entered the water, following the lead line down into the depths.

It still surprises me, that first dive with air after a long hiatus. Free diving is natural, almost instinctive, just a matter of discipline and control as you glide down, the knowledge that you can turn and break for the surface at any moment a reassurance against the pressured depths that surround you. There is no real danger, provided you calculate the air required for the upward rush at the end and don't run out of breath halfway back. It can happen, particularly during spearfishing when the thrill of pursuit might extend you past your safe levels as you chase your prey deeper and longer than you should, but you always have greater reserves than you think, and it is just a matter of clamping down on the panic and hanging on for those few interminable extra seconds as you rise back up to the surface. In the machismo free dive contests, where they test human endurance to the ultimate limits, the very best free dive is considered to be the one where you black out from lack of oxygen just as you hit the surface.

Diving with air is different, more cumbersome and deadly, and a mistake can kill you or leave you with permanent brain damage. The deeper you dive, the more air you use and the less time you can stay on the bottom without a decompression stop. You don't ascend faster than sixty feet a minute, your guide the bubbles that stream up from your mouthpiece. You never overtake them.

Besides the increased danger, there is another downside to diving with air: the strong sense of alienation that overcomes you when you first strap on the gear and enter the water. Gone is the sensation of oneness with the medium, now you are an alien intruder dependent on a complex system for your survival, and the waters are the enemy, lying in wait for your first mistake. You are no longer a free, independent being relying on your own sense and judgment, but rather one part of an intricate interdependence where everything is measured and monitored — depth, pressure, air, time down and time remaining, and all problems are serious ones, and the solutions not always in your hands.

It was strange and disorienting at first, the sounds of my breathing loud in my ears, the distracting bubbles that streamed upwards, the harness and vest and air bottles restricting my free movement. Then, as I descended deeper and left the oxygen and sunlight above me, everything changed aspect and became strange and ghostly. My perceptions shifted, and the gear became a comfort, a link to the world I'd left behind.

Molly and I moved slowly down the sheer face of the reef, keeping just in sight of each other, performing slow revolutions every few feet as we searched for anything out of the ordinary, be it the narrowing circle of an interested shark or the unnatural angles of a man-made object.

As we descended the colours gradually faded, first the brilliant reds and yellows of the upper growth corals, and then the brighter blues and greens, until we moved in a ghostly aquamarine world where everything was toned down, the spectrum of light absent now, and the motion of our passage changed into something altogether quieter and less forceful. The bottom was sandy and uneven, strewn with boulders and shell middens, with the occasional lonely bommie rising up towards the surface. We saw little life present apart from an occasional reef fish, darting back into its cave when we approached, and some small parrotfish nibbling at the coral and shitting almost continuously. They are the prime builders of the tropic beaches, grinding up coral and passing it through themselves in fine particles. A medium-sized parrotfish is capable of creating a ton of sand a year.

We took a compass bearing and swam until we saw the anchored lead line from the buoy that Laura had set from the surface, and then moved ninety degrees off for a timed fifteen seconds, and then took another bearing and returned parallel to our original track until we arrived at the cliff face again and repeated the process, searching in long sweeps. We tried to be precise in our work, knowing how easy it was to misjudge and how we might come within twenty feet of an old wreck overgrown with coral and never recognize it.

We stayed down for an hour, swimming back and forth in tandem, and then we moved slowly back up to the surface where Laura was waiting with a Thermos of tea.

"See anything interesting down there?"

"No. Nothing much at all. Very little marine life, a lot of the coral is dead."

When a reef dies, it turns a pale, ghostly white as the polyps expire, the whole ecosystem gradually disappearing until what remains is nothing but a sparsely inhabited submarine graveyard. It is the eternal causal chain of life and death, beginning with the smallest phytoplankton that feed the reef, and travelling up in a cycle of destruction until the last predator is forced to leave for lack of food. Sometimes it can start with something as simple as a climate-change-induced rise in water temperature, other times it is more obviously man-made — an oil spill a thousand miles distant, or the concussive shock of an underwater explosion.

"What's the visibility like?"

"Pretty good," Molly said. "I think we'll see something if it's down there. It's not easy following the grid, though, especially when there's bommies rising up all over the place. I'm reasonably confident that we can cover the area well enough. What the hell, we're going to need a bit of luck anyway in all of this."

"We're going to need a lot of luck in all of this," I said.

"Hey, cheer up partner. Maybe your pal Joseph will give us some better directions. Look, here he comes now."

She pointed back in the direction of *Arrow*, where a small sail was heading in our direction. With the binoculars I could make out Joseph sitting in the stern with his hand on the tiller and Sinbad occupying his favourite position, teeth clamped on the transom, his humped body flowing out in the water behind. I couldn't help but smile.

"Look at that dumb dog," I said, handing the binoculars across to Laura.

She put them to her eyes and started laughing. "Whoops," she said, "something seems to be happening."

I could see it with my naked eyes now, the little sailboat lurching to the side as Sinbad heaved himself aboard, spun around, and began barking furiously at the water.

"I wonder what's the matter," Laura said.

"Sharks," I said. "He always barks at sharks. They mauled him a couple of times in the Tuamotus where he grew up."

Joseph circled the area for a few minutes, leaning over the side of the boat and looking down into the water, and then altered course towards us.

"Well, I guess we should go back down and get on the grid again," I said.

"We'd better wait. Joseph is signalling us," Laura said.

I had a strong suspicion about what he wanted.

He sailed up and tied off to our dinghy and accepted a cup of tea from Laura's Thermos. I began putting on my tanks, and he shook his head, and I sighed and took them off again.

"Looks like he doesn't want us to dive here anymore," Molly said.

Joseph nodded and motioned back towards the area he had just left.

"You want us to check back there, do you?" Laura asked.

Joseph nodded again.

"And why is that?" I asked.

Joseph put his hands together with the thumbs raised up, and slowly wagged them as he moved them forward. Sinbad barked enthusiastically.

"Sharks," I said. "You want us to dive where the fucking sharks are."

Joseph nodded.

"It's because of his dreams," Laura said.

"What about the sea snakes?" I asked. "Surely if they're not there as well, it doesn't count?"

Joseph shook his head and motioned back towards the shark zone again.

"Have you discussed this with Padraic?" I asked, "He's the dive team leader, you know."

Joseph just stared at me. Laura was trying not to laugh.

"What the hell are you smirking at?"

"Oh, come on, Jared. A few little white tips won't hurt you. People dive among them all the time."

"Oh, so you're an expert, too, now. And who says they're small? They certainly got Sinbad's attention."

The beast looked up at mention of his name and growled.

"What do you think, Molly?"

She shrugged. "This site is a desert; it doesn't feel like we're going to find anything here. Let's try a new spot. Joseph's is as good as any. It's shallower there. We can use the hookah. We'd be covering it in the next couple of days anyway."

"Hey, maybe I can go in there," Laura said. "I'm fine on the hookah."

They were all against me.

The difference at Joseph's site was immediately apparent. Fish were everywhere: tiny triggerfish and wrasse near the surface, the ubiquitous parrotfish farther down, and on the bottom, coral trout and groupers, edging out from beneath the reefs for a quick look before vanishing again with a flick of the tail. Further out, just at the edge of my vision, some larger moving shadows that might have been anything.

There was current present, the seaweeds that streamed out in long flowing fans against the reefs and caves giving the illusion of constant motion, so that your glance was continually pulled in all directions. Small crabs scuttled among the growth, and giant clams rested on the bottom, their lids cracked open, closing when we approached, cautiously opening again after we passed by.

Laura swam parallel to me, thirty feet from my side, attached by a long umbilical cord of air to the same platform that supplied me. It rocked gently thirty feet above our heads and moved in our wake, pulled along by the cord wrapped around my wrist. It was a pleasant way to dive, connected by our regulators to the hoses from the hookah and without the cumbersome tanks. It had the freedom of free diving, the sense of total immersion in another world. A school of tuna blasted by so quickly I felt the pulse of the water and then they were gone; a drift of squid moving past in small explosive bursts of energy; a lone octopus changing colour and texture to match the rock he rested on. Farther on an aggressive moray stuck his head out as we passed his lair, and just beyond him a pair of acrobatic mantas circled lazily at the outer edge of my vision.

I swam over and nudged Laura, and she looked up and smiled at their antics. We continued our search, heading northwest for twenty minutes, then moving laterally for a hundred yards and then coming back again, and keeping it up for an hour that passed like mere minutes, so spectacular was the life and scenery that surrounded us. Finally, the signal from Molly, three sharp tugs on the tow line from the hookah, and we swam back up to the surface. There was no sign of Joseph.

"He and Sinbad took off just after you went down," Molly said. "He headed back across to the other side of the lagoon where the *Golden Dragon* is working. He left you a message."

She handed me a folded over piece of paper with the letter J written on the front. I opened it up.

"What's it say?" Laura asked.

"Five," I said.

"Five?"

"Five."

I passed the piece of paper to Laura who looked at it and handed it across to Molly.

"Five what?"

"Good question. Miles, hours, days, take your pick."

"He didn't say anything?" Laura asked.

"Not that I could understand," Molly replied. "He just looked down into the water after you went in, nodded his head and said something to Sinbad, and then the two of them took off."

"Could you make out any words?"

"Well, maybe something like toonie. As in the two-dollar Canadian coin."

Molly and Laura went back down for another run, and then Molly and I for a short one, but we didn't see anything out of the ordinary. There was a brief moment of excitement when Molly spotted a small boat, but it turned out to be a holed fibreglass panga, probably built in the eighties. There was a long piece of chafed rope attached to it and it had likely drifted off from a village, hit a reef, and foundered in a storm. On the last dive we shot some coral trout and a pair of sweetlips and returned to *Arrow*.

Danny and the others arrived a half hour later, and we all repaired to the saloon for drinks.

"Did you see Joseph?" I asked.

"No. We thought he was with you."

"He was for a while, found us a new area to search, and then took off."

"He changed the dive schedule?" Padraic said.

"Yes."

"Why?"

"Well, I think he felt there was nothing to find in the spot where we were looking," I replied.

"Because of his dreams, I suppose," Padraic said. "We have to talk about this. We can't conduct our search on the confused visions of an eccentric old man. We might just as well throw darts at the charts and search where they strike."

I waited for Danny.

"Well, you see," he said, "Joseph is pretty much the head of the family, and we usually follow his advice."

"It's usually pretty good," I added.

Padraic looked at us and shook his head.

"This is not good," he said. "I am a scientist, you know, and while I hope I'm as open as the next fellow to inspiration, I don't think we can operate under these conditions."

"Well, we'll wait and talk it over with Joseph when he comes back," I said, and Danny nodded in agreement.

But Joseph didn't come back, not that evening, and not the next morning either.

CHAPTER 18

"I don't see how you can just sit there and calmly drink coffee," Laura said. "He could have overturned the skiff and be marooned somewhere, he could have drifted out to sea, he might have had a heart attack or worse, and the two of you just sit there staring at that goddam stupid piece of paper."

Danny and I glanced sheepishly at each other but didn't speak. We'd all waited up until midnight in various degrees of anxiety the previous evening, and Danny and I had got to drinking and stayed up even later and become quite merry, much to the disgust of the others.

To make matters worse, a black squall had come up just before dawn, thirty knots of wind with slanting sheets of rain and a quick bumpy sea. It had only lasted half an hour, but that was more than time enough to swamp a small open boat.

"What's the date today?" Danny asked.

"Wednesday the thirtieth," Elinor replied snippily.

She and Molly were not taking it any better than Laura, while Padraic, who had lifted a few with us the night before, was filled with black remorse for speaking badly about Joseph. He had the Irish facility for maudlin guilt and was wallowing in it like a pig in a trough. You might have thought he was Fletcher Christian sending Bligh off to certain death in a small boat.

"You should never have let him go off in that little skiff," Laura said to me. "It wasn't safe for an old man."

"You think maybe that's what he meant, the fifth, he'll be back then?" I asked Danny.

He shrugged. "Maybe."

"Maybe," Laura exploded. "Jesus. I can't believe you two. Where the hell would he go for five days for Christ's sake? There's not a goddam thing within forty miles except the *Golden Dragon*, and I'm pretty sure he didn't go there. Are the pair of you just going to sit there and do nothing?"

Danny shrugged. "Actually, I was thinking about doing some diving with the hookah in the area that Joseph was interested in. Anybody want to come with me?"

"I'll come," I said.

"I'm taking *Tramp* and looking for Joseph," Molly said, jumping up and striding off with an angry glance back at us.

"I'm coming with you," Padraic chimed in, and Elinor and Laura fell in right behind him. In ten minutes they had untied *Tramp* from *Arrow* and left without another word. We watched them disappear around the little island and away into the distance, the four of them stiff-backed with indignation. The sound of the engine gradually faded and died, and we were alone with our thoughts.

"Seeing as all the dive gear is aboard *Tramp*," Danny said, "we might just as well slip a tot of rum in our coffee to help us pass the time."

I held out my cup.

The others returned at dusk, pointedly ignoring Danny and me. They'd picked up a wahoo on their trolling line and barbecued it on the stern of *Tramp* without even offering us a taste. I was fairly deep into the sauce by then, and not all that interested in food in any case, but my feelings were hurt. Danny appeared as if he couldn't have cared less.

"Look," I said to Laura in our cabin late that evening, "you don't understand. Joseph does what he wants to do. He's out there because of his own free will, and I'm not going to insult him by going out and looking for him."

"That is the stupidest thing I've ever heard, Jared. You said yourself he might be a hundred years old. He's obviously in some kind of trouble, perhaps even dead. If he is still alive, he may not remember where he is or why he's out there. Did he even take food or water with him?"

"Maybe not."

"I can't believe you're behaving like this. It's a side of you I never imagined. Some kind of male macho bullshit thing. As for Danny, all that goddam stoicism is absolute horseshit. Joseph needs help, and all the two of you have done since he left is drink and mope around the boat like a pair of spoiled children."

Her face was flushed, her eyes flashing with anger. I hadn't seen her this mad since I'd thrown her overboard that time in Suva.

"But you had all the dive gear aboard *Tramp*," I whinged.

"Get out of my cabin," she snapped, shoving me back with a stiff arm in the chest and slamming the door in my face.

I left and rejoined Danny in the cockpit where he had already spread out pillows and blankets for the two of us, being more of a realist than I was.

They left again at first light, hurling all the dive gear into *Arrow's* cockpit, where we lay wrapped in blankets and hangovers. I thought I heard Laura say, "I hope you fucking drown yourselves," but it might have been Elinor. After they'd gone we emerged and loaded the gear into the dinghy.

It was a perfect day for diving, ten knots of wind and no chop in the shelter of the fringing reef, a cloudless sky, and the underwater visibility excellent. We picked up the buoy where Laura and Molly had finished off on their last run and slipped into the warm waters and began our search.

We worked ruthlessly, punishing ourselves for our transgressions. We used the hookah and covered a hundred-and-fifty-foot-wide strip at a sweep, swimming steadily back and forth like automatons in fixed half-mile runs. We used the handheld GPS receiver we carried as a backup aboard *Arrow* and took surface bearings before each leg to correct for any drift. The positions were accurate to a few feet and made it easier to work the grid. By the end of the day we were exhausted, but reasonably certain we hadn't missed anything. I had a pounding headache by the time we were done.

"Eight hours with hardly a break, and we barely covered one square mile," Danny said when we were back at *Arrow*. "What, that only leaves about three hundred and eighty?"

"Something like that."

"Great. Another five years, and we'll be through."

"Maybe Joseph will turn up something," I said.

It was the first time either of us had mentioned his name all day.

"Yeah. Maybe."

"Are you worried about him?"

"No, not really. He can look after himself better than anyone I know. We went on a fishing trip up to Haida Gwaii in Erin's boat a few years ago, anchored up in a little cove back of the Sound for three weeks. He'd sometimes take the canoe and disappear for days at a time. Never took any supplies with him, and never said where he went. That's Joseph."

"Where do you think he went this time?"

"I don't know. Kavaroa maybe."

I looked at the chart. It was the closest village.

"Christ, that's over forty miles. He'd have to go back out the pass and stay outside for twenty-five miles to get there. That's a lot of swell for a little boat. What makes you think he even knows about it?"

"He looked at all the charts, seemed interested in that area. Asked me about it that first night."

"What did he want to know, whether it had been mentioned in the journals, or if Padraic had searched there when he was on the *Dragon*?"

This was good news. Joseph had a talent for finding out the truth about things. I wouldn't exactly call it magic, more like an educated guess combined with a long lifetime of experience. He had guided *Arrow* through a reef in a gale when there was zero visibility through the foam and spray. It was impossible to see the opening, we were surfing almost non-stop, and he had directed us precisely to that one narrow place where we had that one slim chance of survival. When I had asked Danny about it later, he said Joseph had once told him the Polynesians could detect the presence of an island a thousand miles away by sensing the change in the rhythm of the waves around their canoes. So maybe that was how he had found the shelf. Or maybe not. All I know is that his eyes were closed at the time, and he was holding up a shaman's rattle and chanting.

"He was interested in the actual village. How big, how many people lived there, if it was Christian." Danny paused for a moment. "Things like that."

"Why the hell would he want to know if it was Christian?"

In all the time I'd known the family, I had never heard anyone talk about organized religion, and none of them attended any church. I knew that some of the aunts and uncles had been forced to attend residential schools, those old colonial-based institutions with their enforced religion, harsh discipline, and well-documented cases of racism and sexual abuse. The family's agnosticism didn't surprise me.

"Damned if I know," Danny said.

The others came back late and anchored a few hundred yards off, not even bothering to come across and speak to us. Danny and I spent another night in the cockpit under the stars, although our cabins were both empty.

The following morning Laura came across to pack her things.

"Giving up already?" I said.

I sat on a trunk in our cabin, watching as she indiscriminately stuffed her clothes into bags, not taking the time to fold or sort.

"This whole thing was a big mistake. The treasure search was always a fool's errand, and now we've killed an old man and a helpless dog."

"A helpless dog and a misguided old man," I said. "What a tragedy. And you, of course, are personally to blame for all of it."

She glared at me. "Don't you dare patronize me, you callous asshole. I can't believe I was ever attracted to you."

"It surprised me as well," I said. "How about the others, are they bailing out too?"

"We're going to search for him for another day. There's still one area we haven't checked. Molly thinks it's just possible they drifted up into the northwest corner, through a pass in the reef. After that Daddy and I are going back to Suva aboard *Tramp*. I don't know what Elinor's plans are. She hasn't said."

"Kind of tough on your dad isn't it? Giving up on his dream and five plus years of his life just like that."

"He feels responsible for Joseph. If it wasn't for this crazy search, he wouldn't have been out here."

"Back home where he belongs, nodding by the fire in a rocking chair," I said, "his faithful dog asleep at his feet."

"He'd be alive," she said, her voice shaking.

"Joseph has been choosing his own path for a long time now," I said. "You lot had absolutely nothing at all to do with any of his choices. If you don't understand that, you don't understand anything. But you just take off anyway. The Irish never were celebrated for their staying power. The agreement still stands, we'll let you know if and when we find something."

She looked at me, her face white, then grabbed her bags and ran out of the cabin.

Danny watched her climb down the ladder and into the dinghy, his face impassive. "So, how are things with you and Elinor, then?" I asked.

"I can't really say. It's been a while since we've talked."

Tramp hauled her anchor and took off, everyone on board staring forward as she circled around and passed us on her way out to resume the search.

"Have a nice day," I muttered under my breath as she clanked by.

Neither of us felt much like working, and we spent the day lazing around, reading, and sleeping. In the late afternoon, Danny went out to the reef and pulled some lobster, and I made a punishing curry in fresh coconut milk sauce, and we ate it with the sweat rolling down our faces, washing it down with beer and bananas to relieve the heat.

Afterwards we lay like stuffed pigs, comatose in the cockpit in the falling darkness, waiting for the sound of *Tramp's* engine. It was ten o'clock when she returned, the full moon and steel hull saving her from the coral as Molly brought her in and anchored up. There were lights aboard for a short time and then they were extinguished.

The following morning *Tramp* didn't leave as usual, and Danny and I sat patiently, drinking coffee and overhauling gear while we waited for something to happen. Two of the neoprene suits had small rips where they'd brushed up against the coral, and I cut and glued on patches while Danny put new rubbers on the spear guns. Sitting there abandoned with our plans crashing down around our ears, it seemed a long time since Suva, and the brave faces with which we had left the harbour and sailed north. With all of us diving it was an exciting prospect; with just Danny and me, an impossible task.

It was three o'clock when they came over in *Tramp's* inflatable.

"Look," Padraic said, "we're taking off early tomorrow morning, and I don't want to leave on a sour note. You've been very generous to us, and we don't want to seem ungrateful."

He stood stiffly, red-faced and perspiring in the heat. Molly, standing beside him, nodded her head and smiled.

"You're welcome," I said.

Elinor had gone over by Danny and was talking to him in a low voice, while Laura stood alone at the rail, gazing off into the distance.

"It's just not good, you see," Padraic said. "This last thing, Joseph, it's made me realize how selfish I've been. That poor soul has perished for my vain ambition. It's time now for me to grow up and accept some responsibility for my life. Stop chasing after foolish dreams. You know what I mean." He offered a shamefaced smile.

"You go along with all this growing up and everything?" I asked Laura. "It seems to me the pair of you were a lot more fun when you were chasing the dreams."

She flushed but remained silent.

"What the hell," I said. "I think we should have a couple of drinks for old times' sake. Call it an Irish wake if you will. What do you say Padraic?"

He shot a glance at Laura. "Well, I don't really know about that," he said.

"Oh, go ahead," Laura snapped. "You know you want to."

"It just so happens I brought a little screech with me, just in case," Molly said, reaching into her knapsack. "By the way," she whispered in an aside, "just for the record, nothing happened back there at Minerva. You passed out and we rolled you into the berth. It was all Danny's idea."

"I'll kill the son of a bitch," I said, and Molly just laughed.

By five o'clock everyone was feeling better, and Elinor had coaxed Laura out of the cabin to join us. She sat quietly by the transom, staring off to sea, and after a while I went over and sat down beside her.

"Hello. What's your name, and what's a pretty girl like you doing sitting here all by herself?"

She smiled and put her hand on mine. "I'm afraid I was a little rough with you the other day. I'm sure you miss Joseph very much."

"I will, that's for sure. If he's missing. And I was egging you on, a bit."

"I'm sorry it didn't work out, Jared."

"You mean the famous treasure hunt?"

"Yes, that as well. It would have been wonderful. But us, mainly."

"Maybe you're giving up too easily."

"No, it's time to end it. I've never seen Daddy as dispirited as he was last night. Losing Joseph has taken the heart right out of him. I think he realizes now it's all over that something was bound to happen. You just can't go blindly crashing about forever. We've spent far too long on this already. Not to mention all the money that's gone into it. And for what?"

"You have to admit there were some good times. A bad day sailing is better than a good day at anything else, as the man said."

She smiled. "And therein lies the problem, Jared. I'm just not built that way, I guess. I need some structure in my life. I can't live from day to day like you and Danny."

"What will you do?"

"Go back to London. Run the antique shop again. It's quite a decent living. I'm good at it and I enjoy it, and there is the satisfaction of discovering the unexpected once in a while there as well."

"What about your father? He and Molly seem like an item."

The two of them were sitting on the cabin top, their heads together, deep in conversation.

"She's been good for him. I don't know what their plans are. Molly talked about them maybe chartering out here, but Jesus, look at the boat."

It wasn't snobbery on Laura's part; *Tramp* just wasn't suited to the enterprise. Apart from being possibly the ugliest thing afloat, her layout was too small to fit two couples comfortably, and that was the absolute minimum required to make a go of it in that business.

"Molly used to collect seashells; there is still serious money being paid for some of the rarer ones, although I can't really see Daddy doing that either. I'd hate to see him go back home to the scholastic world. It would be such a comedown for him after all his high hopes. It's a catty, insular bunch, and they enjoy making him feel small. But enough of that, let's talk about you. What are your plans?"

"I think Danny and I will stick with the treasure thing for a while. We haven't given up on that. Neither of us really wants to go home and fish halibut again, and we need to make some money soon. This is probably our best chance."

There was also a part of me that knew there was still a reckoning to come with Summers, and that running from it was not within me. I'd run once, all the way down the West Coast of America and across to the Tuamotus, and I'd vowed then that I wouldn't run again. Something was holding me here, some sense of impending destiny wrapped up with Summers and the *Golden Dragon*, and the lost treasure of Lapérouse. I didn't know what all the answers were yet, I only knew that I couldn't leave until I found them.

"I don't see how you can stay out here after what's happened. I know Joseph was family to you. And look at Danny. How can he be so light-hearted when he's just lost his grandfather? I don't understand either of you. You're both in some kind of weird denial."

Danny was clowning around on the bowsprit. Elinor had her hand over her mouth stifling giggles as he hung by his ankles hooting and then pulled himself effortlessly up again with one hand.

"Maybe not lost, just misplaced for a while," I said, jumping up and pointing towards the tiny sail on the horizon.

It took the little skiff two hours to reach us, the wind blowing directly down from *Arrow* towards her. She heeled over and tacked, heeled and tacked, and as it approached, it became clear there was more than one person aboard.

"It's not him," Padraic said. "A young man in the bow."

"No, I see Sinbad," Laura cried out, "and there's Joseph, steering in the stern."

She turned and threw her arms around me and then realized and drew stiffly back, her face flushing in confusion.

As the boat approached the young man in the bow became a slender, graceful woman of indeterminate age with short cropped hair.

She wore a yellow pareu with a matching band of colour around her neck. Joseph brought the skiff alongside and she stepped up to *Arrow*'s deck with the painter and tied it off. There was a woven frond basket slung over her shoulder.

Joseph followed her aboard and she moved over next to him, her head slightly bowed, her hands clasped in front of her. There was nothing subservient about her, rather a sense of calm self-possession that surrounded her like an aura, and it would have seemed an impertinence to speak to her.

"Joseph, you old bugger, I was sure you were dead," Padraic cried, throwing his arms around him and doing a little dance of joy.

"Where the hell have you been anyway? I was worried sick."

"Kavaroa," Joseph said. He motioned to the woman who hadn't moved from his side. "Liani," he said.

The woman raised her head and smiled. She was quite beautiful, I realized, with pale green eyes tipped up at the corners, and much older than I had first thought.

"Pleased to meet you," Padraic said. "Kavaroa? How in God's name did you get all the way over there? Not that it matters now," he added. "I'm absolutely delighted to see you again. Now I can leave with a light heart."

Joseph murmured to Liani, and she reached into her basket and took out a silver plate and handed it to Padraic, who stared at it in puzzlement.

"How did you get hold of this? I thought it was stowed safe in my bag aboard *Tramp*."

Laura reached across and took it in her hands and turned it over, polishing it with her sleeve.

"Daddy," she whispered, "it's not ours. It's another one from the set. The engraving is much clearer."

Padraic's face was ludicrous in its amazement, his eyes popping, his mouth opening and closing like a landed fish, and then he leaned back and howled in joy and grabbed Joseph and hugged him.

"Oh Jasus," he screeched, "and aren't you the boyo now. And to think I doubted you, oh Jasus, thank the Lord." He turned his head up again and shrilled out a wild banshee scream and began doing a mad jig on the deck.

"Looks like maybe you're back in the treasure business, darlin'," I said in my best Irish accent, and Laura grinned and hugged me again, the tears running down her cheeks.

Danny winked at me over her head and mouthed "I told you so," and a wave of happiness washed over me.

It lasted until Liani took off her necklace and showed it to Padraic, and he bellowed in excitement once more as he saw the gold coin hanging from it.

"Look, Laura, look. It's the same as the one you had. It's French, 1787, the same date; it's too much of a coincidence not to be from the same minting."

He handed it over to her, and she nodded in agreement.

"This is truly marvellous," Padraic said. "It must be somewhere near her village. Surely we can find it now. Perhaps she even knows exactly where it is. Danny, talk to Joseph, we must find out everything. First, though, we must all have a drink. Oh, Jesus, what a day. What a day."

He beamed at us all, waving his arms as if in blessing, so excited he could barely speak coherently. Molly went over and hugged him and then the two of them went jigging around the deck in gleeful abandonment.

Everybody was laughing and talking at once, one big happy family, all the differences resolved in the excitement of discovery and vindication and the prospect of imminent wealth.

I guess I was the only one who noticed that the weathered yellow leather band that carried the gold piece had tiny iridescent scales on the back and sides.

Sea snakes.

A slim hand gently grasped my arm. There was a thick yellow band around it as well, and it was decorated with shark teeth. Big fucking shark teeth.

The woman looked gravely at me and pointed to the necklace around her neck.

"Dadakulaci," she said.

"Sea snakes," I muttered.

She nodded in agreement and fingered the shark teeth.

"Kallee," she said.

"How big?"

She stood on tiptoe and raised her hand high over my head and moved it upwards.

"Very big," she said.

"And the sea snakes? How big are they? Four feet?" I measured the distance with my hands and she shook her head sadly.

"Dadakulaci very big too," she said. She patted my shoulder in apology and then went and rejoined Joseph.

Padraic and Molly came dancing by, and I took the rum from his hand and half filled my glass, and then I took the screech from hers and topped it right up and drank it down like water. It hit me like a sledgehammer.

When the tears stopped, Laura was in front of me with a disapproving frown on her face.

"Take it easy, Jared, it's going to be a long night."

"Is that a promise, ducky?" I wheezed, when I could speak again.

"Now, now, Jared, I know you're just trying to irritate me. I'm sorry I was rude to you and threw you out of the cabin. I have already apologized for that."

"It's not that. Kalee, very big. And dadakulaci. Very big too."

I stood up and waved my hand above her head and looked about for another drink.

"That's it for you, Jared. Not another drop until you sober up. All the drinking you've been doing for the last few days has caught up to you. You're acting very strangely. The effect of alcohol is cumulative, you know. I've seen it with my father. Come, we'll have some coffee."

"Kalee," I muttered, "very big. And dadakulaci very big too."

She grasped me firmly by the hand and led me down to the galley, pouring out two cups of coffee and allowing me a small tot of rum for flavouring. I sipped morosely, listening to the happy voices on deck, while Laura sat quietly, not speaking.

I told her what Liani had said after we had gone into our cabin. About the sharks and sea snakes. And then I told her about Delaney and the tiger sharks of Tukekoto, and the dreams that haunted me still. She wrapped her arms around me and held me tightly, and we lay there together for a very long time, fully clothed, listening to the slap of the waves against the hull and the gentle murmur of the wind in the rigging.

Gradually I noticed another sound, low and scarcely heard at first, but becoming louder and more intrusive all the time.

"What's that?" Laura whispered.

"I don't know," I whispered back, lying there in the dark. But I had the beginnings of a suspicion.

The slow rhythmic thumping grew louder and accelerated in pace. We lay there in silence. I knew my face was turning red. I put my hand on Laura's forehead and felt the heat there as well.

"Jesus, you'd think they could be a little quieter," Laura whispered. "Their cabin is far enough away."

"Actually," I said, "I don't think it's Danny and Elinor."

Laura turned in surprise, her body against mine.

"You're joking."

The noise was louder now and was clearly coming from the little cabin next to ours where Joseph and Liani had retired a short time earlier.

We lay there in the dark, unwilling listeners, Laura still facing me, arms tight around me as the rhythm built, dark and stirring in the hot tropic night.

"Jesus, Laura," I muttered, embarrassed, as she pressed against me. "Look, I can't . . ."

"Oooh," she giggled, her hand slipping down, "dadakulaci, very big too."

CHAPTER 19

The light filtered into the cabin in restless tendrils, swaying across the bulkheads as the boat gently rocked me up from a dreamless sleep. It was the sudden quiet of first light that had awakened me, the creatures of the night fallen silent and the day birds not yet risen. Only the slight familiar creak of *Arrow*'s timbers and the slap of an errant wave against her hull.

Beside me, Laura, tangled in bedclothes, her breath soft against the back of my neck. The sheet had slipped down, exposing the top of a tanned breast. I bent my head and kissed it and her eyes flew open.

"What are you doing?" she asked.

"Kissing your breast."

"I thought so." She smiled and pressed my head against her.

"Did you dream of sharks and sea snakes last night?"

"No. I slept very well, thank you."

"Good. What time did Daddy call the Council of War for?"

"Nine o'clock."

"What time is it now?"

"Seven o'clock."

"Do you want to get up?"

"Actually, I am up," I said.

"Well, well, so you are."

She threw the covers aside and rose up and straddled me, a sleek brown nymph as quick and sly as a seal.

"How's that then, matey?" she whispered.

I groaned, and she gave a small satisfied smile and began slowly rocking back and forth, her head thrown back, crooning softly, a welcome stranger to myself and the woman she used to be.

The crew was sitting around the big table in *Arrow*'s saloon drinking coffee and thumbing through the jumbled sprawl of charts spread out before them. Liani looked up and smiled. She had changed her pareu for a green one patterned in shells that brought out the colour of her eyes. She didn't look Fijian. Her features finer and her cheekbones higher, as if her Polynesian blood were mixed with something more eastern.

Padraic picked up the dividers and outlined a group of atolls on the northwest corner of Viti Levu that extended outward from the main island in a series of rings, the furthest of them beginning fifteen miles from land.

"From what Liani told Joseph, it seems likely that the plate and gold coins came from somewhere in this area, probably from this particular atoll at the far northern end. Teuini."

The lagoon was a circle four miles in diameter, surrounded by small narrow islands and reefs. There were two passes into the lagoon, one of which looked navigable, the other a cluttered invitation to a wrecking.

"We should be able to take *Arrow* and *Tramp* in there easily enough," I said. "It looks straightforward. This main pass is nearly fifty feet wide and thirty deep."

There was a bommie rising nearly to the surface in the middle, but going in dead slow at noon, with the sun directly overhead, it would be safe enough. *Tramp*, with her steel hull and keel, could lead the way. Padraic looked uneasy. "Yes, so it would appear," he said.

The soundings inside the lagoon ran from twelve to twenty fathoms, with a bowl-shaped recession in the middle, the centre of which ran down an additional forty fathoms according to our chart. It was one of the very old British Admiralty hand-drawn ones surveyed by a centuries-dead naval captain, but even so, it was probably accurate. The lats and longs of the old charts nearly always differ from present day GPS readings, but the actual drawing and soundings are usually spot on.

"A hundred twenty feet," Molly said. "That's getting tricky. If we have to go down farther than that, we won't be able to spend much time on the bottom."

"True," Padraic said. "And there may be a deeper uncharted hole at the centre. At least that's what the locals think."

"They don't know for sure?" Laura asked.

"No. But there is a recent upwelling of warmer water in the centre of the lagoon that was first noticed after an earthquake in 2006. There are the usual Pacific legends about Gods who sleep under the waters, and some of the elders felt that one had awakened. Liani said the young people think that a fissure opened up when the earthquake occurred. It hasn't been surveyed since the eruption."

"We can run the boats over the area before anybody goes down; see what the depth sounders show," I said. "Maybe we'll get lucky and find something in the shallower spots. I gather then that the villagers don't know exactly where the plate and coins came from? What makes them think they're from this particular place?"

A silence descended upon the room. I looked at Danny, but he wouldn't meet my eyes. I sensed that matters had been discussed after Laura and I departed the celebration the night before, and there were things we didn't know.

"All right then. Who is going to tell me what the hell is going on here?"

"Well," Danny said, "the villagers are pretty sure the plate and coins came from Teuini Lagoon." He glanced around. Padraic nodded in encouragement.

"And just why is that?" I prompted.

"They were cut out from the belly of a shark," Danny said.

"The belly of a shark. Okay. And the shark was killed in there, obviously. That's a bit of a stretch, though, isn't it? They are pelagic creatures. The shark could have scavenged the coins and plate anywhere. It could be one that just moved into the area from somewhere else. Pretty much anywhere else actually."

Sharks are not particularly bright, and on the thousands of occasions when they have been caught and killed, and their bellies slit open for inspection, an amazingly diverse number of inedible objects have been discovered, ranging from discarded car tires to galvanized garbage can lids. They will ingest anything, and like most fish, shiny objects catch their attention the quickest. The sparkle of a silver plate could well indicate the flashing scales of prey to a hungry shark.

"The plate and coins were still in fairly good condition," Padraic said. "If they had been in a shark's belly for very long, the juices in the digestive tract would have caused more deterioration."

"Possibly, but still pretty thin," I said. "Better than looking around here, I suppose, but still a long shot."

I tried to keep the disappointment out of my voice. I had been hoping for something more definite.

Joseph spoke out abruptly, and Danny sighed and nodded his head in resignation.

"Actually, the shark wasn't killed in that particular lagoon, but they knew it came from there because it was a man eater, and it was so big," he blurted out.

"Oh," I said.

The villagers had first noticed the difference in the lagoon in the late 1990s. The water was changing, becoming greener than before, and very gradually warming. This was evidently the result of a bubbling, evil smelling, dark green eruption of hot water in the centre of the lagoon, which had occurred at the time of the big earthquake. Some of the older people had declared the place should be made tabu, it was cursed. The chief was not a superstitious man, and he and the headman reasoned that the earthquake must have created a vent in the centre of the lagoon rising up from deep within the earth, resulting in the warming of the lagoon waters.

For generations, the villagers had paddled out to the atoll and fished the lagoon, but now, after the warm water upwelling, they saw that all the species were gradually changing and becoming bigger. After a few years, ten-pound lobsters were common, and even the smallest reef fish had doubled in size.

There had always been sharks in the lagoon, and the fishermen from the village had taken the usual precautions, quickly removing speared fish from the water, and changing sites after a couple of kills. There had been an occasional attack over the years, usually when someone became careless, but nothing out of the ordinary. But as the waters gradually warmed, and the sharks grew larger, they became more aggressive, and began to attack the fishermen unprovoked, sometimes as soon as they entered the water. In less than three years, there were a dozen incidents, two of them fatal. That was unheard of. The sharks had become man eaters.

The villagers stayed away from the lagoon, fishing in other locations, and for a time there were no problems. But the attacks suddenly began again, in the adjacent atolls, and in every instance, it was one of the sharks from the lagoon. They knew this because the fish in the lagoon, as well as being larger, had a different cast to their skin, a faint greenish tinge, as if the warm green water had in some strange fashion dyed their flesh while it increased their size.

"It is a fact," Laura said, "that warmer waters tend to breed larger fish. It's been shown to be true in several studies. I learned that when I was boning up on my marine biology prior to attempting to charter *Arrow* in New Zealand." She smiled at me.

Liani had told Joseph that the chief met with the council, and they reluctantly decided to hunt the big fish down and kill them. They didn't feel good about it, they had been brought up in the old traditions where all life had its own part to play, and the sharks were creatures of the sea like themselves, but they felt they had no choice. The great predators had declared war upon them.

The men of the village fashioned a dozen big steel shark hooks and attached them with long lines to bladders made of bunches of coconuts fastened together. Seven men, including the chief's son, went into the lagoon and baited the hooks with fish and threw them over. They thought the sharks would take the bait and eventually tire from fighting the floats and drown or become so weakened from their struggles they could easily be killed.

The sharks were waiting and took the hooks as soon as they hit the water, and before the men could even clear the lines from the boat, they were racing away with them. In the confusion, a line tangled around one of the men and he went over the side, another line was caught up in one of the proas and ripped it off.

In seconds, another two men were in the water and the boat was crippled. The sharks hit the men and became even more excited and began attacking the boat. Nobody knew how many sharks there were. It was a disaster. In all, four men were killed, including the chief's son. It was a miracle that the other three made it back to shore.

"After that, the chief had the passes blocked off," Danny said. "Some of the men had served in the Second World War and worked with explosives, and they dynamited the pass walls, collapsing them inwards. The remaining openings were filled in by hauling in loads of rocks in their outrigger canoes. It took a while, but in the end the lagoon was sealed off. That was ten years ago."

I waited for someone to say something else, but nobody spoke.

"Am I the only one here who thinks that this lagoon sounds incredibly dangerous, and that only a fucking lunatic would go in there, never mind how much gold might be waiting for them? By the way, what kind of sharks were they?"

"There may not be any sharks left in there," Padraic said. "The lagoon has been closed off for ten years, with little or no seawater getting in. It's a closed system, they have heavy rainfall here for five months, and all that freshwater would affect the salinity dramatically. In fact, there may not be much of anything left alive in there."

He hadn't answered my question. But he didn't have to. I already suspected what kind of sharks they were. Tigers.

"But we don't know that for certain," Laura said. I nodded my encouragement. At least one other rational person was present.

"Not for certain, no, although some of the young men did go back to the lagoon three years ago. They set some shark hooks from the shore but didn't catch anything. Then they tried some small hooks, but again nothing. There were no signs of life anywhere. No birds, no fish, nothing. Even the coral reefs are bleached right out."

"But they didn't actually enter the water," Elinor said.

"No, it's forbidden. After the chief's son and the others were killed, the elders made the lagoon tabu. The young men who went there three years ago were punished, and nobody has been back since."

Nobody spoke for a while.

"Look," I said. "I'd like to recover that treasure as much as anybody. God knows, I could use the money. But there's no way we can do this from small boats, even if the lagoon is safe to dive in. It's impossible."

Molly nodded in agreement. "Yes. We need the boats for our dive base. It would be too dangerous trying to dive out of the inflatables. Especially the deeper dives. Too much backup required."

"Liani says her people might be agreeable to opening a pass for us so we could take *Arrow* and *Tramp* in," Padraic said. "It wouldn't be all that difficult, just a narrow channel a little wider than the boats. Maybe take a week or so, they said."

"Why would they want to do that?"

"Joseph spent a long time in discussions with the chief. It was a real hardship for the village when they lost the fishing. That lagoon was an important source of food for them. Joseph told him we might be able to lift the curse, give them back Teuini." Danny shrugged.

"And just how are we going to do that?"

"He didn't elaborate."

Joseph sat silently, his unlit pipe clamped in his mouth, and his eyes half closed, a million miles away. I knew the old bugger was taking note of every word.

"Just how big were those sharks anyway?"

"They varied somewhat, of course, but usually around twelve feet. The last one they killed before they blocked the pass was sixteen feet long."

"Sixteen feet! My God, that fucker would weigh over fifteen hundred pounds. A man wouldn't have a prayer. And that was ten years ago. Who knows how big they are now."

"Yes, I can see they will present some problems," Padraic said. "But I think with thought and preparation we can overcome them. They might all be dead now, but we must certainly prepare for this as if they are still present. Perhaps a steel cage on a winch to search at first, until we are certain that there are none present, some shark repellents, maybe an anchored net to surround the area if we locate Lapérouse's boat. That's what they use to protect the beaches in parts of Australia and South Africa. They've been very successful."

Of course, Padraic wasn't the one who had to go down there. My understanding was that the great majority of sharks weren't man eaters, and the nets were a mild annoyance that would keep them away, or sometimes even entrap them. They weren't designed to keep out a one ton monster that was actively trying to get through and devour something on the other side.

"And then there's the sea snakes," I said. "And just how big were those mothers?"

"Six feet seemed to be the standard."

"Ten years ago."

"Right."

"And their girth?"

"About as big around as your arm."

I gazed down at my arms. "Marvellous. That would certainly make their mouths big enough to bite a man. I seem to recall that their venom is among the most poisonous in the world. Correct, Professor Laura?"

My sarcasm didn't bother her. "Yes, I believe that's right. There are antidotes available, cultured from horses that have been injected with mild doses and developed antibodies."

"But you have to know the species, right?" I'd done some research on snakes when I first came to the South Pacific. Know thine enemies.

"That's right. The good news is that the sharks and snakes are enemies, according to Liani," Laura said. "The sharks feed aggressively upon them."

"Hmm. And just how aggressive are those snakes, then?"

Silence.

"That's what I thought," I said. "Tell me about the treasure again, Padraic. I really need some motivation here."

"Lapérouse's ship was the *Boussole*," Padraic said obligingly, "and according to the testimony of a French crewman aboard the vessel *Esperance*, three heavy chests were loaded aboard her one stormy night in 1787. They were, I think, the count's share of the family estate, which had been moved out of France to escape the French revolution."

Everybody sat in rapt attention, even Joseph.

"I calculate the estate to have been worth in the neighbourhood of, oh, say," his eyes closed as he calculated. "This is a hell of a thirsty tale," he said.

Joseph reached into his bag and pulled out a bottle of Laphroaig and handed it across to him. Padraic poured a tot into his cup.

"Thank you. Now, where was I?"

"The value of the treasure, dear," Molly said.

"Right, right." He took a long meditative sip.

"In modern-day money, five million pounds," he said.

There was a long collective exhalation from around the table. At that point you could have showed them live videos of forty-foot great whites and sixty-foot sea serpents in mortal combat, and nobody would have given a rat's ass. It looked like we were heading to Teuini Atoll.

I went into the galley and added rum to my coffee and tried to recall everything I could about electric shock fields and big nets and the latest shark defence technology. I could think of no defence against the sea snakes. It seemed to me they would be smarter, more cunning than the primordial shark. Essentially a six-foot poisonous muscle with a brain.

"Well, what do you think about all this, Jared? Isn't it terrific? Don't tell me you aren't at least a little bit excited." Danny, a big smile on his face, ready as always for anything.

Speaking of six-foot muscles with small brains, I thought sourly.

"The day I don't get excited about sixteen-foot sharks and six-foot poisonous sea snakes is the day you can sew me up in a shroud, put the last stitch in my nose, and drop me over the side, old son. I'll be stone cold fucking dead."

"They're probably all gone by now, like Padraic said. It makes sense. Most marine animals can't tolerate much change in their environment. Decreased salinity and increased temperatures; it sounds like it's killed the reefs, could have killed them all off as well."

"It's possible. But what about Joseph's dreams? Sharks and snakes. Have you ever known his visions to be wrong?"

Danny's face sobered. "Right. I'd forgotten about those."

Joseph heard his name and came over and stood beside us, his face impassive.

"Ask him," I said.

"Ah, never mind," Danny said. "I don't want to spoil a good day."

He went back to the table and sat down beside Elinor and jumped back into the discussion about how everyone would spend their money. I heard a lot of talk about big boats and fast cars.

I stared at Joseph until he looked up and put my hands together with the thumbs up and wiggled them, just as he had done that day in the water. I raised my eyebrows.

"Well?" I said.

He looked at me without expression and went out into the cockpit and stood staring northwards, towards Teuini Atoll and the future. Sinbad crept up and leaned his head against his knees and whined.

My feelings exactly.

I looked off down the channel and there, glimpsed faintly through the shimmering haze, I saw the towering masts of the *Golden Dragon*. They had moved and re-anchored closer during the night. In the general celebration of Joseph's return, no one had mentioned the threat she posed to our plans. I wondered if there was a way she might be removed from the equation.

On a sudden impulse, I jumped into the little skiff, raised the main, and set off down the channel towards her. There was a loud splash as Sinbad rose up from the deck and leaped into the water after me. There was scant wind and he soon caught up, the big furred feet efficient paddles as he ploughed through the water. He clamped his teeth on the transom and streamed his body out behind, effectively cutting my speed in half. I wasn't about to argue with him, and we proceeded at a sedate knot and a half towards the far end of the lagoon.

The *Dragon*'s inflatables were less than three miles away, working in a triangle spaced a half mile apart, international diver down flags raised at their sterns. They'd covered close to thirty square miles since we'd last encountered them a week earlier, and it brought home to me once more just how amateurish our operation really was.

I steered towards the nearest Ribby and dropped the sail. Sinbad climbed aboard and shook himself before settling in the bow. As I arrived alongside, a diver broke the surface; the young German who had fought Phueng, the scars on his face where she had slashed him still visible when he raised his mask. He stared at me but didn't speak.

"Hello," I said. "Remember me?"

"I remember," he said.

"How are you doing, found anything yet?"

"You'd have to ask the captain or Mr. Waverly. I don't get paid to gossip."

"Is Waverly aboard?"

"I don't know."

A path of bubbles rose up beside him as his diving partner ascended to the surface. It was the big bald man with the pot belly and dead eyes. Turk pulled himself over the side of the inflatable with a quick flex of his arms and spat out his mouthpiece.

"What the fuck do you want?" he growled.

"Nothing from you," I said.

I raised the sail again and moved off. When I was twenty yards away, the young German called after me.

"Kane. Thanks," he said.

The *Golden Dragon* was anchored behind a small island a mile along. Although I knew her dimensions to the foot from all the articles I'd read, up close she still overwhelmed me. It was not just her size, but the forbidding aspect she presented as well, with steep cambered sides and black tinted port lights which reflected back the sun and gave no glimpse of the interior. It all made her seem even bigger.

Most sailboats present a view of their decks as you approach, but the *Dragon*'s freeboard was so high that there was none. It was like approaching a cliff. No tumblehome and no curve, just a long, angular golden yellow hull that impressed with its commitment to speed and power and gave no hint of the luxury contained within.

The large door centred in her transom dropped outward from the top on hydraulic pistons, creating an extra deck and revealing the huge storage area and workshop that ran forward sixty feet to the steel bulkhead that sealed it off from the rest of the boat. You could have fit

Arrow inside with her mast down. The compartment was filled with sea sleds, diving tanks, air compressors, diving helmets, windsurfers, and a long workbench above which were cabinets filled with tools. Built into the far corner was a decompression tank covered in gleaming gauges and valves, while adjacent to the transom door was a stainless-steel crane for loading and unloading equipment, and chocks alongside where the boats were stored.

I tacked alongside and tied off on the floating dock that connected to the gangway. As I stepped on the first tread a bell sounded on board, and moments later a burly steward appeared at the top of the stairs and barred the way.

"I'd like to speak with Robin Waverly," I said.

"Stay here."

He disappeared from sight and I waited, conscious of the low hum of machinery coming from within the hull. Sinbad's ears rose, and he uttered a low growl and sprang out of the skiff to stand beside me.

"No, boy. Stay."

I grabbed him by the chain around his neck and attempted to put him back in the boat. He lowered his head and growled more deeply, then lifted his goatish eyes and stared into mine, and the growl became more keening.

I released his collar.

The steward returned and stood by the top of the stairs. "Follow me."

I started up the companionway, Sinbad at my heels.

"The dog stays here."

"Okay. You tell him."

The steward took a step towards Sinbad who snaked his head towards him and crouched low and whined eagerly. The man turned abruptly and led me forward.

"Good call," I said.

Waverly sat in a deck chair reading a newspaper. He wore only brief swim trunks, the muscles in his powerful body flexing as he jumped up and shook my hand.

"Jared. How nice of you to drop in. You don't mind if I call you Jared, do you? And you must call me Robin."

His teeth gleamed in his well-trimmed beard, and his eyes shone with pleasure. You would have thought my visit was the best thing that had happened to him in a month of Sundays.

"I love your dog. Mean looking bugger, isn't he? You ever fight him? Hard to tell how they'll do till they're actually in the ring. Sometimes the smaller ones make the best fighters. Not the size of the dog in the fight, but the size of the fight in the dog, as they say."

He spoke rapidly, a pleasant smile on his face.

"And this, of course, is Phueng. I'm sure you remember her. She has to leave now, but she wanted to stay a minute to say hello."

The little Asian girl was stretched out naked on a lounge in the sun, her body glistening with oil. She stood up and approached me, the glowing amber eyes staring into mine. She reached out her hand, and when I clumsily went to shake it she moved it up to my neck and ran those long razor-sharp nails under my chin. She kept them there for a long moment, then drew them across my throat with a little sigh.

I stood motionless as a statue, and all the while she gazed at me without expression, and then she dropped her hand and put on the robe Waverly was holding for her and glided away. The sweat stood out on my body.

Waverly chuckled. "Cute little devil, isn't she? I saw Phueng doing her thing in a Bangkok cage ring a few years back and had to have her. Her name means bee in English, by the way. Can I get you something to drink? You look like you could use one. I'm having Talisker on the rocks."

"That will be fine." I hoped my voice wasn't shaking. The lethal woman terrified me.

He motioned to the steward and we sat without speaking until the man returned with the drinks, set them down on the little table, and left.

"How is the treasure hunt going?" Waverly asked.

"Not very well, actually. That's what I wanted to speak to you about. I think we're in over our heads. I'm trying to talk the others into quitting before somebody gets hurt or maybe even killed. We don't have the experience or the resources, and frankly, I think our search is futile."

"Well, well. You disappoint me, Jared. I didn't take you for a quitter."

"The odds are too poor for us. The chances of finding anything aren't good enough to warrant the risk. I'm willing to come to an agreement with you. I'll give you a copy of the journals in return for twenty percent of the treasure, if you locate it. They haven't been any use to us, but there are a lot of locations specified in there that we will never get to look at. Nowhere near the time or resources. One of them could be the right one."

"The notorious journals, eh? And you're just going to hand them over to us. Well. I must say, that sounds like an interesting offer. We certainly haven't had any luck so far, and the crew is getting a bit restless about our tight work schedule." He grinned. "Not that their complaints matter a tinker's damn to me. But we are ready for some new grounds. I'm going to give this treasure hunt another couple of weeks, and then we're off to Tahiti for the Bastille Day celebrations. There's a race there I want to win."

He paused, his face wrinkled in thought. "Twenty percent if we find anything, you say. I suppose that's fair under the circumstances. Okay, I agree. I'll get Summers to run you back and pick up the journals. I'll have them returned first thing tomorrow morning."

"Agreed. I'll give your man a list of where we've already searched with the GPS settings. Not Summers, though, someone else."

He smiled. "Ah, yes. I'd forgotten your little altercation. I'm afraid Summers doesn't forgive and forget as quickly as me either. But then, I'm a businessman."

His mocking smile said that Summers and I were fools.

He rang for the steward who took me to the rear deck where a crewman had lowered the launch into the water. I took a last look around and then I boarded, and we returned to *Arrow*, the two of us in the launch towing the sailboat with Sinbad sitting in it behind us, his fur all standing straight out in the wind and a foolish, mindless grin on his face.

Padraic and the others were indignant when I told them about the journals, but it wasn't their decision to make. Their safety was my responsibility, whether they liked it or not. I thought Laura might be the most upset of them all, but she just shrugged and said that any deal that kept the assholes on the *Golden Dragon* off our backs for the duration was fine with her. It seemed she had exorcised her personal devils.

The journals were returned early the following morning just as Waverly had promised, and an hour later we hauled our anchors and headed south for Suva to ready our boats for the dangerous search of Teuini Lagoon.

CHAPTER 20

The sun vanished ten miles north of Suva, the sky gradually darkening as we entered the rain shadow on the eastern side of Viti Levu. By the time we reached the pass, we were bucking through driving sheets of rain in a sudden black squall that lasted until we anchored in the main harbour. Fifteen minutes later, the sun was out again, steam rising from the decks in feathery tendrils that slowly dissipated in the dying wind. In another half hour the breeze would disappear once more, and the air, so clean and fresh now, would become hot and humid, and the pressures start to build again and a new cycle begin.

At the moment it was serenely beautiful, the buildings sparkling in the sunlight, the streets washed clean, the emerald mountains behind the city framing the scene in an unearthly shade of green. North of us a hard chine steel ketch from Germany with the yellow Q flag raised at her spreaders ran into the quarantine area and anchored. Threading their way through the anchored fleet were the locals on their way in to the markets, their canoes filled with fish, family, and produce, all of it stacked up in the air and rafted out onto the outriggers as they sculled their way into town.

"Let's go ashore," Laura said.

We took the skiff off the foredeck and lowered it into the water. Sinbad, who'd initially displayed interest, sank back down on his haunches as we bolted the motor onto the transom. He was the purest sailor of us all. After a moment's indecision he soared over the lifelines and swam off towards the mangrove covered beaches that framed the west side of the harbour. We might not see him again for a week.

The outboard sputtered to life and we headed off at a sedate three knots. As we passed *Tramp*'s stern, Joseph raised his hand and he and Liani joined us for the trip ashore. We tied up at Prince's Landing alongside a dozen other tenders from yachts anchored out in the harbour, climbed the stone steps, and were immersed in the teeming streets of Suva. Liani took Joseph's arm, and they moved off down a side street on some business of their own.

In the first block we received a dozen enthusiastic "Bulas," the bestowers of the greeting looking into our eyes and smiling, so that we felt we had not merely received a traditional greeting but made personal contact with another human being. Their culture is the culture of hospitality, and it's claimed the Fijians never forget a person they have met. They have a deep respect for the individual human spirit and will beggar themselves for a casual acquaintance.

Most businesses in Suva are owned and operated by Indians, many of them descendants of the immigrants brought in to work the cane fields by the British in the 1800s. As soon as they took you for a tourist, they descended upon you in a friendly swarm, using everything short of physical force to lure you into their shops. Agents from other stores were nearby, and if you entered a shop and picked up a specific item, one of them would sidle alongside and whisper that you could get a better price down the street. Everybody had "the best price" and we heard the expression a dozen times in the first hundred yards in the good humoured battle for our trade.

The cleverest hustlers were the Fijian street carvers who made the wooden masks, and after a bit of friendly chatter introduced themselves and asked your name. Seconds after you told them, it was carved into the piece they were holding, and it became that much harder to refuse the purchase. The cunning devil who assaulted us carved both our names together, knowing full well that a refusal to purchase by me was now a denial of Laura as well.

"It's up to you, Jared," she said, but of course it wasn't, really. I gave the man half of what he asked, and it was still too much, but the smile on her face made it worthwhile.

We moved slowly along, sampling samosas filled with curry and hot peppers from the street vendors, then stopping at an outdoor café for a beer to cool our mouths before drifting on again without direction, caught up in the constantly shifting rainbow of bright saris and pareus.

The day was becoming hot, and we passed into the covered city market where hundreds of vendors sat on mats woven from coconut fronds, or stood behind long counters, their goods displayed in pyramids before them: bananas, coconuts, cassava, and dalo, the staples of the Fijian diet, as well as breadfruit, jakfruit, mangoes, papayas, avocadoes, duruka, and a dozen other fruits and vegetables that we couldn't put a name to.

In addition to the fruits and vegetables, there were fish, hung up in strings or laid out on ice, with one giant shark on a plank being sold by the piece, the customer tracing an imaginary line and the seller bisecting it with a machete. Salt and freshwater crabs, lobster, clams, squids, cuttlefish, and octopi, a half dozen varieties of shrimp, and one sad tethered turtle rounded out the selection.

We moved slowly along the aisles, stopping to buy a dozen eggs here, some dorado steaks there, a palm frond basket filled with limes farther along. Laura dickered over the price of a pair of squabbling honeyeaters, the little Fijian cousins of the hummingbirds, then lifted the cage high in the air and released them, to the amazement of the vendor. They swooped away and were lost from sight, faster than the eye could follow.

We visited the large stall where replicas of the old tools used by cannibals were sold, gruesome implements with names like brain basher and skull crusher. Specific eating implements for every part of the human body were on display, ranging from delicate long-handled spoons for scooping out the contents of the brain pan to specially shaped forks for digging out the meat between the finger bones. It was hard to reconcile this grisly history with the friendly smiling faces around us.

Laura passed on cannibalism and selected an old conch shell trumpet for Padraic and a pareu for herself, while I couldn't resist a five-foot carved warrior's club with a shark's tooth imbedded in the end. It would look good hung over *Arrow*'s chart table, and might come in handy someday. We were loaded down by now, and after purchasing kava root for the welcoming ceremonies in Kavoa Bay, we retraced our steps to the pier and returned to *Arrow*.

The following morning, we decided to sacrifice caution for convenience and tie up at the Royal Suva Yacht Club while refitting. Waverly had said he was going to continue his search for another two weeks before departing for the race in Tahiti. It would make sense for him to check out at Levuka rather than run the extra miles back down to Suva. In any case, as Padraic had declaimed, "We couldn't carry on a proper search if we lived in fear and trembling of the *Golden Dragon*'s shadow."

We rented space in the boatyard opposite the club and set up a small workshop where Danny and Molly worked on *Tramp*'s diving cage. They'd decided on a unit six feet square by seven high, big enough for two occupants in full dive gear, with half-inch steel rods spaced four inches apart for the top and sides, and two inches apart for the floor. It would have an inward opening door and hold two divers comfortably, four in a pinch.

A roll of steel mesh was fastened on the outside of the cage for protection from sea snakes. We had a heated discussion about what size the mesh should be and finally decided on two inches. Anything smaller would restrict our vision and create extra resistance when towed.

It took Danny and Molly a week to finish the cage and fashion a crude crane that would attach alongside *Tramp*'s pilothouse and swing out to raise and lower it. The steel cable on the crane drum would be powered by the same hydraulic system that worked the anchor.

With *Tramp*, you didn't have to worry about alterations or additions corrupting her overall design as she really didn't have one. It was just a matter of grinding down to clean metal and welding on the new bits, whether it was a crane or the eight-foot steel ladder that extended down to the water underneath it. But under that ugly exterior was a useful boat, one that sailed reasonably well when the wind was up and was virtually indestructible. Her hull was constructed of three-eighths steel plating, and God alone knew what she weighed, but she had a big Cat engine that pushed her along at a steady five knots, and her six-hundred-gallon fuel tanks gave her a range of five hundred miles under power. Her transmission was noisy, and it took an unreasonably long time to get her in and out of gear, but it always engaged in the end.

Molly loved the boat with a passion, and with Padraic's help had made the interior homey, although it would never be charming. They had cleared ten years' worth of junk out of the forecastle and revealed a pair of hinged pipe berths that allowed them guest space should the occasion arise and served as a study in the interim. When Molly wasn't working with Danny, she and Padraic pored over the charts for the lagoon, plotting *Tramp*'s runs.

It became apparent during our first underwater test that there were flaws in the design of our cage. The mesh created a lot of drag in the water, and at speeds over half a knot, the cage trailed out behind *Tramp* at a dangerous angle and spun like a whirling dervish. We attempted to solve the problem by installing a massive swivel purchased from a heavy equipment dealer; that slowed the dangerous careening down, but in the end we had to attach a makeshift rudder on the back of the cage. We found that by hinging the rudder and adding a crude tiller we could manoeuvre the cage from side to side, the amount of travel dependent on the depth.

When we'd finished with the modifications, *Tramp* could do one knot safely when the cage was in the water. That would allow us to make our trial passes across the lagoon, and check for sharks and snakes. God willing there would be none, and we would only require the cage as a base to dive out of if and when we found Lapérouse's boat.

"And for raising up the gold," Padraic added.

While Danny and Molly laboured in the workshop, Elinor and Laura did some research. They took Liani's neckband to the museum of natural history and confirmed that it was the skin of the highly poisonous sea krait. The books at the library weren't specific on habitat, so they posed a hypothetical question to the government department of marine biology. They were told that while sharks probably couldn't survive very long in an environment with increased temperature and lessened salinity, sea kraits spent time ashore and were often found in the mouths of rivers and sometimes a ways up them, so the freshwater would likely pose no problems for them. Although the department head couldn't predict the effect of increased water temperatures on the vipers, he pointed out that it was a well-known fact that snakes sought out heat, and if he had to guess, they would probably enjoy it.

"Marvellous," Danny said when the girls had finished their report. "So what do we do now?"

"We've located some snake antivenom at the hospital in New Caledonia. They're flying it in for us; it will be here in a couple of days. It isn't specifically for sea kraits, but they think it will work." Elinor shrugged. "Apart from that there's not much we can do."

Padraic noticed my glum expression.

"Never mind, lad," he said, "if the worst comes to the worst we can pray to my namesake, good Saint Patrick, to drive out the snakes as he did in Ireland. There's always a shortage of policemen somewhere."

Padraic and I dealt with the problems of communication between the divers in the cage and *Tramp*. Underwater radios were prohibitively expensive, as were the video display cameras, remote terminals, and all the other high-tech items that would have made everything so much safer.

We settled on waterproof buzzers in the cage and aboard *Tramp* that plugged into a wire, which would pay out and retract with the steel cable that raised and lowered the cage. With senders at both ends we set up a basic series of signals that could be relayed back and forth. One buzz for up, two for down, three for stop, and so on. It was not a giant leap forward from two cans and a piece of waxed string, but the best we could achieve under the circumstances. We brushed up on our Morse code in the event we needed to send more complex messages.

The one thing we didn't compromise on was our diving gear. We took it into the big shop run by Carl, an expatriate Aussie, and had him check it all over and renew seals and replace parts that had seen better days. We bought extra spears and cable for the big three-band spear guns, and Carl directed us to an ex-diver who had some of the old bang sticks that were once used as a defence against sharks. These were six-foot rods with explosive charges at the tips which detonated on impact. The charges were powerful, capable of stunning a large shark or killing a medium-sized one.

The drawback is that many experts think that concussion in the water attracts more sharks, and if you draw blood there is the added danger of a feeding frenzy. We decided they could prove useful in an emergency and bought all that he had.

By the time everything was ready, it was July. Elinor phoned the yacht club in Tahiti, and they confirmed that the *Golden Dragon* was registered for the regatta beginning on the fourteenth, although she had not yet arrived for the ten-day event. We loaded the cage aboard *Tramp* and took on supplies for ten weeks. By then it would be nearing time to head off for New Zealand to escape the hurricane season. If we hadn't located the treasure by then, we never would.

Molly and I went to Customs and Immigration and filled out boat clearances, telling the authorities that we were heading to the

Mamanucas for two months. They were courteous and friendly as always, and we left their office mildly ashamed of our falsehoods.

When we returned to the boat, we decided to have a final night ashore and the eight of us went up to the yacht club for dinner. It was bustling with the usual mix of offshore cruisers in cut-offs and jelly sandals interspersed with a smattering of locals stopping in for a drink on their way home after work, and the air was filled with a dozen different accents.

A table of rowdy Americans sat behind us, deeply tanned and engaged in a jeering debate with some Kiwis about the next America's Cup; alongside them the ubiquitous English, playing bridge as if they were the only ones present, while in the far corner a family of new arrivals sprawled out on the couches surrounded by a sheaf of mail. Waitresses in flowered pareus with frangipani woven into their hair darted through the room like brightly coloured birds, carrying plates of food and pitchers of beer.

It was all so damned normal, a scene repeated at any one of a dozen yacht clubs scattered throughout the South Pacific. People with similar interests planning cruises together, giving freely of advice and reminiscing about trips past and pursuing a good time in a congenial atmosphere. In spite of differences in country and tradition, there was a sameness about them, an athleticism, an openness, and sense of adventure that was common to them all.

And there we were, sitting quietly in the middle of it all as if we really belonged to the scene, as if we were not about to engage in an insane search for lost treasure in an area infested with killer sharks and poisonous snakes, with an egocentric madman in a two hundred-million-dollar giant steel sailboat as a rival.

What the hell. I took my glass of beer and drained it and poured myself another from one of the pitchers. You couldn't say life was uninteresting. Our table was the subject of curious glances from many, and as I surveyed my partners, I couldn't blame them.

To my right, our spiritual leader, Joseph, dressed in the fisherman's checked flannels and brown knitted wool pants that were all he ever wore, his long grey hair pulled back in a headband, a glass of single malt in his hand. His collar was open, and in the sunken ridge of his neck was visible the twisted thong that held the knife that was ages older than he was. Sometimes he looked terribly old, his body thin and wasted, his face seamed, and then the eyes snapped upon you, and he lost decades in a second as you felt the force and intelligence of that gaze. He sat stiffly erect as always, his eyes sweeping the room when he wasn't talking to Liani.

She sat beside him, leaning in to whisper in his ear, clad in a brilliant green pareu, perhaps the most beautiful woman in the room, and certainly one of the oldest. She remained a complete mystery to me. From what Danny had said, it appeared that she didn't live in Kavaroa village but was a visitor there. He didn't know how long she had been there, where she had come from, or why she had chosen to leave with Joseph. There was an old faded scar running from just below her ear down past those high cheekbones to the base of her throat that gleamed suddenly in the light as she threw back her head and laughed. Next to her sat Danny, smiling and talking when he wasn't drinking, a big brown dangerous man who looked almost soft, and God help the person who thought he was. He had codes of loyalty and honour branded into his genes that would have shamed a Samurai, and he was the best friend I would ever have. There was a bond of prescience between us, born of our days in prison, and feeling my gaze upon him he looked up and winked.

Alongside him, Elinor, the patrician blond Englishwoman who was the last person in the world you would pick for his paramour, her accent a source of constant though silent amusement to us all, smart as a whip; and then the erudite Professor Padraic, that stage Irishman cradling his beloved Bushmills, the most learned and most naive of us all. But sometimes he showed a hard layer which surprised me, and it was his determination to succeed which drove us all.

Sitting next to him was Molly, whose vocabulary would shame an Irish navvy, her heart as big as her chest. She was the most carefree of us all, moving foursquare through the world in pursuit of what she desired, always open to a good time, and the least likely to become depressed when things went badly.

And lastly, sitting tight alongside me, the dark-haired woman whose smile could stop my heart. Laura. She leaned close and murmured in my ear.

"Easy on the drinking, Jared. It's a long night and a long day following."

We still had a few things to work out between us though.

We tried hard, and there were lots of drinks and laughs, and the food was excellent and the company better, but it was all a bit forced and hollow, and by eleven o'clock we were back aboard the boats.

At first light the following morning we sailed out the pass and headed north to Kavaroa village.

We travelled non-stop in settled weather and twelve-knot trades, keeping well outside the reefs and going the long way around, standing four-hour watches in couples. Joseph and Liani had moved aboard *Tramp* for the overnighter. As *Arrow* pulled away in the light air, we kept contact on the VHF, using the false names we had agreed upon earlier.

It was a beautiful time, night sailing under a waxing moon, the rays so bright you could read by them, and *Arrow* moving tranquilly along under just the main and working jib. The wind was constant on the aft quarter, and for twenty-four hours we never changed a sail or touched a sheet, eating up the effortless miles, sitting together in the cockpit, watching the stars rise up on the horizon and march across the vast curved canopy of sky. No sounds save for the hiss of *Arrow*'s bow slicing through the water, the occasional flap of a sail as we tilted to a swell and the mast outran the wind, the skitter of a flying fish across the decks and the scrabble of Sinbad's feet as he tracked it down.

It was a time for talking, but Laura and I sat silent in the cockpit wrapped in the blanket of night as the hours flew by, content in our company, and near resentful when the change of watch came up and stood us down. I tried to speak of afterwards once, but Laura put her finger on my lips and said not to worry, things would look after themselves, and too many plans for the future had a habit of stealing the present.

We didn't see any traffic on our journey and the passage was uneventful. It was midday when we pulled into the bay in front of the village, and nearing dusk when *Tramp* dropped anchor alongside. The following morning, we took the kava and presents we had brought and went ashore to make Sevusevu with the chiefs and elders.

CHAPTER 21

Kavaroa village nestled in a small bay on the north side of Undu Peninsula and was encircled by a fringing reef that afforded protection from all but the very worst of the winter storms that swept through in hurricane season. Four years earlier, the settlement had been virtually destroyed by strong winds and rising waters, forcing the villagers to move out and seek shelter in higher ground for the three days the tempest blew. When the storm abated, they moved back and rebuilt on the exact same sites, as generations had done before them. It was *Yavu*, the place one comes from, the inherited house site in the village.

A half mile of sandy shoreline fronted the village with clumps of mangroves encroaching on each end before they terminated against the rocky bluffs that bracketed the cove. A dozen bures were scattered along the crescent of the bay and as many again sheltered among the palm trees along the ridge sloping up and back from the sea.

A small group of old men emerged from the largest bure and walked down to greet us as we landed our dinghies. A tall broad-shouldered man with grizzled hair led them. He supported himself on a curiously formed cane as he limped towards us. It was carved in the shape of a pair of intertwined snakes whose juxtaposed heads formed the handle. Part of his right foot was missing, and the remainder was badly scarred.

The headman spoke briefly to Liani and welcomed us to his village in slow and halting English. He accepted the presents of kava and tobacco and led us to the largest of the bures where we sat cross-legged on woven mats while the root was mixed with water and ground into a paste with a stone pestle stained and darkened with age. In the old days it would have been chewed by young virgins and regurgitated into the bowl.

When the preparations were complete, the headman passed the muddy liquid around the circle in an ornate wooden cup and we each drank and clapped in turn as the ritual greetings were performed. It was a slow process, repeated several times over the course of an hour. At the end I felt a tingling in my gums and a modest sensation of well-being, comparable to the effects of a couple of glasses of wine. It affected individuals differently; Padraic's normally ruddy colour had deepened significantly, while Elinor seemed to be striving desperately against an attack of the giggles. When the kava was finished, the headman began to speak in a slow and deliberate voice.

His name was Takli and he was seventy-two years old and had lived in the village all his life. His ancestors were great warriors who had fought many battles along the coast and had once controlled a fifty-mile strip of the territory bordered by the Great Sea Reef, but now his village had only the bay and the atolls to harvest for food. It had been agreed to by his father's father, and the days of war were now past.

His voice was low and wavering, and as he recounted his people's history it rose and fell in a dirge-like song punctuated by the grunts and handclaps and murmured assents of his acolytes. Many of the men were smoking and the air grew thick and stifling.

He spoke about the days when his clan had been rich and powerful, but now they had fallen on bad times. It seemed a well-rehearsed complaint, and I fought to keep my eyes open as his voice droned on. Apparently we were to be given the complete history of his people. I stared up at the woven roof and thought that a hundred years earlier the scene would have been almost the same, nothing had really changed here. Danny nudged me, and I realized the chief was speaking about Teuini Lagoon.

He said that since the green water had come, the catches had been failing everywhere, as if the sea were punishing them for abandoning their traditional grounds. The sea were the supplier of life, a God, and by caging a part of it when they blocked the passes perhaps they were incurring his wrath. It was a difficult choice; they had lost too many people already to the evil creatures of the lagoon. They were not like other sharks and snakes. He fell silent, absently rubbing his damaged foot, as if recalling some distant pain.

He had thought long and hard about what to do, and when Joseph appeared in the little boat and spoke about the lost ship, it was a sign. He commissioned a work party and with the blessing of the elders they set about reopening the entrance into the lagoon. They erected two large walls of logs lashed together and pounded into the sand on each end of the main channel. When they were finished, they had isolated the pass and could safely work at clearing out the rocks that blocked it. The project had taken them three weeks. When they completed their task, they returned to the village, leaving the palisades in place until we arrived. By granting us access to the forbidden area but keeping away themselves, they would not be offending their Gods. It was our destiny.

"I get it," Danny murmured to me, "we're the ones the Gods will be pissed at."

The headman concluded by announcing a feast in our honour that evening and said that the cooking fires would be lit at dusk. He bowed his head to us, and the audience was over. We thanked him and returned to the boats, passing through a crowd of people who had gathered to greet us. Many of them were mutilated.

I'd seen victims of shark attacks in Fijian villages before, but never on the scale displayed here. There were a dozen people missing limbs and others with scars on their backs and bellies where they had been attacked. And that was just the survivors; I wondered how many they had lost.

"Where are all the young men?" Laura said later as we sat in the cockpit eating a late lunch. "I saw only old men and women and children in the village today."

I'd noticed the same thing. Judging from the number of children playing in the compound and larking in the water, there should have been some younger men around.

Liani murmured in Joseph's ear, and he nodded and relayed the message to Danny, annoying me to no end. The old bugger could speak perfect English but chose not to. In all the time I'd known him, he'd spoken exactly ten words to me in my own language, and those only when we both thought they might well be the last words I'd ever hear.

It was all well and good to take the high ground and disdain the language of your conquerors, but we were thousands of miles away from the North American continent at the moment. And what language were he and Liani speaking anyway? Polynesian? Even he wasn't that old. Maybe something he'd picked up from his elders; Joseph spoke several of the old dialects that were now endangered or extinct. At the last census there were only two hundred and forty people left alive who spoke any one of the Haida group of languages. On the other hand, maybe he felt it was acceptable to converse in English with her as she was of Pacific Rim descent. Or maybe because he wasn't in his own land. The whole thing infuriated me.

Joseph saw me scowling at him and smiled as Danny spoke.

"Liani says the men are out to sea, fishing. It's like the old man said, the fish in the lagoons and inside the barrier reef have fallen off drastically in recent years. They subsist mainly on pelagic fish now."

"Well, in that case, let's make damn sure we take in enough supplies tonight to carry the load for the feast," Danny said. "God knows we brought enough."

In addition to a case of the fierce Black River rum which the Fijians loved with a passion, we had brought extra bags of potatoes, onions, and carrots, two sacks of sweet corn and an iced one-hundred-pound pig. This along with two cases of corned beef, which the locals ate like candy. If there wasn't enough food to go around at the feast, it wouldn't be our fault.

Joseph and Liani sailed in early with the pig and the rum, while the rest of us took the dinghies and paddled out for some snorkelling. The reefs themselves were healthy, none of the bleaching we had seen farther south, and only the occasional spiny starfish feeding upon them, but as we dove down, it became apparent that something was wrong. In an area like this, nourished by the outside waters and harvested only by the one small village, you would have expected to find edible fish in abundance. Even the parrotfish and wrasse, marginal food fish at best, had been hunted out in the larger sizes, and nothing over twelve inches was visible.

It was obvious why the men of the village had been forced to fish outside the reefs, but even there the catches would be uncertain; pelagic fish travel in large schools, and there would be times when they were absent.

"What are you looking so serious about?" Laura pulled herself out of the water and flopped down beside me in the dinghy.

"Thinking about the village. The difference between what we perceive as problems and a real problem. We're all trying to get rich, and if it doesn't work out we'll do something else, go back home, get jobs, go on the dole, whatever. These people have a real problem; they're in danger of losing their whole way of life. What are they going to do, move to the city and work at McDonald's?"

"It's happening all the time," Laura said. "Fewer and fewer people can live like this anymore. Global warming, pollution, the decline of life in the ocean, increased expectations. You can't fight it. The days of the noble savage are over, if they ever even existed other than as a romantic Western notion. The kids will be all right; it's the old people it will be the hardest on. They'll probably end up in state homes somewhere, away from their families, living in loneliness and poverty."

"Jesus. Now aren't you the cheerful one? You'll have them all dead or working in T-shirt sweatshops in Suva inside a month."

"Same story at home, in Ireland with the small farmers. They're leaving of their own free will or being bought out by the big agricultural companies. Pretty soon that's all that will be left, except the small boggy holdings that aren't worth anything because nothing will flourish there except a few yuppies with Mercedes in the driveways playing at farming. I've seen it."

"Well, hopefully that's not going to happen here. Not for a few years anyway. Maybe the sharks have gone."

The side of the inflatable suddenly tilted up in the air, and a muscular brown arm raised up and the panicked scream of "sharks" sounded and we fell out into the water, the dinghy rolling over on top of us.

We swam frantically up to the surface and Danny's grinning face.

"Asshole," I sputtered.

After showering and changing aboard *Arrow*, we loaded up the dinghies with our contributions to the feast and went ashore. Preparations were well in progress, some of the women digging fire pits in the sand while others collected driftwood for fuel. Joseph and the headman sat on folding chairs in a cleared area before a small pile of steaming seaweed, a half-empty bottle of Laphroaig beside them. Joseph must have replenished his private stock in Suva. The old bugger had never offered me a drink of it though.

I pulled up a stump and sat next to the two old men. The headman told me that the pig was wrapped in the seaweed, and rested on hot rocks, the lovo, and that it would be very good when it was done in four hours. He said that they used to have many pigs in the village, but they had all drowned in the last hurricane and they hadn't been able to replace them yet. He said this was too bad. I agreed with him. He reached down and took a drink of Scotch and passed the bottle to

Joseph, who took a drink and handed it back. We talked about pigs a while longer then I went off in search of Laura.

A trio of giggling women in the shade of the palm grove were preparing dorado for the feast, slitting open their stomachs with swift practised strokes and chopping them into thick steaks, while beside them another woman rinsed a large woven basket of clams in fresh water. An old withered crone was peeling a jumble of tubular tapered roots which were unknown to me. She pointed a suggestive specimen in my direction and said something and all the women screamed in laughter. I moved on.

The trail through the palm grove climbed upward, winding through a scattering of large pandanus as the sandy soil of the grove turned gravelly before changing into scattered clumps of rock and the beginnings of lava. A pair of goats gave me a bored look and resumed their scavenging, thin unhealthy-looking animals with sparse coats and dull eyes. In good times the villagers sold or traded part of their catch for the crops of the inlanders to obtain what they couldn't catch or fashion from the sea.

It was apparent that the village was struggling. In spite of that, they would make a brave showing at the feast, squandering in one bold gesture supplies that were to have lasted them for days. They were similar to the First Nations of the North Pacific in their proud refusal to surrender to their circumstances, preserving the old traditions of hospitality no matter the cost.

The path opened out into a clearing and a naked sheer-sided black cliff rose up before me, covered with the swirling lava rock that was so common in Fiji. A well-used trail wound around it in long crescents, its slanting cuts clearly visible due to the lack of vegetation. It was as if the cliff had been carefully placed there from somewhere in space, a towering hundred-foot monolith rising above all else, without a blade of grass or shrub upon it.

I wound steadily upwards, curious about what I would find, perhaps an old lookout where they lit the fires to warn the village that enemies were in sight or that their own raiding canoes were back from their sorties. As I went up, the path became narrower and I leaned into to the cliff, my shoulder almost touching the rock as the path shrank.

The last few feet were steps carved into the rock, and I climbed them rapidly, careful not to look down, and emerged at the peak panting for breath. The top was a smooth piece of glassy volcanic rock some two hundred yards in diameter that overlooked the village and the lagoon, and beyond that I saw the atolls, adjoining circles stretching out to sea and vanishing in the distance. It was a stunning vista, the lagoons a dark blue with lighter patches where the reefs rose up near the surface, and the dark green of the motus that surrounded them.

Above Teuini Atoll, just at the farthest limit of my vision, was a small cloud, the only one in the sky. The sun was slanting into the sea, and its rays caught it and there was a sudden flash of green. A sense of unease swept over me, and I shivered in spite of the heat.

In the centre of the lava that crested the cliff was a broad stone platform. I rested for a moment, catching my breath before walking over and studying it. It was formed of huge interlocking stones, each one as high as a man, and I couldn't imagine how they had been brought up the cliff. They must have weighed several tons each, and there were eight of them. An ornately carved wooden chair rested in the middle of the platform, big enough for a giant, and attached to it by a length of woven rope was a large conch shell.

I sat in the chair and it moved slightly, and I realized the base of it rested upon a tapered outcrop of rock in such a fashion that the entire chair could be swivelled a full three hundred sixty degrees. Around the base were the faded remains of an old circle, divided into three sections with illegible drawings set along the edges.

The top of the chair had a canopy of woven leaves over it, so that the occupant could sit out of the sun while he kept watch. Seating myself I had a sudden uneasy feeling that providing a comfortable site for a lookout was not all this chair had been used for, that there was another, darker history to it. There were holes through the arms and legs, and deep striations alongside, as if ropes had been sawing there. It was made of a dark, glistening hardwood that I didn't recognize, discoloured by old stains and the glare of the sun.

"Better not let the elders catch you sitting there, sport. They'll have your balls for breakfast."

I spun around, startled. The laconic voice belonged to a young powerfully built Fijian in his late twenties dressed in a faded T-shirt and a pair of shorts and sporting an orange Denver Broncos cap over a large head of permed yellow hair. He carried a machete slung in his belt, and an old khaki knapsack hooked over one shoulder.

"What is it, the chief's chair, used for some kind of ceremony?"

"Not exactly. It's where the captives were tried in the old days."

He walked over to me and pointed down to the circle.

"The circle of life split into three destinies. They put the men in the chair and spun them. Freedom, death, or captivity. You pays your money and you takes your chances."

"One chance in three. Well, I suppose it was better than nothing. Assuming the chair wasn't rigged."

He smiled. "No, apparently not. But freedom can have different meanings. In this case it was a chance to make the leap."

He walked over to the edge of the cliff and pointed down. There, snuggled in tight at the base of the cliff one hundred plus feet below was a small pool, separated from the rest of the bay by a wall of reef. The water in it was a brilliant blue in the centre, with lighter coloured shallower spots around the edges. Children were swimming in it, their yells echoing faintly up to us.

"Jesus! Did anybody ever survive it?"

"Apparently some did. Tough boys in those days."

He extended his hand.

"Tommo Davids."

"Jared Kane. Pleased to meet you."

He reached into his knapsack and took out a green coconut and whacked the top of it off with his machete and passed it to me.

"Thanks."

The nectar was cool and sweet and damped my thirst.

"I hear you're looking for a lost ship."

"Yes."

"And you think it's in Teuini Lagoon."

"Perhaps. We're not sure, but it seems likely."

He nodded and stared off into the distance. I waited for him to speak again.

"I suppose you've heard the stories?"

"About man-eating sharks? Yes."

"They're true," he said abruptly and raised his shirt.

The scar ran from the base of his neck down to his waist in an ugly curving crescent. Striations ran off it in raised crimson triangles where the skin had ripped.

"I got this ten years ago, when we decided to catch the sharks with baited hooks and buoys. We were a joke."

He rolled a cigarette, lit it, and took long puffs, studying me.

"It was as if they were waiting for us. We were not fools. We had men who had been killing sharks their whole lives with us, but we had no chance. We lost four of our best young men, all of them my friends. After that the elders voted to abandon the area."

"Did you agree?"

"Most of us. Others, no."

He finished his cigarette and pinched it off between his fingers and flicked it over the cliff. It twirled down and disappeared.

"We were hoping to get some of the men from the village to help us search. We could use some more hands. We have a diving cage for protection, good equipment . . ." my voice trailed off.

It was as if I hadn't spoken.

"I've dived all through that area you know. Before the earthquake. It was always the best provider of fish, perhaps because it was the farthest out. And my father dove it before me. He was one of the old pearl divers. He could go down twenty-two rays, he was the best of them. I've been down around fifteen rays."

I knew a ray was six feet. Incredibly, his father could free dive to a hundred thirty feet. I'd heard the stories about Fijian pearl divers. Some of them went down seventy times a day and made a living at it well into their sixties. It seemed unbelievable. Danny and I sometimes free dived to fifty feet and had probably done sixty a few times. One hundred thirty feet was as unreal to me as a trip to the moon.

"What's it like down there?"

He shrugged. "Like any other reef system for the most part. The atoll lagoon is a little different. Sandy bottom, a few gullies, some bommies rising up near the top. Lots of fish, used to be. The gullies all run into a deeper hole in the centre, which is uncommon. I've never been down there; too deep for me. After the earthquake and the green water, everyone talked about the spot. Some of the old men who had dived with my father said there was just a big black hole in there, a quarter mile wide, and much deeper than everywhere else. They said the water was colder there than anywhere else."

And now it was warmer. Strange.

"Didn't anyone consider contacting the authorities, get them to check it out? They might have been able to do something."

"It was discussed, but the elders were against it. Didn't think it was right. They said it was our lagoon, and what happens in there is our business. They thought if the government became involved, they'd regulate it, perhaps even take it away. They said it was our place and our destiny and we had to accept it."

"Why are they letting us in there now?"

"The old man. When he arrived with the dog in that little boat in the middle of the storm, they saw it as a sign. When Joseph saw Liani's necklace with the gold coin and spoke about the ship, they couldn't ignore it."

"So now we're all part of your destiny."

"Yep." He grinned and clapped me on the shoulder. "So now it's all up to you lot. All the sharks and snakes. We locals just get to sit back and watch."

"Marvellous. What if we just say to hell with it and pull out?"

"Oh, you won't do that, sport. It's written."

He grinned again and set off down the path.

I followed him down. Just at the base of the cliff he turned away on a path that disappeared into the bush behind the village.

Several fires were going now, attended by giggling kids with sticks of smoking marshmallows engaged in a competition to see who could eat the blackest one. Their mothers watched, occasionally snatching one, screaming with laughter as the sticky mess scorched their fingers on its way to burning their mouths.

Most of the young men were sitting around the main fire, where Danny had set up bar on an old stump flanked by skeins of green coconuts and a case of Black Heart. A hundred yards away, Joseph performed the same function for the elders.

"Here you go, buddy. Not too strong, just the way you like it."

I took a drink and choked. Danny's idea of strong is not the same as most people's.

"I've been talking to some of the lads. A few of them might be willing to help us search for the boat in spite of the elders. They say we should talk to Tommo Davids about it," Danny said.

"I just met him. Can't say he seemed keen for the job."

"Apparently he's worked off-island for most of the last decade. He was badly chewed up in the shark killing fiasco, stayed on in Suva after he left the hospital, worked at the shipyards for a while. Sounds like he'd be a handy guy to have on our side."

"I'll introduce you later on, see if you can get him on board with us."

But Tommo didn't show up through that long night of feasting and drinking, and when we left the following morning, he still hadn't returned.

CHAPTER 22

It was a fine leave-taking, everyone still in high spirits from the celebrations of the night before, the men singing old chants and rapping their paddles on the sides of the outriggers as they escorted us through the pass, the women ululating from the rocks above. The canoes were decorated with garlands of flowers and woven wreaths of pandan leaves, and when they turned around three miles out and headed back to the village, some of the brightness of the day left with them.

It took us four hours to reach the outer reef, the breeze fluttering and dying as Teuini Atoll rose up on the horizon before us, first the cloud that defined it and then the first few palm trees rising from the water and finally the delineation of the land beneath. The day grew strangely silent, *Arrow* ghosting along, *Tramp* in her wake, no one in a rush to get there, and the heavy complicit air just enough to keep us sailing and dry the nervous sweat from our bodies. Three miles out the last seabird left us.

It took an hour to work our way through the intricate maze that surrounded Teuini Atoll. The channel markers had long since vanished, and we weaved our way carefully in, sometimes taking a false turn into a blind channel and retracing our passage. The water was clear, with schools of tiny reef fish darting over the coral beneath *Arrow* farther out, but as we approached the lagoon a thin green tendril appeared on the water, ebbing down the channel towards us, faint as smoke at first, but gradually strengthening until it became a clearly marked stream ten feet wide drifting on the surface like oil, and in the shadow of that coloured water, no living thing moved.

As we edged closer to the lagoon a thin mist rose up around us, partially obscuring our view. I checked the sea temperature gauge, thinking that perhaps the water had warmed, but it was constant to a degree. Then, as suddenly as it had appeared, the mist vanished under a puff of wind, and Teuini Atoll lay before us, shimmering in the sunlight.

We dropped the sails and took the way off the boats and drifted towards the atoll in an unnatural silence, undisturbed by the cry of a single bird, or the lap of a solitary wave. The atoll and surrounding reefs, those fecund breeding grounds of the South Pacific whose eco-systems are the basis of countless interconnected life forms, should have been vibrant with life, but they were hushed and silent. Competition among seabirds for nesting territory offshore is fierce. The motu should have been strident with bustle and noise in the daylight hours, but there were no birds, no guano on the rocks, no signs of any life. Even the ubiquitous gulls were absent. The ominous silence was unnatural and unsettling.

The palm logs that formed the palisades that guarded the pass were fresh, still bleeding red sap from their recent wounds into the water. As we drifted closer, I saw that the water at the base of the logs was choppy and disturbed and suddenly a large fin broke the surface for a second and then disappeared again, and then another, and another. To my horror I saw that the area in front of the barricade was alive with sharks, dozens of them, jostling and circling and colliding as they sought for passage within. There was none of the frantic threshing of a feeding frenzy, but something deliberate and cold and searching as they bumped up against the logs and then withdrew to continue their restless search for entry. As they swam and circled into the small area of green water and then moved out again, I saw that their attitudes changed as they moved back and forth, enervated as they hit the green water, their movements becoming more exaggerated and aggressive, their speed increasing and their bodies infused with a quivering energy as the green waters passed through their gills. They ignored us, focused solely on that log barrier with a deliberation that was frightening in its intensity.

Padraic and Molly stood by *Tramp*'s wheelhouse, gazing silently down into the water. Even Sinbad, who should have been going crazy with sharks near, was silent, pressed up tight against Joseph's leg.

"Where do you want to anchor?" Danny asked.

"Not here, that's for fucking sure."

We started the diesel and moved *Arrow* away a quarter mile and dropped the hook. In just that short distance everything was changed, the water clear and undisturbed around us, no sign of a single shark. But still that weighted, unnatural silence. We popped a couple of beers and waited for the others.

"It doesn't really change anything," Padraic said at the conference that evening. "It just means it will take us a little longer to get into the lagoon."

The original plan was to pull down the log palisades, a matter of minutes with *Tramp*'s hydraulic winch, and go straight in. Nobody thought that was a good idea now.

"It changes everything," I said. "I've never seen sharks behave like that. It makes me realize that we have absolutely no idea of what is waiting for us inside there. I don't think the normal rules apply here. The green water has changed that."

"It hasn't changed the value of gold," Danny said, "or the fact that if we don't find something soon, we'll be heading back to Canada to find work in the near future."

"Actually, that idea doesn't sound nearly so bad to me anymore. This is no longer fun."

"We can make gates," Molly said. "Go into the pass as if we're entering a lock. Open one gate, go inside and chase out anything that comes in with us then close the gate, and do the same on the other side. I've got lots of spare metal on *Tramp* left over from building the cage, including angle iron and flat plate. We'll weld up some strap hinges. Once we're through we'll close everything up tight again behind us."

"Sounds like a plan," Padraic said. The others nodded in agreement, even Laura. I'd been hoping she would take my side.

"Okay," I said. "First thing tomorrow morning then, the sooner we're done with all of this the better. Let's go ashore and take a look around, maybe we'll see something inside that will bring you all back to your senses."

We landed around the corner from the pass where the beach was sandy, with a gradual slope running forty yards up to the ridge that supported a stunted grove of coconut trees. As we beached the dinghy and stepped ashore, I looked for the shallow curving tracks that indicated the presence of snakes but found none. In fact there were no tracks of any kind present in the white sand. No birds, no lizards, nothing but silence and the pristine white sands that led up the slope. It was as sterile and lifeless as the moon. We walked in silence up to the top of the shallow slope and gazed down for the first time upon the waters of Teuini Lagoon.

The atoll was four miles across, the visibility inside perfect; we could make out each separate motu that enclosed the lagoon and pick out individual palm trees on the ridge directly across from us with the binoculars. The islets sloped uniformly down to the water around the circumference of the lagoon. It was like standing on the rim of an immense bowl of pea soup.

The water was a pale emerald green and as we looked down a section swirled and formed little eddies and whirlpools, then sucked up into little peaks before spinning in on itself and collapsing. I realized that we were not looking at the water, but at a shallow moving blanket of fog or mist that lay above it in random drifting patches from one end of the lagoon to the other. It was thicker and higher in the centre, perhaps reaching up to fifty feet before cascading down on all sides to flow along the surface.

"The fog isn't here all the time, only on still days like this. In the evening it thins out, maybe ten feet above the water. It sometimes disappears altogether for days at a time."

It was Tommo Davids, appearing from out of nowhere with his yellow perm and khaki knapsack.

"Where the hell did you come from?" Danny said.

"I came across late yesterday, spent the night over there. I've decided to lend you a hand. My people can't just keep ignoring this. The village needs the lagoon."

He motioned vaguely across the water.

"I sometimes come out here on my own, have a look around, see if anything's changed."

"Has it?" I asked. "I think I would've remembered if someone had mentioned that a zillion sharks are patrolling the entrance to the lagoon looking for a way in. Is that something new?"

"No, it's not new. Come on, have a look."

He walked ahead of us down to the edge of the lagoon, stretched out, and put his hand in. It disappeared into the green mist as completely as if immersed in paint, and then he pulled it out again and his fingers were dry.

"That is really fucking weird," Danny said.

"Hell, you ain't seen nothin' yet," Tommo said.

He took off his shirt and fanned the water. A small patch cleared, and we looked down into the water of Teuini Lagoon.

It was a translucent emerald green, an unnatural colour seldom seen in nature. The water was clear. It was like looking at white wine through a green bottle held up to the light. There was no trace of sediment or pollution, just that strange unearthly colour. I reached out and immersed my hand in the water. There was no sensation of heat or cold. I put my hand to my nose. Nothing, or perhaps just the faintest hint of sulphur.

"It's the mist that smells, not the water," Tommo said as he crouched down and laid a thermometer on the sand under a foot of water. "It rises out of the centre of the lagoon then spreads out over the water. It takes a fair bit of wind to get rid of it."

He reached down and pulled out the thermometer.

"Ninety-eight point six degrees Fahrenheit," he said. "It's been that for the last seven years. It hasn't changed by a single degree."

"The temperature of human blood," Laura murmured.

I put my arm around her shoulders and fervently wished that we were anywhere but here. But it was too late to stop it all now. We were committed for better or worse.

We stared at the lagoon, the mist suddenly swirling up and thinning, becoming almost transparent, like green smoke rising and twisting while behind it flashes of water showed through and then disappeared, everything in constant motion so that the eye was continuously tricked from one illusion to the next. Suddenly, off in the distance, a heavy splash, and the sound of water folding in upon itself. Nobody spoke.

"I've heard that before," Tommo said finally. "Always out near the centre where the mist is thickest. Impossible to see anything."

In spite of the cloying heat, Laura shivered beside me.

"Let's get back to the boat," I said.

"I'll see you around," Tommo said as he walked off, disappearing into the scrub as abruptly as he'd appeared.

It took us three days. It was unsettling at first, working among the sharks, but it was so apparent that we were not the objects of their obsessive attention that even Sinbad became used to it. At first he lay on *Tramp*'s bow with his head stuck over the bulwarks, growling softly at the shapes that swam around us on all sides, but he soon tired of that and ignored them as did the rest of us.

One of the strangest things in that surreal scene was the size and variety of the patrolling sharks. I saw a thirteen-foot hammerhead, three large tigers, a pair of bull sharks, reef sharks, sand sharks, a mako, several white tips, and another species we couldn't identify. Some of them were natural enemies and yet they swam together, united in their single-minded purpose of gaining access to the lagoon. Even Tommo, who had showed up each day to help us, was at a loss to explain their actions. He said he'd seen nothing like it before. Sometimes sharks would hang around the lobster cages the villagers kept in the water in front of their village to store their catch, but only for a brief period, and never with the concentrated intensity seen here. We cut the lashings of a fifteen-foot section of outer wall and pulled it out, cut it into two equal pieces, and trimmed the bottoms flush. Molly and Danny welded up two pairs of big strap hinges with angle iron and half-inch plate and attached them to the sections and floated them back into place, then pulled them upright with the crane and fastened them back onto the original structure. With the water carrying most of the weight, they opened and closed without difficulty. We were nervous about getting down into the dinghies to chase the sharks back out, but there was no avoiding it. Danny and Molly made the first venture in *Tramp*'s aluminum dinghy, and the sharks paid them no mind at all. It was as if the people inside were invisible, and the little boat just another obstacle to avoid in their restless circling. Emboldened, we lowered *Arrow*'s sailing skiff and dinghy, and the three boats drove the sharks back out of the enclosure with bang sticks and closed the gates behind them with *Tramp* now inside. Even in the uproar and commotion of driving them out, there was no aggressiveness towards us, just that obsessive fixation on the water issuing from the lagoon, and a quick circling back to get up tight against the outer gates again and resume their restless search for an entrance.

We went through the same procedure with the inner gate, although this time there were no sharks to deal with, only the warmth of the water and the faint sulphuric smell. By late afternoon of the third day both boats were through and anchored inside the lagoon. In spite of misgivings about what might lie beneath the water, the lagoon was calm and sheltered with good holding.

"We've got time for a couple of sweeps before dark," Padraic said. "Anyone up for it?"

"Hell yes," Danny said. "Who knows, we could all be millionaires by sunset."

Or dead, I thought. "I'll go down with you," I volunteered with false enthusiasm.

"We'll make our first passes on an axis through the centre of the lagoon," Padraic said. "I think we can eliminate the outer perimeters, anything less than a hundred feet of depth, say. From what Tommo said, that would have been covered by the old pearl divers. They would have spotted anything remotely resembling a boat down there. So that leaves us with a circle slightly over two miles in diameter. Any guesses as to what the visibility will be like?"

"The water seems clear in spite of the coloration," Molly said. "I'm thinking good up to sixty feet, reasonable for another thirty or forty. The chart shows a hundred twenty on average up to that central depression. Let's make the first pass through with the cage at eighty feet. That will give us an idea of the bottom, show us what's changed since the earthquake. We'll go through at one knot, so roughly sixty minutes in the water for the first pass. Off the top of my head, that's around twenty minutes decompression time at ten feet. I'll confirm that. Let's have a look at the charts again so we all know what we're going to do."

In the end we decided to circle at the eighty-foot depth until we encountered one of the gullies Tommo had told us about, and then follow it in towards the centre. While the others loaded the spears, spare cylinders, and bang sticks into the cage and strapped them onto the walls, Danny and I put on our dive gear. The equipment felt heavy and awkward, the sounds of my breathing overloud. We hung our weight belts on the steel bars. We wouldn't be using them unless we went outside and that wasn't going to happen. If Danny did manage to get the cage door open while we were underwater together, it would be over my dead body.

We did one last check-off then swung open the door and climbed in. There was a loud clang as Padraic closed it behind us, and we were trapped, gazing out through the bars of a prison. Two buzzes on our bell, a sudden lurch as the clutch engaged, and we sank slowly down into the green waters.

As we descended the brightness grew rather than lessened for the first few feet, a dazzling green that bathed everything in an eerie fluorescent light. *Tramp*'s rusty hull turned aquamarine as we moved lower, emerald bubbles rolling along her keel and exploding in her wake. It was difficult to estimate distance in the tinted water, the perspectives muted and changed by the colour, the outlines softened so that objects appeared farther away than they actually were. Danny turned and grinned at me, his teeth radioactive in that diffused green light.

Tramp's keel faded from view and there was nothing to see, just the empty water, paler now as the surface light lessened and we hung suspended in a timeless space of depth and silence. We stood upright, clinging to the bars and staring out, the cage slowly revolving as we travelled down.

Danny nudged me and pointed, and there below us lay the ghostly tabled tops of bleached coral, dead stag horn corals and broken whips scattered along the sand, nothing moving, nothing resembling life, just the pale scattered bones of a long-dead reef. Huge weathered rocks were distributed randomly along the bottom, square edged ancient monoliths that could almost have been carved from some prehistoric quarry. Three buzzes sounded, and we jerked to a stop, hanging on to the bars gazing out at a dead alien world. There was a long and a short signal, a sudden lurch, and we began moving forward again. My dive computer read eighty feet. The cage began to revolve, slowly at first, and then more quickly as we came up to speed.

Danny took the tiller and centred it and the spinning stopped, and then he swung it to port and we moved outwards, he moved it back starboard, and we crossed our track and traversed back the other way. He began running the cage from side to side in long parabolic curves, increasing the area *Tramp* covered.

This isn't too bad, I thought, as we moved along, secure in our little cell, scanning the lagoon floor beneath us. I sat down on one of the seats Danny and Molly had welded to the side, braced my legs, leaned back against the bars and surveyed my surroundings.

Tommo had sketched in on our small-scale chart the gullies that ran from the edge of the lagoon into the centre as he remembered them, radiating from the middle of the lagoon and running in towards land like spokes on a wheel until they petered out a half mile from the shore. On our present speed and course, tracking roughly parallel to the beach, we should see one approximately ten minutes into our trip. I looked at my watch. Another five minutes.

The lagoon bottom rose and fell in long gentle slopes, dotted occasionally by patches of dead grass and small outcroppings of bleached-out coral. There was nothing alive. It was like I had imagined Bikini Atoll looked after the nuclear explosions: a lonely grey moonscape filled with ghosts, barren and lifeless, an abomination of everything associated with the South Pacific.

Danny nudged me, and I saw the bottom sloping sharply away just ahead of us, and as he reached for the buzzer to change course it sounded and we swung to port as Molly picked up the gully on the sounder. *Tramp* had one of the fish-finder sonars, more precise and detailed than the simple depth recorder on *Arrow*. The beam projected forward and gave a profile of the bottom ahead of the boat, as well as imaging anything swimming in the water between her and the bottom.

The gully was fifty feet wide and thirty feet deep, the sides nearly vertical. We had dived on similar gullies in South Minerva where they were filled with fish, including the largest groupers we'd ever seen. The undersea coral trenches were a natural gathering place for fish, the drifting phytoplankton that began everything trapped there, the craggy coral affording numerous hiding places for the zooplankton and tiny reef fish that fed upon it, and the undercuts at the bottom a natural hideout for the predators that hunted them in the eternal wheel of pursuit and capture.

Here, there was nothing. Not the slightest motion or hint of life where the waters should have been teeming; no gorgonian fans waving greetings in the slightest trace of current, no nudibranchs floating past, no anemones, no sudden flash of light as a school of cardinal fish wheeled as one, no sudden jet of squid, no parrots, wrasse or even a solitary moray eel. Absolutely nothing as we swung along suspended in our cage, save for the lonely squared rocks that appeared below like tombstones marking a giant undersea graveyard. I shivered in spite of the warmth of the water and vowed once more that in order for me to leave the shelter of the cage, I would have to see enough gold piled up outside of it to purchase Newfoundland.

Danny reached over and tapped my shoulder and mimed wiping sweat off his forehead; it had become warmer. Next time we'd bring a thermometer. I looked at my watch. Twenty-five minutes had passed. We should be getting close to the perimeter of the deeper epicentre. I glanced up again and saw something moving in the water ahead. Something large, spinning and flashing, extending from the bottom all the way up and out of sight.

I punched a stop on the buzzer and gradually the way came off us and we drifted slowly forward and came to a halt and sat there rocking slowly, staring in disbelief at the pulsing phenomenon that confronted us.

It was an immense column springing from the depths below and rising up and out of sight, a huge effervescent upwelling made up of millions and millions of bubbles, some the size of the ones climbing the sides of your champagne glass, some much larger. The edges of the column were sharply delineated, no drift or taper or random motion, just a slow sparkling jet spewing straight upwards from the bottom as if overflowing from some giant underground bottle of champagne.

There was something beautiful and unsettling about it, an implacable, unstoppable force of nature beginning somewhere down towards the pressured centre of the earth and climbing all those lonely miles to freedom. It shimmered before us, beckoning, no gap or change, a moving curtain of encapsulated particles of air or gas. I wished we'd brought a camera. The heat from it was palpable, and I was perspiring freely under my mask. Danny turned and looked at me, then shrugged and pointed forward. I took a deep breath and nodded, and he punched in slow ahead and there was a small jerk and we crept forward.

The column of bubbles was opaque, and there was no telling how thick it was. We inched closer, and I had a sudden impulse to throw open the gate and get out of there, and I lunged towards the door as we moved into the bubbles but by then we were inside and it was too late.

CHAPTER 23

It was like stepping into a giant Jacuzzi, the water hot but not unbearably so, the bubbles pulsing against our bodies like tiny plucking fingers, a strange crackling hiss as they broke against the bars of the cage. It was brighter than before, the illusion of the effervescence, but visibility had decreased, and the bottom had disappeared from sight. Where before the dead and hostile landscape had at least been subject to grid and measurement, now there was only a spinning void with nothing to relate to but the sense of an unfathomable abyss below. We were caught in a freak of nature, like a twig in a whirlpool, and at any second might be dashed down to our destruction. The cable that held us seemed thin and tenuous, *Tramp* and the light and the air a universe away.

We stopped and hung there for long minutes, slowly rotating while we searched for any sign or hint of normalcy, but there was nothing save the column of hissing bubbles rising in that glowing green stream that throbbed with a strange unearthly glow. Danny grimaced at me, his teeth incandescent around the mouthpiece, and reached over and signalled down on the buzzer and we slowly descended. When we reached a hundred and twenty we punched in stop, and still there was no bottom in sight, only the sense of infinite pressured depths beneath us.

We signalled ahead slow and moved a hundred feet into the column when Danny pointed forward and there, faintly outlined in the bubbles, a vague indistinct shape, and he swung the tiller and veered towards it, and I saw it was a table of rock running up from the depths and levelling off just below us, the sides vertical, the top covered with the same bleached-bones coral that lay behind us. Just as we crossed over the edge, there was a sudden crash as something struck the cage, and a piercing high-pitched squeal of rage echoed through the water and chilled my blood. I whirled, but there was nothing. Danny wrenched the bang sticks off the wall and passed me one and we stood there waiting, back to back, our hearts pounding like drums, the sweat on our faces steaming the goggles so that it became even harder to see. I gripped the grab bar so tightly my hands ached as Danny reached for the buzzer to signal our return and as he stretched across, the creature struck again, this time beneath our feet, a loud crack and another angry scream, and still there was nothing to see but the slow-moving bubbles that buffeted and surrounded us. Not seeing made it worse for nothing could be more fearsome than the imagining, and it took an eternity to move back, waiting for another strike and then we were out of the column, like stepping out of a thick drumming shower, and the bottom was there again, sloping up and away from us at a steep angle as we rode back up the side of the central depression towards the first decompression stop. We stayed at the twenty-foot level for five minutes and then the second stop ten feet from the surface for another twenty minutes, and then they winched us back on board, and I was still shaking as I stepped out onto the deck.

They were waiting impatiently, filled with excited chattering questions, but we held them off until we'd had showers to remove the tainted water from our bodies and hot rums to ease the chill from our souls.

Watching the green water sluice down off my body and vanish into the grates below, I recognized it for something foul and contaminated that belonged deep down in the centre of the earth, and I knew in my heart that what had attacked us was the monstrous living embodiment of it.

✿

"So you saw nothing unusual on the sonar?" I said.

They hadn't seen the column of bubbles rising to the surface.

"The sonar picture was intermittent, and we might not have been watching the entire time," Padraic said.

"Why do you ask, Jared?" Laura said.

"Something hit the cage. Twice, just after we entered the column of bubbles," Danny said. "We didn't see what."

"There was a noise as well," I said, my gaze locked on Laura.

"What kind of noise?"

"A pissed off kind of noise," Danny said.

"Can you be more specific?" Elinor asked.

Joseph sat quietly, staring off into space, Liani sitting by his side. She went over and studied the cage carefully, running her hands along the outside edge of it before returning to Joseph and whispering in his ear. He nodded and looked towards me.

I glared at him.

"Sort of an angry squeal," I said. "Not a shark, that's for damned sure. Or anything else that I've ever heard before."

"How big do you think it was?" Molly asked.

A reasonable question. I thought about it. Not huge, the cage hadn't been that shook up, but not something small either. Medium?

"If you'd been paying attention to the fucking sounder, maybe we would know," I griped.

"Yes, that's my fault I'm afraid," Padraic said. "I got a little bit excited when we entered the mist. I do apologize, it won't happen again. Let's make some charting runs over the centre before it gets dark. We'll have

272

somebody watching the sonar, see if we can get a better picture of the bottom before anybody goes back down again."

With the cage out of the water *Tramp* could do her full five knots, and we steamed back and forth across the lagoon for the next three hours, running from the eighty-foot depth on one side to the other in tracks three hundred yards apart. Elinor, who had the best hand, drew a representation of what she saw on the sonar, and at the end of a dozen runs, it was clear that the old charts of Teuini Lagoon bore little resemblance to what was down there now.

Atolls, according to the theory first outlined by Charles Darwin in 1842, are produced by volcanic activity in the ocean floor, which creates a new island as lava climbs to the surface; that in turn provides a shallow substrate on which fringing reefs can form. If the island subsequently submerges, a barrier reef can develop if upward coral growth keeps pace with bedrock submergence. The island ultimately disappears from sight, but the coral keeps growing, live over dead as it, too, subsides over time, and the final resolution is an atoll, that most beautiful and isolated of all coral reefs.

Over the years, tidal action, wind waves, and coral eaters like parrotfish grind down the coral and sand dunes emerge — the motus. A coconut drifts up on the beach, sprouts and grows, other life follows, and you end up with an atoll such as Teuini.

It seemed that what had happened here was that the volcanic activity that created the atoll centuries earlier had resumed deep beneath the earth's surface, and a geothermic vent had reopened. When the tectonic plates shifted in the earthquake of 2006, the fissure through which the heated gas was escaping had been created. I didn't want to think about what else might have hatched and grown down in that hell hole.

"Okay. Near as I can tell, this is what it looks like down there." Elinor plunked down a series of sketches onto the chart table tapping her drawings with the dividers to illustrate her points. "The gullies still run into the middle as shown on the original charts, but the centre appears to have collapsed downwards. How far, we don't know. The sounder images aren't clear, either because of the turbulence in the water, the heat, or a combination of both." She pointed to a rough profile of the lagoon, the centre a jagged mass of rocks and chasms dotted with small bommies.

"The rock table you saw inside the column of gas must be a portion of the original lagoon floor that still stands, while everything else has sunk down around it," Padraic elaborated. "What we have is similar to a butte standing up on a valley floor, but just how far down that floor is from the top of the butte we have no way of telling. The sloping shelf circling the central depression is a quarter mile wide and runs uniformly down from a hundred to a hundred and twenty-five feet before dropping off to the valley floor. Again, no clear soundings so we don't know how far it is from the drop-off at the edge of the shelf to the plateau. A gap of about a hundred yards where Jared and Danny went in. It could be wider or narrower around the rest of the perimeter, although my guess is it will be much the same. What we can chart suggests the centre is concentric."

Elinor sat down and gestured to Padraic to continue.

"Okay. It seems to me that along the edge of this shelf and the gullies that run through it to the drop-off is the logical place to begin our search. If Lapérouse's boat went over the edge, then it's gone for good as far as we're concerned, unless by some miracle it's resting on the plateau inside the column of bubbles. A slim chance and given the lack of visibility and whatever the hell it was you heard down there, not one we should consider taking at the present time. If anything was lying shallower than a hundred feet, then I think it's safe to assume it would have been found by the pearl divers a long time ago."

Joseph stood abruptly and went out on deck. A minute later, I heard the sound of the dinghy entering the water and then the thump as Sinbad jumped into it. Danny and I followed and were in time to see Joseph spin the little boat with a quick stroke of the oars and head off towards the middle of the lagoon. Danny called after him, but he didn't answer, the boat skimming away, the mist covering the bottom half of the boat so completely they appeared to be floating on an emerald cloud. When Sinbad leaned over towards the water and barked, they drifted for a while, and then moved off again, into the faint green mist in the centre that now rose up and hid them completely. There was more barking that faded gradually away into the distance. This time, no one was surprised when they didn't return that evening.

We began our search of the lagoon at nine o'clock the following morning. Since all dives within a twelve-hour period are cumulative and count together up to a point, with time spent decompressing increasing accordingly, there was no sense in getting up at the crack of dawn only to quit at midday when the light was directly overhead and visibility at its best.

Danny and I took the first shift over the objections of Laura and Elinor. We wanted to ensure that whatever had attacked the cage was not out there waiting for us, even though I thought it unlikely. I had a strong feeling that we wouldn't be bothered outside the column of bubbles, although I couldn't have explained why, only that the source of the green water was the key.

Padraic had divided the area into search grids and allowed ninety minutes to cover a segment. With each group capable of two dives a day, he and Molly figured on ten days at most to cover the area and then we would be free to leave. It couldn't come too soon for me; I found the lagoon unsettling and depressing and longed for the old days when life was simple, the waters teemed with life, and dinner was only a spear's length away. Lapérouse and his ghostly crew could keep my share of their treasure.

A breeze was blowing as we motored out from the anchorage, strong enough to dissipate the mist, and for the first time since we'd arrived, the column of bubbles was clearly visible on the surface of the water, a huge rippled ring that formed a circle a quarter mile wide in diameter around the centre of the lagoon. We ran *Tramp* out to the hundred-foot level, lowered the cage, and began making our calibrated runs out to the edge of the column before turning and running back in towards the shore in long parallel sweeps.

Visibility was poor beyond the hundred-foot level and we used the big Mares dive torches to penetrate the gloom. It was tedious work, the landscape unrelieved by colour or movement, just the slow rocking swing at the end of our tether as we guided the cage back and forth across the grid.

The bottom became increasingly fragmented as we moved towards the edge of the perimeter, the gullies deeper and more broken up, some of them narrowing to the point where we were unable to take the cage inside and were forced to run above them, peering downwards into their depths. Once we thought we saw a spar wedged deep back in the under-side of one of the gullies, but it turned out to be an ancient tree trunk, calcified by age and split at one end so that at first glance it appeared man-made. We rang the buzzer and ascended slowly back to the first of our decompression stops.

Molly and Laura were scheduled for the second dive, and I'd run *Tramp* while Danny looked after communications and raised and low-ered the cage at their signal. We were lowering them into the water when we heard an outboard approaching at speed. A large panga with a sixty Yamaha on the transom and Tommo at the wheel emerged from the mist. Behind him sat Joseph and Sinbad, surrounded by a jumble of dive tanks, weights, and gear, the skiff trailing in their wake. Tommo pulled alongside *Tramp* and called up.

"Joseph convinced me I should come and join forces with you," he said. "I took my commercial dive ticket when I worked at the shipyard, and I'm dying to have a look at what's down there. Never fancied going it on my own, but since you're here . . ."

"Glad to have you," I said. "Come aboard."

Tommo proved a welcome addition, his presence giving us the luxury of a third dive unit. He dove with Molly most of the time, the pair of them doing the deeper dives that their experience warranted. To my chagrin, I proved to be the most susceptible to narcosis of the deep, that nervous mental condition resembling alcoholic intoxication, which affects different people in different ways.

It is caused by nitrogen in air under pressure, along with carbon dioxide in the tissues, and begins to have intoxicating effects at about a hundred feet. The symptoms are loss of judgment, a false sense of well-being, and a lack of concern for safety. The rule is simply expressed by "Martini's Law," which states that the effect is roughly equal to consuming one martini for every twenty feet beginning at a hundred feet. To my mortification, I was affected at ninety feet and became quite silly at depths over a hundred and twenty-five feet. Being aware of this I did my best to conceal it, constantly guarding against foolish grins while I swung back and forth in the cage. While this was not a serious problem when restricted to the confines of the cage with my partner, it could be a dangerous liability outside of it.

For the next three days, we worked steadily through the daylight hours, running along our charted tracks, searching some of the more complex areas twice to make sure we hadn't overlooked anything. It was monotonous, exhausting work, carried out under a nervous strain with none of the rewards attached to diving: there wasn't a single sign of life; the water was unnaturally warm so that you were constantly sweating and uncomfortable; the harnesses and straps chafed; and at the back of our minds sat the wild screams we'd heard in the column of bubbles the first time. No one went back inside the column, and we weren't attacked again.

The days merged into a uniform sameness, everything under the water so similar there was no telling where you had been. Only at the surface, where we charted and wheeled *Tramp* through the grids, was there any sense of purpose or accomplishment. We were fortunate in that there were no heavy winds to push *Tramp* off her course, and with the passes blocked, currents were not a factor.

In the evenings we retired to *Arrow* for brief freshwater showers and dinner, but even there we were never free from the constraints of our surroundings, the green water on all sides an alien presence that constantly reminded us of the unknown dangers of the lagoon. Joseph, Liani, and Sinbad had moved ashore and often stayed away from the boat for days at a time, spending their nights in Tommo's bure.

By the end of the seventh day, we were down to the last of the gullies. It was the broadest and deepest, starting out about eighty yards wide at the hundred-foot level and gradually narrowing as it approached the drop-off. The depth inside the gully itself remained fairly constant, averaging around fifteen feet. Laura and I had been diving together, and we caught the final shift of the day. On the third pass, Laura thought she saw something shining in the reflection of her light on the bottom edge of the trench, just where it began to narrow up, but she lost it before we could get the cage stopped. On the next pass we went through lower still, circled slowly, and came back again and stopped when Laura pointed, wide-eyed behind her mask. Then I saw it, lying half-buried in the sand a few scant boat lengths from the drop-off.

A shattered wooden cask and the unmistakable glint of gold.

Then I did what I had sworn I would not do: I opened the cage door.

CHAPTER 24

"How much do you think it's worth?" I asked.

"Gold is selling in the neighbourhood of thirteen hundred U.S. an ounce and back on the rise the last I heard," Padraic said. "The Louis weigh just over eleven pounds, so about two hundred and thirty thousand dollars as a commodity. Considerably more in this minting I would guess. Maybe a quarter million plus. A good start."

The coins were piled up in the middle of *Arrow*'s saloon table on a white towel. Even after all that time in the water they had the soft buttery glow that dreams are made of. We stared reverently at them, as if they were the long-lost icons of our secret religion. Finally, Laura reached out and picked up a handful and ran them through her fingers.

"Say around one hundred and eighty thousand pounds. It was much too easy," she said.

"That's your Catholicism speaking, darling," Padraic said. "It doesn't always have to come hard. Everyone is entitled to a little good fortune once in a while."

He hadn't stopped grinning since we'd come up with the gold in our dive bags.

"And there were no signs of anything else?"

"Not that we could see, but the gully gets tight there," I said.

"How much farther until it runs out over the edge?" Danny asked.

"I don't know for certain. A couple of hundred feet anyway."

"A fair chance, then," Padraic said. "If the ship was lying down in the gully it might well have become snagged, especially as it narrows down on the slope to the edge. I wish we knew how deep that lower shelf that runs out to the gas column is. We should have a better idea by day's end tomorrow."

Laura glanced over at me and I smiled at her, but the look on her face told me that she knew what I was thinking and agreed. There was no way we would be that lucky.

"What should we do with the gold? Shouldn't we stow it away somewhere safe for the time being? I mean, it's an awful lot of money to leave lying around, isn't it?" Elinor said.

She picked up a handful of Louis, a look of fascination on her face that was almost greedy in its focus.

Joseph reached out and took the Louis from her hand and placed them back with the others on the towel and rolled them all up. He handed us one apiece and disappeared below with the remainder. A minute later we heard the sounds of gear being shifted.

"Maybe we can talk Joseph into looking after it," Molly said.

We were all out on *Tramp*'s deck at daybreak, rigging up for the day ahead. A breeze had built the night before, and for the first time there was a slight chop in the lagoon. The weather faxes indicated we might be on the edge of some weather that was building farther north. The isobars were compressing, and while the storm could wheel and swing away from us and go out to sea, there was also the possibility that this was one of the rare ones that sometimes swept through Fiji in the cruising season. They were seldom dangerous, but they often generated winds in excess of forty knots, which would make diving from the cage in the lagoon impossible. I wasn't concerned about the boats, the holding was good, and laying in tight against the weather side of the lagoon with the storm anchors set, *Arrow* and *Tramp* would be secure in anything short of a full-blown hurricane.

Prior to the first dive, Padraic made several runs over the area we'd be searching, trying to get a more exact picture of what was below. Ultimately it was much as Laura and I had thought, the gully narrowing down and the depth constant except for the last twenty yards when it dropped down into a forty-foot hole before rising steeply back up and flattening out again to fall over the edge. That was very different from the other gullies where the final incline to the drop ran smoothly over the edge.

"A natural trap," Padraic said. "That's where we should find the rest of the gold."

He put out a hand and braced himself against the chart table as *Tramp* took a slight roll. The winds were still picking up. If they became much stronger, the cage would be difficult to control on the end of its long tether. *Tramp*'s every pitch and roll would be magnified down below, and it would be nearly impossible to keep the cage positioned over the gully.

"We'd better get down there soon," Danny said, "before the weather puts a stop to everything."

Molly and Tommo took the first dive, running the cage down to the bottom and then moving along the gully and stopping just short of where we'd found the gold Louis. Tommo left the cage on a tether and spent twenty minutes exploring along the bottom. He returned to the cage and they moved it ahead another hundred feet and then Molly went out and down into the hole that Padraic had described. She saw nothing and returned to the cage and they followed the gully to the edge. The bottom sloped gradually then dropped suddenly down to one hundred fifty feet before levelling out again. Surveying it was a slow and tedious process. The visibility was poor, *Tramp* proceeded at a crawl at the hundred-fifty-foot level, and Molly and Tommo could just make out the bottom as they inched along. Their searching time was severely limited at that depth, requiring twice as long in decompression stops at three different levels. When their down time was complete, *Tramp* dropped a weight with a buoy attached at the end of a shot line, marked off and numbered at five fathom intervals. It rose to the surface and marked the spot where Danny and I would continue. We waited until Molly and Tommo returned and held a council of war.

So far it was disappointing. There should have been some sign of Lapérouse's ship close to where we'd found the coins, even after all those years. Some hardware or rigging, even a stray plank, or something from the ship's hold. Some sign. Even if she had been swept off the edge by a heavy storm or, more probably, by the aftershock of the submarine explosion that had created the vent; why only the single bag of gold? Surely the hoard would have been stored in one area of the boat? It was too heavy to roll with the ocean currents. Logically there should be something else, some kind of sign nearby. But with the earthquake and the green water, logic had gone out the window, and we were in a twilight zone four miles in diameter where the natural laws were suspended and green sharks and monstrous sea snakes were possible. The rest of the gold was in the lagoon somewhere, the cask we found proved that, but it might be anywhere by now.

We decided to make one last try before the deteriorating weather shut us down for good. Tommo and Molly estimated their marker to be within a few hundred feet of the plateau. The sonar was near useless in the disturbed waters. It seemed the nearer we came to the epicentre the wilder the readings were.

Danny and I entered the cage and followed the shot rope down to the hundred-fifty-foot level. Visibility was barely thirty feet even with the big cage lights. Padraic was at *Tramp*'s helm and just making forward progress, slipping the engine in and out of gear to keep us moving as slowly as possible as we approached the bluff. It would not be a good thing to come in low and strike the edge with the cage. Peering ahead, we caught a faint glimpse of a cliff rising up and signalled a stop, then rose up sixty feet and halted again twenty feet above the plateau floor that extended out before us. The column of bubbles was much thicker now, rolling slowly to the edge and up. We rested there, straining our eyes as we tried to make something out, but there was nothing apart from the effervescence that enveloped us and the faint pops as the bubbles broke against the cage. We lowered the cage ten more feet, and the bottom came into view.

It was different from anything we had seen before, glassy, whipped up into small peaks and crests in spots and then mirror smooth for a few more feet and then rising again, broken and cracked into numerous gullies and crevasses. It was clear that this was relatively new, there was very little sediment, the lava similar to an enormous piece of peanut brittle that had been struck with a giant hammer and let fall as it may. Even the colour was right: a light shiny brown that assumed a greenish cast under the lights. We sat there watching and listening for a few minutes and then there was nothing for it but to reach for the button and signal slow ahead once more.

As we worked our cautious way forward, it seemed the pressure under us was gradually increasing in tandem with our progress, the bubbles rising faster against us as we drew away from the outer edge and moved towards what lay ahead. Breathless, wired, strung out, and waiting for that initial hit and that first terrifying primordial scream, I had to remind myself to inhale.

Danny stood close beside me, the pair of us almost touching now. We came to the beginning of a large depression that sloped down ahead, and as we moved over the edge of it we could just see the faint glimmer of movement below, the first motion we'd seen since we entered the lagoon seven days earlier. We paused and strained to see, but there was only a faint suggestion at the limits of our lights. We moved ahead another few feet and then stopped and slowly lowered the cage until the scene below came clear.

The hole was less than fifty feet in diameter, but it was impossible to tell its depth for it was swarming from rim to rim with a grotesque writhing ball of sea snakes, their stripes glowing blue and red and yellow in the lights. As the brightness of our lamps fell upon them, their motion slowed and stopped for seconds that seemed to stretch out forever, and then long sinuous twisting necks turned and looked up at us, extending out and upwards from that close-wrapped sphere, their eyes flashing yellow in reflection, and their nostrils flaring as if scenting for prey, the closest of them scant feet away.

"Up," I screamed, and reached for the buzzer and then the ball exploded in one huge piercing shriek and the vipers whirled and struck, and in seconds the cage was overwhelmed with countless numbers of them, the light gone and the cable screaming as it slipped and the cage fell in darkness to the bottom.

We struck on a slant, cushioned by the bodies on all sides and then the cage did a slow half roll and stopped and tilted against one of the glassy protrusions. The dive metre showed one hundred and thirty feet. I unhooked one of the big Mares lights from the side of the cage and flicked the switch and shone the beam into hell. The water was roiling with snakes, scales everywhere, glinting and falling and reflecting back amongst them, blue and black and yellow banded kraits, some with their heads pressed against the mesh that surrounded the spaced steel bars, others bulging the mesh with their hungry force and others behind, the force that drove them inwards. Danny grabbed a bang stick and shoved it against one of the biggest of the wedged heads, the detonation loud in that cramped cell, the smoke trapped, and the green water now tinted with a swirling red and blue. The head fell away and another took its place. The screams had stopped with that first onslaught, and it was silent now save for the creak of the mesh under the weight and the sound of the buzzer, the rapid WTF, WTF query repeated continuously. I replied WAIT and turned to Danny.

He looked at me and shrugged and made the sign for slow up. There was nothing else for it, and I nodded in agreement. We waited and then *Tramp* took up the slack and the cable straightened and trembled under the load, and the cage groaned and shook under the strain, but the inside corner wouldn't release from the overhang and there was a crack from the top corner as a bar sprang loose from its weld and I frantically signalled stop. The mesh had pushed aside and created a six-inch gap and a krait wiggled through. Danny pulled his knife and cut off the head with a quick slash and it drifted to the floor and glared viciously at us, its fangs opening and closing in spasms while its length coiled and threshed alongside. Immediately another one took its place, this one bigger. Christ, it had to be near a foot thick in the middle. Its head came through and the slimmest part of it followed and the rest of the body jammed in the opening. I took a bang stick and blew half its head off and left the body trapped and writhing in place.

Danny tapped me on the shoulder and shone the light past the reptile's body into the damaged corner and beyond, and I looked out. My heart stopped. We were dead men! The molten lava had curled and peaked that fateful day and extended up under all that pressure forming an overarching rock waterfall curving down over the edge into the hole we lay in. The glistening petrified cascade was stunningly beautiful if only our viewing platform hadn't hit just outside it and the corner tipped just enough on the bias to be trapped underneath. The only way to release the cage was to push it back three feet to clear the edge or to remove the overhang. Pulling at an angle with *Tramp* wouldn't do it. There wasn't enough slack in the cable at this depth to move us back the few necessary feet, and not enough time to jury rig aboard *Tramp* even if we had the communication system and equipment in place to do so.

Danny must have reached the same conclusion because he picked up one of the big pry bars off the wall and began to thrust through the bars at the lava in heavy furious blows, but he was only wasting air and energy, and after a couple of minutes of futile effort I reached across and stopped him. It was intensely hot in the cage now, stifling, and our masks fogged up continuously. The fact that we were surrounded on all sides by an impenetrable wall of snakes only reinforced the claustrophobic heat. A thousand glaring yellow eyes focused on us, all of them with a single thought.

Dinner.

How much air? Danny signed.

I held up one finger. *An hour.*

Likewise.

We sat for a while, and then Danny jumped up and released the catch on the roof opening where the creatures seemed less thick, and the two of us strained upwards but we couldn't gain an inch against the press. Truth told, I was relieved. The thought of going out against those monsters was infinitely more terrifying to me than the alternative of slowly choking for lack of air. The buzzer started tapping out Morse again.

WTF WTF

SNAGGED NEED TIME. I responded.

I looked at my dive computer.

Forty minutes.

Danny would have a bit less; he was bigger and had used more energy. We sat for another bit.

WTF WTF

WAIT FIFTEEN MINUTES LET OUT ALL CABLE SLACK. STEAM FULL THROTTLE NE.

OK. GOOD LUCK.

Nothing to do now but wait. Lethargy and a shameful resignation consumed me in the close and heat. Depression, guilt, Danny dying alongside me. My boat, my trip, my choices. For the first time, I was thankful we didn't have voice communication with the surface. No sad complicated goodbyes, no apologies, no "my fault," "your fault," no "I'm sorry," "you're sorry," "we're sorry." Just a slow extinguishing, a dying of the light. Maybe not so bad. I almost resented the quick jerk to come, the brief surge of false hope, the steel cable jumping and stretching, then thinning before it parted and flashed away and disappeared. I closed my eyes and waited for the end.

We sat slumped over for another five minutes in lethargy and then I jumped to my feet and yelled *Fuck This!* and grabbed some bang sticks and my knife and jumped to the bars. Danny's teeth flashed, and he reared up with me and the two of us flew into them. I banged two dead with the sticks and stabbed others and I heard a scream from one and Danny had knives in both hands now and the shrieks were louder as we gutted and slashed and I thought, *Good, you fuckers.* And I worked faster and the screams went up another scale and some of them were mine now and the water was filled with blood and smoke and scales and slashing knives and I thought, *This is better,* and the screams became deafening, and I could taste the blood and scales in the water now, and I spat out my mouthpiece and embraced it all and the madness overwhelmed me. There was a sudden crash and I stumbled and I thought, *No, it's not time yet,* and I fought harder and slashed more wildly, and then a quick flash of white beyond the snakes and the cage rocked and bucked once more, the impact driving me to the floor and slamming me up against the wall. My head snapped back against the cage and the cage trembled and shook and slid back under the impact and Danny raised me up and slapped me across the face and shoved my mouthpiece back in and we slowly rose up and I saw the vipers falling out of sight beneath us and then everything faded into the black with them and I was gone.

CHAPTER 25

I awoke coughing and spitting, my head aching, my face stinging, my mouth a foul combination of sulphur and blood and something worse. There was a large tender bump on the back of my head.

"Maybe one more good slap," someone said.

"Stop that, Danny. It's not helping."

Then Laura leaned down and kissed me.

"I wouldn't do that if I were you," Danny muttered. Molly passed me a glass of rum and I took a mouthful and rinsed and spat it out into *Tramp*'s gutters. Laura frowned. I lay on a blanket on *Tramp*'s deck, surrounded by, for the most part, concerned faces. It felt like every bone in my body was aching.

"What happened?"

"The cage broke free, and you were knocked out, Danny brought the cage up to the first decompression stop, we went down with spare tanks, hooked you both up, waited, then went up to the next one, same routine. You were out cold."

"Ah. It caught me off guard. You were early on the cable."

Again the shifty glances. Joseph watched impassively.

"Actually, that wasn't us."

"What do you mean it wasn't you?"

Joseph put his hands together with the thumbs up and moved them sinuously back and forth. Sinbad uttered a loud bark.

"No fucking way," I said.

"Way," Danny said. "Biggest white mother you've ever seen. Thirty feet. At least. Had to have been three tons. Came at the blood and snakes, smashed into the cage, never even slowed down. Moved us a good ten feet."

I thought about it for a minute. Nobody spoke.

"Oh well, a cool quarter million ain't half bad. We'll never find Lapérouse's ship now. The lava will have destroyed every trace on the plateau. If she was ever there she's gone now. It's as bare as a baby's bum. Besides which, we couldn't go back even if we were insane enough to want to. Cage has to be overhauled before any more dives, storm coming, monster sharks, monster sea snakes, who knows what else might be down there. Monster squid? Could be, right? Nope, we're done. Finito." I drained my glass and handed it to Molly for a refill and tried to look as if I felt bad about it all.

"Party time. We'll leave first thing in the morning, or at least, when we're awake and capable of rational thought." I raised my glass and toasted the assemblage.

They were all looking down upon me with pity in their eyes.

"Come and take a look at the cage, Jared. There's something you need to see."

The cage was winched up just out of the water alongside *Tramp*'s hull; there was no way it would have slotted into the chocks that usually held her. The cage had been struck so hard its shape was out of square, condensed and flattened on the one corner, the bars all loose from their welds and popped on the other. There were two large dents imploding where the door opening used to be, and the top had bent down over that. The lower bars had pushed into the steering rudder, which was now folded in upon itself. Just to complete the destruction, a twenty-foot chunk of fossilized log had somehow impaled the cage and ran right through one side and out the other. A pair of decapitated sea krait carcasses were jammed in one corner where the mesh had been peeled back.

"See, that's what I'm talking about. No fucking way we're going back down in that fucking wreck again. Not without some major repairs, maybe not even then."

Laura gave me a reproving look. I sensed my near-death language credits were used up.

"Take a closer look at that piece of wood," Elinor said.

I looked back and saw the fresh wood at the end of the log where it had been broken off — the log was evenly tapered, I belatedly noticed, and what I'd taken for seaweed was actually a chunk of rotted rope.

It was a goddammed motherfucking ship's spar!

"It's off an old sailing vessel," Padraic said.

I nodded.

"It was broken off by the cage. You can see the fresh wood."

I nodded.

"If the spar was unattached down there, it would have come up in one piece."

Maybe the end was jammed under a rock. Encased in the lava even. Probably not.

I nodded.

"It has to be Lapérouse. What are the chances it could be another ship when we found the gold so near?"

It could be another ship, I wanted to say. A lot can happen in two hundred and fifty years. Tides, currents, storms. Probably not, though.

I nodded.

"Say something, Jared!" Laura snapped.

I raised my glass and said, "I need another drink," and she whirled and stamped away.

Danny came over and sat down beside me. "I think I have the answer," he said, as he topped us up.

"What?" I inquired sourly.

"Blue paint. In a little portable spray can. You always carry it with you and whenever you're about to go batshit like you did in the pub at Opua or in the cage just now, you paint your face like your forefathers did. Think Gibson in *Braveheart*. It would give me a little heads up. Donning a kilt would be outstanding, but that might take too long. Although maybe you could always wear it under your shorts. Kind of like Superman. Rip 'em off when the time came."

"Fuck you, Daniel MacLean, and the canoe you paddled in on."

He grinned. "Lame, Jared, very lame."

I returned to *Arrow* and showered and had a nap and awoke feeling almost human. While I slept they had moved the boats out of the lagoon and sealed the gates behind them. We were anchored two miles away from Teuini in another of the atolls that were strung out in a long crescent chain, the water sparkling clean, a building breeze blowing across our decks and the nightmare memories already fading into a half-remembered dream. Looking out over the lagoon, it seemed that everyone was seeking normalcy by engaging in those mundane activities that define the cruising life for most sailors. Laura and Elinor were in the little skiff sailing among the reefs that dotted the lagoon; Joseph and Liani were just visible walking along the far shore, Sinbad fishing the edge beside them in stiff-legged jumps. Danny and Tommo were spearfishing by a bommie out in the middle, using the panga for their diving base. Just as I put the Steiners on them, Tommo surfaced with a lobster. Padraic and Molly were nowhere in sight. I grabbed a snorkel and goggles from the dive locker and went over *Arrow*'s side and swam into the shore.

By the time I'd walked around to the far side, Joseph and Liani had dug a small pit in the loose sand and lined it with rocks. I gathered firewood and we lit a fire and sat watching while it burned down to coals. Joseph reached into his bag and pulled out a bottle of Laphroaig and two glasses and poured drinks, passing one to me.

"Thank you," I said, as surprised by the offer as by his seemingly unlimited stash. He smiled and murmured softly.

"You're welcome," Liani said.

Joseph leaned over and clinked my glass with his and drank it down. I did the same. He reached across a second time and poured us both another. I became wary.

"What's the occasion?"

Again with the murmuring.

"He's just glad to be here with you."

I stared across at him and felt the annoyance rising as always with his language of the conquerors act and readied myself to have a go at him when Elinor and Laura sailed the skiff up onto the beach and the opportunity was lost. Danny and Tommo showed up right behind them with lobsters and coral trout, and then Padraic and Molly with yams and taro from the ship's stores as well as ample supplies of drink, and the feast was officially on. It might have been one of the best nights of my life — the food was superb, everyone was in high spirits, and nobody drank too much, even me. Laura never left my side all night. By mutual consent nobody mentioned Teuini until the last lobster was eaten and the last coconut split for the last drink.

Padraic cleared his throat. "Well then," he said and paused. There was a long silence.

Damned if I would be the one to break it.

"We can't just leave it without knowing," he burst out. Another long silence.

"I agree," I said, to my own surprise.

And then there was a burst of talk, led mostly by Tommo and Molly. We'd head back to Suva, refit, bigger cage, better equipment, a grapple, voice communications, maybe hire a couple more divers, explosives, shark repellents, underwater acetylene torches, etcetera, etcetera. Now that we knew what we were facing, more or less, everyone seemed confident we could eliminate most of the risk from the enterprise. I didn't take any part in the planning. From here on in I was strictly Captain

Kane, master of the S.V. *Arrow*, and underwater expeditions only concerned me inasmuch as they affected the safety of my vessel. No power on earth could induce me to enter the green waters of the lagoon once more. It was decided we'd stay for one more day and leave the following morning for Suva. At midnight everyone split up and went their separate ways and Laura and I returned to our cabin aboard *Arrow*. She was happier than I'd ever seen her, a giddy mixture of relief at the day's outcomes and excitement for our prospects. It was the best time together we'd ever had. When she finally fell asleep, I whispered in her ear that I loved her.

I awoke early and slipped out of the bunk, leaving Laura asleep. I put on a sweater and made a pot of coffee and sat on the stern rail watching the sun rise through *Arrow's* rigging. It was eerily quiet, just the sound of a loose halyard tapping and the usual creaks and groans of an old wooden boat, and then, as the sun tipped the top of the mast, it was as if a switch had been turned and all the sights and sounds of lagoon life rose up around us. Seabirds stirring, the quick flash and skitter of a school of juvenile tuna, a heavy hunting splash out near the middle, the far away keening cry of a sea hawk. All of it so damned nice and normal.

The sea was quiet, but the tops of the palms were swaying under the trades. The wind was up, and it would be a quick passage back to Suva. I leaned back and closed my eyes and fell into a dreamless sleep.

I was awakened by the sounds of Elinor and Laura emerging from below, arm in arm, the pair of them laughing about something, Danny trailing behind in their wake. Laura bent down and kissed me.

"Cheer up, old man, life is good. We're going to find the treasure and get rich and live happily ever after. That's an order by the way. I've got it all figured out; six months sailing and six months in the antiques business in London. That's fair enough isn't it? Has to beat six months sailing and six months fishing halibut."

She smiled down at me, and my mood lifted at the sight of her happiness, and the responsibility for it settled over me like a jurisdiction. To my surprise I found I didn't mind, and even welcomed it, and I sensed in that moment how rich my life could be.

"Daddy and Molly have decided to leave a day early and get a head start for Suva. They say they're both so wound up they won't get any sleep tonight anyway, so they might as well get underway. Elinor and I are going to have breakfast with them on their way out to the pass and sail back in the skiff. Troll a line, maybe pick up something for dinner. You want to come along?"

"No, I think not. I'll tidy things up a bit, get *Arrow* ready to leave in the morning."

Elinor appeared on deck and the two of them took the skiff across to *Tramp*. Padraic and Molly came out of the cabin and yelled across about meeting at the yacht club in Suva and a few minutes later *Tramp* headed off towards the channel.

"I'm glad you and Laura have worked things out. It's about time," Danny said.

"Yes, it is. You know, I miss her already. I'm not used to that feeling."

"You should get used to it," he said. "She's a keeper."

"How about you and Elinor?"

"You know me, Jared. A shiftless drifter incapable of sustaining a permanent relationship. Although I think this time Elinor is going to beat me to it. When she left just now it was as if she was apologizing to me."

I felt a twinge of unease and stood up and waited for *Tramp* to reappear around the island. Finally it did, just barely in sight now, a blond head and a dark one just visible on deck as *Tramp* motored into the slanting rays of the morning sun. I watched them until they disappeared from sight and resisted a sudden urge to jump into the inflatable and power out to the pass and escort them back. What was acceptable from a concerned friend could easily become a question of trust and control with a partner and lover. It was a new place for me, and I wasn't comfortable with the boundaries yet. Maybe I never would be.

I lay in the sun, thinking about it all, then Joseph and Liani came out and paddled off in *Tramp*'s aluminum skiff, and it was only Danny and me left aboard, like old times. We broke out the beer and talked and dozed under the bimini. Danny changed the main halyard where it was showing chafe at the mast pulley while I adjusted some of the baggy wrinkles on the shrouds. Just idling away the time in what passed for toil in the cruising life. The sun rose gradually up overhead and began its slow fall to the west as we puttered, and I was just beginning to think it was getting past time for the girls to show up when the call came over the VHF.

CHAPTER 26

"*Arrow*. This is *Golden Dragon*."

A chill passed over me at the sound of Waverly's voice. I think something deep inside me was half expecting it and to my horror there was a shaming sense of anticipation, a grim dark thing that raised its ugly head and sickened me.

Danny picked up the handheld.

"*Golden Dragon*, this is *Arrow*."

"Go to sixty-eight, *Arrow*. Low power."

Danny switched over and we waited. Waverly wasted no time on small talk.

"Time to finish the dance, lads. Partners all lined up and waiting."

"Why would we want to do that?"

"Some of your friends have already consented to join us. I'm sure you wouldn't want them to get lonely now, would you? One of them is an old flame of Summers's. He's a bit of a devil with the ladies you know, don't know how much longer I can hold him in check."

Danny closed his eyes and slowly shook his head. I reached over and snatched the handset away from him.

"We're on our way," I said.

I took all thoughts of Laura and our time together and wrapped them up and put them in a safe place and brought out the picture of Summers, and let the picture expand and fill my consciousness until there wasn't room for anything else.

"Are we taking the inflatable?" Danny asked.

"No. *Arrow.*"

I fired up the engine as he sprang to the foredeck and hauled the anchor, the muscles on his back jumping as he pumped it up. I jammed the engine into gear and powered into the channel, Danny cursing as the anchor bounced in the shallow passage, the chain slack and then shrieking on the sheave as we went around the island and out into the main channel.

The *Golden Dragon* lay directly ahead of us a scant mile away. As we approached, I saw the little sailing skiff rocking alongside her stern. There was no sign of *Tramp*, and for a brief instant I considered radioing her but realized that would be pointless. There was nothing that Padraic or Molly could do that would change anything. They would only be another pair of hostages.

Keep it simple.

I let my mind play back over the first contest with Summers in the North Island bar and recreated the quick mongoose bounce of his moves, the way his slender, muscular body slanted back from my forays and then countered in fast sidelong thrusts, the superior mocking smile always seen in profile as he presented the smallest possible point of attack. He had been so sure of me.

"Starboard tie," I said, and Danny dropped the bumpers down as we approached the *Golden Dragon* at full speed ahead, and I slammed the old Perkins into full reverse and she shrieked in furious protest as I laid the tiller over and we made a foaming ninety degree turn and slammed up against the yellow bitch's gleaming sides and made fast and went up and over the rails in a quick rush.

"Easy now, lads," Summers said. He stood with Turk and the young

German who had fought Phueng. The scars of her nails still disfigured his face. They all had pistols trained on us. We had brought none. There were too many of them. Our best hope was negotiation. Trade the location of the ship for our freedom.

"Search them, Turk."

The man ran his hands over me as I stood motionless watching Summers, and then he turned to Danny and Danny slapped his hands away.

"Don't touch me, you fat fucking eunuch. I'm not armed."

Turk swung a big fist at Danny's head and Danny ducked down and carefully uppercut him in the groin and the man screamed in a high-pitched voice and fell to the deck, cradling himself.

"That the best help you can get?" Danny asked.

Summers stepped forward, his pistol raised.

"That's enough," Waverly said, immaculate in whites and a red silk shirt, as he stepped out of the pilothouse, a smile on his face.

"I must apologize for Summers. Sometimes he lets his personal feelings interfere with the proper courtesy toward guests aboard the *Dragon*," he said.

"We're not guests and we're not here of our own free will and we're tired of playing your games," I said. "Give us the women and we'll leave. We don't need the trouble. You've got the journals. There's no need for any of this. We're pulling out in the morning anyway."

Waverly shrugged. "I'm sorry you feel that way, Jared, but things aren't quite that simple anymore, now, are they? There's the treasure to consider now that we have a fix on its whereabouts. Your Joseph is really quite an amazing fellow. Of course, you know I want it all. Need it actually. Slumping London real estate, Brexit, a downturn in the market, a couple of high-tech companies gone bad, boring story, really, not one you need to know in any detail." He shook his head and raised his hands in a mocking gesture. "Did you think I wouldn't find out? You've underestimated me rather badly, I'm afraid. If you know only one thing about me, know this: I seldom lose at all, and never in the long-term. I always cover my bets. Think about that. I'm afraid you will have to be locked up until the entertainments begin. A pity, really. I do so enjoy our little conversations."

He motioned to the young German who came over and stood close behind us. Turk, still bent over and gasping for air through his open mouth, joined him.

"Lock them in the cabin next to Summers's and post a guard at the door. If they cause any trouble, kill them. Send a man to search their boat for the gold coins, Friedrich. I want them all."

They took us below and into a large stateroom. As we stepped through the door, Turk hit Danny in the back of the neck with his pistol, knocked him to the floor and kicked him.

"That's enough," Friedrich said and shoved him away. He bent close to me and whispered, the scars thin red lines on his face. "The girl has drugs on her nails. Hallucinogens. If she cuts you, you're finished."

He grabbed Turk, and they went out the door and slammed it behind them and then there was the clang of twin bolts being dropped into their slots. Everything in the cabin was solid steel or aluminum and welded in, even the bed and table; there was nothing we could detach and use for a weapon or as a tool for escape. A locked door led to an adjoining cabin with a thick Lexan window looking in, a shutter screening it from the other side.

Danny raised his head and groaned. I squatted down beside him. "You look like shit," I said.

He wheezed a curse and pulled himself up onto his knees, his head down, panting heavily. I went over to the fridge and took some ice and wrapped it in a towel and handed it to him. He applied it carefully to the back of his neck and then pulled himself up and collapsed into an easy chair bolted to the deck.

"I'll be all right. Give me a minute."

There was a stocked minibar in the corner and I handed him a couple of the little plastic bottles. He drank one down and sighed.

"That's better."

He looked around. "I don't suppose there's much chance of getting out of here."

"I think not. They've probably got surveillance in here as well."

I looked at my watch. Almost five o'clock.

"I wonder how the girls are doing," Danny said.

As if in answer to his question, there was a noise from the cabin next to ours, a woman's voice raised and a muffled slap. An awful knowledge rose within me. I took a quick step and hurled myself at the steel door, but it never even quivered under the impact. I reared back again and Danny grabbed and held me. I heard the sound of a coarse grunting and then the shutter rose in the adjoining cabin. I knew before I looked.

She was lying on the bed in the centre of the room, her hands and feet tied out on both sides of her, her eyes staring vacantly upwards as Summers laboured above her. I hammered on the window and screamed her name, but she didn't respond, her head slowly swinging from side to side in dumb negation.

Danny grabbed my arm and tried to pull me away, but I was turned to stone. If Laura could suffer it, I could watch it. She never moved or screamed the whole time, even when he struck her, only staring mindlessly at the ceiling and her head slowly moving from side to side as he writhed above her.

It seemed to go on forever, a brutal mechanical coupling, Summers's cold face turning to grin at me over her body, his thin lips twisting as he mouthed obscenities and the sweat from his face dripped down onto her body. He had no satisfaction from my masked agony as I took the measure of every plunging stroke and added them to his private tally and calibrated every separate straining muscle on his body and marked it for my own.

Finally he was done, and he stood up and moved away from her. She stayed as she was, passive save for that frightening motion of her head and he looked down at her and screamed "stop" and struck her and it made no difference at all. He took the ripped dress and wiped himself down and threw it over her body and left. A few minutes later, Elinor entered, her head bent away from us, and came over to the window and pulled down the blind. Danny hammered on the window and shouted her name, but she wouldn't look up or speak. A few minutes later, we heard the cabin door close again, and we sat there in silence as the quick tropic darkness fell. Danny tried to say something once but stopped partway. I wanted nothing but oblivion, but I didn't touch a drop.

It was two hours later when they finally came for us.

CHAPTER 27

They'd set up a proper ring this time, three braided nylon ropes enclosing a squared-off area in front of the dining table. Thin tatami mats were spread out inside, with a large circle outlined in red in the centre of the ring. In two opposing corners were stools with buckets of water and sponges. Behind each stood an armed man, with another pair at the entrance.

Waverly sat at the big table, Laura and Elinor on each side of him. Elinor was gazing down at the tablecloth while Laura stared in front of her. Her shoulders were slumped and her movements slow and hesitant, and I wondered if she was drugged. Elinor raised her head and glanced quickly at us, and I saw her face was bruised and one eye blackened. Phueng stood behind Laura, massaging her neck and shoulders. She saw me watching and slipped her hand down and caressed Laura's breast and smiled knowingly at me.

Waverly looked on in approval, then spoke. "You're probably wondering how I knew about the treasure, so let me set your minds at rest on that point; Elinor told me this afternoon, when she delivered Laura to us. You mustn't blame her too much; she has a brother in parliament, married, there were some private meetings with a page, we obtained pictures, you can certainly imagine the rest. Of course, I'd told her nobody would be harmed. Silly cunt actually believed me. As a matter of fact, she was very loyal to you up to a point, even tried to get Laura away." He shook his head in mock disapproval.

"We couldn't have that, of course. Not when I had promised her to Barclay. If you don't keep your promises to your men, how can you expect to retain their loyalty?"

Each time he mentioned Laura's name her eyes swung slowly in his direction and then back straight ahead, her face as blank and lifeless as a doll's. She simply wasn't there. Waverly smiled at me.

"You'll get your chance with Summers soon enough, Jared, but there's an agenda to the evening. Violence without form is merely barbarism, and you must be patient for a little while. I think we'll have your friend up first off. Turk wants him."

Danny rose up and went to the table and two of the men moved quickly in on him, but he simply touched Elinor's bent head and said, "Don't sweat it," and vaulted lightly over the ropes into the ring.

"How about you and me, Waverly? You've got to fancy yourself a little don't you? You're in good shape, same size as me near enough, what do you think? Tell you what, you gutless piece of shit, you can tie one arm behind my back." Danny smiled mockingly, his eyes hard as stone.

"Don't push your luck," Waverly snarled.

"Or what? You're going to let us go after we kick your ass? Don't insult my intelligence."

"There are different ways to die," Waverly said, his composure back. He glanced at Phueng, who smiled back at him. I noticed for the first time that her incisors were filed into points.

"You mean that freak show sitting alongside you? If I can't take her I'll cut my fucking throat myself, I promise. Come on, bring her on, then afterwards, I'll take you."

Danny ragged and taunted him, and I felt a surge of love for him for I knew what he was doing, even as I knew it wouldn't work. Phueng had marked me for her own that first time, when I'd interrupted her pleasure with the young German, and she wouldn't be cheated again. As for Waverly, he was a proud man who thought highly of himself, but Danny had taken his measure that first time they met and shook hands, and he would never risk himself in an even contest.

Waverly clapped his hands and the door at the end of the hall opened and Summers and Turk entered. They were stripped and oiled, barefoot and wearing only shorts, Summers lean and sinewy as a stalking cat, Turk sumo-like with his great haunches and swinging belly. They moved up in front of Waverly and bowed to him and then Turk ducked through the ropes into the ring where Danny stood waiting. He looked almost small beside the other man. Turk was a good three inches taller and outweighed him by fifty pounds. Danny was good, but this guy was awfully big.

"How're the nuts feeling, big fella?" Danny inquired. "Still got a twinge or two? Never mind, in a few minutes you won't feel a thing."

"No talking in the ring," Waverly snapped.

"And fuck you too," Danny responded.

Waverly gestured and the man in the corner behind Danny raised the barrel of his pistol and chopped down on the back of his neck. Danny fell to his knees, stunned, and rolled over onto his side.

"You gutless bastard," I hissed at Waverly.

"The rules inside the ring, apart from silence, are this: there are none," Waverly said. "The contest begins when the clock strikes the quarter hour and ends when one of you is dead. I'll sound the rounds on this bell."

Danny was back on his knees, his head bowed, shaking it slowly from side to side as he struggled to regain his senses. The ship's clock on the wall behind him showed there was less than a minute to go.

"He's still groggy, give him another few minutes, you bastard."

Waverly shrugged. "He disobeyed the rules, Jared. We mustn't have that. On the quarter hour."

I stared at the clock as the second hand made its final sweep. Danny was up, rolling his neck to loosen the muscles. He took a half step forward and staggered slightly, and then the bell sounded and Turk was upon him.

He came across the ring in a quick shambling run, fast for a big man, a cruel smile on his face as he lifted his elbow and smashed Danny across the throat. Danny moved sideways at the last moment and caught some of it on his shoulder, but it spun him sideways and knocked him to his knees. He ducked under a vicious kick and managed to catch the foot and twist Turk off balance. The big man fell, but Danny was still too slow to take any advantage.

They came to their feet, and Turk took a boxing stance and moved in, his oiled body gleaming in the light as he feinted left and swung a roundhouse right that caught Danny under the ribs and elicited a grunt of pain. Danny jabbed, but his timing was off, and Turk lowered his shaved head and planted his feet and swung heavy chopping blows to Danny's midsection, loud meaty jolts that left red welts behind. Danny crouched under the punches and tried to grapple with Turk, but his grip slipped on the oiled body and Turk shook loose and came in again, delivering those heavy thudding body blows, and Danny went down once more.

Turk stood over him grinning, and as Danny struggled to his knees, threw a side kick at his head that caught him square on the ear and stretched his length out on the mats. Turk knelt beside him and locked his fists together and raised them high over his head for the finishing stroke, but before he could bring them down a bell rang out.

"Round one, I think," Waverly said. "We don't want the performance to end too quickly, now, do we? You may assist your friend, Jared. You have sixty seconds."

I sprang over the ropes and dragged Danny onto the stool in his corner and took some water and poured it over him.

"How am I doing?" he mumbled. His eyes were dazed and unfocused, his speech slurred. A thin trace of blood leaked from his nostrils.

"You're getting your ass whipped. Big time." I put my hands on his neck where the guard had struck him and massaged the rubbery muscles.

"That's what I figured."

"Stay away from him; try to work from the outside. He's too big to trade shots with."

"Yeah. My legs aren't quite right yet though."

The bell rang and Turk stormed out again, using his weight to force Danny into the corner, pounding him with short heavy body blows. Danny crouched low under them, sagging down as Turk bored in, all defences gone before the onslaught, and the fat man opened up and reached back for a finishing roundhouse. Danny suddenly straightened and swung his head upwards with the spring of his legs and butted him under his chin. Turk reeled back and Danny was upon him, swinging heavy vicious blows to his stomach. Turk staggered and fell forward and as he went down, Danny caught him with a knee in the face. As the head arched back he delivered a backhand to the throat, and over the frantic ringing of the bell I heard the crack of cartilage, as sharp and final as a rifle shot.

In the sudden silence there was the choking rasp of a long-drawn shuddering breath and then nothing.

"Round two, I think," Danny said into the quiet.

Waverly stared at him, his face twisted with rage. He motioned to two of the guards and they stepped into the ring and ran Danny back into the corner and bent his arms back over the ropes and held him there.

"Keep him still," Waverly hissed, "and tie up the other one. Dump that carrion over the side."

Two of the guards seized me and tied my hands behind my back while two others each took a leg of Turk and dragged the body out through the entrance doors. There was a muted splash and then they returned.

Waverly took off his shirt and entered the ring. He pulled on a thin pair of leather gloves and walked over to Danny's corner.

"Aren't we the brave fellow now," Danny said.

Waverly grinned and threw out a jabbing left that caught Danny on the cheek, and then feinted left and threw a sharp right-hander that struck him in the stomach. Danny grunted and his nostrils flared and his eyes never left Waverly's.

"Why don't you let me loose and try some of that," he said.

"Maybe later," Waverly said. "Save your breath now, you're going to need it."

He worked Danny like a body bag, dancing back with long flickering jabs and crosses then coming in close for the heavy pounding combinations to the ribs and stomach, turning Danny and opening up his kidneys for vicious slanting shots that staggered and finally dropped him.

Danny never spoke again, twisting his head trying to avert the main thrust of the punches, slanting his body, his eyes always on Waverly as his features thickened and coarsened under the onslaught. Each time he fell he rose up again, his eyes blazing, his face a red mask of blood.

"Stay down, you fool," I murmured, but I knew he never would.

Finally it ended, Danny bent over on his knees, head down, Waverly panting above him exhausted.

"Throw water on him, Friedrich. I want him conscious for the next act."

Waverly took a drink from the bucket and the young crewman dumped the rest on Danny then lifted him to his feet and ran him over to the big table and set him back in an armchair. He sagged forward, and Summers shoved him back and threw a drink in his face and the liquor burned in his cuts and he grunted and his eyes jerked open and Danny was back. Elinor went over and wiped his face, tears running down her cheeks, and he might have tried to smile up at her.

Friedrich shoved her away and reached down and tied Danny's wrists to the back of the chair. He whispered something in his ear and jerked the rope tight and Danny grunted in pain. Waverly nodded in approval. He took a small, almost dainty drink.

"Well, Act Two," he said, and they picked me up and untied me then threw me over the ropes and into the ring where Summers stood waiting.

CHAPTER 28

I rolled to my feet and turned to face Summers. He stood in his corner with a faint supercilious sneer, relaxed and waiting. I went across to the opposite corner and waited for the bell that would toll the start of this insane charade. The guards who stood around the ring seemed bored by it all, their faces impassive, their pistols held loosely in front of them. They'd seen this show before.

Waverly was in no hurry to begin things and took another little sip of his drink and dabbed his lips with his handkerchief as he surveyed the scene with approval. It was reminiscent of something from the fall of the Roman Empire, Waverly the maddest Nero of them all. All that was missing was a raised dais, some grapes, and a wreath of laurel around his brow. I found the thought strangely comforting.

"I'm glad you're enjoying this, Jared."

"Not so much. Just thinking what a crazy bastard you really are."

"Well, enjoy it while you can. I imagine it's not going to end all that well. Phueng is waiting for her kick at the can, so to speak, should you be fortunate enough to get past Summers."

He patted her shoulder and she twisted and looked up at him, her filed teeth gleaming in the cabin light, then turned those glowing eyes upon me, her nostrils flaring as she ran her tongue slowly around her lips, as if already tasting my blood.

I felt a cold paralysis under that gaze, as if those long scarlet nails had already ticked my body and poisoned my mind, and I knew then for a certainty I would have no chance against her. She held my glance, reading my mind and raised her free hand and stroked Laura's throat with those long slender fingers. Laura never flinched or moved away from her touch but sat quietly, facing straight forward, her vacant gaze lost somewhere above the ring where I stood and waited for death.

Waverly took a long, well-satisfied look around, paused theatrically, then struck the bell. I turned to face Summers. He took three quick steps into the centre of the ring then began the dancing sidelong hops I remembered so well. His oiled body glistened in the light, even his head shaved and gleaming now, showing the raised purple scar previously hidden by the long blond hair. He looked every inch the martial arts warrior, calm and confident of his victory.

I stood and waited for him, no plan really, just a grim hope that whatever awaited Laura, Danny, and me this day, he wouldn't be around to enjoy it. But first things first. I breathed in deeply and summoned my resolve and took a slow step forward and he spun and kicked out, the blow grazing my throat and knocking me backwards into the corner post. He was lightning fast, out of my range before I could even begin to format a response. I shook my head to clear it and he moved in, dancing, feinting, a hard punch to the ribs then away once more.

I felt already drugged; leaden, stupid, a quarter second slow and a half step late. Summers minced in again and aimed a quick knee at my groin. I turned away and took it on the thigh. He whirled again as I drew back and chopped my neck with the edge of his hand, as hard and calloused as a club. I shook my head to clear it and he turned his back on me and glided away untouched.

I glanced towards the table. Waverly was scowling, presumably at the lack of contest and spectacle his gladiators were providing. You could hardly blame him. Danny was frowning as well.

"Think blue," Danny yelled suddenly.

At the disruption, Waverly turned and nodded, and the young German struck Danny in the back of the neck with the barrel of the pistol and he grunted in pain and mouthed the words again. I almost smiled until I turned towards Laura. Her unfocused gaze had moved down from the ceiling and now rested blankly upon me and there was nothing there, no recognition, no feeling, a lost hopeless mannequin, and then her eyes rose up into space once more. My heart sank, and despair rose up and overwhelmed me.

"Laura!" I screamed, and the crewman leaned over the ropes and struck me. I fell to my knees and Summers drifted in and kicked me under the chin and I flew back against the ropes and collapsed. He smiled mockingly and came leisurely in for the kill and then the bell rang, and I stumbled back to the stool in my corner. I gazed down at the mats, vowing not to look again, but I couldn't help myself. When I glanced up, Laura's gaze remained on the ceiling above her, her face clear and untroubled and I rejoiced. None of this was affecting her. She was gone to some safe private place where they couldn't hurt her anymore.

A weary fatalism descended upon me, and the last energy drained from my body and there was nothing remaining to take its place. Phueng's arm was cradling Laura's shoulders, her own little doll now, and I tried to raise up some anger, some outrage or thirst for revenge, something to fuel my passion and spur my body, but there was nothing there to build upon, nothing save a hopeless aching nihilism and a shaming desire for an end to it all. I was as empty and lost as Laura. The only thing left in my life was a quick death.

The bell sounded, and Summers danced towards me in those prancing sidelong moves, willing and eager to grant my final request. A shadow of self-contempt rose up from some other person locked deep inside and it aimed a slow kick at his groin, but he brushed it contemptuously aside and landed a savage blow to my neck that staggered me, and then dropped me with a kick to the midriff. He turned his back and strutted away as I lay there and fought for breath. Waverly clapped his hands in approval and took another drink.

Summers turned and glided back towards me with deadly purpose. His leg took me in the throat and the cold shadows enfolded me. My heart froze as I lay there dazed and waiting for an end to it all.

Summers bent over me. "I'm going to kill you now, mate, and then I'm going to fuck your Irish bitch until I'm tired of her and then I'm going to give her to the crew."

I gazed up at him through the blood and sweat and tears. *She won't even know you're there, mate*, I thought. He gave me a contemptuous kick in the ribs and walked away.

"Finish him," Waverly said. "He's pathetic."

I rolled onto my back and struggled up for my last look at the woman who'd been Laura. Her gaze had dropped upon me now, and where there'd been blankness before, I saw confusion.

Jesus, no, I prayed. *Please God, not now. Leave her be, for pity's sake.*

She bent slightly towards me and I saw I was mistaken. Her face was frozen, expressionless; it was just a trick of the lights. I sighed in thanksgiving then saw the glistening tears that belied the mask as she gazed upon me.

"Laura," I screamed in horror and rolled desperately away. Summers charged, and the numbing coldness that had enveloped me exploded into a red-hot pain.

He caught me on the thigh and staggered me, then whipped a sweeping cat-quick heel to my head that smashed my cheek and exploded my vision in blood. I focused on Laura's face and took that pain and rolled it in with the other and banked the fuel and fed upon it. I took a deep breath and the cracked rib screamed and I breathed more deeply. The ring was growing now, with more room to move. The air had thickened, and Waverly yelled but his words floated slowly away and didn't reach me. I rose to my feet with a world of time and slipped past Summers's clumsy charge and let his flailing fist catch my mouth for added fuel and smiled through the blood and caught the faint first scent of a hesitant fear and my nostrils expanded to savour the taste.

"Come on, mate," I whispered.

He paused, uncertain now, then advanced in cautious sidelong hops and as he kicked I caught his leg and could have broken it but I didn't. I backhanded him and he fell and glanced at Waverly who glared coldly and waved him upwards.

"No joy there, mate," I said. He sprang erect and came at me and I swept his feet out from under him and elbow-smashed his face and he skidded and went down. The sneer disappeared under a mask of blood. I turned my back on him and walked towards my corner, and I heard the sound of his rise and the slow whisper of each tread as he rushed. I ducked and swerved as he went past and caught him in the ribs and heard the crack and the gasp of pain he tried to muffle. He crouched and bent sideways and now I was the stalker and he the prey. He looked to Waverly again, more urgently now, and Waverly assessed him impassively and did nothing. I studied Laura's face as I waited, searching for her assent to the task in hand, but nothing showed, she was frozen in time and yet she didn't look away, the eyes empty but upon us, and I took this for permission and turned to kill him.

Phueng reached under the table and released a knife, a long, curved kris dagger, and threw it to Summers who caught it by the handle and held it out before him. Waverly looked at me and shrugged and held his hands up in mock surrender.

"What can you do?" he said, gazing fondly down at Phueng like a loving parent upon a naughty child.

Summers shook his head to clear it, the blood flying, then advanced towards me, crouched and favouring his left side, the knife extended before him in a slow sweeping arc. I feinted left and moved right, and Summers went the wrong way. I kicked the kris up and out of his grasp; the blade tip just nicked my wrist on the way down and left a faint trace of blood.

"Ten seconds, Kane," Summers hissed. "Mind the snakes now."

Time enough, I thought, and went for the kill, but in my eagerness I slipped in the blood and fell and Summers caught me with a kick that dazed me. He was much slimmer and quicker now and as I shook my head to clear it, he shifted shape and when I went to strike him he was no longer there. I scrambled back against the ropes, slow and clumsy as the thick air turned a smoky green and then he was before me, his face lengthened, his forehead sloped and triangular, his eyes shining golden. His tongue was forked as he opened his mouth and laughed and struck me, my body falling in slow motion now, his fangs emerging as he leaned down to finish me and then a long-toothed wolf with blazing eyes hurdled the ropes and seized him by the throat and then there were more snakes, flying through the air and falling about me, the ring filled with writhing nightmares in electric blue and red and yellow bands.

A guard raised his pistol, his face frantic as he ran off bursts, and I rolled clumsily under the ropes towards him, but he was firing into the ring and then a snake flew through the air and caught him around the neck and he dropped the gun and scrambled to remove it and then another one landed on him and he staggered and fell screaming amongst the vipers. I tried to crawl to Laura and something burned my ankle and then again and there was more firing and Danny was beside me and he had a gun now. He seized me and dragged me from the ring where Joseph and Liani were standing with Sinbad beside them, and I thought, *So this is what it's like, you see the ones you love at the end*, and I turned to tell this comfort to Laura but she'd vanished, and then I followed her headlong into the welcoming darkness.

CHAPTER 29

"He's coming around."

I awoke to darkness and pain, my head throbbing, my legs stiff and swollen. I was lying in *Arrow*'s cockpit and we were flying upwind, the motion quick and pounding, the hull shivering as we slammed into the waves. Danny smiled down at me from a bruised and bandaged face.

"What happened?"

"Joseph and Liani came aboard with baskets of sea kraits, threw them into the ring just as Summers was about to finish you. They'd been collecting them for a while."

"Drugs."

"Yeah. The knife was poisoned. Hallucinogens, like Friedrich said. You got a couple of snake bites too. Elinor gave you the antidote."

"Summers?"

"Dead. Sinbad and the snakes got him."

Good.

"Didn't get the witch though. She just walked away as though she was on a summer stroll when it was all going batshit. We managed to get away in *Arrow* in the confusion. Friedrich had tied me loosely, said he owed you, so I got to pitch in and help some. The bad news is Waverly and most of his crew are still out there. Two miles back and gaining fast. Joseph is at the tiller."

I tried to stand and staggered as *Arrow* came off the shoulder of a wave. My legs were pretty much useless. "Wind is up." I grabbed the cup of coffee he passed me and bolted it down.

"Yep. Looks like the edge of the storm is here. It's up and down. Twenty knots and gusting. Still building. Hopefully too much for them to launch their Zodiacs and run us down. We can dodge the *Dragon*."

For a while anyway, I thought. I asked: "Laura?"

"Sedated and asleep below with Sinbad," Elinor said. "I think she's still in shock. Jared, I'm so sorry about all of this."

It was always going to happen with or without you, I thought, but couldn't bring myself to utter the forgiveness.

It was near three in the morning, a full moon shining on eight-foot seas with the occasional larger one coming at us right down the moon's track on the water and putting spray on the deck. Danny and Joseph had somehow managed to get the skiff aboard and stowed in its chocks. The radar showed us doing eight knots two miles off the linked crescent beaches and pounding surf that spun away for fifteen miles on the port side. *Arrow* was sheeted hard in and approaching them at a thirty-degree angle. The *Golden Dragon* was a mile back, off our starboard quarter and closing. She hadn't bothered to put her sails up and was overhauling us with ease.

"Waverly wants to force us into the surf, have us break up and founder. He probably doesn't want to put bullet holes in *Arrow* in case some trace of her is found," Danny said.

Joseph nodded. He had his unlit pipe in his mouth, as calm and relaxed as if he were on his front porch.

"If we were a few miles farther along we might be able to duck around the last atoll, get a little room to manoeuvre among the islands. But she's making almost two miles to our one. No chance. She'll be on us long before then," I said.

Danny and Joseph nodded in agreement.

"No passes anywhere along this chain, according to the chart."

They nodded again.

"And no place to sneak in and hide. We'll be lighting up his radar like a Christmas tree. We're not going to lose him. Daylight in less than two hours."

They nodded again.

"You don't have to be so fucking agreeable," I said.

"Sorry," Danny said. Joseph nodded.

I stared at the old chart, then compared it with the one showing on the GPS. They were identical, no slim chance there. Sometimes the old ones were more detailed. A narrow half-hidden pass would have been a good thing right about now. We'd be overhauled in another few minutes.

"We'll loose the sheets, slow *Arrow* down a couple of knots, and let the *Dragon* come up on us faster. Then do a one eighty."

It might not change anything in the long run, but it would gain us some space and time and it was better than doing nothing. We slacked the sheets and brought *Arrow* into the wind a few degrees and the sails shivered and luffed, and *Arrow* slowed. The *Dragon* was a mile back now, bearing directly for our stern.

"Three hundred yards, and then we'll dummy a tack to starboard, if she swings off to head us, we fall off towards the beach, jibe around, pop the chute, take off back down the chain. Bring the rifles up, no reason we shouldn't have a go at him."

Not that we had any chance of hitting anybody inside that steel hull, but what the hell. Take your pleasures where you find them. Maybe we could take out his radar, knock out some of his antennas for what that was worth. Cut down on his TV channels. Or just put some caution in him.

"Four hundred yards," Danny called.

He was crouched near the mainmast, the spinnaker turtle at the bow covered by a piece of old tarp in case anybody aboard the *Dragon* was watching. I took the tiller and Joseph picked up and checked out the rifles, his face impassive.

"Three hundred yards," Danny yelled.

I shoved the tiller to port and the bow swung and I waited long seconds and then the *Dragon* shot up one hundred yards aft of our stern and turned to starboard to head us back and we fell off and came around as she passed, Elinor working the sheets, Joseph firing steadily, first one rifle then the other. I saw the dome around the biggest satellite receiver explode, and then the radome lost one of its wings and stopped its rotation.

"Fucking A," I screamed, then settled *Arrow* onto her new course as Elinor dropped the jib and Danny hauled up the big chute and it popped its ties and billowed out, the reds and yellows shining in the moonlight. *Arrow*'s shrouds thrummed under the extra load and her bows lifted and we swung the boom out and tracked back along the chain, the foam fluorescent along *Arrow*'s waist and sides as she surfed and settled back and then surfed again. We were doing twelve knots in the surges. By the time the *Golden Dragon* turned back onto our track we had gained back a half mile of our lead.

"She won't fall for that again," Elinor said.

"No."

I studied the charts again, but there was no hope there. The two little lagoons we had time to get into would be traps, barely a mile in diameter with only the one entrance and scant room for manoeuvring. Within those tiny arenas the *Dragon* would ride us over with her steel hull or herd us onto the rocks. They could launch the Zodiacs with riflemen in the calmer seas inside and that would be the end.

I looked aft. The *Dragon* had every light blazing and shone huge in the moonlight as she powered after us. The difference in speed between us downwind wasn't as great and she was overtaking us at a slower rate, but she was still a good five knots faster.

"So, what do we have, maybe thirty minutes?" Danny asked.

"Pretty much."

Nobody spoke for a while.

"So what's the plan?" Danny inquired.

"I guess we just run until we can't, then head in to the beach."

We were on our own out here. No one was coming to save us in the final moments. I wanted to try and get Elinor and Laura away in the inflatable that sat ready on the foredeck with the big Honda bolted on up, but at this speed, in these seas, there wasn't a prayer.

I tapped the chart on the screen that showed the reefs in large scale.

"Here looks to be the best chance: sandy, not so many rocks, and shoals up gradually, maybe a little shelter from the seas. Everybody tie yourselves down for the impact, then head ashore with the rifles and the rest of the weapons."

I tried to sound optimistic. If *Arrow* managed to miss the bigger rocks, somebody might just make it ashore, you never know. It wouldn't be me though. I'd be down below with Laura for those few final moments.

"No."

A slender brown hand moved towards the screen and a finger tapped it.

"Here."

I gawped at Joseph in amazement. It was the first time he'd spoken to me directly.

"Teuini? You're mad," I said. "The gates are closed. Remember how big those logs are? *Arrow* will never break through them without sinking or suffering critical damage. We won't have the time to open them. We'll be dead in the water after the first wall, never mind that we'd still have the second wall to get through. Even if by some miracle we do manage to break through, the *Dragon* will just follow us after she's knocked down the rest of the wall. Same story inside as the other lagoons except it's also filled with snakes and sharks when the mad bastard finally does catch up with us and run us over."

"Teuini," Joseph said.

I looked to Danny for support. He shrugged. "Doesn't sound any worse than the other thing, breaking up and drowning in the surf with a marginal chance of making it ashore to get hunted down and killed.

Bigger space to move around if we can make it inside, maybe some mist to hide and a chance to get in a few licks."

Liani stood by Joseph's side as always and nodded when I caught her eye. Elinor glanced away.

I knew when I was beaten.

"All right then," I muttered.

"Good." Joseph clapped me on the shoulder and smiled. I glared at him. Four fucking words. Actually, only three as Teuini was the same in any language and didn't really count as spoken English.

"You want to enlarge upon your plan?" I snarled.

He grinned at me. "You steer," he said. "I shoot." And he went back to his seat beside Liani and lit his pipe behind cupped hands.

"Okay, then," I said. "Bring Laura up; we'll put her in the Avon with Elinor. When we get through" — *if we get through*, I thought — "she and Elinor can take off to the other side, hide out in the scrub. With any luck Waverly won't even know they've left the boat. Maybe they can bring some sort of justice to all of this if the rest of us don't make it."

"Agreed," Elinor said. "I'm all for justice. Revenge would do equally well for that matter," she added.

"A thousand yards to the pass."

"Right."

I glanced behind us. The *Golden Dragon* was a half mile back but slowly gaining. Elinor went below and emerged with Laura. She was bent over with her eyes tightly shut, clutching a blanket wrapped tightly around her. She was completely foreign to the woman I cared about. I hoped it was just the drugs Elinor had given her, but in my heart I knew it wasn't. Laura's world had crashed down and broken upon her and she had retreated to another one, a safe and private place of close boundaries that had no room in it for anyone else and probably never would. I hoped that if she somehow survived all of this, she could find some semblance of peace inside there. I reached down and picked her up and she put her arms around my neck as I carried her forward.

I set her in the Avon and cushioned her tightly with life jackets, and she looked up at me as a child to its parent and the knowledge crashed down upon me that she had become the child we might have had. I kissed her goodbye on the top of her head and turned away as Elinor climbed in alongside her.

"Four hundred yards."

"Right. Throw the spinnaker sheets off when we're abeam, and we'll jibe the main and go through on starboard tack. We'll be about five hundred yards out, too close for them to cut us off, even if they wanted to."

But why would they want to? Much easier for them to let us dash ourselves against the gates and power in at their leisure to clean up the mess.

"Another ten seconds and we're abeam."

"Okay. Let her go."

Danny slipped the sheets and the spinnaker flew out and trailed aft from the masthead like a giant windsock.

"Jibing!" I screamed.

I threw the tiller over and brought *Arrow* onto the starboard tack as the boom slammed across, and Joseph pulled the slack from the main-sheet as we flew towards the gates.

"Three hundred yards."

I squinted through the spray as *Arrow* rolled in the cross seas, trying to keep her on course. The gates were tiny in the sea and swell, the palm-tree logs looming large in the moonlight beyond *Arrow's* bowsprit. If we hit the wall, we were done; the gates might give us a slight chance. I lined up on the narrow gap where they came together and suppressed the nightmare vision of *Arrow's* bowsprit impaled on the logs like a dart as the *Golden Dragon's* massive bow ran us over. I hoped the inflatable wouldn't fly off in the collision. I should have lashed it down. Far too late now. But it was all a matter of luck anyway.

The noise crescendoed with the pounding surf and the wind's howling, and the seas that had been astern now crashed and broke alongside *Arrow's* hull as the bottom shoaled and the waves piled up and compressed against it. A heavy gust caught *Arrow* and laid her over on her side, and water spilled over the rail and drenched us. We lay there for long seconds, the cockpit awash, the tiller light in my hands as she near broached, then Danny slacked the mainsheet and *Arrow* rose up again and shook herself and thundered on.

God help us, I thought, and as I formed the words, the gates shuddered and danced and disappeared in a cloud of foam and water, and a split second later I heard the concussive boom and pieces of the gates were flying through the air and raining down around us.

I strained to hold the tiller as *Arrow* ran through the debris, the larger pieces pounding along her sides and others knocking loudly as they passed under her keel. A few chunks fell onto the deck and there was a crash as one went through the saloon hatch, the least of our worries.

"Look out!" Danny yelled, and a quartering green capped wave curled up half again as high as the others and foamed and broke against the starboard quarter. *Arrow*'s bows turned towards the rocks with the impact, and Danny threw his weight against the tiller with me and we fought her back as the bowsprit grazed the remnant of wall that framed the narrow opening and we bounced back and through. I looked ahead for the next set of gates, but they were already open and then we were by them, the seas dropping down immediately as we went through. Another hundred yards further and *Arrow* was gliding quietly under the lee of the rock bluff, and I let out the breath I'd been holding.

"Hallelujah!" Danny yelled. "We made it."

I brought *Arrow* around into the wind and we sat there, the main luffing gently. It seemed eerily quiet after the maelstrom of the pass.

"Yes. We made it." Out of the frying pan and into the fire.

"Have you glanced over the side?"

Danny stepped to the rail and hung onto the lifelines as he gazed down. There was a steady procession of fins cutting purposefully through the water and heading out to the centre, where, in spite of the increased wind, the green mist swirled as steadily as ever.

"Ah. Well, at least we have a while to get ready, it will take some time for Waverly's crew to clear the bommie and take down the second . . ." his voice broke off as the high-pitched scream of a big outboard sounded, and I thought, *Jesus Christ, not already*, and reached for a rifle. Joseph shook his head and a minute later Tommo pulled up alongside and tied off.

"Welcome back. Wasn't sure if I'd be seeing you guys again. Joseph said you might be coming back in a bit of a rush."

His boat was piled up with floats and ropes, with three dusty old wooden crates stamped with skulls and warnings in the bow. "The last of the council's stash from the Second World War," he said, motioning towards them. "I ran back to the village and picked it up after I spoke to Joseph. Dynamite is still good, fuses a bit tricky though, gates were supposed to blow a few minutes earlier. Cutting it a bit fine there."

"No shit," Elinor said. She and Laura had moved back to the cockpit. Laura sat passively, her head bowed, her face a blank slate.

Tommo regarded her thoughtfully. "So, everyone's okay?" he asked.

"For the moment," Danny said. "The *Dragon*'s still out there though. And she's not going to leave until we've all been dealt with. How long do you think for them to get through? She's got a twenty-foot draught with the board up, about forty feet of beam. She's close on the clearance it looks like, but there's that bommie that rises up in the middle. She'll have to take that out first to have enough water. Does she have explosives on board?"

"Yes. We heard them blasting the reefs at Kandavu," Danny said.

"Assholes," Tommo said. "Well then, say at least a couple . . ."

He was interrupted by a loud explosion from the pass and then seconds later the sound of big diesels accelerating up to speed. The turbos kicked in, and they whined up another notch, a high-pitched keening rising above the sound of the wind and seas. There was a loud crash and the squealing grating sounds of metal on rock. We stared at the pass as the yellow bow of the *Golden Dragon* slowly appeared in the faint predawn light, and then shuddered, slowed, and stopped.

"She's run aground," Danny said, and she hung there for long moments as the engines roared, and then her bow lifted on a through swell and she shuddered and lurched and there was a crunching squealing sound as she ground her way forward the last thirty feet and sprang free.

CHAPTER 30

I cursed and reached down and turned the key and pumped the throttle and waited and then pressed the button and the old Perkins growled into life. I threw her into gear and the RPMs spun up, but way too fast. I throttled right back down but it didn't matter. The prop was gone. A piece of log must have knocked it off on our way in. We were dead in the water in every sense of the phrase.

"Fuck. Set the jib," I screamed, but Danny already had the halyard and the sail was flying up. We were caught in irons and Elinor ran up the little mizzen sail and shoved the boom across to turn us off the wind. The stern swung agonizingly slowly and finally the main caught the wind and we moved off. There were around ten knots of wind inside the lagoon, not nearly enough for *Arrow* in that arena. Fifteen knots and we might have the ghost of a chance. The *Golden Dragon* would run us down in minutes.

"She's not moving," Elinor said. I turned and saw the *Golden Dragon* slowly drifting broadside to the wind. A crewman came out and ran forward to release the fastenings on the anchors.

"She's lost power," Tommo said.

"Looks like."

Joseph picked up the .308, sighted through the scope, and fired, and the crewman dropped down onto the deck and started crawling aft. Joseph fired again and he lay still. A fusillade of shots rang out, and we ducked down but were out of range for their pistols and the shots fell short and then we were into the green fog. As we entered the darker water, we seemed to slow, as if the liquid was somehow denser and required more force to pass through, but surely that was only imagination. The air was warmer and closer, moist and cloying as you breathed it in, with a faint coppery taste that lingered. The wind gusted and the mist swirled and the *Dragon*'s masts suddenly showed above it, the sails extending slowly out along her booms.

"She won't be long," I said.

Tommo jumped down into the panga and lifted one of the wooden crates up onto the rails where Danny grabbed it and laid it carefully down on a cockpit seat.

"Hand grenades," Tommo said.

"Ah."

Danny grabbed a winch handle and carefully levered off the lid. "Actually, they don't look all that bad," he said. They were the old Second World War pineapple style, individually wrapped in heavy greased brown paper and, apart from some slight rust flaking, seemed in reasonable condition. "What's the time delay on these things?"

"Three or four seconds," Tommo said. "We used to steal the occasional one when I was a kid."

"So what, say a couple hundred yards in the air after the pin is released?"

"Something like that. We dropped one off a four-hundred-foot cliff once, went off just before it hit the water. Brought home a hell of a bunch of fish; the elders were impressed."

"They'll give us another weapon, add to the surprise, maybe a chance to do some real damage."

The *Dragon*'s hull and decks were steel, and I didn't know what a grenade could do against them, but the masts were carbon fibre. An explosion anywhere close could do those some serious harm. I felt a stirring of hope and thought that we might have just the slimmest of chances.

"Look, Tommo, take Laura and Elinor with you, put them ashore and blow a passage in the north pass. Pick them up afterwards and make a run for it while we tie up the *Dragon*. Worst case, they might have a Zodiac and a couple of crew on the passes, we've got rifles and ammo for you and Elinor. You should have a real chance."

"I'm good," Tommo said. "Got more fire power than we can use. I saved a few grenades."

"I'm not leaving," Elinor said.

"You have to look out for Laura," Danny said.

"I'm not running from that bastard," Elinor vowed. "I owe him."

"Look, love," Danny said. He leaned forward and held the back of her head and gently brought her near and popped her on the chin. She sagged down unconscious and he picked her up and laid her down in the panga.

I held Laura and looked into those blank doll's eyes and wanted to say goodbye, but she wasn't there. I took a last look and turned away, and Tommo led her down into the panga and they motored off. The green mist swirled and surrounded them, and she faded away and was gone. I put her from my mind and swung *Arrow* back towards the *Dragon*.

"Let's go sailing," Danny said.

I looked at the screen and saw the *Dragon* moving slowly across the lagoon towards us.

I wondered if she still had her radar. Joseph had shattered the main radome and damaged one of the others, but there was still one pod left. No telling what was in there. Our masts were covered by the mist and we swung to port and moved across the *Dragon*'s path. She was six hundred yards away coming directly for us and didn't alter course. I kept our heading for another minute, doing a slow four knots. We were barely leaving a wake. The mist coalesced on the sails and ran down onto the decks in pale green rivulets. The silence seemed threatening and unnatural after the chaos of the pass. We were thirty degrees off Waverly's bow now and moving away and still he hadn't altered course. He couldn't see us.

"Joseph must have taken down all the radar," Danny said. He had the skiff paddles out and was lashing them into a Y with half-inch line. Liani had taken one of the heavy three-band spear guns out of the locker and was removing the rubbers.

"Either that or he's being cute. Let me guess, you're making a slingshot."

"No. A catapult. Much more scientific."

He began fastening the heavy rubber bands to the forks with whipping twine. There was a puff and *Arrow* heeled five degrees for ten seconds and then straightened up again. The *Dragon* still hadn't altered course.

"Excellent!" I said. "Shifting tilting platform, seventy-five-year-old explosives with rusted moving parts, and rubber bands and a brace of paddles to launch them with. It's perfect. What could possibly go wrong?"

The *Dragon* was four hundred yards away, on our port quarter, doing six knots, invisible save for the tips of her masts. It was eerily quiet, the only sounds the slight hiss of our bows cutting the water and the soft soughing of the wind in the rigging. A stronger gust came down on us and *Arrow* heeled sharply, and the mist shredded away. There was a shout and the *Dragon*'s bow swung towards us. Joseph began firing, and there was an answering barrage of shots. We heard the chunk of them striking *Arrow*'s mast above our heads and then there was a crash and pieces of our radome fell on the deck and the radar screen went blank. There was the twang of rubber and a grenade shot up and out and splashed and sank in front of the *Dragon*; a muffled thump, a minor upwelling.

Danny muttered a curse and took the grenade Liani held out and launched again and the grenade soared and came down perfectly on the *Dragon*'s wheelhouse, bounced twice and fell harmlessly over the side. She was a hundred and fifty yards away now and heading directly towards us.

"Fuck," Danny screamed, and the rubber twanged once more, and another grenade flew through the air and exploded ten feet above the *Dragon*'s foredeck and she swerved violently.

"Hah!"

Danny quickly reloaded and hurled another, and this one hit the big pilot house and bounced forward down the slanted Lexan windows and rolled up beside the towering centre mast and laid there for a long second as we held our breath. A crewman emerged and ran towards it and then there was a loud explosion, and the bottom ten feet of the mast disappeared in a cloud of smoke and then it tilted and fell in slow motion over the side and into the lagoon.

"Fucking A," Danny yelled. "How's that then?" He threw his arms up into the air and high fived me in jubilation.

The *Dragon* suddenly veered off one hundred twenty degrees and headed back towards the pass. If she'd had a tail, it would have been between her legs. We'd hurt her, and although she was still faster than us with her remaining sail, we'd levelled the playing field a bit. She'd have to be more cautious now. If she lost her second mast we'd have her. Even now, with her slower and less manoeuvreable with just the one, we might be able to keep some distance between us. The explosions likely hadn't damaged her hull, but the loss of the mast would have unnerved Waverly. What had seemed an easy kill was now less certain. The wind was gusting upwards of fifteen knots now, and *Arrow* would be at her nimble best. If he tried to send the Zodiacs against us, we could take them out before they got close enough to do any damage. Shooting from *Arrow*'s relatively stable platform would be easier than trying to hit something from a bouncing, slamming rubber dinghy. When Tommo blew the second pass we might have some options. I wondered what was taking him so long.

Arrow was running on a beam reach, just on the edge of the swirling green mist that now barely covered the bottom foot of her hull. She was doing a nice six and a half knots as I called the tack. *Arrow* swung around, and as the boom came across there was a loud crack and the top third of the mast broke off above the triatic stay and fell onto the deck in a tangle of shrouds and lines and sails. The burst that took out our radar had stitched the mast and weakened it. In seconds the mainsail was over the side and dragging in the water and *Arrow*'s speed died. Joseph had his knife out cutting the tangled lines in seconds, and I grabbed the knife at the compass binnacle and handed it to Liani as Danny worked the big Feldspars, severing the stays and upper shrouds. In five minutes of desperate effort the four of us had the whole ungodly mess clear and floating away downwind. The rest of the mast would hold with the lower shrouds, but we wouldn't be able to fly anything from it without a lot of work and time, something we were out of. We would be lucky to do much over a knot downwind with just the little mizzen. Our only hope was the mist, and I turned *Arrow* and slowly headed for the centre of the lagoon where it had been the thickest, but with the rising wind it had all but vanished. We lay there, barely moving, naked and vulnerable, and just when it seemed that things couldn't get any worse there was the sound of a starter spinning over and then the uneven staccato cough of a diesel slowly coming online. We watched in silence as the bow of the *Dragon* swung back towards us and she ran up to speed. She turned away and did a wide three-sixty to port and then turned to starboard and circled back again and halted facing us.

"Everything looks fine to me," Danny said. "Maybe only the one engine though."

"I think so. Still more than enough to finish the job."

Joseph and Liani moved forward and slid the little skiff over the lifelines and into the water, then climbed in and set the mast and raised the sail. Why not. They took a rifle and a shotgun and a half dozen grenades, and sat alongside, the little sail luffing gently under the lee of *Arrow*'s hull.

"What's Joseph waiting for?" Danny said. "They should make a run for it ashore. Hook up with Tommo and Elinor."

The *Dragon* had finished her test runs and was heading directly towards us. She was a half mile away with her one remaining sail neatly furled.

"Doing eight knots at least."

Arrow was doing under one and a half. Downwind we'd barely have steerage. We were all out of options. Danny adjusted the paddles, setting the trajectory, and placed his box of grenades next to him in the cockpit. When we went into the water under the *Golden Dragon's* hull I would take one with me just to make sure the snakes didn't get me. Maybe two, with my luck I'd probably get a dud.

The *Dragon* approached to within five hundred yards and then slowed and stopped and rested there, the sound of her engine drifting down to us on the wind. The RPMs rose up and dropped down and then rose and dropped again, as if taunting us.

"Waverly is enjoying this," Danny said.

She idled slowly, just drifting.

"She's raising her transom door. Launching the Zodiacs." Danny said. He picked up a rifle and waited.

"They'll shelter behind her when she comes for *Arrow*, clean up when she rides over us. If there's anything left." I said.

Joseph shoved off downwind from *Arrow*, caught the breeze and flew off on a beam reach. He handed Liani the tiller and knelt down in the bow, his rifle resting on the gunwales. He was probably a good five hundred yards clear of the *Dragon*.

"He'll try and neutralize the Zodiacs," Danny said.

Why not.

We could just glimpse them now and again; the three of them huddled in the *Dragon's* lee like chicks to their mother hen, still too far away for any remote chance of hitting them. But they weren't really the problem. When we went into the water, their bullets might be a mercy.

The *Dragon's* engine rose to a scream once more, then idled back down and into gear. She moved towards us gradually increasing her speed. A dinghy moved out from behind her and laid down a quick burst of fire then moved back again. The engine howled as the turbo kicked in and the stern settled as the props bit and then the noise suddenly died down once more as they backed the engine off. The yellow bitch slowed and stopped and lay there a scant three hundred yards off. We could hear her engine idling over, the sound coming down to us on the wind. Her transom suddenly raised again, and the hydraulic ramp was lowered down once more.

"Now what?" Danny said. He was sweating and brushed the drops away as he struggled to see.

And then I saw Tommo's panga coming out from the shore, slowly approaching the *Dragon*, a white flag flying from an oar strapped at her transom.

"That's not smart," I said.

Danny raised the glasses. "What the fuck does Tommo think he's doing? They'll shoot him down long before he gets anywhere near."

He paused, looked again, then sighed. "No. That would be Elinor at the controls. I guess she had second thoughts about her best option. Oh, dear Christ, she's got Laura with her."

My world crashed down around me, and I raised my rifle to use the scope to see and there in the circle was Laura. She was gripping Elinor's hand and her head was raised and she was looking towards the *Dragon*. Her face was tranquil, and I thought there was almost the hint of a smile, but that was impossible. Grief and horror overwhelmed me.

Laura stood with Elinor at the wheel as the panga crept within a hundred yards of the *Dragon*'s stern, idling slowly along as two of the Zodiacs approached it, one from each side, armed men inside laughing. Everything was moving in slow motion now, the scene burned into my brain. It was deathly quiet, only the muffled sounds of the idling engines as the seconds stretched out and the dinghies approached the girls. When they came alongside, the women suddenly stooped and flipped grenades into the inflatables. I saw Elinor jam the throttle forward and the panga's bow shot up into the air as the engine screamed and then it slammed back down, and the screw bit and the boat bucked and jumped up onto a plane. It flew away from the explosions, the girls' hair streaming behind in the wind, one blond, one dark, their arms intertwined for eternity, and their faces turning towards us as they hit the *Dragon's* ramp and rocketed up it in a grinding screech of metal and disappeared inside.

There was a split-second silence as my world stopped and then a series of deafening explosions from inside the *Dragon* and her stern rose up out of the water and the aft deck peeled back like the lid of a sardine can. She slammed back down, and the green water boiled and foamed into the gaping hole where her transom had been. In seconds, her stern was down below the waterline. The *Dragon's* engine rose up into a roar, and her bow swung, and she jerked towards us, then the diesel coughed and sputtered and died, and she drifted slowly on for another fifty sluggish yards.

"Water in the engine room," Danny said.

He put down the grenade he had been readying and picked up his rifle. The *Dragon's* stern was now completely underwater, and the bow pointed upwards at an unnatural angle.

"Yes. They've sunk her, Danny." My voice was choked, and I could barely see.

Laura.

We stood transfixed, stunned, staring in shock and disbelief. She was gone now, and I couldn't think about that and what it might make me into, but a small part of the horror was the sight of a magnificent creation in its death throes. The *Golden Dragon* was one of the most beautiful sailboats ever built, a stunning marriage of advanced engineering combined with an artist's eye and an obscene budget. To see her stricken and dying for no reason but maniacal ego was sad and abhorrent.

Danny suddenly snapped out of his reverie and raised his rifle and began firing. The last Zodiac had come out from behind the *Dragon* and was flying towards shore. The little sailboat moved into her path, Liani at the tiller and Joseph crouched and firing from the bow. The dinghy swerved suddenly and pounded on, then slowed as the tubes began collapsing under Joseph's and Danny's combined assault. The crew yelled and cursed as they pumped and bailed and the water rose up inside. Then something hit them from underneath and the dinghy spun up and flipped over and they were all in the water screaming as it boiled and frothed around them. Then the noise stopped, and it was calm.

"Jesus," I said, "what was that?"

"I'm not sure," Danny said, "but I think it was large and white."

Joseph had raised the sails again and was making his way back towards us.

"Look," Danny said.

The *Dragon's* stern was now underwater as far as the pilothouse, the bow slanting upwards at a thirty-degree angle. In another minute she would be gone. Two figures came out of the wheelhouse and ran forward, the woman lithe and graceful, the man awkward and stumbling. Waverly went to the bow, a mere fifty yards from us and pleaded and screamed, his voice frantic. Phueng glanced at him scornfully and stepped up onto the railing and waved to us and dove over the side. She entered the water with barely a splash, surfaced, and headed towards the shore in an unhurried measured stroke.

"Damned if I don't almost hope she makes it," Danny said, lowering his rifle.

There was a sudden jetting of air from the *Dragon* as her pilothouse disappeared and the bow rose straight up ninety degrees, Waverly clinging desperately to it, fifty feet up in the air now. She began to go down, dead vertical, slowly at first then faster and faster, Waverly's arms wrapped around the pulpit as it disappeared under the green waters. The last thing we saw was his frantic screaming face and then he plunged out of sight and was gone.

We sat there for a minute, stunned by what had transpired and what had been lost. Even the wind had died with the *Golden Dragon*, and the last circles of her fall spread out and vanished in widening ripples across the lagoon. In minutes it was as if nothing had ever happened there. Joseph and Liani came aboard and tied off the dinghy, and we began to make our slow way back to shore when the waters came suddenly alive and exploded beneath *Arrow*'s hull.

One moment we were resting virtually becalmed in the middle of the lagoon, and the next the tiller wrenched and jumped away from me. I shot backwards and slammed up against the mizzenmast as *Arrow* turned crossways thirty feet up on the crest of a surging tsunami, her bow hanging out in space, the green water bunched beneath her stern like a balled fist.

"What the fuck?" Danny screamed as he threw his weight beside me on the tiller and we fought to straighten her out. It was hopeless. *Arrow* had no way upon her and no steerage; we were as helpless as a piece of driftwood caught in a breaking wave. I looked back and saw the huge whirlpool where the *Dragon* had vanished, a full three hundred yards in width frothing and spiralling downwards and out of sight.

The shore approached at frightening speed, and still we rode the foaming forward edge of the wave. A coloured ball of entwined sea kraits rose up alongside *Arrow* and over the top of the wave and then fell back. Even if we could make it to the bow, there was no time to launch an anchor, and we had only a pathetic hope if we did. Suddenly *Arrow*'s bows rose up an additional thirty degrees and we hung on and the wave passed under her and *Arrow* dropped back stern down and sat rocking in its wake two hundred yards from the shore. The wave rose even higher as it raised the shallows then crashed and broke on the sand, foaming across the beach and up into the scrub line before slowly retreating back into the lagoon.

Nobody spoke for a full minute.

"Are we done yet?" Danny said finally.

I looked behind. The funnel had closed and filled and the seas had calmed, only a few gentle waves rocking *Arrow* now, each one marginally smaller than the last.

"I think so. I'm not seeing any frogs or locusts just yet anyway."

"Okay." He stared out into the centre of the lagoon, his face a blank mask and then he went to the bow and we set the anchor.

CHAPTER 31

Joseph ran the Avon ashore and picked up Tommo and brought him back to *Arrow*. When he saw the tsunami forming, he had headed for the high ground.

"Seen those before," he said. "One took our village out when I was a boy. I'm sorry about Elinor. Wasn't expecting it. She surprised me." He touched his swollen lip. "When I tried to stop her, she whacked me with the butt of her rifle. Threatened to shoot me. I think she would have."

"We'd all be dead if not for her," Danny said.

"Yes."

There was a long silence.

"Did Laura go willingly?" I finally asked.

"Yes. When Elinor said she was going to end this, Laura went over and took her hand. Didn't speak but wouldn't let go. Clung to her. She was not going to be left behind."

So at least she got to make some kind of a choice. Perhaps that's the best any of us can hope for when the time comes.

Joseph went below and emerged with bottles. The wind had died almost completely. I thought there was not enough whisky in the world now to grant me peace.

"The mist has gone," Liani said.

Already the water was clearer, with less of a tint. There was a strong current flushing through the lagoon as the water and temperature equalized.

"Fissure closed I guess," I said. "When the *Dragon* went down. She carried a lot of explosives on board. Blew up down inside there. Lapérouse and the gold must be gone forever now. Good riddance."

"When's *Tramp* due?" Danny asked.

"Day after tomorrow, I think. VHF is on, she'll be in range in the afternoon if she's coming."

The day's tragedy hung over the evening like a pall and after some desultory conversation I turned in. I lay sweating in my barren bunk and remembered Laura and I thought about our brief journey on the blue seas together and how it could have been changed a hundred different times by any one of a hundred different things. Like a thousand-mile ocean voyage where one degree of change can completely transform the outcome, one click of the windvane that determines whether or not you hit your mark or continue on into the blue unknown. The journals, Summers, Waverly, the *Golden Dragon*, everything falling exactly right to land me precisely where I now was. Alone and falling in the abyss. When the others had retired for the night, I went back out on deck and stared out towards the middle of the lagoon and thought about what was gone and what might have been.

In the morning Danny and I dove on *Arrow* and checked her hull for damage. There were a few scrapes where logs had threshed alongside and one serious gouge that would have to be attended to in the boatyard, but she had been lucky for the most part. The prop shaft was bent and would have to be pulled before we could put a new prop on. No matter, we could still sail back to Lautoka. The broken top of the mast had kept the sails and shrouds afloat and the whole mess had ended up tangled high in the brush in the aftermath of the tsunami. We pulled it out and cleared it and by evening we had run shortened stays and shrouds and *Arrow* could fly a small jib and furled main in a decent wind. Not pretty, but adequate. What was the hurry when you had nowhere to go?

Tramp hailed *Arrow* on the radio the following morning, and by noon was tied up alongside. Tommo went out in the Avon to meet them, and when they came aboard it was evident he had told them everything. When I saw him, Padraic looked twenty years older and held me for the longest time as Molly murmured her soft regrets. He finally released me, wiping a tear from his eye.

"Be careful of what you wish for, boyo. To think it has come to this. My poor girl gone just when she was the happiest I've seen her for years. And Elinor as well, dear God. You can rest assured I'm going to make certain everyone knows about those monsters. There'll be no Westminster high masses and praising eulogies for those fuckers when I'm done, believe me. We've got the spar and the coins that prove the tale, never mind the rest is gone. I'll set a trust up to honour the girls' memory and keep the story alive. Too bad that bastard Waverly took our coins from *Arrow* though," he added. "It would have been a help in the short term."

Joseph stood up and went below and returned carrying four of the large dive weights and set them carefully on the cockpit grating before me.

"If you think any of us are going back down there, you're out of your mind," I said slowly and deliberately, as if speaking to a small child. "Haven't you been listening? There is absolutely zero chance of finding anything anymore. Everything down there is sealed up and buried forever."

He stared at me impassively then pulled out the old knife he always carried in the scabbard that hung around his neck. He reached forward and scraped away at the bottom of one of the weights. It showed yellow beneath a thin skin of lead. The old bugger had put the gold coins into Molly's loaf pans and covered them with lead melted down in her still. Mixed in amidst the random jumble of dive weights in *Arrow's* locker you'd never have guessed. Waverly's crewman had missed it in his search of *Arrow*.

"Well fuck me for an Orangeman," Padraic said. Molly brought a hammer and cold chisel over from *Tramp* and soon the coins were spread out in a glittering heap in front of us. Padraic divided it into three equal piles.

"One share for Tommo and the village; one for *Tramp*, Molly, and me; and one for *Arrow*, Joseph, and Danny. Is that fair?"

"More than fair," Tommo said. "Getting the lagoon back is reward enough, but we could use some new outboards for our pangas. Not to mention the antique village genset."

I tried to give Padraic my share for the memorial fund, but he wouldn't hear of it. He said he knew Laura would have wanted me to have it. "Just promise me you won't write a book or go on speaking tours," he said with his first faint smile. "I'm going to make buckets out of this, never mind the joy of seeing the College Board kiss my ass, which is truly a treasure beyond price."

"You have my solemn word."

We agreed Padraic would market the gold; he reckoned by releasing the coins in small amounts over time he could get close to four hundred thousand American. Beneath the curly mop and the stage Irishman act lay a shrewd man, and I didn't doubt he would make good on his promise. It made no matter to me. I had enough on hand to rerig with a new mast and stays, straighten the prop shaft, repair a few dints and scrapes, and get *Arrow* shipshape again. A week in the yard in Lautoka would see the job finished.

We'll leave in the morning. Joseph is going to spend some time in the village with Liani. Danny is flying back to Canada. Elinor's death has affected him more than he lets on. Even Tommo can't lighten his dark mood. I'd hoped he would choose to stay with *Arrow*. The thought of a single-handed journey reliving the sad past and foreseeing the bleak future overwhelms me, but I can't bring myself to cajole him. I want only to leave Teuini Lagoon and its memories behind. The future stretches out before me as blank and empty as Laura's eyes.

Azure skies, a gentle swell, the even bellows of the trades sighing on the beam, and *Arrow* running at five knots under jury rig towards Lautoka. It is another of those perfect Pacific days, the vane set, never a tweak to sheets or sails.

Danny comes up from below, the now ever-present drink in his hand, he passes mine across and gazes blankly around before leaning back against the coaming. The sun completes its arc across the sky and plunges out of sight without a word exchanged between us. As night comes on the wind shifts forward and *Arrow* alters her course in concert. The loom of Lautoka's lights falls off to starboard and we begin to sail away.

I wait for Danny to reset the vane and guide us back towards safe harbour and his ticket home.

He does not.

I lean back, complicit.

So we beat on.

Into the blue abyss.